Finishing Touches

By

John Yates

Published by New Generation Publishing in 2022

Copyright © John Yates 2022

First Edition

ISBN
Paperback	978-1-80369-543-3
Hardback	978-1-80369-544-0
Ebook	978-1-80369-545-7

www.newgeneration-publishing.com

 New Generation Publishing

Chapter 1

Peter expectantly drew back the curtains and was greeted by another gloriously sunny day. He looked at the sky and was pleased to see that it was virtually cloudless with only a few wispy flecks of white here and there on an otherwise unspoiled ceiling of blue. It was still quite early, but he sensed it was going to be another hot day, which was, he thought to himself, exactly what he had hoped for when he had booked the holiday. Feeling curiously satisfied that the good weather in some way constituted the cruise line keeping up their side of the bargain, he eagerly picked up the grey plastic-handled hairbrush that seemed to have followed him everywhere for the last twenty years or so. Then, turning to face the full-length mirror on the wardrobe door, he carelessly flicked the top of his head in a bid to make what little hair he had left appear to be an adequate covering. Peter comforted himself with the thought that his grey was tinged with patches of the black waves that had been there since he was in his teens. He looked pretty good for his age and was dressed casually but smartly in a pair of beige chinos and a light blue cotton shirt. He certainly would not need a jacket today, so one last check that there was nothing unseemly attached to his face or that the fly on his trousers was undone was all that was required.

Heading for the door, he checked the time and realised that he had not put on his watch. Noticing it on the bedside table, he slapped the silver strap firmly around his wrist and clicked it shut. He then grabbed the linen bag that contained his pad and a few pens, which was hanging next to the notice that he had not yet read but which he assumed explained how to put on a life jacket in case of emergency, and opened the cabin door.

Exiting the room, he narrowly avoided knocking over a trolley which was rather haphazardly positioned in the hallway. He banged his leg and just managed to stop halfway through an inappropriate expletive when a young girl, who had heard the noise, poked her head out of the cabin next door to see what was happening. Peter recognised her immediately as one of the maids who cleaned the rooms and replaced toiletries for the guests. She was, he had surmised when he had previously heard her speak, Eastern European, but he could not precisely identify her nationality. His anger was temporarily overcome by embarrassment as he hoped she had not guessed what he had intended to shout.

"Meester Davees, I am so sorry. I didn't know you were in there." She was young, probably in her mid-twenties, slim and very pretty. Her jet-black hair was tied back neatly in a ponytail except for a few strands which had temporarily escaped and fallen over her face. As she pushed them back into place, Peter gazed at her glossy, pink lips, grappling unsuccessfully to try and remember her name so that he could at least respond. Settling instead for a smile by way of delay, he noticed that she was wearing a name badge. Unfortunately, his failing eyesight and lack of glasses (although Joan often reminded him to wear them) meant that he could not read it. He thought it looked like it might begin with a K or was it an N? Trying not to be too obvious, he moved slightly nearer to her and trained his eyes on the area a few inches above her left breast where the badge was positioned. It was still no good, so he stretched his head forward a foot or so in a final attempt to avoid having to confess to not recalling her name. Unfortunately, Karolina, the beautiful Latvian maid, possessed a rather formidable bosom both in proportion and shape. It ran in her family and her mother, who had owned a small café on the coast in Liepaja, used hers to great commercial advantage. She ensured that the counter behind which she worked was at precisely the right height to form a platform on which it could rest. This allowed her to display just the right amount of alabaster flesh for ogling male and female admirers alike. She was always popular with the locals and became something of a tourist attraction for those visiting the local beach. She did extremely well until, as she entered her fifties, her assets inevitably headed south and the takings in the café regrettably followed. Her daughter, however, possessed neither her mother's ambition for commercial success nor, unfortunately for Peter, her desire for the attention of admiring eyes.

Matters were made worse in that Karolina's labours of the morning had involved rather a lot of strenuous bending and stretching which, in tandem with her natural attributes, had forced open not one but two buttons of her tight-fitting scarlet tunic.

"Good morning," he offered unconvincingly, followed by hesitation, as his eyes continued to focus, Karolina thought, much closer on the undone buttons than her face. Had he been looking a little higher, he would have noticed her smile being replaced by a threatening scowl as she stooped to pick up some boxes of tissues that had fallen on the floor. Now completely flustered, Peter tentatively passed her two miniature bottles of shampoo that had stopped rolling and come to rest awkwardly by his left shoe.

Karolina had three younger brothers and was all too well acquainted with the fascination young boys had with the female form. She had long since reached the conclusion, as had her mother, that this was a preoccupation that continued into manhood and ultimately, she realised, into dotage. Fixing her now stern gaze on him, she hissed in pidgin English through pursed lips, "You are naughty man, Meester Davees, aren't you? Very naughty man. I know what you look at."

Realising what the girl was saying and simultaneously acknowledging that she was making a fair point, Peter jettisoned all thoughts of trying to remember her name and, in a hideous wave of embarrassment, could only resort to damage limitation in the wake of her damning accusation.

"Oh no. No, please... I didn't mean to... I wasn't..." He was flustered. But, of course, he was, and he had. He might not have meant it, but the fact hit him like thunderbolt that it could only have looked to any unbiased observer like one thing. He could see the headlines now, 'The lecherous old man and the gorgeous young girl going innocently about her duties'.

To add insult to injury, the intense stabbing pain emanating from his shin reminded him all too unkindly that only a few seconds ago the steel ledge of the trolley had collided with his lower leg. It had now acquired an accompanying throb and Peter's only option was to retreat gracefully or at least limp away as best he could. Head down, avoiding eye contact and coughing abruptly in an attempt to bring closure to the sorry episode, he made a rapid escape down the carpeted corridor.

Glancing over his shoulder tentatively to assess the scene, Peter saw the maid disappear into the cabin next to his and hastily accelerated towards the left turn that would take him out of view. Then, relaxing somewhat, he continued along the hallway before gingerly easing himself down a short flight of steps which led to the relative sanctuary of the ship's café.

This place, thought Peter, was his favourite on the whole ship. Of course, he enjoyed the theatre and the cinema and naturally the restaurants were pretty good, but here he felt he could really relax. It was the perfect place for him to kill a few hours while Joan was at one of her classes, and, quite apart from anything else, they served great coffee. His wife had left early that morning, explaining that she had signed up for arts and crafts sessions all week. They were apparently being run by a lovely lady who in a previous life had been in one of Joan's favourite soap operas playing the part of the beautiful wife of the village rogue. In the programme, the woman, fed up with his criminality, had killed her thoroughly unpleasant husband by smashing him over the head with an antique last while he was in the bath. She had then evaded prosecution by disposing of the lifeless body in a pit on a nearby building site upon which a supermarket car park was subsequently erected. Peter found it very amusing that this woman was now showing his wife how to make a delicate macramé plant hanger.

Joan had always been the gregarious one, ready to talk to anyone and everyone, and loved not only the making and doing but also meeting and chatting with new people. Peter, on the other hand, had been shy as a child and, as he had grown into a man, this same trait displayed itself in a reserved manner based on cautious suspicion of encounters with acquaintances. With those he knew, however, he could be easy-going and his quick wit endeared him to their close friends.

Finding a comfortable-looking chair by the window, Peter flopped down, feeling unusually out of breath. Moments later a young man, dressed smartly in the ubiquitous white uniform of the ship's employees, came over to his table to take his order.

"Hello, Mr Davis. What would you like this morning?" he asked politely.

Peter was always astonished that, with so many guests on the ship, the staff were able to remember individual names so well. He had been in here most mornings, but it was nevertheless quite an impressive feat of memory. He recalled seeing a man on television some years ago who could remember people by associating parts of their appearance with a particular name. The main part of his 'act' had been to greet two hundred people as they took their seats before one of his shows, examining each one for only a couple of seconds. An hour later he asked them to stand up for the rest of the audience to see and reeled off all of their Christian names, asking each to sit as he did. The two hundredth sat down in under five minutes and he had not made a single mistake. The trick was apparently to relate either what the person was wearing or another unique attribute to a separate picture that represented a list of names that he knew already. He would link the picture of the item of clothing or personal feature with that of the picture of the relevant name which he had already memorised. He explained later in the show that the memory remembers pictures better than words or numbers and that the more outlandish and animated they were, the easier they were to recall. Provided he did not encounter too many odd first names that were not on his list, it was simply a matter of creating the pictures. Over the years he had a huge list of names for which he had devised memorable images, so he rarely failed. Peter had tried it later that week with a much smaller number at an office function and it had worked. He smiled as he remembered the grey suited 'Jim' who had been introduced to him. The man had huge ears that seemed much too big for his modest-sized head. Peter associated the name Jim with jam. The picture he created of a jar of strawberry jam with enormous ears flying around the room was not a difficult one to recollect when he introduced him to another colleague twenty minutes later. He practised this method regularly and once had managed to memorise a full deck of cards in the correct order. He made a mental note to have another go since he had not had the opportunity to use the technique for a while.

"Good morning," said Peter. "Could I have a strong white coffee, please?"

The array of options in coffee shops constantly confused him and he struggled to remember what differentiated a flat white from a latte or an espresso from a normal black coffee. He knew vaguely what a cappuccino was, but the nuances of this new vocabulary were to him still something of a mystery. For this reason, he preferred not to be too ambitious but instead tended to describe the coffee he wanted in simple terms. He was content in the knowledge that although sacrificing an opportunity to fit in or appear to be trendy, he had, on the balance of probability, a greater chance of receiving something that was drinkable rather than unidentifiable.

As the waiter smiled in acknowledgement, Peter, who had now put on his glasses and laid out some pens and his pad in front of him, noticed his name badge, which read Norbert. His eyes could not help but linger on a brown odd-shaped birthmark above the man's left eyebrow which, Peter thought, bore an uncanny resemblance to the coastline of New Zealand. As Norbert disappeared into the kitchen, Peter began to wonder what pictures the memory man would have conjured up to remember his name when he became conscious of a tightness in his chest. He coughed lightly in an attempt to clear it, but nothing happened. He tried again, harder and louder this time. It seemed to do the trick, but he hoped his drink would come soon as his throat was sore after the exertion.

To pass the time until his coffee arrived, Peter took up his pad and leant it against the edge of the table with the bottom resting in his lap. As he smoothed down a page with the heel of his hand, his tummy rumbled loudly and he realised how hungry he was. He decided that when the waiter returned, it might be an idea to order some breakfast.

A few minutes later, Norbert reappeared and placed the steaming coffee on the table. Peter breathed deeply, allowing the aroma to delight his senses.

"Could you do me some Welsh rarebit by any chance?" Peter asked, wondering if the waiter would understand what he meant.

"I'm sure we can manage that for you, Mr Davis."

"With plenty of Worcester sauce, please," Peter added hopefully.

"No problem at all," said Norbert, reaching across to remove a discarded mug from the other side of the table.

Alone again, Peter began to scan the café properly, looking for something interesting to draw. After discounting both 'sugar bowl with spoon' and 'carnations in blue vase' as rather uninspiring still life options, he settled on a table ten or fifteen feet away at which two elderly ladies were playing cards. He had always drawn people well and, in many ways, preferred animate subjects. These two individuals seemed to fit the bill, so, with pencil poised, he examined them closely. They were an intriguing pair. The woman on the left was not only tall (even sitting down) but she was solidly built with strong-looking shoulders that provided a firm base for an oversized head, which was made all the bigger by the addition of a vast curly mass of grey hair that Peter suspected was probably a wig. A bright pink tee shirt covered her square torso and it reminded Peter of one of those boiled sweets from his childhood that could be bought by the quarter ounce. What were they called? he thought... the jar was always full to the brim because no one ever bought them... Winter Selection – that was it. He smiled to himself contentedly as he remembered the pink, blue and yellow pillows of flavoured sugar. Her partner, in contrast, was of average build and dressed as though she had just stepped out of one of those adverts for stair lifts or reading lamps for the elderly that he had seen in the back of the *Sunday Times* supplement. She was immaculate in a round-necked blue polyester dress with large brooch and a neat, tightly fitting white cardigan. Around her neck was draped a set of extremely large, bright orange beads. Her inevitable thick, flesh-coloured tights were wrinkling slightly around the ankles and her tiny feet were nicely cushioned in a pair of flat slip-on shoes. Her grey hair was perfectly washed and set, backcombed and heavily sprayed.

An unlikely couple, but it takes all sorts, Peter thought to himself as he began to skim his 5B pencil over the paper, producing a reasonable outline of the card players. He never scrimped on paper quality and although he did not quite go for the top of the range cotton-based variety, he did like to use a fairly heavy two-ply wood pulp. He could see the ladies moving their pegs in a wooden board and he was pretty sure they were playing cribbage. When he heard 'the Pink Tee Shirt' declare in a loud voice, "Fifteen two, fifteen four, fifteen six and a pair's eight!" his suspicions were confirmed.

A few minutes passed and the women, having finished their game, had already started another when Norbert arrived once again at Peter's table.

"Your Welsh rarebit, Mr Davis," he declared, carefully positioning the plate to the right of a pile of pencils that had now been brought into commission by Peter as he sought to add some detail to what was turning out to be a rather good picture.

"Do be careful, please, it's very hot," said Norbert, smiling as he scanned the drawing quickly, immediately noticing the resemblance it bore to the occupants of table three.

"That is very good, Mr Davis. You have certainly captured the scene extremely well," he said hesitantly. "Particularly..." he continued, "how should I say it – the larger lady."

Peter turned his head, looked directly at Norbert and, with a grin on his face, replied, "Yes, I think so. I just draw what I see."

The private joke and accompanying schoolboy grins exchanged, Peter asked for another cup of coffee and returned to the drawing. Five minutes later coffee number two materialised and assumed the place on the table that had been occupied by its predecessor. Peter added a few little squiggles to the sketch and leant back in his seat, exhaling with satisfaction.

"That'll do, I think. It's not too bad."

"Mr Davis, it's better than not bad. You've captured them perfectly," said Norbert, marvelling at the amazingly detailed representation of table three that had been produced in such a short space of time. "You are very talented. I think it's brilliant."

Peter added his signature in the bottom right-hand corner and, in inverted commas, wrote 'Table Three' underneath. He then tore the sheet from his pad with a well-practised flourish and handed it to Norbert.

"Here. Take it."

Norbert looked uncertain and Peter assumed he was inwardly debating the ethics of accepting a gift from a guest. Assessing there was no harm and also that he would really rather like the picture, he replied politely, "Are you sure?"

"Yes, of course. It's just a doodle. I'm glad you like it."

Satisfied that he wasn't taking advantage of the elderly man and committing a potentially dismissible offence, Norbert gleefully took the picture.

"Thank you so much, Mr Davis. Wait until my wife sees it. She'll love it." Secretly Norbert also wanted to show the picture to his colleagues Stefan and Paul with whom he had discussed the two ladies in question on several occasions and whom he was sure would be equally amused by 'Table Three'. The high standard of professionalism he set himself, however, prevented him from sharing this additional information with Peter.

Realising that he had neglected his food, Peter took a quick swig from the fresh coffee, picked up the cutlery on the plate next to him and began to eat. After a few mouthfuls of the very tasty Welsh rarebit, he felt full. He obviously was not as hungry as he thought, or perhaps he should not have had so much coffee first. Either way, leaving the majority of it, he placed the knife and fork neatly parallel in the centre of the plate and pushed it to the side of the table. Leaning back in the surprisingly comfortable chair, he shut his eyes. Seeing how pleased the waiter was with the sketch had made Peter happy. He smiled remembering the time when selling his pictures brought in enough money to enable him to pay off his mortgage early.

Peter's parents, like many, had thrust pencils and paint brushes into his hand at an early age, encouraging him to produce a masterpiece or at least something good enough to be pinned up in the kitchen so that it could be admired by all who entered. In truth, Peter's creations were much the same as any other three- or four-year-old – indeterminate splashes and blobs of colour that could only be identified as the animal, building or person that they were assured was the subject by screwing up one's eyes or tilting the picture at the correct angle to fully appreciate it.

It was not until he gained a much sought-after boarding scholarship to Rosehill Grammar School in West Sussex that his artistic ability was spotted and then carefully nurtured. In contrast to his previous school, Rosehill was ideally suited to a pupil like Peter. Boys were judged on what they did rather than who they were and, when talent was apparent, it was supported so that the very best was obtained from it. The main school building had an imposing façade with arched porticos and enormous leaded windows surrounded by ivy that hid the ancient brickwork. Settling in to a new school was never going to be without its challenges, but Peter managed things well. By midway through the Michaelmas Term, he was able to successfully navigate the labyrinth of corridors that connected classrooms and dormitories without getting lost and had even managed to make friends with most of the other boys in his class. He had been selected to play in goal for the school's under-twelve football team and had joined the chess club, which was run by a young Polish science teacher who played competitively and who would later become one of his nation's first ever Grandmasters. He did well in all his lessons, although he found Latin difficult, but by the end of that first term, Peter felt like he belonged at Rosehill.

At the first school assembly after the Christmas holidays, the headmaster, Mr Milson, introduced some new appointments to the teaching staff, one of whom was to have an enormous impact on Peter's life. Mr Albrighton, the art teacher, who had already noticed Peter's obvious talent for drawing, had taken a post in his home town of Scarborough, the headmaster explained, so that he could be near to his mother whose health was failing. His replacement came in the form of the diminutive figure of Mr Anton Carling, who made up for what he lacked in height (he couldn't have been an inch over five foot three) with a personality that oozed confidence and a wardrobe that matched. He always wore black or grey trousers but possessed an enormous array of different coloured smocks which he rotated frequently and which were used as much as a fashion statement as they were a garment to protect the white shirt that he favoured underneath. His outfit was always completed by a paisley cravat which was worn jauntily around his neck as a reminder to those who needed one that he was an artist rather than a man of books.

Mr Carling soon recognised that Peter possessed a raw artistic flair, and over the years that followed, he helped him to refine his technique whilst ensuring that his natural ability was encouraged to flourish. By the time Peter left Rosehill, he had been transformed into a promising artist whose work formed the centrepiece of an exhibition of students' art which was displayed for parents to admire at Speech Day. Drawing and painting became a constant for Peter and a welcome refuge to which he would retreat when he wanted to relax.

As the years passed, Peter began to sell his pictures to friends and acquaintances. He received commissions, most of which were for landscapes, which he found quite easy to produce. On one occasion in the early 1970s, he was introduced to a 'really hip dude' by someone at work. This 'guy' who owned a night club was apparently also 'cool' and, according to the colleague in question, he 'dug Peter's art'. This all made good sense until he told Peter that he wanted him to paint a nude. To be precise, a completely naked woman reclining on a settee. Sensing Peter's reticence, he produced a large cardboard box, explaining that he did not expect him to use a live model and he could probably find everything he needed in the magazines that filled the container to the brim. Peter had never seen so much pornography in one place and, over the course of the next few weeks, painted, as requested, the three feet by four feet reproduction of a blonde, sun-tanned woman sprawled invitingly on a red satin sheet draped over a black chaise longue. It was, Peter later reflected, the tackiest thing he had ever done. The client, however, was delighted, announcing that it would adorn the wall in his office at 'The Club'. Most importantly he paid handsomely and insisted with an 'I bet I know what you'll do with them' wink that Peter could also keep the magazines. He could hardly wait for the man to leave with his picture (although the overpowering smell of Blue Stratos took some time longer to depart) so that he could throw them on a bonfire at the end of the garden.

Peter was not an art snob, but he knew what he liked and developed a style of his own influenced by some of his favourite artists, such as Renoir, Dufy and Chagall. As his portfolio of work continued to grow, he held a few small exhibitions at home which proved very profitable, with his work being snapped up by friends of friends who had attended. Peter had always bought his art supplies from a shop in Walthamstow which was about a twenty-minute drive from home, and he had built up a good rapport with the owner, who had often given him discounts, particularly when he bought large quantities. He knew that old Mr Crompton could not go on forever and that Mrs Crompton had her sights set on a move to a cottage in the country, but it still came as a disappointment when he told Peter that he was selling up. The good news was that the new owner intended to keep the art shop going, which Peter thought made a lot of sense based on the good will built up by the Cromptons over the twenty years they had been there.

Peter's contented smile broadened as he leant back further in his chair, concentrating hard to try and picture old man Crompton. He had met a lot of people through his artwork. Most, he reflected, were innately good and Mr Crompton was one of the best. Sadly, though, there was one very notable exception that Peter would never be able to forget.

Chapter 2

I seem to be on the deck of a boat. No, it's much bigger than a boat and there are crowds of people looking over the side at the water. There is an enormous funnel protruding upwards from the middle, so perhaps it's a ship or a cruise liner. When I look more closely, I realise there are not as many people as I first thought, just a few groups milling about the deck, looking out to sea. A cluster of three men are pointing at the coastline ahead, which is fast approaching. I am sitting on a rounded wooden bench which is one in a block of six. I glance up and, perched on the bench opposite me, I can see Zhechev. He is grinning smugly at me and he looks like the cat that has got the cream. In return, I do my best to scowl, although I am not entirely sure why. It has little effect because he seems completely oblivious to my aggression. Quite suddenly it occurs to me precisely where we both are. This is a ferry, not a ship, and we are crossing the Channel, heading for France.

I stare once again at the face of Dimitar Zhechev, the art dealer who took over the shop from the Cromptons. His self-satisfied, condescending smirk somehow exudes confidence and control. It's as though he knows something that I don't, something that is going to happen. That worries me, which I assume is precisely his intention. Neither of us speak, but I am conscious now of more than his face. His smart dark grey blazer and spotted tie. No, it's not a tie; it's a cravat. And spilling out from his top pocket is a handkerchief with the same pattern on it. That detestable trickster that I have grown to loath, perfectly dressed as always. As I watch, the two items of clothing merge into one enormous garment that obscures his face, and he disappears. Zhechev has gone, and I am surrounded for a moment by a mass of polka dots that have been left where he was. Then, in a flash, he returns like a magician. The dots are around his neck again and have reformed into an even more impressive silk cravat. I half expect him to take a bow, but there is no applause because no one except me is paying attention – perhaps the crowd has seen this illusion before.

I didn't notice before, but he has a pair of sunglasses perched on his head even though it doesn't seem particularly bright on deck. In fact, the sky is grey and it looks very much like it is about to rain. I'm not aware of what I am wearing, but judging by his superior glances in my direction, I am not as well dressed as him. I feel a little uncomfortable but go along with things because he is still smiling and seems to like me in spite of the revulsion that I feel towards him. He opens his mouth and now, quite unexpectedly, I can hear him speaking.

"Your pictures are wonderful. They are going to love them."

I say nothing in response, but I manage the sort of smile you give to someone speaking a foreign language, hoping that in their next sentence you can latch on to a few familiar words that help you to form a sensible response. He is oblivious to my tactic and simply carries on with his flattery.

"Well done, Peter," he says, his smile becoming broader. He reaches across to shake my hand, but as he does, it begins to rain, gently at first and then much heavier. Big drops begin to explode all around me like the water bombs we used to make as children. In seconds I am soaked to the skin, so I jump up and run towards a door in search of shelter. For some inexplicable reason, Zhechev stays seated, laughing contentedly to himself. He's a fool, I think, he'll be drenched in no time. But as I look back towards the seat, I can see that he is perfectly dry and his clothes are as immaculate as before. He has pulled his sunglasses down to shield his eyes from a solitary ray of sunlight, isolated from the downpour, which has settled directly on him while the rain continues to bounce off the deck.

I go through the doorway, leaving him outside, or so I think. This does not make any sense, but Zhechev is in here with me. I consider going back on deck to check whether he is still there and this is actually an imposter, but the door has disappeared, so I'm not going to be able to do that. I am stuck in here. He has seen me, of course, and because I can't think of anything else to do, I nod to him in recognition. A crowd of people is gathered around him, urgently pushing and shouting to make themselves heard. Ignoring the clamour surrounding him, with a stylish swish of the hand, he beckons me to join them. Presumably this is the real Zhechev because he definitely knows me and his charm offensive on deck is continuing with smiles and introductions. His companions are all dressed very smartly. Men in suits and ladies in long dresses. I don't know any of them, but it feels like they are all staring at me. There is an enormous chandelier above us which is giving off much less light than it ought to. I struggle to see Zhechev in the gloom and can only just make out his face. I look at the others around me, but I can't see properly what any of them look like either. They're shadows of movement but don't seem to possess any obvious human qualities that might help me recognise who they are.

And then one of them comes towards me and I do not have time to move away. I am glad that I did not take evasive action on reflection, however, as next to me, so close she is almost touching me, is a beautiful young woman with perfectly tanned skin. Her blonde hair falls onto her shoulders and extends to her breasts – she is naked. I gaze at her body and drink in its perfection. Noticing, she smiles encouragingly and leans over to whisper something to me. Her face is close to mine and as her mouth moves, I can't take my eyes off her lips. I think about kissing her because I definitely sense she wants me to. A coy smile of glossy red lipstick invites me and I touch the softness of her shoulder and lean my mouth towards hers. The people who moments ago were nearby have faded into the distance; even Zhechev is no longer visible. Right now, the only things that matter are those voluptuous lips. I kiss her passionately and lose control as yearning becomes desire. Looking directly into her beautiful eyes, I am desperate for more. I pull her close so that I can feel her lips on mine again and I can see her tongue and her bright white teeth. She is magnificent. But then, without warning, the gap between our open mouths closes abruptly and instead of her tongue sliding sensually against mine, it hits me hard in the face like a chameleon in search of a juicy fly. It is rough and stings painfully. Suddenly I feel myself falling into an enormous hole that has appeared from nowhere beneath my feet.

The chandelier has gone and the room I find myself in now is much smaller with hardly any illumination at all. The beautiful woman is still here though and she is wearing a very tight-fitting dress that shimmers as she moves. If anything, she is even more sexy than when she was naked. She turns and stares at me and all I can see are two perfect breasts peeking out at me from her dress. Is she nodding at me? Urging me to do what she seems to know I want. Is she telling me to touch them? I think she is and although I know it is probably not right and I've got a nagging feeling that the people in the other room are going to see, I stretch out my arm and my hand cups her soft flesh. She doesn't flinch and I can see her smiling and appearing to enjoy it even though all I am really doing is pawing her like a clumsy adolescent. I notice that there's someone standing next to her, and I *see polka dots – the Bulgarian is back, and he is grinning at me knowingly.*

I sense immediately that he approves of me touching the young woman, but it occurs to me that I ought to stop now, mainly because I am afraid of that tongue of hers. In any case, the moment is gone, and he is here, very much playing the gooseberry. Nice while it lasted, but it's over now. What's next? They exchange glances and I am left in no doubt that they know each other. She is less interested in me now, which is a little deflating for me, and appears to be fixated on him instead. They are leading me towards a wall that is covered in paintings, and I definitely get the impression now that the woman knows her way around this place – perhaps she lives here. They are laughing as though at the punchline of a private joke and I feel a wave of sadness because I am being excluded. He kisses her and she yields to him in front of me. I feel completely ostracised and utterly desolate. She obviously wants to be with him and not me. Then, as though feeling my distress, they each take one of my arms and pull me over to the wall. I can't see much of the detail of the pictures, but they are pointing at one in particular and it looks familiar to me. I don't know why, but I've definitely seen that orange sun that dominates the landscape somewhere before.

Then the penny drops – it was one of my paintings. Actually, it's not just any one of my paintings – it's THE painting. It has been so long since I've seen it that I had almost forgotten what it looked like. I am being stupid – how could I forget that scene? Everything floods back in an instant as every minute brush stroke reveals itself to me. The white stone of the ruins in that glorious garden. The majestic trees like sentinels guarding the ancient edifice and reaching up to a dark blue sky, perhaps the prelude to a thunderstorm to end that hot summer day. The flowers, the grass and again I am drawn inexorably to the orange of that sun, still powerful but about to give way to the inevitable dusk, and beyond that the blackness of night. And then, without any obvious interference or disturbance, it's gone and Zhechev is holding the woman in his arms again. They embrace tightly and all I can see is a mixture of polka dots, blonde hair and tanned skin combining and gradually, in front of me, becoming an ugly black monster. I have to escape from this hideous beast. I run as fast as I can through a big door and I am safe.

It's sunny outside and the street I am standing in is busy. I see stalls and assume it must be market day. The young woman is there with me and she is wearing clothes this time. Somehow, I feel less threatened by her, but I am not sure why considering her previous actions. She looks just as stunning as before, but I don't really want to go too close in case she whips me again with that tongue of hers. People are staring at the two of us as we walk, apparently happy together, hand in hand away from the market and up a steep hill. It feels good to hold her and as we carry on our journey, we pass a group of soldiers firing guns into the distance. Some of them fall over dead. Presumably someone is shooting back at them, although I can't see anyone. There is no sign of Zhechev, which relaxes me. Eventually we reach the top of the hill, but there is nothing there. She turns to face me and I see her smile. She unzips her top, revealing her naked breasts, and I want to touch them, to caress their warm, smooth softness. She must want me to touch her, otherwise she would not have unveiled them for me. I look up at her face again, but her hideous tongue is forcing its way past those perfect teeth. She unleashes it in my direction, and I have to dodge so that it misses me.

She has disappeared and thank goodness I seem to have evaded her again. I can't help but wonder where she has gone and I feel a strange sense of loss even though I know full well I should avoid her at all costs. I am in a room I don't recognise. It could be a hotel, or an office, or possibly someone's home. The door in front of me, which is ajar, catches my attention. It's the only thing here, so it would be stupid not to open it a little further so that I can see what is going on inside. Part relieved that there is not a giant tongue-wielding woman in the room and part inexplicably angry, I see polka dots. They clear, revealing an almost empty room. It is not obvious to me if the floor is carpeted or if anyone is in here. There is a very plain-looking wooden table in the middle of the room and not much else by the looks of it. A noise is coming from the far side of the room, but there is no one there. As I am about to enter, I notice that there is a painting leaning against one of the table legs. Although I try, I am unable to see it clearly at this distance; however, I can make out an orange light which is shining brightly from it. The light becomes more intense and fills the room so that now the table is not even visible. I want to go and take a closer look, but as I try, I begin to move further away from the door or perhaps it is moving further away from me. It's as though I am being dragged helplessly backwards on an invisible conveyor belt. I could nearly touch the handle a moment ago, but even if I stretch now, I can't reach it.

I'm determined to get inside so that I can see the picture. I want it and I intend to have it, although I am not sure why. But I'm moving slowly, so slowly in fact that I am not getting any nearer the door. This is ridiculous. I'm walking through treacle. I reach for the open door. If I can grab the handle, I might be able to pull myself nearer. What has happened to my legs? They are not working properly. And then just as it feels like I am about to get there, the door slams shut right in front of me and suddenly the room and the picture have gone.

Nothingness for a while and then I am clearly somewhere else. I am in another street which seems vaguely familiar but equally not a location that I can pinpoint precisely. I am facing a row of shops, but they all look grey, and I can't read any of the names above them. The odd car goes by, but other than that, it is completely deserted. No people, no noise, and now that I look a little closer, all the shops seem empty. None of them have any stock in the window. There are no people inside, no lighting, and I can only assume they are all shut or possibly even closed down completely. Without making a conscious decision, I move towards one particular shop. There is no logic to my selection because it looks just like all the others around it.

Very abruptly, it feels as though night has fallen and I have a sudden impulse to enter the shop. I push at the door, but it does not yield. It has been locked and I notice some of the windows have boards over them. Nonetheless I am not deterred in my quest to get inside or at the very least to alert anyone who might be in the shop to my presence. So, I bang on the door. A knock or a tap at first, but then when there is no response, I hit the door harder. It is like hitting a wall. The thud of my blows reverberates as though the door is made of some high tensile metal. I hit it again, with both hands, one after the other as hard as I can, but it is no use. All I can hear is the bang, bang, bang of my clenched fists against the impregnable barrier.

Chapter 3

Peter was woken by a loud banging noise and as he opened his eyes, he became aware that there was some sort of disturbance going on in the café. After a few moments he realised that what he had heard was someone thumping their hand very firmly on one of the wooden tables. His eyes gradually focused on the man who was evidently the culprit and was now also shouting frantically. He was standing some distance away, waving his arms and pointing at the large window behind him. Peter's first thought was that it was probably a yob complaining about something. He bristled disapprovingly, considering for a moment how the quality of the clientele on these cruises had fallen now that lower prices had made them an affordable alternative to Benidorm or Torremolinos for such people. He certainly did not consider himself superior despite this reaction, but he did like people to behave themselves properly. Looking across he half expected to see shorts and a vest, tattoos, and to hear the estuary English that defined the type of individual he was imagining. To his surprise, however, the troublemaker was smartly dressed in sharply creased grey trousers and a navy-blue blazer. Under the blazer was a seemingly spotless, bright white shirt and a navy-blue and green striped tie with some sort of emblem or insignia on it. His black shoes had been so thoroughly polished that there was no question they could be used as a mirror if one was needed in an emergency. Having assessed his attire, Peter was next struck by his physique. He was solidly built and appeared considerably younger than the majority of his fellow passengers. Although not very nearby, he was close enough for Peter to hear the odd word and the decibel level of his voice rising as the cause of his agitation became audible to the other patrons.

He spoke clearly and in what Peter used to call BBC English before standards fell even there. What was most odd, Peter thought, was that he did not appear to be addressing anyone in particular and there was no one on any of the tables surrounding him that had been singled out as the target for his tirade.

"Look at these windows. They're not secure!" he was yelling, apparently to anyone who would listen. "This wouldn't have happened in my day. These locks are not good enough. They're not safe."

By now most of the café goers were, in true British style, desperately trying to avoid eye contact with the man who was beginning to sound rather angry. One poor couple who were sitting closest were spotted by him as they got up to move to another table.

"Don't walk away," he hollered. "There's something wrong with these windows and there is no point ignoring it."

Peter wondered if perhaps he was concerned about rising sea levels. They were on one of the higher decks though, so that did not seem to make much sense. He had heard about freak tidal waves coming over the higher decks in extreme storms and high winds. In fact, one of Joan's friends had, according to her version of events, been sunbathing on an Adriatic cruise with her husband when a wave had thundered over the deck and washed them and their fellow sunseekers into the pool, around which they had previously been relaxing. "Sunbeds and all," he remembered her explaining to Joan in order to leave her in no doubt as to the severity of the onslaught they had faced. Surely though, something like that was unlikely, especially in this sort of weather. There wasn't a cloud in the sky and the sea was like a mill pond. Of course, it was possible that the man knew something he did not about the forecast. Nevertheless, such a dramatic change to the current conditions seemed highly unlikely.

The man was becoming more proactive now, shouting increasingly loudly and confronting other guests, moving as he did from table to table. Peter was reminded of an occasion on his way home from work one evening when a man on his tube train had terrorised passengers by telling them the world was going to end. He recalled how miraculously the other commuters had found books to read or crosswords to do in order to avoid any engagement with him. The relief was palpable when the miscreant alighted at Liverpool Street to allow a new group of unsuspecting travellers on the platform there to share the benefit of the herald of Armageddon's insight.

That individual, though, wore dirty clothes and had long unwashed hair. And, if Peter remembered rightly, he was also clutching a can of Tennant's Extra very tightly, the contents of which occasionally spilled out as his passion about the world's impending doom intensified. This man was a very different kettle of fish, thought Peter. Dapper, intelligent-sounding and delivering his message in a structured, if somewhat obstreperous, manner.

"We need to take this up with the management!" he bawled at one poor chap, who, flinching from the oncoming broadside, dropped his glasses and was now grappling around on the floor in search of them.

People were becoming uneasy, and although Peter remained some distance from the epicentre of the man's invective, he began to pack up his pencils in case a speedy exit became necessary. Relief for all came in the shape of two crew members who, breaking off from their debate about whether oat or almond milk tasted better in tea, came out of the kitchen door and at pace advanced towards the man. The arrival of a third uniformed liberator confirmed that some strong-arm tactics could be in the offing. The blazered man was now flailing his arms around, and had also augmented his repertoire of sound by occasionally stamping on the floor while continuing to point intermittently at the window. As they approached him the three slowed, intending to try and calm him, and it soon became apparent, much to the reassurance of those watching, that the man was known to them.

"Okay, Mr Chadwick, could we quieten it down a bit, please? I'm sure we can sort everything out," said the smaller of the waiters as he cautiously but confidently addressed the man.

The scene that followed would not have been out of place had the protagonists been well-practised clowns in a circus act. The man, sensing that the oncoming group were about to attempt to curtail his protestations, stopped shouting, stood still for a second, turned to his right, and in what could only have been an attempt to bamboozle, thought Peter, crouched and performed a perfect forward roll on the soft carpet beneath him. This had the desired effect as all three pursuers were completely blindsided by the manoeuvre, managing only to stare, in some admiration no doubt, as the man stood up with a jump between tables fourteen and fifteen. Apparently satisfied, he then stayed completely still as a pincer movement comprising the other two chasers carefully approached and ensured both of his arms were firmly restrained.

"Right then, Mr Chadwick, why don't you come with us now?" said the third waiter, who had now joined his colleagues. "It's all going to be fine. There's no need to worry. We'll ask our maintenance team to check things out and make sure all the windows are secure."

Mr Chadwick nodded meekly in approval, now curiously subdued all of a sudden as though someone had thrown a switch that turned him off at the mains. Maybe, thought Peter, he was exhausted by his acrobatic performance or perhaps, more likely, he had done himself an injury.

"Let's find you somewhere to have a sit down for a bit and we'll fetch your wife," the waiter continued as he and his colleagues escorted Mr Chadwick, who now looked somewhat bewildered by the extent of his new-found fame, out of the café.

Things returned to normal surprisingly quickly. Readers picked up their magazines and books, gazers again looked dreamily out of the windows as others turned their attention once more to their food and drinks. On table three the smartly dressed lady declared "One for his knob!" and adjusted the position of her peg in the board in front of her accordingly.

A waiter was clearing cups and plates from a table nearby and at the same time reassuring another lady who had been so alarmed that she had dropped her blackcurrant yoghurt on the floor.

"Please don't worry yourself, Mrs Dalrymple, we are very used to Mr Chadwick's behaviour. He worked for many years in the Health and Safety industry and sometimes can get a bit carried away if you know what I mean. I'll be back in a moment to clean the floor and bring you another yoghurt."

Mrs Dalrymple was still in a state of shock but managed a mumble of acknowledgement which was not quite a full endorsement of what she had heard but did, if nothing else, establish that she had not lost the power of speech altogether.

"He'll be fine once he gets some fresh air," the man added with a series of encouraging nods in an attempt to convince her further as he headed off in the direction of the kitchen.

A short while passed and a few people left and were duly replaced by newcomers who were unaware of the kerfuffle that had taken place only minutes earlier. Peter looked around the room with no great purpose. He felt restless and a little on edge, which was strange because he was not particularly bothered by Mr Chadwick's outburst. If anything, now that it was over, he thought the whole incident had been quite comical in a way. He could not put his finger on the reason for the anxiety that was consuming him and this disturbed him all the more. It was only then that he remembered his dream. That was why he felt uncomfortable. The dream itself was decidedly unpleasant, but some of the memories it provoked inside him were much more distressing to him.

It was in early 1977 that he first met Mr Zhechev, who was the new owner of the Cromptons' art shop. He had been pleasant enough, if a bit smarmy with his flashy suit and pocket handkerchief. Peter recalled that he had explained he was really an art dealer primarily and that the shop was only a side line for him. Apparently, he had bought a Victorian town house in Dalston which was being renovated, so he was currently living in the flat above the shop until it was finished. Mr Crompton had left notes about some of his better customers, and the new owner had been alerted, therefore, to the fact that Peter was having considerable success selling his pictures. Insisting that Peter should call him Dimitar, he went on to describe his plans to turn part of the large storeroom at the rear of the shop into a gallery. His intention was to sell his customers' art there predominantly and he wondered if Peter would be interested in exhibiting. It seemed like a great idea and having agreed what he thought was a pretty reasonable commission of twenty-five percent, Peter dropped off the first few pictures the following week.

A few months later, having sold three or four of Peter's pictures, Dimitar said he thought that the style of Peter's painting might be well received on the Continent. The impressionist influence on his landscapes and scenes that included people appealed to the French sense of history, he explained, as long as they were original enough to be interesting. He thought that Peter's work could be perfect for the French market and suggested he put them in an exhibition in Paris that was to take place in the summer. Dimitar enthusiastically explained that he would be able to make all the necessary arrangements as he knew someone on the organising committee and he was quite happy to take the same commission on anything that sold if that was agreeable to Peter.

The exhibition was arranged over a weekend and all pictures had to be at the venue by the Friday evening at the latest. They decided that Peter would pick up Dimitar early on the Friday morning for the drive to Dover where they could catch the first ferry of the day to Boulogne. Rather than risk damaging the pictures by loading and unloading them, they planned to take the car across and drive again to the small town of Suresnes just to the west of Paris where the exhibition was being held. It would be a tiring journey, but provided they had worked out their timings correctly, they should arrive by late afternoon. That would give them plenty of time to settle into the hotel, have something to eat and deliver the pictures to the exhibition that evening.

The exact location of the exhibition was a very grand chateau which, they were informed, had been inhabited by the local gentry since the sixteenth century. To the rear it was surrounded by gardens with parcels of hedging that each enveloped a different splash of colour from the flowers planted within them. It was the epitome of historic French chic with no detail out of place and when the colours in the boxwood parterre ran out, the manicured lawns continued until they could just be seen in the distance reaching the banks of the Seine. To the front was a large entrance courtyard which had no doubt served as a defence against unwanted visitors in the past. For the weekend in question, however, it was home to temporary signs providing directions to the car park and a man in a yellow jacket occasionally waving his arms should anyone require additional clarification.

As they went through the main doors, their names were taken by a middle-aged woman in tortoiseshell spectacles who, having ticked the sheet of paper on the clip board she had previously held tightly to her chest, invited them, and the paintings they held, to enter. Inside the chateau was equally glamorous and stylish. The exquisite decorative detail of the entrance hall with its hand painted chinoiserie mural and sumptuous antique carpet was breathtaking. Mahogany tables and hand carved chairs were positioned for maximum effect. Delftware and Sevres porcelain elegantly adorned sideboards and mantelpieces and wonderful sculptures filled alcoves arranged opposite one another to create a feeling of symmetry. Peter made a mental note to have a closer look later at a stunning equestrian painting by Eugene Delacroix as Dimitar hurried him past it. He gazed in appreciation at the huge windows, designed and strategically placed to ensure that every available particle of light came through them to illuminate the neo-classical opulence and old-world grandeur inside. There were, hanging from the astonishingly high ceiling, eight gigantic chandeliers that sprayed light extravagantly around the room, to ensure that this continued when day gave way to evening.

Two magnificent Louis XV chairs upholstered a la Reine stood at the foot of the grand staircase that led to the first floor. Peter admired them as he passed, but once again, to his disappointment, Dimitar did not pause to appreciate their surroundings. Instead, he continued to walk a step or two in front of Peter, encouraging him to follow or become detached. The reason became clear when a young woman approached and greeted him with a kiss on either cheek. As though they were caught in a revolving door, they then turned as one to face him. Dimitar introduced the vision that exuded sophistication and expensive perfume as Sophie Leclaire, the curator of the exhibition. She had blonde hair that seemed almost white under the glare of the chandeliers. It fell delicately on the tanned skin of her shoulders and rested above her firm breasts, which shone like beacons of forbidden fruit from the decolletage of her tight blue satin dress. She fixed him with her green eyes and smiled at him, revealing perfectly aligned white teeth. Peter was stunned by her beauty and realised that he had temporarily lost the power of both movement and speech.

Sophie showed them into another large room where the lighting was provided for the most part by bright spotlights that shone on the pictures that had already been hung and the blank spaces ready for those which had not yet arrived. Dimitar nodded knowingly while she explained how things would work as Peter handed over his three pictures to a man wearing white gloves. In addition to the exhibition there would be a competition, after which the paintings could be purchased. A representative of the Louvre would attend on Saturday and announce the result on Sunday morning. Prices would be agreed for each picture so that visitors could acquire them if they wished. It was, Peter realised, evidently quite a prestigious event with the Medaille D'Or being awarded to the winner with silver and bronze medals for the runners up. Sophie then flashed her enchanting smile again, apologising that she needed to go and deal with another exhibitor who had just arrived from Italy.

When they were alone again, Peter was curious to find out how well Dimitar knew Sophie, and the art dealer was only too pleased to tell him. He explained that their relationship was purely professional and that she had curated a number of exhibitions that he had attended over the years. Whilst Peter was trying to work out whether he was telling the truth, Dimitar casually mentioned that he had arranged for her to give Peter a tour of Suresnes in the morning. He had one or two things he had to sort out and she was not needed at the chateau until noon, so he had asked her to meet Peter at the café opposite the hotel for coffee at nine. Peter was simultaneously flabbergasted, excited and worried. Why had Dimitar done this? Why did she want to spend time with him? Was there an ulterior motive? What about Joan? If he went along with this, was he being disloyal to her? Fortunately, common sense then kicked in and he managed to rationalise the situation. He concluded that provided he treated it as a kindness from a local rather than a romantic assignation, all would be fine. In any case, how could a woman like that possibly be interested in him?

The next morning, after breakfast, Peter nodded to the concierge as he left the hotel and crossed the street, which was bathed in the sunshine of early summer. He was a little early, but as he approached the café, he caught sight of Sophie, who was already waiting for him at a shaded table outside. She was sitting with one leg crossed over the other, wearing a tangerine leisure suit. A pair of black-rimmed oversized sunglasses perched on top of her head and whisps of her bright blonde hair were temporarily displaced by them. She waved gently in case he had not seen her, smiling enthusiastically as she did so. He noticed that her top was fastened at the front by a zip which had been casually pulled up so that it barely covered her breasts. Peter smiled back, desperately trying not to stare at her as she nonchalantly oozed chic. Feeling embarrassed by her beauty, Peter extended a hand to her when she stood up to greet him. Ignoring this, she smiled again and, placing a manicured hand on his shoulder, kissed him softly on each cheek. They sat down and Peter became immediately conscious of the glances cast towards them by some of the other patrons. He allowed himself to bask proudly in the attention of the onlookers even though he knew full well that they were not at all interested in him.

They ordered coffee and, as they drank, she outlined her ideas for the morning. The main landmarks in town were the cemetery and memorial to American soldiers killed in the world wars and Fort Mont-Valérien, with another memorial commemorating French soldiers and Resistance fighters. This interested Peter as he had heard a lot about the Resistance, but he did not want to appear overexcited about such a sombre subject. Sophie lightened the atmosphere by adding that from the high ground there you could look across to Paris and on a day like this they should be able to see the Eiffel Tower quite clearly.

As they finished their coffees and Sophie rose again, Peter could feel the stares of both men, who simultaneously sat up straight in their chairs and thrust out their chests, and women who gazed at Sophie with a mixture of admiration and envy.

They strolled slowly through the cemetery and past the memorials, pausing respectfully from time to time for Sophie to explain things that were of particular importance. Peter tried to put thoughts of Sophie's beauty out of his head and began to think of her as a tour

25

guide and her words those of a matronly history teacher. It was difficult. The smell of her perfume, her hair fluttering in the faint breeze or simply the curves of her body pressing tightly against her clothes continually invaded and teased his senses. He thought of Joan, oblivious to all this, at home with the children while he paraded through the town with this stunningly gorgeous and charming Frenchwoman. The guilt nagged away at him, but he kept telling himself that this was all very innocent even though he knew deep down that many of his thoughts were not. They stood and looked towards Paris and, as she extended her arm in the direction of the Eiffel Tower, her top stretched – revealing, for just a moment, the top of a suntanned breast as it pressed against her zip. He hastily averted his eyes, hoping he had done so before she had noticed him looking at her.

On the way back to the hotel, they chatted about his painting, occasionally stopping to say hello to someone she knew or to look in a shop window. She was sorry that it was only a quick tour, but she needed to go home and change before returning to the chateau. He said that he understood and was sure he and Dimitar would pop in later to see how things were going at the exhibition.

When she had left, Peter scoured the hotel but could not find Dimitar anywhere, so he ordered a beer and a sandwich which he ate in the lounge. When he had finished, Dimitar had still not appeared, so he headed back to his room to relax after the morning's exertions. Just as he was getting into the lift, he heard his name being called and turned to see the Bulgarian art dealer walking briskly towards him. He looked very smart in a grey flannel suit and carried a leather briefcase in his left hand. Peter assumed he had been to a business meeting of some kind but did not like to ask, preferring instead to let Dimitar tell him if he wanted him to know. They agreed to meet at three o'clock so that they could head back to the chateau where the Louvre's expert would probably be coming towards the end of his initial assessment.

On the way to the exhibition, Dimitar asked about the morning and Peter told him what he had learnt of the town and where Sophie had taken him. He was clearly pleased they had enjoyed their morning but did not volunteer any information concerning his own activities or why they involved such formal attire. Peter decided not to press him, concluding that, odd though it was, it was really none of his business.

When they arrived, there were a lot of people milling about and Dimitar explained that they were mostly press covering the exhibition for various newspapers. Large vans were parked by the elaborate formal gardens. Cameras and lights were being hauled past the delicate marquetry of the doors and it occurred to Peter that this combination, spanning as it did about three hundred years, provided a truly surreal contrast.

Inside, a television crew were setting up their equipment at the bottom of the staircase. Peter had not imagined that there would be so much interest, but clearly the presence of someone from the Louvre was quite a coup for Suresnes. Dimitar breezed through the crowd looking only vaguely over his shoulder every now and again to make sure Peter was following him. They passed the television cameras and headed into the main exhibition room. Sophie was there talking to a plump middle-aged woman who had squeezed herself into a skirt and blouse, both of which looked at least two sizes too small for her. A few moments later Sophie came over and thanked them for saving her. She was wearing a cream blouse which despite having the top three buttons undone was smart rather than sexy. With her knee-length skirt and medium-heeled black shoes, she was clearly in business mode. Peter felt himself relax a little. The lady she had dodged was, they learnt, apparently a reporter from Paris Match who had overindulged on the complimentary champagne on offer and consequently would not stop talking.

Dimitar was extremely keen to know if there was any word as to which pictures the Louvre expert seemed to favour. She explained that Monsieur Lefevre had walked the room twice, spending a few moments looking at each of the ninety pictures on display and making notes on a small pad. He had then moved to the middle of the room where he stood, contemplating them at distance before revisiting about fifteen of them, spending longer with each and scribbling on his pad as he did so. To pre-empt the question that they were about to ask, she added with an enthusiastic smile that one of the fifteen was Peter's painting of 'The Ruins at Cowdray Park'.

Peter was thrilled that he had potentially made the top fifteen and better than that, a cultured eye had seen something special in what he had produced. Dimitar was pleased too and allowed himself a modest grin before Sophie apologised that she could not stop to chat because she had to find Monsieur Lefevre and make sure he had everything he needed. She was attending a dinner that evening which had been organised in his honour and she would of course let them know if he said anything about his deliberations.

Peter and Dimitar wandered around assessing the competition for half an hour or so before deciding to return to the hotel for dinner and an early night.

The next morning, just as Peter was finishing his breakfast, Dimitar rushed excitedly into the hotel restaurant. He had already spoken to Sophie on the telephone that morning and she told him that Monsieur Lefevre, who clearly enjoyed the sound of his own voice, was very happy to tell the table about some of his favourite pictures. Sophie had made a mental note and she counted six that he had talked about particularly enthusiastically. The good news was, Dimitar explained, that Peter's was one of that smaller group.

At 10.00 am the two men met in the hotel lobby and headed for the chateau. The result was scheduled to be announced at around eleven, so they wanted to be there in plenty of time. A small stage had been erected in the hall overnight and shortly before eleven a group of local dignitaries began to take their seats and were then joined on the platform by Monsieur Lefevre and Sophie. A few minutes passed and Sophie approached the microphone, thanked those who were present, outlined the events of the day and then invited Monsieur Lefevre to announce the result of the contest.

Peter listened intently, his expectations significantly buoyed by Sophie's report from the previous evening. Dimitar fidgeted nervously as the bronze medal went to a local artist of some repute for his picture of yachts in the harbour at Port Vauban. An elderly Belgian lady was then awarded the silver medal for a very modern painting of interlocking coloured squares and rectangles which had caught Peter's eye when he had wandered around on Friday evening. Many people in the audience nodded approvingly at the artists as they collected their medals and took their seats on the stage. There was palpable tension as all eyes focused on Monsieur Lefevre, who explained that first prize and the gold medal was to go to an artist from England. Peter was aware that he was now holding his breath. He was by no means the only English artist there and some of the others were much better known than him, so he was not going to get carried away. And then it happened. The winner was announced as… *The Ruins at Cowdray Park* by Peter Davis and the room was suddenly filled with tumultuous applause as Peter exhaled in disbelief.

He did not remember too much about the next few minutes. Collecting his medal, being photographed with Monsieur Lefevre and the mayor and receiving the congratulations of the other artists on the stage. He did, however, recall Sophie kissing him on both cheeks again and the smile on her face when Dimitar almost lifted him off his feet as he hugged him in celebration. Eventually things calmed down and the stage was vacated so that the sale could begin.

Peter noticed a short man with a bushy beard talking to the Belgian lady, who was smiling and nodding animatedly. Then they shook hands and the woman's husband came over and embraced her warmly. The third-place French artist had also been approached by a tall, angular lady with an enormous nose and they too seemed deep in conversation. At that moment Peter could see three people he did not recognise coming towards him at pace. Trying to beat the opposition to the punch, they began to call to him. Peter heard one shout "Thirty thousand francs!" And then another countered with "Thirty-five thousand." Peter was rooted to the spot as they approached. At that moment Dimitar appeared, arms outstretched, both obstructing their progress and rounding them up in one movement. He said something to them in French and they stood still, waiting, it seemed, for him to continue. Turning to Peter he explained quite calmly that they all wanted to buy the winning picture and if Peter was in agreement, he would broker a deal for him.

Before Peter could say anything, Sophie arrived and, taking him by the hand, whisked him quickly away. She eagerly informed him that the press, including someone from *Le Figaro*, wanted to hear his reaction to winning. Over his shoulder he could see Dimitar talking to the group of possible purchasers which had now grown to five or six. Things were becoming heated as the buyers argued with one another and he was very glad not to be involved, especially since the alternative was to be with Sophie.

Using an interpreter, Peter answered questions from the press about his inspiration for the picture, the medium he had used and how it felt to win the gold medal. Cameras clicked and bulbs flashed. In a corner of the hall, his picture had been placed on a large easel and he and Sophie were encouraged to stand in front of it with the press gathered around them. Questions continued for the next three quarters of an hour. The journalists wanted to know about his choice of subject, how long he had been painting and the techniques he liked to employ. Sophie translated for him as journalists scribbled notes for their stories and photographs were taken. Eventually, Sophie called a halt to proceedings, explaining that the sale of pictures was due to start shortly, and she had to ensure that everything was ready for that.

As the last reporter wandered away, she took Peter to one side, thanked him and made a point of telling him how well he had done with the press. She embraced and congratulated him again then said that she was looking forward to catching up with him later once the sale was finished. Peter wondered if this comment was as innocent as it sounded and found himself, as if hypnotised, inhaling deeply in order to savour every last particle of her perfume as it lingered in the air she left behind. In fact, although he did not know it at the time, Peter would never see Sophie again.

The champagne and all that talking had made Peter thirsty, so he headed in search of a glass of water. Dimitar was in a corner, chatting to a man and woman, neither of whom he recognised. When Peter approached, they dissolved into another circle nearby and Dimitar turned towards him and asked how the press conference had been. They discussed this for a few minutes and Peter inquired how he was getting on with selling the picture. Dimitar explained that there were at least three interested parties and he was certain he could get a minimum of forty thousand francs but was hoping to play the purchasers off against each so that someone might pay fifty. He told Peter that he had arranged second viewings of the picture tomorrow and he should then be able to finalise the deal. Peter was a little concerned knowing that he had to leave early in the morning to travel home for work on Tuesday, but Dimitar reassured him that he was only too happy to make his own way home later in the week once he had completed the sale. This made perfect sense to Peter and even though he would rather have been involved in the process, he conceded that this was the best way forward. Dimitar assured him that he would telephone to keep him updated and to let him know the final figure as soon as it had been agreed.

As planned, Peter left after breakfast, retracing his journey and arriving home, gold medal in hand, around five o'clock that afternoon. Joan was delighted and that night they washed down the shepherd's pie she had made with a bottle of French wine Peter had bought at the ferry port. They chatted about what they might do with the money from the picture which, even after Dimitar's commission, was going to be at least £3,500. That would easily be enough for the conservatory that Joan wanted and they might even be able to use the rest to update the car.

A few days passed without any news from Dimitar. The days became a week and by the following Wednesday Peter was beginning to wonder why he had not heard anything from Dimitar. He decided to telephone him in case there was a problem, but when he did so there was no answer at the shop. He tried again after work on Thursday and there was still no reply, which Peter thought was very strange. Perhaps he had been delayed in France or was still in negotiations with prospective buyers. Unfortunately, the following week Peter's boss had arranged for him to attend a course at Head Office, but he periodically tried to contact Dimitar from his hotel. Each time he called, no one answered. When he tried on Friday afternoon, before leaving the hotel, the tone he heard had changed to unobtainable.

Peter was obviously concerned but assumed that there must be something wrong with the phone line. He did think it was odd, though, that Dimitar had not contacted him yet. He could have used another telephone or driven over to see him. Something did not feel right and he decided the best way to find out what was actually happening was to go to the shop in person. First thing on Saturday morning, Peter arrived at the art shop and was relieved to see some activity. It was open and a large van outside was making a delivery. As he approached, he looked again and realised he had been mistaken and that it was not a delivery at all. Instead, two burly men were carrying out boxes of paint and armfuls of frames. He went inside, but there was no sign of Dimitar, so Peter asked if either of the men knew where he was. They checked with each other and agreed that neither of them had heard of anyone by that name. They worked for a local removals firm and were transferring the contents of the shop and flat to a storage unit. They were expecting some colleagues to return with the other van any minute, so perhaps one of them might know something.

Peter waited patiently for the other men to arrive, but they could not help either and suggested Peter spoke to their boss, who might be able to shed some light on the matter. A few hundred yards down the road, he found a pay phone and called the office number they had given him. The owner apologised but explained that he was unable to tell him who his client was or divulge any details about them. The story was the same at the storage depot. No one could help Peter. There was no sign of Dimitar or Peter's picture.

Over the next few months, Peter continued looking for Dimitar, but it seemed that he had vanished and taken with him either Peter's picture or the money he had received for selling it. He told the police, but all they were able to do was to take details and said they would let him know if they heard anything. One of the officers thought they might be able to liaise with the French authorities, but time slipped by and there was still no news. Eventually he contacted the police again and was told that they had decided that the case could not be investigated further due to lack of resources.

To this point Peter had concentrated his efforts on finding Dimitar, but as a last resort he wrote to Sophie care of the chateau, hoping that she might know something. Eventually after a few weeks had passed, he received a reply from her office in Paris explaining that she no longer worked there and that they had no record of where she was now employed. Apparently, she had left quite abruptly and they had not been asked to provide her with a reference.

When, after about six months, the art shop became a hairdresser's, Peter had given up all hope of ever finding Dimitar or his painting. He popped into the salon one Saturday morning, but none of the young girls working there knew anything about the previous occupant. That night he and Joan had a heart-to-heart discussion and she told him in no uncertain terms that his efforts to find Dimitar were becoming rather obsessive. She tactfully suggested that although the whole thing was awful, it was perhaps time to put it behind him and move on. He knew that she was right, and although it did not sit well with him, he reluctantly agreed.

Time passed and the memory faded. Very occasionally, though, something would remind him. Perhaps a mention of Cowdray Park or someone they knew going on a trip to Paris, but he learnt to cope by turning his mind as quickly as he could to another subject. Deep down he knew he would never completely be able to eradicate the thought of Dimitar, Sophie and the theft of his painting. The only way he could truly resolve things was to find them, but as the years went by, that never happened, and he had to accept that the injustice he felt would always be with him.

Chapter 4

Opening his eyes slowly, Peter again took in his surroundings. He was pleased that everything seemed to be as usual, and people were apparently oblivious to him having been asleep. Although he felt less tired, his dream had left him a little anxious. He rarely reflected on that episode in his life and he had even put his winner's medal away in a box so that he was not reminded of it. The dream, though, had brought it all back. He had never seen Dimitar Zhechev or the picture again, although he recalled reading an article in the paper a few years later about the death of the lady whose painting came second in the contest. Evidently, she had also been a very successful author of children's books and was more famous for that than her painting. There was, however, a small version of her picture from the exhibition next to the piece and Peter thought how original her style had been. According to the newspaper, she had held on to it for some time and sold it later for seventy-five thousand francs, splitting the proceeds between her nine grandchildren.

It was not just the money; after all, he had done alright for himself since then. It was the injustice of it all that rankled. He was convinced that Dimitar and Sophie had been working together, and being distracted by her obvious charms had made him feel stupid. He had been flattered by her attention and could never shake the mental picture he had developed of the two of them laughing behind his back as they divided the proceeds of the sale. He felt embarrassed that he had been so gullible as to trust Dimitar, a man he hardly knew. How naïve he was to trust him to sell the painting on his behalf. He was comforted a little by reminding himself that he had been young and was caught up in the moment of victory. It had taken him by surprise and his judgement had been impaired. Did they know he had a chance of winning? Was that why they worked on him? Was Sophie sweet talking some of the other artists too, just in case one of them won? The local chap and the elderly Belgian lady would not have been suitable prey, of course, but perhaps some of the other foreign artists were targeted. So many unanswered questions still existed and that added to his dissatisfaction and prevented him forgetting completely. Regardless of all those things, the money, losing the picture and being duped like a fool, the other thing that hurt him in particular was the guilt of that morning with Sophie. Nothing had happened, of course. Just two people seeing the sights, talking and enjoying a coffee. He might have been daft, but no one could accuse him of being anything other than a gentleman. The problem was that he always remembered how he had felt with her. He might not have acted on those feelings, but the memory of his thoughts about her tortured him still. He had not told anyone what he was imagining, although he suspected that Sophie had a fair idea from the looks he gave her (she and Dimitar probably laughed about that too), so why did he feel so helplessly guilty? It was as though he had committed adultery in his mind with that woman, and Joan, loyal, loving Joan, did not deserve that.

He spent another hour or so sitting in the café, sketching whatever he saw. He wished he had been able to take a photograph to capture what had happened earlier with Mr Chadwick as he thought it would have made a good picture. Unfortunately, it all happened so quickly he could not even properly recall the appearance of the main protagonist now. He settled instead for a few caricatures of other passengers and an extremely accurate representation of an elegant standard lamp with a green tasselled shade, which peered out from behind a brown faux leather armchair. The scene was completed by the addition of a dark wood side table upon which stood a small silver vase containing a spray of pink carnations and white freesias.

Peter thought it was probably time that he should stretch his legs, so he collected his belongings and headed out of the café. Judging by the number of people in the corridor, he assumed it was probably lunchtime. There were groups of passengers chatting about their morning and others on their own focusing on making a beeline for the buffet. All were moving inevitably, like iron filings to a magnet in the direction of the restaurant. Peter looked to the head of the throng, half expecting to see a man dressed in breeches and a funny hat casting a musical spell on his hungry followers. Instead, he caught sight of Joan with two other ladies he assumed must be fellow crafters. He paused for a moment, looking at her laughing with them. What a smile, he thought. Apart from a few extra wrinkles at the corners of her mouth and on her cheeks, it had not changed in the fifty years they had been married. How could he have ever wanted anyone else?

In his eagerness to catch her up, he tripped slightly on a loose piece of carpet and had to steady himself on a short man in a dark green sweatshirt and baseball cap, who, having acted as a temporary buffer, did not break stride despite the unexpected nudge and hand on his shoulder. Peter did not want to call out to Joan for fear of embarrassing her. Instead he settled now for a mild acceleration, which took him past the man. Turning as he passed to smile his thanks, Peter noticed his cap was emblazoned in large letters with what looked like the words 'Shire Loss Adjustors', but without his glasses, he thought it could easily have said Spire or possibly Squire. His mind was suddenly filled with a variety of other words that it could have been. He fleetingly remembered his friend Phil whom he had met on holiday one year. Despite being a very serious senior accountant for one of the UK's leading food manufacturers, he always had a ready supply of appropriate insults in his verbal armoury. He loved football and smiled as he recalled his favourite description of his team's local rivals. Peter smiled as he imagined the baseball cap reading 'Shite Loss Adjustors'. What a brilliant marketing ploy that would be for the firm – complete honesty with prospective clients.

Pressing on now, he was only a few feet from Joan, and as she and her friends went through the doorway, he sidled in behind her, looking forward to hearing all about her activities that morning. Peter did not want anything to eat as he was not particularly hungry. The Welsh rarebit and coffee had filled him up and Joan was deep in conversation. He settled for catching her eye by waving his hand energetically above his head. She smiled but did not wave back at him and, sensing she felt a little self-conscious, he decided to leave her to it.

At the door he waited to allow three other women to enter as he exited. One clutched a plant hanger and was obviously considering her next project as she excitedly asked the friend who squeezed through the doorway by her side about the needle felted toadstools that she and the third woman were proudly grasping. So engrossed were they that they did not even bother to acknowledge Peter's courtesy. Enjoying being chivalrous rather than needing to be thanked for it, Peter was not at all affronted. He did, however, take greater offence at the overpowering smell of what he called 'old lady's perfume' that accompanied them, and which seemed to follow him as he took his turn through the door. They had evidently been a touch overzealous with their atomisers that morning, he thought to himself.

Even though he was not a particularly avid reader nowadays, Peter thought he would go to the library for a while. The main attraction of this for him was that there was usually a puzzle or two laid out on one of the tables in the centre of the room. This allowed passengers to while away spare time by contributing a small segment to perhaps a five-thousand-piece recreation of Constable's *Hay Wain* or a ridiculously difficult picture of baked beans or chocolate buttons. Once completed, the puzzles would be removed and replaced with new ones. As he had not been there for a few days, he was eager to see what the choices might be. When he arrived, he found two rather stern-looking men in tracksuits hunched over a traditional English village scene complete with thatched cottages, pigs, geese and children playing what appeared to be hopscotch. The shorter of the two stretched confidently to insert a piece, revealing as he did so the top third of his buttocks, which had escaped from the loose-fitting tracksuit bottoms he wore and had become displaced by this exertion.

Two other puzzles were about half done and both unattended. Peter immediately ignored the impressive but rather boring view of St Paul's Cathedral at night, settling instead for the more interesting task of adding whatever he could to Turner's *The Fighting Temeraire*.

Thirty minutes and only three successful piece placements later, he realised that although he knew the sea would be tricky, he had not considered how difficult it was going to be to differentiate between the subtle variation of the colours of smoke coming from the ship's guns or the numerous blues and greys of the sky. He marvelled at the brilliance of the artist that shone through even though it was replicated here on the paperboard of the puzzle.

He did not feel he had used up an awful lot of energy so was surprised that he felt a little drowsy. Concentrating closely on the puzzle pieces could be oddly tiring, he thought, and he decided to turn his attention to the other great appeal of the library, the marvellously comfortable array of seating. He chose an inviting, high-backed armchair with a thick cushioned seat that accepted his backside gratefully. As he eased himself in, it was as though the chair welcomed his body with a comforting embrace and the only sensible course of action available to him was to submit entirely to its softness.

There were a few magazines on the table next to him and he slid the copy of *Classic Cars*, not a subject that had or was ever likely to interest him, from the top of the pile to reveal the other two. *Cake Making Monthly* underneath, with its headline about the secret of making the perfect angel cake, was almost as likely to send him to sleep, so he had to settle for *National Geographic*, which he thought had an outside chance of containing something of interest. He scanned an article about climate change and the rising sea levels in the Arctic. He found himself unable to absorb much of the information about carbon dioxide and greenhouse gases. Had he been able to, he might well have appreciated the irony of being on a massive cruise liner which, in addition to using huge amounts of fuel, no doubt had numerous adverse effects on the ocean and its inhabitants. He flipped forward a few pages to a picture of a grey whale and the accompanying text which outlined their twelve-thousand-mile annual migration from the warm waters of Mexico to the cooler temperatures around Alaska. They had been hunted and were a critically endangered species now. Once again, though, Peter was unable to take in much of the content despite being fascinated by the large colour picture of these astonishing mammals.

As he reached over to replace the magazine, he coughed loudly. He probably had a cold coming on because his throat had felt a bit tickly for a day or two. *Great*, he thought sarcastically. *Just what you want on holiday*. He coughed again and this time it was deeper and lasted longer, winding him for a moment. His eyes were watering as the librarian came over to see what was happening. Fortunately, no one else seemed to have heard, so hopefully she would not issue him with a reminder of the need for silence.

"Are you okay? That was quite a cough."

"Yes, I think so, thanks. I just needed to catch my breath for a moment," Peter replied, pleased that he was not about to be reprimanded.

"I'll bring you a glass of water," she said, the concern on her face subsiding slightly.

Peter thanked her and a few minutes later she returned with the water accompanied by a colleague. This lady was older than the first and she asked him how he felt.

"I'm fine, honestly. I'll just sit here and have a rest while I get my breath back."

Seemingly content that he was okay, the two women retreated behind their desks and carried on working. The younger of the two had a huge pile of books scattered on the floor around her desk. She picked each up in turn and then ticked the piece of paper in front of her, presumably checking it off a list. Occasionally she would add a short note alongside her tick. When writing she leaned forward, tilting her head slightly as though she was listening to something the page was saying. The pen was clasped as if in a vice, with the pen resting on her fingers and being pressed in place by her thumb. Peter wondered how much dexterity was possible with this grip, watching her hand, arm and shoulder move in unison as words were strenuously formed.

He absentmindedly picked up the magazine again and looked at a few pages without reading before putting it back down. He reached for the glass of water, filling his mouth and taking a satisfying gulp. The water soothed his throat temporarily and he decided he might go for a wander outside to clear the fuzziness in his head. As he edged forward to push himself out of the chair, his left arm gave way under his weight and, feeling rather foolish, he glanced towards the librarian guiltily. He was pleased that she had not appeared to notice because he hated fuss. Perhaps he would go outside later, he decided as he flopped back into the snugness of his chair. Within seconds his eyes were shut.

Fatigue overcame him quite quickly, but as he was enjoying the blissful haze of semi-consciousness, he gradually became aware of an unusual sensation. He could not identify it, but it was in him, becoming part of his being. It was immediately familiar yet strange and nefarious. It seized his body, permeating his skin, tiptoeing silently around him. It weaved itself into all that he felt but managed to retain a distinct and curious energy. Then suddenly it took on an existence of its own. A smell, something undoubtedly familiar. It was musty and dusty but unexpectedly comforting. It was stronger now and was mutating. In his brain the smell was forming something almost palpable. The memory became clearer but frustratingly still would not reveal itself completely. It was gaining strength now and as it did so, it became overwhelming. Then in a flash, the obstinate veil of thick fog dissolved and in its place appeared with absolute clarity the memory of his first day at school.

His older sister Pat was two years ahead of him at Longcross Junior School and she had been allowed to go into class with him on his first day. Sitting on the wooden floor of Miss Martin's classroom, the children were oblivious to the fact that the previous month the Olympic Games had been staged only a few miles away in London. They were equally unaware of who Aneurin Bevan was or what the National Health Service had been set up to do. The arrival of four hundred and ninety-two Jamaican immigrants on HMT Empire Windrush and the impending birth to Princess Elizabeth of the heir to the throne were not of concern to Peter as he sat there with the other children.

He strained his memory, but try as he might he could not see the whole room in his mind's eye, just small snippets of random objects and colours. Light brown wooden blocks, a yellow wooden bridge and dust on the floor. Pale green walls and large windows and children wearing grey, green and brown. Peter had not yet experienced the delights of rice pudding on Tuesdays or the mid-morning miniature bottle of milk he would receive complete with his own straw. Catching the bus home, being bullied by a greasy-haired boy called Darren whose hands were covered in warts, and reciting times tables for hours on end in the playground were all things that would come later.

At that moment, just as the smell was at its most potent, he could picture his hands moving uncertainly as he began to construct a house with the building blocks. Others helped him. And he remembered them as Lee and Samantha who, although he had not even spoken to them yet, were to be his best friends in those early years. Samantha would become a highly successful designer later in life and produce, with her husband Jim, three beautiful daughters, each of whom had the same emerald-green eyes as their mother. Lee would make a fortune as an estate agent and property developer before he was thirty, only to lose it all when he was sent to prison, having been found guilty of spying on a female tenant with a miniature camera hidden inside a can of anti-perspirant in her bathroom. Sitting there on that first day, things were so simple. Little of life was behind them. Everything was ahead.

He had not been anywhere other than at home or at the house where his grandparents lived. He certainly had never been to a place like this before with its hard floors and big windows that were too high for him to see through. He recalled poor Miss Martin's hand which had been horribly disfigured during the war. He had not seen that many hands in his short life, but he knew that none of them had looked like that. He remembered being frightened but at the same time fascinated by it. He would later discover that she was an incredibly kind and gentle young woman who had, whilst an auxiliary air raid warden, saved a teenage girl's life by shielding her from the collapsing roof of a public lavatory in Hackney. Unfortunately, the brickwork had shattered her arm and damaged her left hand so badly that three of her fingers had to be removed. She was a heroine, but to Peter she was just another part of this strange conveyor belt of sights, sounds and smells. He had no idea why or how, but he knew that he needed to survive, and in Lee and Samantha he had found friends, as they both had, in this most frightening of worlds into which they had all been thrust.

The bricks. It's the bricks, thought Peter as his eyes, now open again, slowly became accustomed to the light of the library. *That's the smell*. His nose could still recall it after more than seventy years, although he had never encountered it since. The dust and dirt of hundreds of children that had played with them before him was ingrained in them. Innocence, anxiety, fear, relief and gratitude were embedded deep in those dusty old bricks and the smell those emotions created could not be washed off. As the memory of their smell had become part of Peter, those feelings that had been absorbed by the bricks had transferred themselves to him forever. He felt comfort but at the same time a sense of loss. That time had gone and that sensation of absolute innocence was barely a flicker in his memory. Although he was grateful for those days, he regretted now, like so many that had lived most of their life, that he had not appreciated how wonderous they were at the time.

Peter noticed that a tall skinny woman was standing over the puzzle, examining it intently. She wore a pink and yellow checked jumper and her hair was pulled tightly back from her forehead and secured behind with a yellow hair tie. Peter thought she looked like a slice of Battenburg. She had bony hands which held the pieces by their edges as though trying to avoid smudging the picture printed on them.

Peter was thirsty and his throat felt dry. He coughed and produced a blob of stale-tasting phlegm in his mouth. He took out his handkerchief, which required him to turn onto his left thigh so that he could thrust deep into the right pocket where he usually kept it. He put it to his mouth and spat out the gloopy substance, which was an angry green colour. Replacing the handkerchief, being careful to ensure that the recent addition remained contained within it, he realised his chest was sore. *That was some cough*, he thought as he instinctively rubbed the source of the pain.

He scanned the room searching for the disapproving looks that would have been completely justified following his noisy cough and subsequent spit, but there did not seem to be any. Pleased that any indiscretion on his part had gone largely unnoticed, he leaned forward and tried to push himself out of the chair. His first attempt was unsuccessful and he fell back down as he had done earlier. What was wrong with him today? He had no energy.

He rubbed his throat, assessing that its dryness and the accompanying ache in his legs might be symptomatic of something other than open-mouthed breathing. *That's all I need*, he thought, *a cold while I'm on holiday*. An annoying thought occurred to him about the shore excursions that he could miss and how he might not see some of the wonderful places they had booked to visit if he was not well enough to leave the ship. He dearly wanted to get out in the sun and take in some of the sights and resolved to try and nip things in the bud. So, with a concerted effort, he managed to haul himself from the chair and head back to the café in search of a hot drink.

When he arrived, he was glad to see that Norbert was still there and explained to him what he needed.

"I feel a bit weak, and I think I might have the beginnings of a cold. Could you possibly do me a hot drink with lemon juice and honey in a large mug?"

Norbert listened to the instructions attentively. As he headed off Peter called to him.

"If you could pop a tot of whisky in there too, that would be great."

Raising his eyebrows slightly at the request, the waiter disappeared into the kitchens. Five minutes later he returned with a mug containing the piping hot honey and lemon, deposited it on the table with a smile and left again. Eager to start the preventative process, Peter assessed after a couple of minutes that the drink had probably cooled sufficiently to try. He was wrong and his tentative first sip burnt his lips, causing him to jerk the mug away from his mouth, narrowly avoiding a spillage. Eventually the steam from the drink subsided and he tried again, managing this time to swallow some of the hot liquid which he was sure would soothe his throat. It did. Thirty seconds later he took a bigger gulp. He could not taste much whisky and although he was sure Norbert was trustworthy, he suspected the whisky had been forgotten. Of course, nothing was ever paid for with money on these cruises. All purchases were carefully allocated to a passenger's bill and settled at the end of the holiday. He seemed to recall from previous voyages that a running total was occasionally popped under the cabin door every few days so that people could get a rough idea of the state of their account rather than receive an unwelcome shock when they disembarked. So as not to appear ungrateful, he would not mention anything to Norbert but would instead have a good look at the items on the list in due course and query it later if he felt a mistake had been made.

Sipping the honey and lemon drink made him feel slightly better, although his legs still ached. He rubbed them gently to get some blood circulating and warm them.

"Thanks," Peter said absentmindedly as Norbert removed the mug from the table.

"Has that done the trick, Mr Davis?" Norbert asked.

"Not really," he said. "Although it tasted very nice," he added so as not to cause offence.

"Well, it will be dinner time in a few hours, so perhaps what you need is a good hot meal."

Peter was not sure that Norbert was right. All he really wanted to do was curl up in bed and go to sleep in the hope that he would feel better in the morning. Perhaps he would be able to eat something light, but for now he could not think beyond the tiredness he felt.

Chapter 5

At dinner that evening Peter managed most of a bowl of French onion soup and then picked at some risotto, eventually admitting defeat after eating a couple of forkfuls, mashing a considerable amount of it up and prodding at it expertly in an attempt to camouflage it in the pattern of his plate. He did not want Joan to think there was something wrong, so he called on one of his favoured excuses when he was faced with a dish that was not to his taste by explaining to the others on the table that there was a little too much garlic in it for his liking.

A man, who in essence was bald but had, with considerable dexterity, managed to cultivate the small piece of brownish grey hair that grew a few inches above his ears into a comb-over of great distinction, nodded at the explanation, clearly believing it to be completely plausible. The others were too preoccupied by their meals to respond, although he noticed that Joan smiled knowingly at him as she added some sliced parsnip to the piece of salmon on her fork in preparation for her next mouthful.

Dessert was apple pie, which was one of Peter's absolute favourites. He always made a point of asking for vanilla ice cream in restaurants if it were available rather than the ubiquitous cream or occasional custard alternatives. However, on this occasion he could not even countenance that and he was hugely relieved when the plates were finally cleared away and he was able to drop his pretence. Some of the guests drifted into the lounge for coffee, but Peter made his excuses, explaining that the sea air must have made him tired, and headed off for an early night. Joan stayed up with a few of her crafting friends. Although he never liked being separated from her for long, he was pleased by this as he knew how happy it made her to chat with like-minded people. As he gingerly weaved in and out of the now mainly vacated tables and chairs, his aching joints confirmed that he had made a good decision to make his way to bed.

He was relieved to leave the warm dining room and move into the comparative coolness of the corridor. A couple of paces down the hall, he felt like he was losing his balance and had to pause for a moment to catch his breath. Initially he propped himself against the wall, leaning as he did so on his shoulder. Feeling the need for greater stability, he rolled around so that his whole back was now securely pressed against the wall. It occurred to him that anyone passing might have suspected he was suffering from sea sickness, which, for some reason, seemed hugely embarrassing to him. In order to avoid the perceived ignominy of this, he gathered himself and pushed away, determined to get to his room before he felt any worse. As he did so, he stumbled slightly but managed to propel himself forward and gradually began to edge down the corridor.

After forty or fifty short deliberate steps, he reached a dead end that he did not recognise and was forced to turn left through some swing doors which had been propped open with a small wooden wedge. To his left was a staircase which presumably led to the deck above. It was cordoned off with a rope, over which hung a sign which read 'Private'. His only option was straight ahead down another long corridor, and he wondered if he had the strength to carry on or whether he should ask someone to help him. He did not want to be a nuisance, deciding instead to plod slowly onwards. As he did so, he realised that his surroundings were now completely unfamiliar and that he was in fact quite lost. There was wallpaper rather than the usual plain white paint on the walls, which was certainly something he did not remember seeing on the ship before. Peter looked at the green floral pattern that contrasted well with the deep red of the carpet stretching in front of him. The rest of the ship was smartly decorated, but this décor was definitely of a superior quality, he thought. He was worried that he might have encroached into one of the VIP sections intended for guests who had qualified for some club or the other by sailing frequently with the cruise line. If that was the case, though, where was everyone? An even worse thought struck him. Perhaps this area was reserved for senior officers and at any minute he might find himself outside the captain's quarters. He began to feel nauseous at the thought of the humiliation of having to explain his presence to someone in authority and again had to use the wall for support.

As he surveyed the locale, he glimpsed a short, thin man with a walking stick halfway down the long hallway. He was wearing a white tee shirt which swamped his frail body, and a pair of baggy pyjama bottoms. Feeling hopeful that perhaps this man might be able to direct him to his cabin, he summoned up all the energy he could muster and shouted in his direction.

"Hello."

As there was no response from the man or even any discernible recognition, he tried again, a little louder this time.

"Hello. Excuse me."

The man still seemed not to hear and simply kept shuffling steadily down the corridor, moving further and further away from Peter. Perhaps he was hard of hearing or maybe even deaf, Peter thought. With a monumental effort Peter took a few quick strides to try and catch him so that he could make his presence known. Again, though, he was thwarted. The old man, oblivious to Peter's attempted communication, opened a door on his left, walked through it and, with a deftness that belied his age, disappeared from view. Peter slumped again against the wall, exhausted. He had not noticed the doors until now and, as he tried to regain his composure, he examined the one to his right curiously. There was no number on it. It was plain white with a brass handle. Feeling the last remnants of energy draining from his body, he decided to throw caution to the wind and stretched his arm out to try and open it.

Before he managed to even touch the door let alone push, it was flung open and a much younger man poked his head out. Peter caught the briefest of peeks into the room behind the man, but he saw enough to realise that it was much fancier than any of the cabins he had seen in the cruise line's brochure. In the blink of an eye, the man was in the corridor and the door was shut behind him. He was immaculately dressed in a grey twill suit and an expertly shined pair of black brogues. His bright white shirt was secured at the neck by a purple and gold striped tie. Peter assumed he was leaving his cabin for a late dinner or possibly going to the casino.

"Good evening, Sir. Sorry to startle you." The man beamed, revealing a set of apparently perfect teeth behind his warm smile.

"That's quite alright," Peter mumbled awkwardly.

"Is everything okay? You look a bit under the weather if you don't mind me saying so," the man continued. "I am a doctor. Perhaps I can help."

What a stroke of luck, Peter thought to himself. It all made sense. Of course the ship's doctor would have prestigious quarters. They would not put him on the same deck as the regular crew. Feeling a huge weight suddenly being lifted from his shoulders, Peter smiled back weakly.

"I don't feel very well, I'm afraid. Only a touch of the flu probably, but I am very tired, and I can't seem to find my cabin. Quite honestly,

I feel a bit of a fool, but I think I am lost. I don't want to put you to any trouble. You must be very busy with…" Peter added croakily.

His sentence was interrupted by a rasping cough which felt as though he had been stabbed in the chest. Like a magician, the doctor produced a handkerchief from his pocket and nimbly handed it to Peter just in time. Peter grabbed it thankfully and proceeded to fill it with the same thick dark mucus that he had produced earlier. It took a while for him to regain his breath in order to speak properly.

"I'm so sorry. Your handkerchief…"

"Please don't worry. I can assure you It's no problem at all, but I do think you really ought to be in bed rather than out here, don't you?"

Without waiting for a needless reply to his rhetorical question, the doctor put an arm around Peter's shoulder and with the other began leading him slowly back down the corridor.

Hoping that he had managed to avoid looking entirely foolish, Peter held on gratefully. The doctor was having to take short staccato steps to ensure that their strides were synchronised as closely as they could be in order that Peter's progress was not hindered.

"By the way, I'm Dr Edgeman," the man volunteered.

"Davis. Peter Davis."

"Ah yes, Mr Davis. I think I've seen you around occasionally, but it is always good to put a name to the face."

Peter smiled in acknowledgement, flattered that he was worthy of note, and the two men continued on their way. They had only walked for what seemed like a minute or two when Dr Edgeman twisted a hundred and eighty degrees and expertly pushed open a set of double swing doors with his hip. Nice move, Peter thought as they walked through still linked together. Peter felt bad that he had obviously strayed into a private area of the ship and wanted to apologise.

"I'm so sorry," he began. "I don't know how I ended up at your door. I don't normally ignore signs – I was so tired I must have missed them."

"No need to apologise. It happens all the time. I'm just glad you found me, even if you hadn't intended to," the doctor replied reassuringly.

"Anyway, here we are," he said, indicating Peter's door to him.

That was quick. He had obviously not been too far away from his cabin, Peter thought to himself, feeling pleased that his sense of direction had not entirely deserted him despite his fatigue.

"I'll use my pass key if that's okay with you, Mr Davis. I expect that you want to get into bed as soon as possible and I'd like to check you over quickly while I'm here."

"Yes, of course, that's absolutely fine," said Peter, glad that he did not have to try and remember which pocket his key was in.

The room was in complete darkness and the curtains were drawn. Somehow Dr Edgeman managed to manoeuvre Peter in spite of this added difficulty and deposit him gently on the bed. As he did so Peter felt the man's arms leave him and sensed he was leaning across to the bedside table. Suddenly the room was filled with a bright light as he turned on the lamp and it took Peter's eyes a few moments to adjust.

He could have happily gone to sleep fully dressed sitting there on the bed, and encouraged by the doctor, he flopped his head down onto the pillow, his feet still hanging over the side of the bed.

"That's it, Mr Davis, please relax," he said as he lifted Peter's legs and swung them onto the bed so they could join the rest of his body.

He then stooped a little and began to loosen Peter's shoes, which were sticking up in the air like a shiny, black number eleven at the end of the bed. Having unfastened them, he eased them off and, in one continuous motion, carefully placed them on the floor.

Released from their incarceration, Peter's feet began to breathe blissfully. He tried to reach down to remove his socks but only managed to raise his body a few inches before slumping back down on the soft mattress. Even though the room was warm and Peter was virtually fully clothed, he became aware that he was now shivering uncontrollably.

"Right, let's get you into bed now, Mr Davis," the doctor said with authority.

Peter was in no fit state to argue as he helped him off with his jacket, shirt, trousers and socks. He gently pushed Peter onto his side and folded down the sheets where he had been lying. He then rolled him back onto the under sheet that had been revealed and repeated the process on the other side. He was then able to pull the sheet up and over so that Peter's body was now fully covered. Nonchalantly, he tucked in both sides where the sheets had been pulled out and looked at Peter, who now had his eyes shut.

"There, that's better, isn't it?" he said, not anticipating a reply.

"Mr Davis," he said, raising his voice almost imperceptibly to ensure Peter was listening.

"You need to sleep now, and I'll come back in a few hours to check on you. Before I go, though, I want you to take a couple of these," he said, removing a small bottle of pills from his jacket pocket. He filled the glass that was on the bedside table with water and, having extracted two pills from the bottle, put his hand under Peter's head and carefully raised it.

"Swallow these, Mr Davis," he said, popping them into Peter's mouth and putting the glass to his lips.

Peter obediently gulped down the water and pills then allowed his head to drop back to the pillow. He was asleep within seconds.

I am immediately aware that I am holding something in my hand. I look down and see that it is a wooden brick – a building block. It's dusty and incredibly heavy, so heavy that it seems I am having trouble gripping it. It falls from my grasp and shatters on the floor in front of me as though it was in fact made of glass. I look warily across at the children sitting with me and see that they are all smiling, so I pick up another brick. For some reason this one turns to dust as soon as I touch it. The other young children are having fun, intently building something with their bricks and encouraging me to do the same. I can't tell what it is we are supposed to be making, but I desperately want to play my part in its construction whatever it is. I notice a boy with very closely cropped brown hair sitting cross-legged on the floor opposite me. He nods supportively, which I take as an invitation to get involved. I reach for another block and, this time, can hold it without difficulty. It's a blue wooden bridge, which I place rather precariously on the top of the pile of bricks, pleased with myself when it does not collapse. I take a deep breath – I can remember the distinctive smell of those wooden shapes and I invite it to fill my nostrils. Nothing happens, so I try again, longing for that musty smell of my past, but it's no good. There is no smell at all, but I am only mildly disappointed because I love being in this place. This is Longcross Junior School and I am totally safe and very happy. A small green car, released to glide on its plastic wheels by someone nearby, gently hits my shoe and I flinch with a start.

The classroom and the bricks have disappeared now, and I am outside with the other children. We are standing in the playground, dressed in our mostly home-made school uniforms and organised efficiently in long lines. Rows and rows of hand knitted pullovers and trousers and skirts, some no doubt handed down by older siblings, others newly created by our mothers. I sense the presence of someone in front of me and another behind, but I can't actually see them. My eyes are unable to focus and all I can make out are outlines and shadows – unidentifiable but unmistakable figures. I can hear a rhythmical sound and I understand then why we are here. We are with our teacher Miss Martin, reciting our times tables, and I can hear the chanting. My mouth is moving and I seem to know all the answers. Seven fives are thirty-five… eight fives are forty… nine fives are forty-five… I look to my right and my friend Lee is standing in the next line drinking his milk out of a miniature bottle with a blue plastic straw. That's weird – we never have our milk outside, presumably because a dropped bottle could smash and leave dozens of shards for unsuspecting young hands and knees. I tell Lee that he shouldn't have brought the bottle into the playground and he smiles and points at me. "You're a fine one to talk." He chuckles. I look down at my hands and see that I am clutching a bottle too. I drink, savouring the sweet creaminess of the liquid. I don't know why I made so much fuss; everyone else has their milk out here. Even Miss Martin is drinking some.

That milk tasted so good, but it has vanished now and so has Lee. Suddenly a wave of sadness overwhelms me and I am rooted to the spot. I don't think I can move my legs. The sun is still shining though, and I can feel a small piece of paper in my hand. I look down to see what it is and immediately recognise that it's a bus ticket. Being unable to move is worrying, but the familiarity of the surroundings that are beginning to reveal themselves are curiously comforting. I look again at the paper with its unforgettable blue ink which confirms how much I have paid. The picture around me is almost complete and I can see where I am. It's the bus stop at the end of our road – Wilton Avenue, where I lived as a boy. Hearing a loud noise, I look round and watch the number 262 moving slowly away, having dropped me off after school. I am relieved to discover that I can move again now and walk happily round a corner even though there were no corners between the bus stop and my house. It should be a straight stroll home down the tree-lined avenue, so I don't understand where this is all coming from. In front of me are some men dressed in black cloaks. I don't recognise them and then realise that the reason for this is that I can't see their faces. They are engrossed in conversation and don't notice me as a walk past them. I must be invisible because I am sure they were looking straight at me for a moment. Another corner. This is definitely not the walk from the bus stop I remember, but I carry on anyway. I am pleased that I did because I see the familiar face of my mother running towards me now, her long black hair in a plait which is swinging metronomically behind her as she runs. She is wearing a light blue cotton apron and I think to myself, great, she has been baking. I hope she has made Chelsea Buns. As she gets nearer, I can see she is excited to see me, but the large envelope she is waving in her hand seems to be the cause of her pleasure, rather than her son's arrival home. She has never met me at the bus stop before, but she has the broadest smile imaginable on her face today. The distance between us disappears in a flash and she is in front of me with her arms open wide. I reach out towards her and am overcome by the intense love we have for each other. But before I can touch her let alone hug her tightly, she disappears and I am alone again, surrounded by a blank canvas.

Peter woke up with a jolt, wide-eyed in the half-light around him and aware of someone approaching his bed. He was just trying to place the face when the doctor saved him the trouble.

"Hello, Mr Davis. Sorry to disturb you, but I just wanted to see how you were," said Dr Edgeman cheerfully.

Having only been awake for some ten seconds or so, Peter's body had not yet given him any obvious indication as to how he could answer the question accurately. However, the doctor was standing by his bedside and he thought that he should try and respond. He opened his mouth to speak, but all that he managed was a harsh, raking cough which left him short of breath and with a sharp pain in his chest.

"That's okay," the doctor reassured him, assessing that the need for an answer no longer existed. "Please don't try to speak."

Refilling the glass with water, he again encouraged Peter to drink.

"Just take a few small sips, Mr Davis."

After a few moments Peter could breathe again, albeit only being able to take small gulps of air with each inhalation. The doctor gave him another two tablets, which he washed down with a mouthful of water that was considerably bigger than a sip. He asked Peter if he needed the toilet, but feeling relatively comfortable, he declined, pleased to avoid whatever strategy the doctor had planned for him to fulfil the task. Instead, he rested his head on the pillow and, feeling momentarily alert due mainly to the pain in his chest but also because of the doctor's presence, he felt able to speak.

"I was just dreaming about when I was a child at primary school, I think. I can't remember it all, but my mother was in the dream…"

The doctor smiled, but Peter was too exhausted to try and understand his dream let alone tell him about his friends, the break time milk and how they all learnt their times tables by rote. He could not stay awake long enough to begin to think about what was in the envelope that his mother was waving so happily.

When it had happened, he had been as pleased as his parents. The joy on his mother's face the day she ran to meet him at the bus stop was something he thought about often – it was the happiest he ever remembered her. The envelope contained the results of the examination he had taken a few months earlier and the offer of a scholarship to attend any one of a number of private schools near London. There was no way his parents could have afforded the fees to such places even though his father had recently been promoted to office manager at Stradbrook's, a local firm of solicitors. The scholarship meant all his boarding fees and food, even his books, were waived by the school they chose simply because he had managed to be in the top five percent of boys taking the examination.

Most of the day was a bit of a blur to him, although he recalled it was in three parts. Mathematics was straightforward. He had always done well in primary school and found it logical and easy to understand and explain. English was harder for him, although his technical knowledge of the subject made up for any lack of creativity in his competent if not particularly exciting short composition. The third element was called an Intelligence Test. Peter was vaguely aware of MENSA but had no idea of the types of question associated with membership. He found them quite interesting and enjoyed the variety of problems that needed to be solved. He was one of the first to finish, although of course he did not know how well he had done. In fact, it transpired that his marks were outstanding and, apparently, he had been second overall out of the two hundred boys involved. The other thing he always remembered and which never failed to make him laugh out loud was an incident involving a boy named Wesley Tricklebotham.

Everything was organised to the letter that day and it was very clear to all the boys that certain procedures had to be strictly observed by everyone. There was a roll call to ensure that all those who had entered was there. Ensuring everything went according to plan and that no rules were broken was a team of invigilators, most of whom were teachers and other academics employed by Tinniswood Manor, the school where the examination was held. Their leader was a gruff man with wiry grey hair and an enormous nose. His face was redder than any Peter had encountered up to that point in his life, although later he would understand the relationship between it and the hip flask of whisky that accompanied the man everywhere he went. All those in attendance were asked to confirm their presence and, as his father had told him he should, he responded with a confident "Yes, Sir" when the ruddy-faced man called his name. As the invigilator was approaching the end of his list, everything had gone smoothly and there had been no absentees. "Nicholas Taylor... Yes, Sir... Andrew Thomas... Yes, Sir." But then when the man enquired, "William Tricklebotham?" there was no reply. He tried again, but still there was silence. He looked around, but with only a Vincent, Walters and Williams left on the list, he decided to press on, assuming that Master Tricklebotham was not in the room. When the remaining few had acknowledged their names, the man, who had never experienced anything but full attendance during the eight previous sittings of the scholarship examinations in which he had been involved, felt he ought to check again, given the enormous financial rewards at stake. The quickest way of dealing with this was to ask for a show of hands to ascertain whether there was anyone whose name had not been called. If no hands went up, then he would know that only one hundred and ninety-nine candidates were present.

It was very obvious that he did not enjoy inefficiency, particularly if it had anything to do with his own actions. The redness of his face, which now seemed slightly deeper in colour, had spread to his neck and throat as he said in a loud voice, "Put your hand up if your name has not been called." There were a lot of desks to search, but then one of his colleagues alerted him to a raised hand two thirds of the way back on the right side of the room. The man, who was now almost entirely red above the shoulders, advanced halfway down the aisle so that he could see the owner of the hand with its index figure pointing to the ceiling.

"What's your name, boy?" he demanded, obviously annoyed at this delay.

"Wesley Tricklebotham, Sir," the boy replied.

Glancing down at his list for confirmation, the man, in a slightly louder voice, said, "Yes, Tricklebotham. I called your name twice. Why did you not respond?"

"My name is Wesley Tricklebotham, Sir, not William Tricklebotham."

At this extraordinary admission the man was temporarily lost for words and with his face now looking like a volcano about to erupt, he could only stare in disbelief as he wondered how many Tricklebothams there were in the whole country let alone in this room. Taking the silence, during which the man continued to try and make sense of the situation, as a need for further clarification, the boy timidly added, "My middle name is William, Sir, if that helps." Red now turned to purple and the man raced towards the boy shouting.

"You damned fool," he bawled as he descended on the still unsuspecting Tricklebotham, intent on clipping him hard around the ear with the signet ring that glinted on his chubby finger. Sensing the impending danger, two of the other invigilators were just in time to intercept their enraged superior, successfully halting his progress before he could reach his target. Very carefully they coaxed him back to the front of the room, thus averting the assault and catastrophic outcome that might have followed for both examiner and examinee. Some boys began to snigger, others simply stared bewildered as they were by the sight of the chief invigilator retreating from the scene. At one point he bumped into the corner of a desk that had presumably been arranged slightly out of line with those in front and behind. He turned and glared menacingly at the nervous-looking individual behind it whom he had already decided was responsible for moving the obstacle deliberately in order to impede him. Fortunately, his colleagues were able to pull him away again, narrowly avoiding the prospect of the physical assault that might otherwise have followed. Eventually they succeeded in navigating the journey back to the front of the room where they deposited the now dishevelled man in the seat that he had previously occupied. The man had not calmed down at all as he grabbed the register of attendees and called, much to the dismay of all those that had hoped for a peaceful end to the saga, for the boy to answer his name.

"William Tricklebotham?"

There was silence, not least from the boy himself, as the enormity of what the man had just said hit all those observing and listening.

"William Tricklebotham?" he yelled a second time, directly towards the area where the boy was sitting.

The bravest of the other invigilators approached the man and leant forward to whisper something in his ear. His only intention, of course, was to defuse the situation, of which all but the head invigilator was aware by now. Unfortunately, and not wholly surprisingly, his words had precisely the opposite effect as the man, realising his blunder, erupted uncontrollably and screamed at the top of his voice, saliva bursting from his mouth as he did so,

"WESLEY TRICKLEBOTHAM?"

He stood up, furiously daring the boy to answer. For a second or two, there was silence as the room awaited the response.

"Present, Sir," proclaimed Wesley cheerfully as though the events of the previous few minutes had never happened.

It was the last straw for the invigilator who, grabbing his red pen, scrawled a huge tick on the page, before ripping it out, screwing it up and throwing it and the book in which it had been contained across the room, narrowly missing the head of a pimply child called Trevor, before storming out and slamming the door behind him.

Whenever Peter told the story, which he did on many occasions, he always qualified it with the statement "You had to be there." Nevertheless, it was one of the funniest incidents he could remember. Young Wesley Tricklebotham, a boy to whom detail was all, had the ultimate last laugh, finishing a very creditable seventh that day and joining Peter at Tinniswood. Although they would later lose touch, Peter followed his career in the papers as he joined the Royal Engineers after obtaining a double first at Cambridge and rose to the rank of colonel by the time he retired.

Peter often recalled those days fondly. Everything was simple. He was popular, loved playing with his friends and, with the exception of only a few subjects, found his schoolwork very easy. The difference between right and wrong was instilled in him at a very early age by his parents and when reminders were required, they were promptly administered. Honesty, truth and fairness were ingrained in him and remained embedded in his psyche even now.

Perhaps it was something to do with the pills the doctor had given him, but Peter could not keep his eyelids open, and it was not long before he dozed off again.

Another place I could never forget. We are in the car. Dad is driving and Mum is in the front passenger seat. She turns round to speak to me. "You look so smart. My little boy is so grown up." She is wearing a hat and lipstick, both of which tell me that we are going somewhere special. I don't feel particularly grown up and the blue blazer I am wearing is as uncomfortable as the tie which is done up so tightly around my neck that I can hardly speak. I realise that I am also wearing a cap, which seems unnecessary in the car, but then I understand why when we arrive. Dad has parked the car and the three of us are now standing by the boot as my father heaves out a huge wooden box which he presents to me. Other boys, all with the same blazer and cap, are filing in through a huge door in the distance. There are so many of them and relentlessly they continue their procession through the door. I am relieved to see that they are all dragging one of the big wooden boxes behind them just like me.

My parents have gone now and although I don't remember entering the building or anything specific about that enormous door, I appear to have made it inside. More than that, I am in my bedroom. Wait. Perhaps it's not my bedroom as there are lots of boys in here and, as I look around, there are lots of beds too. On the floor next to my bed is my box and I can see that it is open. It's full of food, mostly biscuits, cakes and sweets. There are two boys relaxing nearby on beds which have thick iron frames that make them look uncomfortable. They have boxes, just like mine, open on the floor next to them. This is great fun. We are laughing and joking with each other, stuffing our faces with the contents of our tuck boxes. I don't recognise the other boys and as I try to work out who they are, they turn their heads away so that I can't see them properly.

The beds have gone, but the boys are still there and now it seems they have been joined by lots of others. Chairs are rowed up back-to-back and we are running as fast as we can around them – musical chairs. Again, no faces are visible, but there is a boy who is not running. He is instead hovering by a vacant chair with his back to us, hoping we can't see him. "Don't cheat," I yell at him, pushing him with both hands so that he reluctantly starts to move again. I have obviously pushed him too hard and he falls over, crashing into a chair in the process. Broken pieces of wood are strewn all over the floor – indisputable proof of my heavy handedness. No one has noticed the wreckage though and everyone seems quite happy again. We are all tearing wrapping paper from presents, although I have no idea who gave them to us. The boy I pushed over is gorging on a massive box of sweets and I notice him sneaking away so that he doesn't have to share them with us.

"Oi!" I shout in his direction, but he doesn't hear or pretends not to anyway. "Don't take all the sweets away. We won't have any."

Then I am wearing the same uniform and looking in the window of a sweet shop. There's a theme here, I take pleasure in thinking to myself. The sky is grey and heavy as if it is just about to rain, so I push the door open and go inside. The click of the latch is familiar, as is the bell that rings to announce my arrival. No need for the bell as the shopkeeper, Mr Fenwick, who I recognise immediately, is already serving someone, another boy. Old Mr Fenwick is welcoming as always, smiling and making suggestions as to what sweets I might want. At the other counter the boy who had cheated at musical chairs is on his own, helping himself to sweets. He is not wearing his cap and his hair looks greasy. I am about to remind him that it's a rule that caps must be worn at all times if you are not on school premises when I notice what he is doing. Under one arm he is holding a jar of Liquorice Allsorts which is full to the brim. With his other hand he is scooping handfuls of Fruit Salads and Black Jacks which he then crams into the pockets of his blazer. He has taken so many that they are spilling out onto the floor of the shop. He glares at me menacingly as if daring me to say something, and as he does this, I see that his mouth is full of gobstoppers. He then starts to take money from the till and stuffs it into his pockets so that they bulge. I open my mouth to warn the shopkeeper, but no words come out. So, I point again and then wave my hands frantically trying to alert Mr Fenwick, but he is laughing at me and doesn't notice. The greasy-haired boy runs over and grabs my cap then charges out of the door, slamming it behind him so the bell falls off. Suddenly everything is dark and I am no longer in the sweet shop.

My parents have come to collect me and my father is putting the big wooden box in the back of the car. Happily, I assume it must be the end of term and I am going home for the holidays, but why is it dark? Why am I leaving at night-time? Most importantly, why does my father look so unhappy?

He slams the boot shut. He slams his door shut, puts on the headlights and we drive out of the school gates in silence.

Chapter 6

Peter had no idea how long he had been asleep let alone the time, but the curtains were open and the glorious Mediterranean sun was pouring in through the windows, filling every corner of his cabin. He loved the sunshine and breathed as deeply as he could as if trying to absorb it, but the effort hurt his chest and he coughed. The air smelled fresher, and he glimpsed an open window which was clearly the source of the vast improvement on the mustiness in the cabin previously. It was so bright that his first reaction was to squint slightly as he began to gently ease himself towards a sitting position in the bed. It was obviously morning, and by the look of it, another hot day was in store. He was alone and, as his brain began to slowly function, he assumed Joan had probably already left for her craft class. He had a vague memory of dinner the night before but could not recall any of the conversation or the people involved, although he was certain Joan had been there. The oddest thing was that he could not remember how he had transitioned from dinner, to bed, to morning.

He reflected that he had often heard people say that they could not remember what had happened the night before, attributing it inevitably to the excess of alcohol they had consumed. That was most certainly not likely to be the case with him as he had always been careful about how much he drank. His rule was to stop as soon as everything started to move in slow motion. The main sign that tended to accompany this for him was a numbing of his mouth and tongue which, if ignored, was likely to lead to him saying something that was either incomprehensible or very stupid. At the first indication of 'cotton wool mouth', as he called it, he made a mental note to stop drinking and to remember to have at least two pints of water before he went to bed. In this way he always knew what was going on and was much less inclined to experience a hangover.

Why was it, he thought, that so many men (it was almost always men) judged the level of their manhood by their ability to drink so much that they made themselves ill? The whole thing made no sense to him. He had attended conferences where delegates would crawl into breakfast the next morning looking barely alive and announce in the most serious voice they could muster that they had been up until

4.30 drinking. Unfortunately, some idiot or another would usually say something or perhaps effect a knowing smile that was sufficient to suggest that what the individual had managed was indeed impressive. This ensured the drinker gained both the recognition he sought and, he almost always assumed, some sort of respect amongst his peers. In reality, of course, those with a modicum of intelligence were actually thinking to themselves that the individual in question was not only someone to avoid but was also possibly one of the biggest dickheads they had ever had the misfortune to encounter. Peter could never understand the correlation these people believed existed between drinking to excess and being either more worthy of the admiration of either sexes or more successful in life. From his perspective they were silly little men, and very occasionally women, who presumably used this means to establish their credentials because they were too stupid to do so in any other manner.

His mind wandered to one of the few times he could remember drinking much more than he should have done. He was thirteen years old and had been selected to play in the Saturday third eleven for his local cricket club. Apart from one other lad in his early twenties, all his teammates were in their thirties or forties and a couple were over fifty. These were experienced men whose best playing days were behind them and who, although capable of the occasional good innings or bowling performance, were most attracted now by the social aspect of the game.

The opposition did not score many runs due in no small part to the fact that Peter took six wickets with his gentle medium pace swing bowling. An early tea was taken, after which his team's openers steadily accumulated the runs needed to win by ten wickets. There was briefly talk of a 'beer match' (the losers of which would buy the beer for the winners) because it was still not quite five o'clock, but this was quashed by murmurings from some of the senior players who wanted to repair to the bar immediately in order to 'socialise' and for whom the shorter than usual playing time was the ideal excuse to do precisely that.

Peter had sipped wine and beer before at home, but that night he was introduced to beer drinking cricket club style. The older men, Peter thought, seemed disproportionately pleased with him as he followed a few of his teammates into the clubhouse, where two trays of pint mugs, eleven on each, were positioned prominently in the middle of the bar. Next to each tray was a huge jug of beer and when

Peter arrived a couple of players who had decided to have a drink before showering were preparing to pour the jugs. A glass was thrust in his direction and promptly filled. Peter was thirsty, so he drank and discovered almost immediately that he liked the taste. Although there was a huge variety of sandwiches, fruit and cakes at tea, he had not been able to eat much because he was so nervous about the prospect of having to bat against fully grown men. Although Peter was oblivious to the fact at the time, this unfortunate twist of fate now had the unwelcome consequence of accelerating the effect of the alcohol on his body.

The jugs were emptied relatively quickly and two more were filled to replace them. Match fees were collected to cover the cost of tea, but the captain told Peter that because of his age, he was not expected to pay. As his father had given him enough that morning to cover the cost, and now feeling hungry and a little dizzy, he decided to buy some crisps and nuts. One of the opposing players had scored fifty and was at the bar buying another jug, some of which was soon used to top up Peter's glass and quench the thirst caused by the saltiness of the snacks. He was having trouble speaking by this time, but one of the older players explained to him that a 'personal' jug was expected from any player scoring a fifty, taking five wickets or holding on to three catches. This fact vaguely registered with Peter as he felt in his pockets to see how much money he had left.

The recollection of the precise events around his purchase of the twelve-pint jug had long since faded from Peter's memory. He did remember, however, that his remaining match fee money was insufficient, and he had to ask one of his teammates to negotiate for him, assuring the barman that Peter's father would settle up when he came to collect him. The weight of the jug and Peter's relaxed state meant that the first few pours from his jug were a little wayward, but no one seemed to notice. As it emptied things became easier. Plenty was left once he had completed a circuit of the bar and he took the opportunity to refill his own glass. Another round of the bar left a small amount remaining for himself before the jug was finished. He seemed to recall that a third personal jug was bought by someone who had taken three catches, but the exact details were sketchy enough at the time, let alone now.

At about 7.30, Peter's father arrived in the hope of catching the end of the game. He was no doubt surprised by the early finish but not as shocked as he was to be greeted by the sight of his thirteen-year-old son half on, half sliding down a bar stool, desperately clinging on to anything he could in order to remain relatively upright. Everything from that point became a bit foggy, but Peter did remember his father sitting with him, holding a pint of his own and congratulating him on his wickets before driving them both home. Few words were exchanged on the short journey and when they arrived his father encouraged Peter to go to bed, although a memorable visit to the bathroom was required on the way. Peter still retained the mental picture of himself, head thrust in the direction of the toilet, making the acquaintance of Messrs Armitage and Shanks face to face for the first time. This association was rekindled on and off over the course of the next few hours as he shared the fruits of his evening's labours generously with his new friends.

He was never totally sure whether his mother knew what had happened, but her concerned look and offer of dry toast when he came down for breakfast the next morning led him to suspect that his father had been pressed to divulge at least part of the story.

His thoughts continued to drift for a while as he connected this memory with others like an intricate dot to dot puzzle in which only he knew the location of the next number. He thought about his schoolfriend Chris who played some games for the club later in the year. He was a leg spin bowler and was able to turn the ball a yard if he pitched it right. What had happened to him? Peter never went to the reunions once they had all left school, so they had lost touch. He was always good at art too and Peter imagined that he had probably become a graphic designer or cartoonist, running his own business from a purpose built shed in his garden. He winced as he recalled the time Chris had been caned in front of the whole school by an Australian supply teacher called Mr Haigh because he had taken the lid off a box of giant stick insects they were examining in a nature studies lesson.

Memories of the teachers at Rosehill Grammar School started appearing in his mind. Mr Winter, who carried his cane with him at all times just in case the need to use it should arise. Mr Paxman the English teacher, a pasty-faced man who insisted that his chair should be cleaned before every lesson and even appointed a 'chair monitor' in each form to ensure that this requirement was not overlooked. And of course, the trendy History teacher Mr Johnston, who was the master of balancing humour with fear, a talent that made him both popular and respected by all the students. His disciplinary methods included a punishment for miscreants in which they had to keep their noses an inch above their desks. As he wandered around the classroom explaining about the Treaty of Versailles or who Turnip Townshend was, he would apply a gentle pat on the back of the head should they move from their prescribed position, thus introducing tender skin, bone and gristle to unyielding oak. Peter remembered the coloured pencils he encouraged them to use in their exercise books to highlight key points because he said it would make them easier to remember. He was absolutely right, Peter thought. He could remember to this day the names of most of the main contributors to the agrarian and industrial revolutions, not to mention all the leaders and political figures in nineteenth century Europe.

He was recalling the ridicule and subsequent punishment Mr Johnston heaped on one boy who wrote about the renowned Italian general and republican Gary Baldi in an essay, when he heard a loud click as the door of his room was opened. Although Peter was too tired to lift his head from the pillow, he knew that someone had entered and was creeping slowly towards the bed, obviously trying not to disturb him.

"How are you feeling, Mr Davis?" Dr Edgeman enquired, noticing that Peter's eyes were open.

"Not all that great actually," said Peter, making a wheezing sound as he spoke.

He tried to sit up properly and as he did, he let out a cough that burnt his chest painfully. His mouth filled with mucus. Seeing this the doctor reached for a paper handkerchief and passed it to Peter, who spat the contents of his mouth into it. The gunk was green and looked angrily back at Peter as he inspected it. The thick solution began forcing its way through the thin layers of tissue and into Peter's hand. Having pre-empted this possible mishap, Dr Edgeman advanced stealthily with reinforcements, passing two more tissues to Peter and wiping the bed sheet, on which some of the gloopy mess had been deposited. Peter choked as a further cough tried to escape his lungs.

"Thanks," he managed with a croak.

"No problem at all. I'll leave these next to you," he said, plucking a wad of tissues from the box and placing them on the bed within easy reach. Peter nodded his gratitude as another sharp cough erupted from his chest. Less green this time, he noticed, but he thought it looked dark, almost bloody. The doctor held his head up and helped him to some water, which momentarily soothed the rawness in his throat.

Peter remained propped up on his pillow, feeling slightly better now that his lungs had cleared a little, and was virtually at eye level with the doctor, who sat on the chair next to the bed silently assessing his patient. Dr Edgeman surveyed Peter carefully and, noticing a blue tinge to his lips, asked him to put out his hands so that he could check whether his fingertips were similarly discoloured. With some effort, and helped by the doctor, Peter managed to extend his arms far enough so that his fingers could be examined. They looked okay at the moment, thought the doctor, but he was concerned about the colour of Peter's lips. The raking cough and difficulty breathing were also worrying him, as was his temperature, which was still much higher than normal.

"I'll be back very soon to see you again," Dr Edgeman whispered as Peter dropped his head onto the pillow and shut his eyes once again. Producing a plastic bag from his pocket, the doctor tipped Peter's soiled tissues inside then sealed the top. He did not like the look of what he had seen when Peter coughed and was keen to have the gunk tested as he saw some pus in it. Quietly he crept out and headed off to organise the relevant tests and to arrange some intravenous antibiotics. Peter was so exhausted that he did not even hear the click of the door as it shut behind him.

Chapter 7

Peter woke to darkness. The curtains in his room were drawn, but as his eyes adapted, he began to make out some familiar-looking shapes. He felt less fatigued now and wondered how long he had been asleep. Those pills Dr Edgeman gave him certainly seemed to have the desired effect. He thought he might be able to sit up, so, very carefully, keen not to overdo things, he slid himself into an upright position with his arms and manoeuvred a pillow behind his back for support. He reached across and turned on the bedside lamp just as there was a knock on his door.

He was pleasantly surprised to discover that he was able to inhale sufficiently well to make a noise slightly louder than his normal voice.

"Come in," he called out firmly, wondering who on earth this could be since the doctor had not knocked on his previous visits.

As invited, the person outside opened the door and entered. The lamp next to him provided only a modicum of light around the bed and the majority of the room was therefore rather gloomy, which made the newcomer difficult to see at first. The person's voice when it came was not one that Peter recognised.

"Good morning, Mr Davis."

As he was trying to place both the accent and its owner, the man stepped out of the shadows and approached the bed so that he could be seen. Peter was taken aback as he took in the sight of the person before him. Was this man a thief who was about to relieve him of his possessions? Or perhaps he was lost, but then how would he know his name? Peter stared at the man, temporarily unable to speak. He was tall. Six foot four at least, Peter estimated. The wide smile on his face was enveloped by a bushy red beard that matched the mop of hair on the other end of his head. A pair of green corduroy trousers encased muscular legs while a beige cotton shirt did its best to do the same with his torso, failing only to conceal the red chest hair that burst out of the top where two buttons were undone. The two were joined by a thick brown belt with a chunky gold buckle that was engraved with a picture that Peter could not decipher at this distance.

Peter emitted a polite good morning in reply and the man stretched out an enormous arm, grabbed the chair that was positioned in front of the dressing table, flipped it around with a flick of his powerful wrist and sat down next to Peter's bed still wearing the same cheerful smile.

"Sorry if I startled you. The name's Souter, Mr Davis, Archibald Souter."

Then as if to address what was clearly on Peter's mind, he continued, "Perhaps I ought to explain what's going on. Dr Edgeman, who was looking after you while you were unwell, has had to attend to some other patients, so I am here as his replacement to assist with your recuperation."

Peter was relieved by the realisation that his cabin had in fact not been invaded by either a burglar, an assassin or a madman, and gave a polite nod to invite the man to continue.

"Oh, I see," said Peter. "You're his locum."

"Yes, in a manner of speaking, that's precisely what I am. Although I am what you might call a specialist in this phase of things rather than a general practitioner like Dr Edgeman."

Peter was comforted by the word specialist although still a little perturbed by the arrival of this great hulk of a man in his cabin. His somewhat informal dress was also rather distracting. Peter had never quite managed to come to terms with the acceptance in society that professional men such as solicitors, accountants and in this case, a doctor, were not expected to wear a tie or even a jacket. He remembered how, when he was this man's age, a blazer and trousers instead of a suit was considered unduly casual for work. Souter looked, to Peter, more like he was dressed ready for a night club than the serious task of making him better. But things change, as Joan constantly reminded him when he became stuffy about such matters, and he understood that sometimes you have to embrace the future rather than live in the past. In any case, he pondered to himself, it sounded as though this man knew what he was doing and there was no way on earth the cruise line was going to let a sub-standard medic loose on their clients.

"How are you feeling, Mr Davis?" the man enquired in a relaxed tone that suggested he already had a pretty good idea what the answer to his question would be.

"Much, much better, thank you, Doctor," Peter replied. "In fact," he continued, "I feel stronger than I have done for a while."

"Good, I am very pleased to hear that."

"Yes," said Peter and then he added eagerly, "I've slept well and being able to relax has given me time to think about all sorts of things."

As Souter did not immediately respond, Peter thought for a few seconds, contemplating how much, if anything, he was comfortable sharing with his new acquaintance. The man was physically intimidating, and his presence seemed to fill the room, but there was also something approachable about him that made Peter feel comfortable enough to continue.

"I've just been thinking about my old school days." And then remembering, he added, "Come to think of it, I just had a dream about my early school days too."

"Oh, yes? That's interesting. What happened in your dream?"

"I don't think I can remember really," Peter said evasively. "Dreams are often just a series of disconnected pictures, aren't they, like different scenes in a play."

"Yes, I know what you mean. I suspect most people probably dream like that. Can you remember any of the scenes?" Then sensing that Peter probably felt the conversation was becoming a little personal, he decided to try and reassure him.

"I hope you don't think I'm prying. It's just that dreams and the subconscious in general are a particular area of interest and expertise of mine. I've studied the subject for many years and worked with a great many people, helping them to make sense of the things that they see when they are asleep."

Souter's obvious sincerity when he spoke convinced Peter to be open with him and, after all, he thought he might have some interesting insights to share with him.

"Well, I often dream about my earliest memories of school. I must have been about four years old when I started at Longcross Junior School. It was quite soon after the war, so things were not easy, but I enjoyed my time there. When I dream it's usually about playing with wooden bricks, sitting on the floor of the classroom. Another scene that often crops up is of us learning our times tables by rote, lined up in the playground. We used to start with our twos and go all the way up to the twelve times table. It's amazing really that the constant repetition of those numbers became indelibly printed in my mind. I have always been able to respond almost immediately to any simple multiplication – it was quite useful."

"They sound like happy memories."

"Oh yes, they were good times. Everything was simple then and the world was a safer place than it is now, I think. There were bad people in society, but there seemed to be fewer of them. Perhaps we simply didn't hear about them. I often think the newspapers, television and the internet are a big part of the problem and have a lot to answer for. Children played outside because they didn't have computers and families looked out for each other. My parents even let me take the bus to and from school on my own from the age of about seven or eight. Sadly, I don't think that sort of thing is possible nowadays – the lack of care and respect we have for one another today is so sad."

Peter paused while the mention of those bus rides unlocked the memory of the rest of his dream. "Actually, one of those bus rides featured in the second part of my dream. It was about what happened when I left primary school. That was not such a good time actually."

"Oh really? In what way?"

Peter was concerned that he had been monopolising the conversation, but this man clearly was keen for him to talk. Perhaps, he thought, it was part of his treatment and the doctor was seeing how long he could speak without coughing and spluttering. Whatever the case, he had asked Peter to explain, so he decided to do precisely that and to tell him about the events in reality that had probably triggered his dream.

Peter was eight years old and he loved primary school. Lessons and learning came easily to him and the teachers often gave him extra work, especially in maths where he seemed to understand things much quicker than most of his classmates. He liked everyone and they all seemed to like him, but his closest friends were Lee and Bernard. The three of them would team up at school whenever possible and often went to one another's house to play. They were pretty much inseparable and never seemed to argue or fight, not even when all three of them took a shine to the prettiest girl in the class, Samantha. Without needing to discuss her, they ignored their feelings, as eight-year-old boys can, choosing instead to prioritise their friendship. In the same way they compromised to avoid disputes over toys or the rules of the games they played, any competition for her affections was put aside because they understood it could damage the bond that they had developed between them.

The boys would often catch the bus home from school together. Both the 262 and the 69 took them to stops close to their houses.

Bernard would get off first, Lee a few stops later and finally Peter, whose stop was at the end of his road. From there it was a short walk past the park then the fire station to his house. In his dream, Peter remembered the bus had been the 262. Whether that had been the actual bus on the day in question he could not be sure, but he was absolutely certain that there was only one occasion on which his mother had met him at the bus stop.

The headmistress had informed Peter's parents that he was working at a level in all subjects well beyond his age and that, in her opinion, his understanding of mathematics was exceptional. She explained that she could put him up two years but cautioned them that occasionally children as young as Peter were often adversely affected by the separation from their natural peer group. Having weighed up the various options over a number of weeks, Mr and Mrs Davis decided to enter Peter for a scholarship examination. Their view was that were he successful, he might be able to gain a place at a school that could better accommodate a child of his ability. There was no way, at that time, they could afford to pay the fees that were required for schools of this type, but if he could win a scholarship, then his fees would be waived. If Peter was unsuccessful, then he would stay at Longcross where he was clearly happy and then move on to a local secondary school with his friends when he was eleven. However, they were extremely well aware that success could change his life and, as his parents, they did not feel it would be fair to pass up that opportunity for their son.

They agreed to say nothing to him until a few days before the examination to avoid causing him undue worry and when they did, they explained that all they wanted was for him to try his best. They had certainly not told him much about the schools he might go to or that this could involve living away from home as a boarder. There was no point, in their minds, worrying him about that either. He would take the exam and if he did manage to win a scholarship, they would then cross those particular bridges.

On the bus ride home that early spring day, the three boys had been eating a piece of left-over sponge pudding that Lee's mother, who was one of the dinner ladies, had given him. With the restrictions of food rationing still in place, they had long since made a pact to share any windfalls of this kind with each other. With some difficulty, Lee had divided the sponge as evenly as he could by prising it apart. His hands were not particularly clean, as the boys had been playing marbles on the pavement while they waited for the bus, but no one cared. Pleased enough with the fairness of the result, the three had gleefully enjoyed the unexpected treat.

When his stop was approaching, Peter headed for the open exit where he could hold on to the pole that ran from the floor to the ceiling as the bus slowed to a halt. He jumped off into the warm haze of the afternoon sun and began the short walk home. He had only taken a few steps when he was surprised to see his mother about twenty yards ahead, near the park. She had been running and slowed down as she came nearer, waving above her head a brown envelope. She explained as she stopped in front of him that the result of the examination had arrived. She admitted that she was so excited that she had opened it already, but the great news was that he had been awarded one of the available scholarships. Smiling with pride she stooped and squeezed him as tightly as he could ever recall her doing. The memory of his mother's elation and happiness that warm spring afternoon was one that would stay with Peter forever.

That weekend, Peter was summoned by his parents to sit with them in the dining room. On the table was a pile of pamphlets that he had not seen before. His parents explained to him that these were prospectuses from the various schools that they were considering for Peter. They wanted to look through them together and talk to him about the options before making any firm decisions.

His father held one out to Peter for Tinniswood Manor, the school where the scholarship examination had taken place. He told him that, having looked into things carefully, he and his mother both thought this school might be the best choice. His mother added enthusiastically that the school had been in existence since 1690 and had an excellent reputation academically. It looked fine to Peter, and he readily agreed with their selection, much to their delight. In truth, he was more concerned that he had arranged to meet Lee and Bernard at the park for a kick about – Bernard had recently been given a new football from his grandmother for his ninth birthday and he wanted to see what it was like. Oddly enough, Peter remembered the games of 'three-and-in' that afternoon much clearer than the conversation with his parents. They had played for hours and Peter came home caked from head to toe in mud. On Monday at school the others had told him about the bus conductor who did not want to let them on his nice clean bus. Only after their assurances that the mud on them had mostly dried and the removal of their muddy boots (which they each had to hold on the journey) did the grumpy man grudgingly acquiesce.

It was decided that Peter would start at Tinniswood Manor in September and because the school was so far away, his parents explained that he would have to board. Peter did not really appreciate what this would entail, but he could apparently come home some weekends, so he thought it sounded okay.

In the summer holiday his mother had taken him to the school outfitters. Peter was quite excited when she had told him that they would need to go by train because the shop was in Regent's Street. They caught the bus at the end of the road to the station where they took the train into London. From there they took a short underground ride, which was Peter's first taste of the tube. He loved it and there was no question he enjoyed the experience considerably more than the ordeal of being measured for his uniform. The tailor, a skinny, unpleasant man with a crimson spot on his nose, pushed and pulled him angrily into position for each measurement. Peter's mother had not been invited to comment throughout the process other than to clarify which items she required from the list provided by the school and, when the man had finished, she was as relieved as Peter to leave. To cheer him up she suggested they celebrated with lunch at the Lyons Corner House in Oxford Street before catching the return train home.

The last few weeks of the summer holidays were spent getting everything ready for the start of term. His mother sewed name tags into all his clothes and sports kit, ticking off each item on her list as it was completed. She gave him a particularly severe haircut with a large pair of dressmaking scissors, presumably in the hope that he would not need another one before Christmas, and began the process of filling the large wooden tuck box that Peter was required to take with him. The fare was limited because it was so difficult for his mother to source the ingredients to bake a cake, so he had to settle for whatever she was able to find or create. The cavernous box was only about half full, but when she added three chocolate bars Peter's grandmother had contributed, he was overjoyed.

Boarders were due to return to school on the first Sunday in September and Peter and the other new pupils had been asked to arrive in the morning. His father had loaded up the car the night before and the plan was for the whole family to make a day of the trip to the Hertfordshire countryside. With Peter's mother navigating efficiently, they made good time and as his father drove through the gates and along the short driveway to the parking area, Peter held his breath. He was flabbergasted by the sheer size of the place let alone the splendour of the ancient buildings. The only time he had seen anything like it was in books or in the magazines his mother sometimes bought.

He was naturally sad when his parents left him there for the first time, but it soon became apparent that he and the other new boys simply had to get on with it. Sympathy was in short supply among the staff, and boys who mentioned or displayed signs of home sickness were soon ridiculed by the seasoned campaigners who had known only this life since the age of four. Fortunately for Peter, he was tall for his age and quite obviously one of the cleverest boys in his class. This gave him something of a protective aura and those inclined to bully tended to find easier prey elsewhere.

As the weeks turned into months, Peter began to prosper. He was often invited to midnight feasts in the dormitory when one of his fellow classmates had been the beneficiary of a food parcel from a distant relative or a parent feeling guilty. He had also set up a rather profitable side-line, helping some of the less gifted boys with homework or tuition, particularly with maths. Payment was made in cakes, sweets and fruit most of the time and thanks to the intricacies of algebra, trigonometry and fractions, his tuck box was constantly replenished. In fact, he did so well that it occurred to him that he might need a second tuck box to accommodate his hard-earned booty. It soon became apparent that money seemed to be of little consequence to most of the boys, but he knew there was no way his parents could afford to buy him another. He settled instead for contributing generously to dormitory feasts whenever his tuck box was overflowing, and this had the welcome effect of further enhancing his popularity.

The highlight of the end of the first term at Tinniswood Manor was the Christmas party. There were too many boys for the whole school to celebrate together, so multiple parties were organised during the final week. Peter's class was paired with the form above them for their party, which was to run from three o'clock to five o'clock. Teachers oversaw proceedings in shifts so that, following a clear-up operation, the ten- and eleven-year-olds could have their party afterwards, between six and eight. He had been told by his classmates to expect lots of food and games and a present that he could take home. Despite this inside information, nothing could have prepared him for the extravagance of that afternoon.

In an attempt to tire out fifty or so young boys, some of the teachers were charged with organising party games which were not only fun in themselves but included the added attraction of prizes for the winners. Unfortunately, the tail a dizzy, blindfolded Peter attempted to pin on the picture of a donkey ended up nearer the beast's nose than its rear end. He was then, he felt, rather harshly eliminated from dead lions, being adjudged by the geography teacher Mr French to have moved his foot. His prospects of a prize, which were small packets of sweets for second and third place and a more significant parcel containing sweets, biscuits and a gift for the winners were beginning to diminish as the games went by.

Then without trying particularly hard, he found himself one of only about ten boys left in the game of musical chairs. Sensing his chance, he carefully navigated his way around the chairs as gradually ten reduced to five, then to four and three. He knew he was going to win at least a packet of sweets and was reasonably content with that, but he could tell by the look on the other boys' faces that second and third place were of no interest to them. The first prize for musical chairs, it transpired, was a huge bag of sweets and a fruit cake. These were riches enough in Peter's eyes, but accompanying them was a miniature cricket bat signed not only by the England cricket team but also the Australians who toured in 1948. The two other boys left were older than Peter. One was clearly an athlete who was by far the quickest and most nimble as he effortlessly circled the chairs. The other was a stocky boy with greasy, dark curly hair and a spotty chin, who glared threateningly at him when he caught his eye. Peter quickly assessed that the latter would do him physical harm rather than lose and the former was so fleet of foot that he could never match him.

The music started up again and, to Peter's surprise, when it suddenly stopped, the agile boy reacted so quickly that he tripped himself up in his haste to reach a chair and ended up prone on the floor as first Peter and the greasy boy easily took the two available seats. Boys from both forms seemed to be cheering for Peter. His classmates because he was their friend and the older boys who, apart from a few hangers on, knew that their form's representative was an arrogant, spiteful bully.

The boy, whose name was Blackshaw, deliberately bumped into Peter, pushing him momentarily off balance while the teacher, having turned his back on them, removed one of the remaining two chairs. The threat was plain to see and it had the desired effect of unnerving

Peter. However, when he heard the music, Peter instinctively ignored the glare of his opponent and began to walk cautiously around the solitary chair. Both slowed slightly as they approached the seat and accelerated again so that they rounded it as quickly as possible to return to their goal. The music went on longer this time as if to convey to everyone the importance of what they were watching. Round and round they went, ten times, twenty times. Every time Blackshaw went past, he ran to return, sometimes so quickly that he pushed Peter out of the way, meaning that, even if the music had stopped, he would not have been able to take the seat. Very suddenly, there was silence followed by a split second of panic. Peter was behind the chair, about to round it, and Blackshaw had just walked beyond it. It was against the rules to move backwards, so the bully charged around the chair, pushing Peter hard in the back in an attempt to get past him. Having experienced this a few moments earlier, Peter was prepared this time and, instead of falling, managed to divert his weight towards the vacant chair, spinning slightly as he did so with the result that he landed perfectly on the seat. A second or two of realisation elapsed as the spectators took in the sight they had witnessed. Then came the roar of celebration as Peter was simultaneously proclaimed the winner by Mr French and mobbed by boys celebrating, in equal measure, their friend's victory and the defeat of the loathsome Blackshaw.

The prizes were awarded and as Blackshaw ungratefully collected his sweets for second place, he shoved Peter again and whispered in his ear words to the effect that one day he would regret beating him. Ignoring the threat, Peter collected his prize, marvelling at the names on the cricket bat.

The final game involved throwing bean bags through hoops and scoring points based on the difficulty of their position. Peter sat it out, unable to stop gazing at the bat. He had heard his father talk about the feats of Don Bradman and Len Hutton and now he had something that they had both also touched. Not only that, but they had both signed it. The bean bag through the hoops game finished with an older boy, who had an extremely long body, scoring seven hundred and ninety points and duly being awarded first prize.

Afterwards, everyone adjourned to the refectory for their Christmas tea. Peter had never seen food like it, certainly not at home. Sandwiches, cold meats, sausage rolls, pies and all manner of other fare adorned the tables at one end of the refectory. At the other end there were as many tables piled high with cakes, biscuits and jelly.

There was even talk of ice cream, which Peter had only ever tasted once before when he visited his grandmother. Each boy had a cracker, which they opened with whoever was sitting next to them. Paper hats were donned and laughter filled the room as jokes were read to one another. The boys ate and ate until they reached the point where just an additional roast potato or mouthful of jelly might tip them over the precipice from being replete to a pre-vomitous state of queasiness. Unfortunately, some boys misjudged this fine balance and were forced to return to their dormitories tentatively clutching their bellies.

After Christmas, the Spring Term passed in a flash. Peter continued to do well academically, friendships were cemented and now that it was warmer, dormitory feasts were supplemented courtesy of visits to the local shop for sweets. Most boys, Peter included, returned from the Easter holidays looking forward to a Summer Term of sunshine, cricket and swimming. Even the thought of the inevitable end of term exams could not dampen the atmosphere of enthusiasm and optimism that existed.

It transpired that they were much easier than the scholarship examination Peter had taken and although most of the results would not be known for a week or two, he felt he had done well. One of the last to be sat was maths. With over an hour remaining, the invigilating master approached Peter's desk and enquired as to why he had stopped writing. When he explained that he had not only finished but had also double-checked his answers, he was told that he could leave, provided he was certain and on the proviso that he did so quietly.

It was a blistering hot June afternoon and Peter was glad to be out of the oppressive fug of the examination room. His grandmother had sent him some money at the weekend, so he decided to take the short walk to the shop to buy some ice lollies which would, he was sure, be gratefully received by his friends David and Edward after the exam. His plan was to buy the lollies, run back to the dormitory and present them to his friends before they melted.

Having calculated the time to coincide with the end of the exam, he strolled through the school gates and down the road to the shop. As he entered, the familiar bell above the door chimed, alerting the owner to his presence. The owner was Mr Fenwick, a small man in his late sixties, whose size belied the strength of his wiry body and his determined character. He had lost an eye at the Battle of Arras in 1917 and spent the next six months in a convalescent home. Fortunately for him, he inherited money from his grandfather in the mid-1920s and invested it in the shop which he and his wife had run until her death three years previously. As Peter entered, Mr Fenwick turned away from the group he was serving so that he could see the new arrival with his good eye. The three boys, Peter noticed, were all in the year above him at school. Glancing at them, his eyes momentarily met those of Blackshaw, who was arguing with two of his lackeys about which sweets they should buy. Realising that their debate was likely to continue for a while, Mr Fenwick came over to serve Peter.

Peter asked him for the lollies, which necessitated a trip to the fridge. Mr Fenwick slid the lid across and stretched deep into the freezer to reach them. As he did so, Peter noticed that the three boys were taking advantage of the fact that the shopkeeper had turned his back and filling their pockets with Fruit Salads and any other sweets they could easily access. As Peter opened his mouth to speak, Blackshaw stared at him menacingly and slowly shook his head in warning. Then the two other boys turned and glared at him, making it very clear that they would not take kindly to him snitching on them. Mr Fenwick finally managed to retrieve the required items from the depths of the freezer and as he extracted his head and shoulders from the cold, Peter considered telling him what had happened. The two miscreants with Blackshaw continued to stare at him as their leader reached behind the counter to the makeshift cash box that Mr Fenwick preferred to a till. He grabbed some notes and before Mr Fenwick, having handed Peter the lollies, turned around, he slipped them hastily into his jacket pocket. The three coolly walked out of the shop without saying a word, leaving Peter to pay, which he duly did. It had all happened so quickly and for once Peter was unsure what to do. He should tell Mr Fenwick (in hindsight he would always regret that he did not), but he was scared of what Blackshaw and his cronies would do to him if he did.

Outside, Peter looked up the road and saw the boys fifty yards ahead scoffing the sweets they had stolen, occasionally patting one another on the back in congratulation. He did not want to catch them up even though his idea of sharing the lollies with his friends relied on him running back to school. He felt numb and confused and was relieved to see them keeping up a good pace and ultimately disappearing through the school gates.

A few days later, Peter was summoned to the headmaster's office. He had never been inside the room that lay behind the big oak door but had spoken to plenty of other boys who had. The experience was rarely a good one and usually resulted in a punishment of some kind, often the cane.

The headmaster sat behind his desk and was flanked on either side by two men Peter had never seen before. Both of them wore dark suits and glared severely at him as he entered. The one on the left was skinny and had red hair. The man on the right was overweight and sweaty with a thick mop of dark curly hair. Seated in front of them sat the familiar figure of Mr Fenwick. Peter smiled at him, but the acknowledgement of his presence was not returned. He assumed he was going to be asked to confirm that he had seen the other boys stealing and began to feel worried about the beating they would give him when he did.

Standing in front of the four men, Peter heard the headmaster explain that some money had gone missing from Mr Fenwick's shop. He had been to the bank on the day in question and had been able to pinpoint quite precisely when the alleged theft might have occurred. Mr Fenwick recalled that a number of boys from the school had visited his shop that afternoon and the headmaster had been making enquiries in order to establish who the thief might be. He had interviewed other pupils and been told by three boys that they had seen Peter take the money while the shopkeeper's back was turned. Nodding in the direction of the other men, he continued to explain that he, the chairman and the vice chairman of the board of governors believed that Peter was the culprit.

He was dumbstruck but knew that he had to defend himself against this charge and tell the men what had really happened. Stating his complete innocence, he pointed out that even if he had the inclination, which he did not, he would not need to steal since he had received some money from his grandmother only a matter of days before the incident. He explained that he had been in the shop and seen the money stolen by Blackshaw and that he and the other boys had also stolen sweets. He knew he should have said something to Mr Fenwick, but they had threatened him if he did so. As he was about to apologise to Mr Fenwick for not coming forward, the headmaster put up his hand, making it evident that he wanted Peter to stop talking. Glancing at his colleagues, he told Peter that they had predicted that he would try and blame the other boys as it was them that had informed the headmaster and governors of Peter's guilt. They said they had seen Peter take the money but had been too frightened to say anything. Peter was silent, unable to speak, trying desperately to absorb the enormity of the treachery of their story. He tried hard to speak but realised that even if he did, he would also be unable to stop himself crying, such was his frustration at the injustice of the situation. Taking his silence as an admission of guilt, Peter was dismissed but not before the headmaster told him that he had sent for his parents, who would be coming to school the next day to discuss the matter.

Peter was beside himself. He was powerless, the thieves had pointed the finger at him and the headmaster had swallowed their lie. Telling the truth was useless when you were one voice against three, each of which was prepared to say you were lying. He could not sleep that night. He knew now that he should have told the headmaster what he had seen when it happened, but Blackshaw had scared him, and he did not want the beating that would have inevitably followed if he had snitched.

It transpired that the headmaster had telephoned Peter's parents informing them of the events that had taken place and that, following assiduous enquiries, he was convinced that Peter had undoubtedly stolen the money. He had discussed the matter with the school's governors and the only option available to them was to expel their son immediately. The next morning a prefect had been sent to Peter's dormitory with the message that he did not have to go to his scheduled lessons. Instead, he was to pack his belonging as his parents would be arriving to take him home at ten o'clock.

When they arrived, Mr and Mrs Davis were embarrassed and furious. His father angrily packed his things in the boot then told him to wait in the car while they went inside to speak to the headmaster and governors.

Afterwards they returned to the car without saying a word and as they drove away Peter tried to explain that he had seen a group of other boys stealing the money but that they had ganged up and blamed him. His parents wanted to believe him, and they knew he was an honest boy, but the evidence put before them was quite compelling. Perhaps the school had changed him and without them there he had gone off the rails. One thing was for sure: they were going to have to find a new school for Peter as Tinniswood Manor was not likely to allow him to return.

The next day a letter arrived from the school confirming unequivocally that he was to be permanently expelled. Peter's mother left it on the dining room table for her husband to see when he came home in the evening and although Peter did not really want to look at it, out of some macabre curiosity, he forced himself to while his mother was outside hanging some washing on the line. The school's crest on the note paper made the document undoubtedly official and the few sentences of writing condemned him to exile from Tinniswood Manor forever. So as to formalise things fully, it was signed not only by the headmaster, Mr James, but also the chairman of the governing body. Peter scanned the words quickly, pretty much knowing what it would say. He was about to put the letter back on the table when his eyes fell on the signatures at the bottom of the page. Two illegible squiggles, one of which he recognised as the headmaster's. As he stared at the other, his body went cold, and he was hit by the full realisation of what had happened to him. He had to read it twice to be sure, but there was no mistake. Underneath the signature in bold letters was printed the name of the chairman of governors – Mr D A Blackshaw.

Chapter 8

"That sounds like quite an ordeal for a young boy. What happened after you were expelled?"

"Yes, it was," replied Peter thoughtfully. "My parents contacted the headmaster and put my version of events to him and enquired as to whether Mr Blackshaw had been involved in the investigation, explaining that they felt this would have been inappropriate. The headmaster stuck to his story that the decision was based purely on the statements he had received, and as other boys had corroborated Blackshaw's explanation, the matter was closed and that my expulsion stood."

"That must have been difficult for your parents to take."

"It certainly was, but they knew I had not done anything wrong and that it had been a stitch up. Apparently, Mr Blackshaw had made a fortune rebuilding houses after the war. A family like mine couldn't possibly compete with the Blackshaws. A boy from a lower middle-class family who had only been admitted because of his academic ability was dispensable and they closed ranks. There was nothing my parents could do about it."

"That is a shame. What happened next?"

"My parents talked to the head at the local school, who said that he would happily take me. The attraction was that most of my old primary school friends were there, so I would not feel like a complete stranger. The problem was that I had changed in the short time I had been at boarding school. It had made me more independent and I had been pushed harder academically than I would be at a regular school. My father's boss, Mr Stradbrook, was sympathetic to our situation and, I suspect, wanted to look after one of his most reliable employees. He spoke to a friend of his who had recently been appointed headmaster of a private school that might be willing to accept me. Rosehill Grammar was, however, in Sussex, so not only would full-time boarding be the only option, but I was also required to pass an entrance examination and an interview to secure a place. It seemed like a good solution, apart from the fees which my parents could not afford. Mr Stradbrook again came to our rescue by negotiating on our behalf with the school, and it was agreed that provided I was in the top five percent of those sitting the exam, my fees would be reduced by seventy-five percent."

Peter reached over for his beaker of water, which he sipped. It tasted good and he took another quick gulp, keen to tell the whole story now he had started.

"Of course, we had to try the entrance examination and the local school was still there as a back-up if things didn't go well. The headmaster had confided in Mr Stradbrook that he expected around a hundred boys to apply, so I knew I had to be in the top five. I was never told my actual position, but I was awarded the subsidised place. At my interview, the headmaster had asked about the circumstances surrounding my expulsion from Tinniswood Manor and seemed happy enough with my explanation of events, no doubt because it corroborated what Mr Stradbrook had already told him."

"What was the new school like?"

"In many ways Rosehill Grammar was much the same as Tinniswood Manor. It had also been established for centuries and day to day life was similar. There were strict teachers and friendly teachers, but the main difference was that the prevailing atmosphere seemed less hostile, both from the teachers, although they did use the cane quite regularly, but also from the other boys. Perhaps I had become like them, but I think it was really that most of us appreciated being there. At Tinniswood Manor there were so many pupils who seemed to think that their family's wealth or social standing would save them if they didn't do well academically or if they misbehaved. Exactly as it did with Blackshaw, I suppose. Of course, there were boys from wealthy families at Rosehill, but the importance of being the best we could be as individuals was instilled in us constantly. I made new friends, and had a great time. I became captain of the school cricket team and played football and rugby too. We had a terrific art master who was kind to me and I improved my drawing and painting through working closely with him. I did well academically too and when I left, I was offered places at a number of top universities."

"It sounds to me as though it was probably meant to be that you ended up there."

"Yes, I suppose so. It didn't seem like it at the time. I felt so ashamed when I was expelled, but my parents were understanding and incredibly supportive even though I didn't see them as often as I would have liked. They were very determined and hugely protective of me. They knew I had been hard done by and did everything they could to make sure I was given the best possible opportunities in life – opportunities they didn't have themselves. After school I went to university, and it wasn't long after that I met my wife, Joan."

"I'd like to hear about that later, but for now I suspect you could do with some time alone and perhaps some rest."

"Mmm," agreed Peter, vaguely settling his head on the soft white pillow. He did not feel as though he needed more rest, but all this talking had made him a little tired.

"Perhaps we can speak again later, Mr Davis. I'd love to hear how you met your wife."

With that he wandered over to the window and pulled the curtains shut so that the room was in semi-darkness. Glancing over his shoulder, he could see that Peter had his eyes shut, so he crept carefully out of the room, turning the knob slowly and then very quietly shutting the door as he left.

Peter lay for a while thinking about that night at the dance and smiling as the memories came flooding back to him. His eyes were shut now and he felt incredibly relaxed, concentrating hard on remembering every detail he could and savouring each one as he drifted into a comforting sleep.

It's sunny and there are lots of people running around me, some of them so quickly I can't even see their faces. To my surprise, someone stands directly in front of me and starts talking. I don't recognise him at all, but he seems to know me. He is wearing red trousers and a vest and, judging by his friendly demeanour, he is obviously pleased to see me. I look again at his vest and notice that I am wearing an identical one. Perhaps we are teammates of some sort, but what is the game? I can see white plimsolls on my feet, like the ones I had at school, and I'm also wearing a pair of shorts. This is my old athletics kit. I look again at the man, hoping that he might tell me what event I am supposed to be doing and now I am able to see his face much clearer. It's Andy. He is young and smiling happily. I am excited that we are on the same team, just like the old days. But just as he is about to say something, someone jumps, narrowly missing us, and lands in a pile of yellow sand that has appeared to our right. In the sand is a young woman who I immediately recognise as Joan. Rather oddly, she is chatting to an old man who is dressed in a thick winter coat and a dark hat. What a strange outfit to be wearing here, I think. He seems quite cheerful though, smiling with Joan and every now and then taking a puff from a pipe he is holding. As he exhales, a vast cloud of

80

smoke hangs in the air above his head then suddenly disappears. To my astonishment, the man jumps to his feet athletically and pulls out a golf club from a bag next to him. Still smiling, he thrusts it into Andy's hand. Gleefully Andy jumps into the sand and starts swinging the club expertly. Golf balls fly in all directions except towards me. He hits some of them so far that we can't see where they land. Then I notice that one flies past a group of men who are running on orange track. They carry on and speed past us, apparently oblivious to their narrow escape from injury. Andy takes his time with the next shot, lining it up before he whacks the white ball into the distance. It bounces off the dusty orange surface and hits a Rolls-Royce which is parked next to a big red sports car. A smartly dressed man jumps out from the driver's side to check the damage, but Andy does not seem too bothered and continues swinging his club. The man obviously did not see who was responsible because instead of rebuking Andy he is shouting and screaming at a young man who, it would appear, has ridden his motorbike into the side of the Rolls.

Andy must have stopped or run away, perhaps fearful that he would be blamed, because I can't see him now. I am aware, though, of some bright lights and two young girls who are dancing nearby. Noticing me watching, they stop and one of them walks towards me purposefully. Quite suddenly she is standing next to me, close enough that I could touch her. She is older than I thought at first but quite unmistakable. It's Joan. I want to hold her tight, so I throw my arms around her and kiss her red lips hard. They are soft and she pulls me tightly towards her, kissing me hungrily.

Peter had a knack of being able to deliberately wake himself up from a dream when he needed to. It was not usually the joy of a moment like this but something worrying or dangerous that prompted him to do this. Sometimes he was kissing a sexy young woman who was obviously trying to seduce him. Or if someone fired a gun at him and a bullet hit him, he could wake himself up before it actually killed him. The same happened when he dreamt that he was about to drown or if he was falling uncontrollably into a deep chasm. He could always open his eyes and be alive.

Even though he had only been asleep for a few minutes, it took a while for his eyes to gradually focus on the objects around him. He was in bed and the bright light of the sun outside was sending a thin sliver of light through a narrow gap in the curtains where they had not quite been drawn shut. It looked like a laser beam as it hit the plastic jug full of water on the table next to him and he was reminded of using a magnifying glass of his father's to burn twigs and paper with his sister Pat one sunny day when they were young.

He knew he was alone, but the residual happiness of his embrace with Joan, albeit in his dream, filled him with warmth and comfort. It was almost as though she was still there with him, hugging him tightly. He pictured her face in his mind and was overcome for a moment by a surge of love for her. Her presence was everything to him and he never felt quite complete when they were apart. What would he do without her? How lucky they were to have found each other.

He knew that he sometimes struggled to remember mundane things nowadays, but he would never forget the first time he saw Joan. It was the 15th of October 1964, the day of the general election which would bring a Labour government and a new prime minister, Harold Wilson, to replace Alec Douglas-Home's Conservatives. It truly was the end of an era politically as Sir Winston Churchill had retired the previous month at the age of almost ninety. The war had finished twenty years before and a new normality had begun to exist in Britain. Society was changing and young people became obsessed by these changes, championing some things and condemning others. There seemed to be no middle ground. Earlier that year the conflict between mods and rockers had erupted as youngsters the same age as those who such a short time before were fighting as one and giving their lives to vanquish the same evil foe became divided by the frivolities of fashion and music. In October those who were not interested in the country's political landscape, and many that were, turned their gaze, or at least their ears via the radio, to Japan where the Games of the XVIII Olympiad in Tokyo had been opened by Emperor Hirohito earlier that week. It seemed so perverse that a defeated wartime enemy now welcomed athletes from Britain, America, France and Russia to her shores. The intense societal unrest at home in Britain, one of the principal victors in that war, brought this stark contrast into even sharper focus.

Peter had turned twenty in May and was about to head back to university for the third year of his maths degree. The start of term had been delayed because of the general election, which meant that he had been able to stay on and earn some extra money continuing his summer job at Daniels and Sylvester Limited, a firm of insurance brokers in North London. Much of the work was mundane, but when he was given the opportunity, he enjoyed talking to clients on the telephone and sometimes in person, mainly helping them with queries and referring them to one of the partners when appropriate.

On that particular day Peter had taken the afternoon off for a dental appointment and had returned home in time to see some of the Olympic Games coverage on the BBC. The programme was introduced by Alan Weeks and two young commentators, David Coleman and Harry Carpenter, who provided their inimitable descriptions of the events of the previous day. The programme was dominated by the achievement of Mary Bignal-Rand, who had not only won a gold medal in the long jump but had also set a new world record of 6.76 metres in the process.

That evening Peter had been invited by his best friend Andy to go with him to a dance at the golf club where he played. Andy made it sound like a good evening and although they were both single, he had assured Peter that there would be plenty of girls in attendance. Peter had never played golf or even been to the club before, but he knew that Andy's father had introduced him to the game years ago and he spent quite a bit of his spare time there. As he pondered the merits of golf versus cricket, Peter looked at the clock and decided that he ought to get changed as he wanted to leave for Andy's as soon as they had eaten. He was vaguely aware of Cliff Michelmore telling everyone about an engineer from Sutton Coldfield called Ken Matthews, who had taken paid leave from his job to compete in the 20 km walk. Apparently, he was one of the favourites to win the gold medal. Peter switched off the set, making a mental note to check the result tomorrow.

Peter and Andy had lived a few doors from each for the past nine years and although Peter had been away at boarding school and now university for a lot of that time, when he returned, they spent as much time together as possible. They were inseparable during the long summer holidays of their early teenage years, playing football or cricket in each other's gardens and going on long bike rides together. Other than Peter playing cricket and Andy going to the golf club at the weekends, the two were seldom apart. Interestingly neither had been tempted to try the other's sport. Beyond confirmation that they had a good game or a good round, when they met they hardly discussed these periods of time when they were not together, preferring to concentrate on whatever they were planning to do next.

Around 6.45, Peter ambled down the road, dressed in his best slim-fitting grey trousers and a pale blue polo shirt. He let himself in through the gate, wandered up the path and rang the doorbell of Andy's house. His friend came to the door looking extremely trendy in a pair of red polyester trousers which Peter thought seemed a bit tighter than was comfortable, an orange shirt and his favourite brown suede lace-up Oxfords. They greeted each other, staring casually at what the other was wearing, and finally nodding as if to confirm that their chances of finding girls who would dance with them were above average. A rattle of car keys came from the kitchen at the end of the hall and Andy's dad, who had agreed to be their chauffeur for the night, appeared with a smile on his face. By the time they shut the front door behind them, he was already getting into the driver's seat of the blue Vauxhall Victor estate that was parked on the drive.

It was only a short drive to the golf club and as they pulled in through the gates, Peter was amazed by the sweeping driveway that led through a majestic avenue of poplars before cutting across the eighteenth fairway and ending at the car park in front of the clubhouse. Mr Wakely dropped them off and Peter gazed at the magnificent building that looked to him more like a stately home than somewhere you would meet for a friendly round of golf. He was temporarily transfixed by the cars that surrounded him. He could see at least two E-types, a Humber Super Snipe, a Sunbeam Alpine or two, a huge dark blue Alvis that seemed as big as a tank, and three rows ahead he could have sworn was a shiny, red Aston Martin Vantage. This was a very different world to the one he usually inhabited at the cricket club, and he suddenly felt relieved that he had not asked his dad to take them in his shabby Ford Anglia.

"Alright, mate?" Andy asked, seeing Peter's mouth widen.

"Yeah, fine. It's just not quite what I expected."

"Don't even think about it, Peter. There are some very wealthy people at this club, men that run big businesses and even a few politicians. But when they are standing over an eight-foot putt to win a match, they are all just as nervous as the rest of us. I play some of these guys at the weekends because they like to be seen out with us low handicappers. It's all show. They go and brag to their friends about it, but they never mention that they lost every hole and went round in ninety-five."

"Just posers, eh?" Peter said.

"Exactly. It must be the same at the cricket club."

"Well, yes, I suppose it is – just with fewer Aston Martins."

Andy laughed, put his arm round his friend and they walked across the gravel walkway that led into the clubhouse. Inside they passed through an oak-panelled hallway containing cabinets full of silver trophies and display cases which housed numerous old-fashioned golf clubs and golf balls. Each one had a label or card attached with a description and date on it. It was like being in a museum. Through a set of double doors at the end was a lounge area where Peter noticed there was a bar, behind which a man in his fifties was pouring a pint and simultaneously calling to a colleague to come and help him serve. The walls in this area were covered with honours boards declaring in gold letters the names of club captains and secretaries going back to the 1920s. There were also dozens of names of the winners of the various club competitions and Peter's eyes settled on the list of club champions, at the bottom of which, alongside the year 1964, was Andy's name. *He kept that quiet*, thought Peter as he began to relax a little, in the knowledge that he was accompanied not only by his best friend but also the current club champion.

As they approached the bar, there was a fork to the right with a sign above a huge set of double doors indicating the way to the members' lounge and a much smaller door to the right, which they took, on which was written in navy-blue lettering, 'Spike Bar'.

They were greeted by the sound of Herman's Hermits proclaiming 'I'm into something good', so it was fair to assume that this was obviously where the dance was being held. Peter had feared that this might be a stuffy affair, but as Herman and his Hermits were replaced by the Beach Boys singing one of their classics, he felt very optimistic that it might indeed turn out to be 'Fun, Fun, Fun'.

He was surprised how large the Spike Bar was and how many people were already in there. As was usual at this sort of event, the room was divided into two distinct camps. The girls were on the far side chatting and smiling with one another in small groups. Occasionally one or two would glance at the bar area or the other side of the room where the boys had gathered. A nervous wave of testosterone on legs dressed in a variety of bright casual tops and trousers oozing bravado that belied their complete lack of confidence with the opposite sex. The no man's land that divided the two factions was occupied by a middle-aged man with a vast brown beard that threatened to take over his whole face. He wore a red and blue horizontally striped tee shirt which was impossible to ignore.

Surrounding him were dozens of boxes of records and in front of him was a square lectern, around which rotated blue, green and red flashing lights, illuminating the sign that read 'Mellow Mike's Mobile Music'. Two large speakers were strategically placed either side to ensure that all parts of the wooden rectangle of dance floor would receive their full blast. At present, however, only one brave couple and a group of three girls were on it, casually oscillating on the spot to the unmistakable harmonies of the boys from California.

With an almost imperceptible glance, or so they thought, towards the girls gathered opposite, Peter and Andy headed for the security of the bar.

"What can I get you, Andy?" asked the man in the blazer and club tie behind the bar, ignoring two other lads who were hoping to be served, one of whom was frantically waving one of the newly printed £10 notes. The other, clearly disgruntled, shouted, "Oi, I was here first."

The barman half turned towards him, placing a meaty hand on the bar, using his left eye only to fix him with a stare. He allowed a few seconds to pass, during which time the unruly youth had the opportunity to consider the size of the man he was addressing and to notice the scar that covered a large portion of his left cheek. Concluding that the barman had almost certainly received his injuries from a fight in which he had no doubt ultimately been victorious, probably against multiple opponents, the boy swallowed and looked away to avoid the man's attention. He might have been surprised to know that, in fact, the injury had been acquired falling from his push bike a couple of years earlier while riding to the post office with a letter to his mother in Eastbourne. The bins had been collected that morning and he caught his face on a jagged piece of wire that had been dropped by a careless dustman and was strewn on the pavement precisely where rider and bike had parted company.

Turning back to Andy, he raised his eyebrows and widened his eyes, encouraging a response to his earlier enquiry with a broad smile on his face.

"Evening, Joe. Two pints of Red Barrel, please," said Andy.

As the bar steward began to pour the drinks, Andy rested his elbow on the bar casually and swivelled to face Peter. "What do you think? Anyone you like the look of?"

Peter nodded his head towards two girls who were chatting alone by the window that looked out onto the putting green. "The girl in the lime-green dress over there. She is stunning, isn't she?"

"Oh yes, I see her. Not bad at all and her friend is pretty tidy. Let's get over there and see if we can make up a foursome."

Joe returned with the drinks. "Three bob, please, Andy."

Andy duly passed across the requisite coins and handed Peter his beer. The lad with the £10 note piped up again, now aiming his displeasure in Andy's direction rather than the barman's.

"We were charged three and six for two of those earlier," he said accusingly.

Before Peter could respond, Joe intervened with a steely look. "Yes, you were, young man, but he's a club member and you're not." This, and Joe's considerable bulk, seemed to satisfy the lad, who withdrew slightly, edging up the bar with his £10 note, hoping to be served by someone else.

"That's a result," said Peter. "I didn't realise that there were reduced prices for members."

"I didn't either, mate," said Andy, who looked at Joe with a smirk.

Joe winked in reply. "Oh, didn't you know, Andy, the rule came in a few minutes ago. Apparently, it's intended to annoy tossers who wave new £10 notes in the faces of the bar staff," he said very seriously before roaring with laughter.

Two mods who, Peter calculated, were probably a year or so older than him and Andy had just been served at the other end of the bar and were wandering in the direction of the two girls Peter and Andy had been discussing. They were both tall, one thick set and the other wiry. The bigger of the two wore grey tailored trousers which made him look thinner than he actually was, a pale blue polo shirt and grey lace-up shoes with a single black horizontal band over the toe. He was attractive with short brown hair and green eyes and exuded an air of confidence. As he strolled across the dance floor, girls certainly seemed more inclined to admire him than his slightly pale-looking friend, who had been unsuccessful that evening in taming his unruly shock of blond hair. The sidekick was dressed in a tight-fitting blue suit which, instead of enhancing his appearance, made him look like a moving pipe-cleaner. Their sights were firmly set on the two girls and within seconds they were next to them. The good-looking one was doing the talking, smiling at the girl in the green dress and offering her his hand for a dance.

Much to Peter's dismay she took it and followed him onto the dance floor where a number of other couples had been persuaded to venture by Mellow Mike, who, in a moment of inspiration, had put on the current number-one hit by Roy Orbison. She moved gracefully if somewhat reluctantly to the beat next to the lad whose main aim seemed to be to move as little as possible and touch her as much as he could. Peter could not avert his eyes. She was gorgeous and Peter did not need Mr Orbison's constant reminder to see that she was most definitely an extremely 'Pretty Woman'.

"Those bastards have beaten us to it," he said to Andy. A moment later his despair was compounded as the two remained together for the slow song that followed.

"Well, actually, mate, I think I might be alright," said Andy, nodding in the direction of the other girl, who was desperately trying to avoid eye contact with the skinny boy, who she feared might offer her a similar fate to her friend. Closer inspection proved that she had little to worry about. His charm offensive, in stark contrast to his more direct friend, consisted of looking at the floor a lot while twiddling with one of the buttons on his jacket as he wondered why his voice had suddenly stopped working.

"Do you know who those blokes are?" Peter asked.

"I don't know the beanpole," Andy replied, "but the big guy is a member here. His name's Gary Carr. Not much of a golfer – from what I hear he spends most of his time riding around on his brand new Lambretta with all the other local mods. I heard him bragging to one of the juniors the other week that they all went to Brighton in May and beat up a load of rockers. Complete bollocks if you ask me. His family is loaded though. His old man inherited a fortune from his parents and set up 'Carr and Son' the estate agents. Gary runs one of the branches, but when his dad retires, he'll probably take over the whole operation."

This news did not make Peter any less gloomy. Not only was this interloper well-dressed, but he also had what sounded like unlimited funds with which to impress a girl.

On the other side of the bar, the members' lounge had suddenly become busier, Peter noticed, as a group of middle-aged men in suits and blazers had arrived and the bar staff were struggling to cope.

"You should go and talk to the other girl, Andy. Rescue her from that idiot at least. Go on, I'll get us another round of drinks."

Andy glanced across at the poor girl, who, clearly fed up with the lanky hanger-on she had unwittingly attracted, now seemed to be explaining to him angrily that his attentions were not welcome. Andy could not quite read her lips, but he got the gist of what she had said and so, fortunately, did the pipe-cleaner.

"That's tempting, thanks, Peter, but I have a feeling she'll be able to look after herself for a while. Anyhow I think we shouldn't settle for anything less than that foursome we talked about."

"That doesn't look very likely though, does it?" said Peter, staring across the room at Gary Carr, who was unleashing his full repertoire of chat on the girl in the green dress. That said, Peter thought the girl did look rather bored and she had glanced towards her friend a couple of times for support. Perhaps there might be chance to speak to her but not while Gary bloody Carr was there.

"I think I've got an idea," said Andy. "Get the drinks in. Joe knows we are mates, so you'll get the members' discount. I'll just be a couple of minutes."

With that, he headed out of the Spike Bar. While he was waiting to be served, Peter could see him in the hall outside the entrance to the members' bar chatting to a man in a grey pin-striped suit. A few minutes later Andy returned with a satisfied grin on his face, just as Joe placed another two pints on the bar.

"Cheers, Peter," said Andy, picking up his pint while simultaneously putting his arm on his friend's back and leading him conspiratorially to a quieter area where they could not be overheard.

Peter looked at his friend expectantly, waiting to hear what he had been up to.

"Did you see that man I was talking to outside?"

"Yes, I did," Peter replied, looking intently at his friend. "Who was he?"

"That was the club secretary and he has just told me that there is a committee meeting at the club tonight. You might have noticed that group of blokes assembling over the other side of the bar."

Peter nodded to confirm that he had but looked questioningly at his friend, waiting for him to explain the relevance.

"All the club officials come to these meetings. The secretary obviously, the club captain, and the various sub-committee officers. Sometimes the president puts in an appearance if he is in the country, and tonight is one of those nights."

"Go on," Peter said, now beginning to become intrigued.

"He's a big cheese. You might have heard of him, Sir Martin Parfitt?"

The name did not mean anything to Peter.

"Parfitt foods? Crunchy crisps, chocolate peanut clusters, fancy fondant creams?"

"The biscuits?" Peter said as the penny dropped.

"The very same – and much, much more besides. The Parfitts make biscuits and cakes but are into lots of other things as well. They export all around the world now and Sir Martin spends most of his time, from what I can gather, on his yacht in Monte Carlo. Apparently, it's fully equipped with an office suite so that he can run his business from it. He has a private chef and entertains some of the wealthiest people in Europe on board."

"Wow, that is impressive," Peter agreed.

"Yes, I've met him a few times, but he's not the sort of man you go and introduce yourself to. He's a bit like royalty – you have to wait for him to talk to you first. Loves his golf and is an absolute stickler for all the traditions and etiquette that surround it. He likes everything to be 'just so' if you know what I mean, but apparently he's a decent old boy. I wouldn't cross him though. I've heard he's got a heck of a temper when he gets going. Joe saw him rip into one of the members who let two of his guests go into the lounge in their spikes. I haven't seen the guy playing here since and I'm pretty sure Sir Martin had him kicked out."

"Crikey, he sounds scary, but how does that help with getting Gary over there to leave that girl alone?"

"I'm glad you asked, Peter. That is the brilliance of my plan. It's what they call in golf, 'local knowledge'."

Peter looked at his friend expectantly and Andy continued.

"The meeting starts at 8.30. Sir Martin will arrive no earlier than 8.25 apparently. He likes everyone to know how busy he is and that he can't waste time hanging around, so he always makes a bit of an entrance, spot on time – he hates lateness. It's ten past now, so I reckon we've got a window of ten or fifteen minutes to set everything up."

Peter liked what Andy was saying but still looked puzzled.

"Probably easier if I explain as we go along," said Andy. "Come on," he said, putting his half-finished pint on the bar. "We'll be back for these, Joe," he called to the barman. Peter did the same and eagerly followed him out of the room.

Andy led him all the way out to the car park. It was dark now and turning a little chilly, which made both boys shiver slightly. Rubbing his hands together for warmth, Peter dutifully followed as Andy led him through the car park, past the Aston Martin that Peter had noticed earlier. Once again he stared longingly at it as they passed.

"No time for that now, Peter. We've got things to do," Andy said urgently.

The car park was well lit with knee-high block lamps so that members could easily navigate their way back to their cars even when inebriated. Andy led Peter to a small covered area beyond the cars, which was the designated parking area for bicycles. The bikes were arranged in two rows. At the far end of the second of these were the motorbikes. Andy glanced at his watch. Just after 8.15. When they were in front of them, he turned to his friend.

"We are going to move Gary's bike."

"Great," said Peter, "but how's that going to help me talk to that girl?"

Smiling at Peter, Andy could not resist continuing the subterfuge a while longer. "All will be revealed in due course. Come on, let's get his bike."

Peter scanned the rows and saw three Lambrettas, two next to each other and another a little further away. "Okay, great, so which one is his?"

Andy smiled and grabbed the handlebars of the silver Li150 in front of him. "This one."

"How do you know?" Peter asked.

"Simple. Firstly, it's the newest one and Gary is, as I explained, two things: a flash git and loaded."

Peter looked a little unconvinced because the other two looked new to him too.

Noticing his friend's uncertainty, Andy added, "And if that doesn't convince you, have a look at the registration plate."

Peter did and as he did so a smile appeared on his face. It read 'GDC 897B'. "What does the D stand for, I wonder, 'Dickhead'?."

As they laughed Peter stood aside to allow Andy space to kick away the brake and wheel the machine out of the shed.

"Where are we going to put it?" Peter asked, still not fully understanding the plan.

"Follow me," Andy said. "We'd better be quick," he added, breaking into a trot and retracing their steps with the bike towards the entrance to the clubhouse.

Peter noticed there was an area outside the building where no one had parked, and Andy was heading straight for it. The car park was empty apart from a couple that were taking a stroll, hand in hand, towards the first tee, but they had their backs to them. Andy deposited the Lambretta in the middle of what Peter could now see was a marked parking bay. A wooden plaque at the front read simply 'President'.

"That should do the trick," Peter declared. "I don't think Sir Martin is going to take too kindly to someone parking in his space."

Peter laughed with conspiratorial glee as he understood.

"Quick, let's get inside," Andy said as some headlights appeared at the end of the long driveway. The blue touch paper well and truly lit, the two retired to the safety of the Spike Bar to await the fireworks.

Sir Martin never used his chauffeur when he was at home, preferring instead to drive himself. The satisfying crackle of the tyres of the Rolls-Royce Silver Cloud on the gravel in the car park pleased him as he guided the 6.2 litre symbol of his enormous wealth towards its parking bay next to that of the club captain. As he approached, the new four headlamp layout of the Rolls shone brightly on an object that seemed to be occupying his space. *What the bloody hell is that?* he thought to himself as he stopped the car and got out to investigate. As he did so he glanced at the clock, which confirmed it was 8.25. Five minutes until the meeting. He did not have time for this nonsense.

Sir Martin had never seen a Lambretta up close, but he knew what it was because he had seen pictures in the newspapers and on the television. He had also formed an opinion that people who rode them could be trouble. He considered moving it himself but thought that might represent some sort of acceptance on his part that this was a simple error by the owner. "Couldn't they read?" he seethed to himself. Or was the owner some thug trying to prove a point about authority? Either way he was not going to stand for this. Sir Martin's temperature began to rise as he strode through the doors like a prize-fighter stalking his man. His face was flushed now and he was perspiring in his thick woollen suit. Grimacing at the noise coming from the Spike Bar, he assumed that the culprit was bound to be inside. He certainly was not, however, going to lower himself by going in there to confront him. Instead, he veered left towards the lounge bar in search of someone at whom he could bark his instructions. The lucky man who, seeing Sir Martin in his peripheral vision, came to greet him, was the secretary.

"Good evening, Sir Martin. How lovely to…" The man was cut off by an eruption worthy of any firecracker, rocket or roman candle.

"Some bloody hoodlum has left their motorcycle in my parking space," Sir Martin bawled at the poor man. And as if to emphasise his contempt, he added, "If you call it a motorcycle. Looks more like a bloody hairdryer on wheels. Get it moved, Simpson, and I want the idiot responsible to be dealt with."

The club secretary nodded to confirm his understanding. "Yes, of course, Sir Martin. I'll see to it."

He headed straight for the Spike Bar as he too was sure the offender must be one of the youngsters at the dance. It took him less than ten seconds to establish from Joe that the owner of the Lambretta was indeed 'that obnoxious poser Gary Carr' and that he could be found on the dance floor 'trying to chat up that pretty girl in the green dress'.

The secretary, who was a long-legged man of six foot five, advanced on the unsuspecting Mr Carr and was by his side in a couple of huge strides. There was a glimmer of recognition on the boy's face as the man began to speak. This soon developed into full awareness of his predicament as very calmly but very firmly he was asked, "Do you own a motorcycle with the registration number GDC 897B?"

"Yes, that's my Lambretta. Nice, isn't it?"

Most of the people in the room were by now staring intently at the events unfolding on the dance floor. Only two of them knew what was about to happen. Peter and Andy winced as they overheard Gary's response to the secretary's question.

"Listen to me, you little shit. I don't give a monkey's if it's nice or not. All I want to know is why it is parked in the president's parking space?"

Gary found himself unable to speak as he tried to process the words that had been directed towards him. Surprise turned to bemusement and then manifested itself in utter panic. Sir Martin Parfitt's reputation had filtered as far down the food chain as the place that was inhabited by the Garys of this world.

'I… I…' he stuttered, trying to form a sentence. "It's not parked there," he managed.

Although the secretary had not seen the bike for himself, he considered that he was probably quite safe in believing the word of a

Knight of the Realm in preference to that of the smarmy toe rag in front of him.

"Come with me, young man," the secretary said, grabbing Gary's arm, dragging him out into the hallway in a matter of seconds.

The Spike Bar emptied as everyone inside followed as one to observe proceedings. Even Mellow Mike joined the throng, leaving Gerry and the Pacemakers to ironically assure an empty room that they would 'never walk alone'.

Peter did not see Gary's face or precisely what happened in the car park because he and Andy had made sure they were standing near to the girl in the green dress and her friend. Andy thought the girls looked relieved to have extricated themselves from Gary and his lapdog and decided to speak to them straight away. "What an idiot," he said, directing his words to the friend.

"Couldn't agree more," the girl, whose name they subsequently found out was Teresa, said in response.

"He's been all over my friend for the past half an hour and she's been trying to get away from him," she added, looking towards Joan.

People seemed to be drifting back inside, so Andy thought he would take his chance. "Do you fancy a dance with me?"

"Yeah, why not? As long as you'll be okay, Joan?"

Peter jumped in, glancing over his shoulder towards the open door to the car park where the forlorn figure of Gary could just be seen wheeling his Lambretta slowly away.

"I don't think he's going to be bothering you for a while," he said to Joan. "Perhaps we could have a dance too, if you have recovered from your ordeal?"

She smiled. "I could do with a quick drink first if it's okay with you and then, yes, a dance would be lovely."

Chapter 9

Peter opened his eyes a crack, but the brightness of the room made him shut them again almost immediately. He allowed his closed eyelids to shield his vision, hoping that the eyes underneath would eventually be able to cope with the onslaught. Then like an astronaut carefully removing his helmet in an alien atmosphere, he tentatively allowed the light through. After a few seconds he gradually began to focus. He looked at the patterned bedclothes, which dulled things, and was eventually able to open his eyes fully. He caught sight of a shadow moving towards the window and looked across to where he thought the doctor must be.

"Sorry, Peter, I thought you would appreciate some sun, but perhaps it's a little too much," he said, shutting the thin curtains with a flick of first his right wrist then his left. A narrow gap was left in the centre where in his haste the doctor had not quite shut the curtains completely. A determined fragment of the sun's rays glinted against the vase on the table as if to make its point that they would have to do better than that if they wanted to obscure it.

Peter assumed he had been sleeping, judging by the difficulty he had experienced trying to open his eyes. He could not remember and decided that he had probably only been resting or at most had a very quick snooze – a power nap, as people called it nowadays.

"It looks beautiful out there again," said Peter, now much more alert.

"Oh yes, it's a wonderful day. It's a shame to shut it out really. Would you rather I hadn't drawn the curtains? I can easily open them again."

"Why not, but perhaps leave one shut, otherwise it might get a little too hot in here."

Once this had been done, half the room was immediately filled with the balmy heat and light from outside. The bed, and the area around it, was now enveloped in the warm half-darkness that only occurred on a summer's day.

Neither man said anything for a minute or two and, feeling slightly uncomfortable with the silence, Peter surveyed the room, his gaze darting around inquisitively, ensuring that he did not make eye contact with the doctor who had now pulled up a chair by the bed. The momentary air of embarrassment was eventually broken by the other man.

"What did you read at university?" he asked randomly.

"Mathematics," Peter replied in the apologetic manner of those who chose to study the subject.

"I guess that's not everyone's cup of tea."

"No, you're right. Most of my friends thought I was some kind of freak, but I always found maths easy to understand. It just seemed logical to me. At school things like algebra and geometry made sense and I loved the completeness of the subject. There was an answer to every question and I enjoyed the process of solving each one. At university we learnt ways of applying maths to the real world, which was interesting, but I always preferred a puzzle and a solution. Give me a nice differential equation and I was in my element."

"I steered clear of maths as much as possible, although I had to do some, as you can imagine. I guess I couldn't see the benefit in it other than the obvious – adding things up correctly and checking figures balanced."

"You'd be surprised. There are lots of ways of using mathematics outside the academic world."

"Oh really?"

"Yes, I'll give you an example. I used the laws of probability to work out how to increase my chances of winning the Pools."

Seeing the blank look on the doctor's face, he added, "The Football Pools?" in an attempt to clarify what he meant much as one would with a small child.

"No, I'm sorry, I've never heard of that."

"Oh, I see, well, perhaps they don't do it anymore. I stopped years ago. The idea was to select eight football matches that would finish in a score draw to win what was called the treble chance jackpot. Each week an agent from the Pools company would deliver a coupon and then collect it with however much money I wanted to stake that week. I used probability theorem to produce permutations of lines to improve the odds of winning."

Encouraged sufficiently by the doctor's apparent attention, he continued enthusiastically.

"If your line contained eight score draws, you would win a share of the jackpot, which was often hundreds of thousands of pounds. Occasionally someone would win a million."

"And did you ever win?"

"Not really. I won £150 one week, but the problem with my system was that you had to make certain decisions about a number of what seemed straightforward wins or losses for it to work. I didn't know an awful lot about football, but I soon learnt it was very unpredictable. A game you thought the home side couldn't lose, they did – or a team that notoriously couldn't score away from home would do so one week and ruin the whole thing."

Watching the doctor lean forward in his chair and place the yellow cushion that sat on it behind his back for support, it occurred to Peter that he might be sounding like a bit of a maths bore.

"Come to think of it, you could say I was a bit obsessed by mathematics. Perhaps I still am."

"Obsessed. How so?"

Peter was quiet for a few moments as he decided whether he was prepared to share this sort of private information with a man he had only known for a relatively short time. For no good reason he could identify, he decided to answer.

"The thing is that adding and subtracting as a young child were simple for me. I could always do them quicker than the other children in my class. As time went on and we learnt about geometry and trigonometry at school, I realised that these were easy for me to understand. It was almost as though I had been pre-programmed with information and knowledge that other people had to work hard to learn. Algebra and, later on, complex topics like calculus were just straightforward to me. Quite honestly, I didn't have to work particularly hard to be the top of every class I was in. It wasn't really until university that I met other students who were the same."

It was clear that Peter had something else to say but was reluctant to continue. He hesitated for a few seconds and then decided that having said this much there was little point in not telling the doctor everything, especially since he seemed such a good listener.

"I realised I had a gift in that I could do something better than everyone else. You come across people who are great sportsmen, or perhaps play the piano like some of these young musical prodigies you hear about, but with me it was maths. The problem is that no one prepares you for having this unusual ability. Why should they? It was difficult for others to understand and easier for them to think you were simply clever. I began to feel guilty because it was so much easier for me than my friends. I skipped lessons because I already understood perfectly the topics that needed to be drummed into my friends by teachers. Sometimes I felt afraid that I might lose this God-given talent and occasionally this worry could lead to elementary mistakes. Of course, it didn't make much difference whether I got ninety-five percent or one hundred percent in terms of grades, but I knew when I slipped up and it began to bother me."

Sensing the doctor raise both his eyebrows as a bidder might to let the auctioneer know that he was still interested in the lot that was being sold, Peter was encouraged to finish what he had to say.

"Since I've told you this much, I might as let you in on a secret. I still have dreams about school and the guilt. The recurring dream I have had for as long as I can remember is of me skipping a maths class and being alone in the house room. I am not doing anything in particular; I just know that I have not gone to the scheduled lesson with everyone else. In the dream I see the pupils, even the teacher Mr Partridge, who was my maths teacher at Rosehill Grammar, but I am not there. What makes things worse is that no one, least of all Mr Partridge, realises I am not in the classroom. My friends come out and I meet them and we go to the next lesson together. No one ever says anything to me about it and I feel guilty that they haven't noticed my absence and that the teacher hasn't either. Sometimes in the dream I have a sudden urge to go to the class just in case there is something I need to learn, that there is a gap in my knowledge that will be exposed in the next exam or test that I take. It's like I understand I don't need to be there, but I am also worried that I could miss something crucial. I've probably had that dream hundreds of times in the past sixty years."

"That's very interesting, Peter. Has this tended to be at specific times? Perhaps when you are worried or preoccupied with something, or do the dreams just happen as and when?"

"I don't know. I mean, I haven't really thought about it. I've always had quite vivid dreams though."

This time Peter's pause was longer. There was no turning back if he told the doctor what was on his mind.

"Is there something else, Peter?"

"Well, yes, there is. This is probably going to sound a bit stupid, but lately I have been dreaming a lot. Much more than normal and not just my usual ones. I've been dreaming about all sorts of things. In fact, they have been so vivid I can actually remember most of them.

That rarely happens. At most the only indication as to whether I've even dreamt is a feeling of dread or depression when I first wake up."

"So, they're often bad dreams then?"

"I suppose they must be, but recently I have had some good ones too. For example, I dreamt about the night I first met my wife Joan. My friend Andy and I had gone to a dance and she was there. The dream almost felt like it was real and I was actually there again."

"Ah yes, we were talking about that earlier. And is it unusual that you dream about something pleasant like that?"

"Yes, very. Most of my other dreams have felt just as real, but they have tended to be about things I would probably rather forget. When I have woken up, I've experienced that immediate uneasiness I mentioned, but it goes after a few seconds. Come to think of it, a lot of them were real things that have caused me to be either depressed or angry or sometimes both whenever I have thought about them. I've tried to forget them as best I can, but they were horrible events at the time and had a lasting impact on my life."

"Those memories must be difficult for you."

Peter reached across for the beaker of water on his bedside table. He took a few sips, replaced it then pushed himself into a more upright position on his pillow.

"It must be a blessing to go through life being able to avoid conflict with others and not to encounter nasty people doing unkind things. I wonder if anyone actually manages it. At Tinniswood Manor, I was something of an outsider – most of the other boys had rich parents and I was only there because I had won a scholarship. I made a couple of decent friends while I was there, but I think my face never really fitted."

He paused and reflected for a second before continuing to speak.

"It was my background, my upbringing that set me apart from the others. These boys were from the upper classes. They all knew each other and their parents moved in the same circles. At best my parents aspired to be middle class. Anyway, the upshot of the whole affair was that I was expelled, as I explained. I had to leave and Blackshaw stayed there, protected by his father. The normal rules of society didn't apply in those days to those people. There was an unwritten rule that the upper classes, the wealthy, controlled society at the time, particularly since the gap in prosperity between them and the working class had become a chasm thanks to the war. The hardest thing to bear then, and it still is now incidentally after all this time, is that I hadn't done anything wrong. It was the injustice of what happened and our helplessness to challenge it that causes the most pain. What gave those people the right to throw me out on the say-so of a liar simply because he was one of them?"

The response when it came was both prophetic and pragmatic.

"People can be odd, can't they? On the face of it, those with money and power have great lives. They are immune to many of the worries that most of society has. Financial security is so important in society today and from what you say, this boy and his family had monetary wealth which made this of no concern to them. Their behaviour does seem almost immoral when you think about it. So many around the world then and now unable to feed, shelter or clothe themselves, yet there is a minority for whom such simple necessities are irrelevant."

"Exactly. Why can't people be more generous with what they have?" said Peter, pleased that the doctor was on his wavelength.

"It's a good question for which I don't have an ideal answer, I'm afraid. What I do wonder, though, is whether these individuals stick together for security of a different kind. Perhaps they see financial wealth as their gift and because they have it, their main concern is to ensure they don't lose it."

Peter considered this theory and hesitantly nodded his head in agreement. It was a decent explanation, which if it were true might give him a modicum of appreciation for what the Blackshaws did to him. While Peter was assimilating, he watched as the doctor picked up the plastic jug on the bedside table and wandered to the sink, where he filled it up with cold water. Returning it to the table carefully, he saw that Peter was still deep in thought, so he picked up the small vase on the table, which contained some carnations that were beginning to turn brown, and took it over to the dressing table.

"Looks like these could do with replacing," he said cheerfully in an attempt to lighten the somewhat sombre atmosphere that had developed. "I'll see if I can get some new ones for you."

"Thanks," said Peter without taking much interest.

"I have one or two things to do, so I'll let you have some time to yourself and come back later if that's okay with you."

"Okay, thanks, Doctor, that's fine."

As he lay there, warmed by the sun which had progressed on its daily journey and was now flickering on the bedclothes that covered his feet, he reviewed in his mind what he and the doctor had discussed. He had told him things he had never confided in as much detail to anyone else. He and Joan had talked about his childhood, of course, as indeed they had about hers. He had shared his feelings and emotions with her, which was perfectly natural for a husband and a wife. The only other man he had been so open with was Andy, which again was nothing out of the ordinary. Andy was his best friend. They were closer than brothers in many ways. He always remembered hearing someone say that friends are chosen carefully, selected from the whole range of people that one encounters in life, whereas family is simply inherited.

His friendship with Andy was incredibly special to him and was quite unlike the relationships he had with many of his other friends, both male and female. They never went to the same school, like so many close friends do, so they never knew each other in that environment. They had been at different primary schools and Andy went to the local secondary school that Peter would have attended had he not won the scholarship to Rosehill. They were virtually neighbours though and, because they did not see much of each other in term time, were even keener to spend time together in the holidays. They had a lot in common. Both were sports lovers and preferred being outdoors instead of cooped up inside. Even in this regard they were not always together, Peter preferring cricket and Andy golf. They made other friends, but none had the close understanding that the two of them shared. It was no effort for them to be friends. Neither of them had to try; it just happened naturally and over time they formed an unbreakable bond.

Perhaps he was looking back with rose-tinted spectacles, but he could not remember a time when they disagreed on anything. If one of them wanted to do something and the other didn't, one would give in, accepting that it was their turn to do so or that it was the best option for them both.

The nostalgia of those wonderful days growing up was as good to remember now as it was to experience then. He had never felt so helpless and so utterly distraught as he did the day Andy died. His friend was cheated out of life and Peter felt angry that his best friend had been taken from him so early. His death left so many unanswered questions – what would Andy have done with the rest of his life? Who would he have married? What would his children have looked like? Would their families have been as close now as the two of them had been as boys?

Peter shut his eyes as a defence against the sun's rays which were becoming even brighter now than before. Even though he was not especially tired, the sun sapped his desire to do anything other than sit there and relax. In a matter of minutes, sleep overtook him once again.

This is my kind of dream. Here comes Andy heading towards me with a pint in each hand, one of which is almost certainly for me. He moves away from the bar and looks down, seeing that there is a girl on the floor in front of him. She is wearing a pink mini skirt with white knee-length boots, and she has a woolly scarf around her neck. An interesting combination, I think to myself. Andy has to step over her to get to me and as he nimbly does so, she smiles at him. He makes it safely enough and, pleased with himself, he presents me with my beer. The bar is full of people who are laughing and joking, but I can't hear any of their conversations. Some couples are dancing, presumably to music that is also inaudible to me. In a smoky corner a group of men are playing some sort of game which involves them running around and waving at each other. One of them smiles triumphantly, almost losing the cigarette from his mouth in the process, and I assume he must have just won.

I try to take a sip from my drink, but there is no beer in my glass. Andy holds his empty glass up in front of his face. It's obviously my round, so I head for the bar. The girl is still on the floor and I raise my leg to step over her. As I do, she changes into some kind of hideous monster – it looks like a wolf, or at least it has a wolf's mouth, and it tries to bite me. That was close, but I manage to get away and make it to the bar. I ask the barman for another two beers, which appear in front of me almost immediately. I didn't even see him pour them. Andy is still over the other side of the bar and the wolf-faced monster is positioned menacingly between us. If I try to walk around it, I feel sure it will go for me again. The only thing to do is to step over it once more, but this time it will be made even harder because of the glasses I am carrying. Keen not to waste time thinking about what it could do to me, I run towards it, shut my eyes and jump. The wolf jumps too and this time manages to sink its teeth into my thigh. My whole leg feels unbearably hot and there is a lot of blood.

Somehow, I seem to have survived, because I am in the living room of my parents' house with Joan. She is young and so am I. The doorbell rings, so I go to answer it. Walking down the hall, which is much longer than I remember, I look at the striped wallpaper that I knew so well in my childhood. There is someone at the door, so naturally enough I want to open it. Without thinking I remember the trick of pressing the handle in the correct place with my thumb, which is the only way it works. On the doorstep is Andy smiling back at me, smiling enthusiastically. It's a beautifully sunny day outside and he is wearing a short-sleeved shirt and a pair of shorts. Behind him there are lots of people in the street. Children are playing and there is a long line of them queueing in front of an ice cream van. For some reason I am not appropriately dressed. I realise that I have a shirt and tie on under the heavy grey suit I usually wear for work. The sun is so strong that I begin to feel uncomfortably hot and thirsty. Andy tells me I should take my jacket and tie off. This seems a sensible thing to do, but my arms are stuck in the jacket and the tie is becoming tighter around my neck. They won't come off and I panic as I am beginning to choke. Andy walks away, apparently oblivious to what is happening, and I try to call after him, but no words come out of my mouth. I can't make him hear and he closes the gate at the end of the path and heads back towards his house, still smiling. He wanders away happily, oblivious to my plight. Then suddenly the wolf monster appears on the path, and I am unable to move. It looks angry and is salivating. It charges towards me bearing a mouthful of terrifyingly sharp teeth. Desperately I attempt to run back inside, but for some reason I am moving in slow motion. Expecting the teeth to sink into my flesh any moment, I somehow manage to reach the door and slam it in the beast's face. I wait for it to burst through the closed door, but nothing happens. I listen for any noise, but it is quiet, and I assume the monster must have gone.

Safely inside, I run back down the hallway and Joan is in the living room sitting at a dining table which I don't recognise. It's made of metal, so it's not the dark wood table we usually had in the dining room. Joan's parents are sitting there and are eating, which is odd because I can't recall them ever coming to my parent's house. Joan waves at me to come and sit down too, so I do. The food looks fantastic. Joan spoons some roast potatoes onto my plate and her father, who rarely smiles, has a broad grin on his face as he pours me a glass of wine. He isn't looking properly and the glass overflows, which just makes him laugh even more. Most unlike him, I think to myself. Joan and her mother join in, but I am still recovering from my ordeal outside. The wine dribbles off the table and into my lap, making my trousers wet. The three of them are laughing hysterically and that annoys me and I feel angry. I shout at them to stop, but they just laugh even louder. I don't know how to make them stop and I begin to cry uncontrollably.

Joan and her parents disappear, and the dining table suddenly turns into my desk at work. I immediately recognise the old-fashioned red telephone that sits in the top right-hand corner. I am amazed that there is nothing else on the desk because it's usually covered with documents and other bits of paper. I know that people always think that my desk is untidy, but I understand where everything is. This is a bit extreme though – it's never been this tidy. I swivel around to look out of the window. It's absolutely tipping down with rain and the sky is dark. It's a blue-black colour and I can hear thunder overhead. There are people outside in the street being soaked by the torrential rain and a very long lorry appears, travelling much too quickly for these conditions. Inevitably it skids on the water as its driver attempts to avoid some cars in front of it. The lorry continues its slide and smashes into the cars, flinging them to the side of the road, then disappears from view. Two men in dark suits and top hats get out of one of the cars and step into the pouring rain. They walk towards our building, and I can see them below at the front entrance. They must be absolutely drenched.

A flash of lightning fills the sky, creating a dramatic contrast against the darkness. Simultaneously, or so it seems, the telephone starts to ring very loudly, and I turn my chair around in alarm. The noise is incredibly loud now, so in an effort to preserve my eardrums, I stretch across to answer it. As I hold the receiver in my hand, I notice that it has become bigger as though my touch has caused it to increase in size. It's so huge that I have to use both hands to hold it to my ear. I say hello and announce myself with my full name to the caller but can't make out what they are saying. There is someone there, but the voice is muffled and none of the words make any sense. It's so frustrating, but all I can do is say hello again. The indistinct words continue unabated and without realising it I begin to cry once again. There are people now in the doorway and I recognise my in-laws. I have a sudden impulse to get rid of the telephone receiver, so I summon up all my strength and hurl it across the room at them. It falls at their feet like a grenade and they are gone. In their place is the wolf. It is looking straight at me with its yellow eyes and is moving closer with its mouth open. All I can see now is those enormous teeth.

I am terrified and, in the hope that this is a dream, I force myself to open my eyes in an attempt to make it disappear.

It works this time and for now the wolf is gone.

Chapter 10

Peter lay for a few seconds with his eyes wide open, staring at the ceiling. He felt hot and anxious as he often did when he had that dream. Easing his top half out from under the bedclothes, he reached across to the bedside table and flicked on the lamp. As he did this, he noticed a cobweb hanging from the shade. Picking up his glasses, he inspected it further and saw that it was connected to the stem of the lamp. He muttered to himself words to the effect that standards were clearly falling and that whoever was supposed to be cleaning his cabin was obviously not doing a very good job.

He looked closer and was transported momentarily in his mind to the perfect autumn cobwebs he remembered from his childhood. They would appear overnight like magic on hedges and the laurel bushes in the front garden, spun with such precision that their structure was perfect. So many of them and every single one a masterpiece. He used to imagine that the spiders that crafted them possessed skills far greater than most other species. This, though, was not one of those cobwebs. Leaning forward, he assessed that this was more like a smudge of fibre that lacked cohesion and any semblance of artistry. The confused, wispy strands were stuck together like a piece of grey candy floss discarded by an ungrateful child.

A fleeting annoyance at the cabin steward's carelessness invaded his perusal again. It left as quickly as it had arrived as he moved closer to inspect the cobweb. Just above its centre there was a fragment of something he did not immediately recognise. Two more long thin objects below it provided the solution to the conundrum. It was clear that they were legs and that the other item, logically because of its shape, was a wing. These remnants, now motionless and without purpose, he surmised used to form part of a fly or some other unfortunate insect that had been no match for the trap laid by its arachnid assassin. Peter imagined the last moments of the poor thing, immobilised, powerlessly waiting for the inevitable fate that was to befall it. The fly had been devoured by the spider who, apparently sated, had not bothered with the wing and legs that were now strewn across the shamble of threads.

Part of a Shakespeare quotation he had learnt at school flashed into his mind as he considered the death and destruction wreaked on the fly. 'Out, out, brief candle, life's but a walking shadow, a poor player that struts and frets his hour upon the stage and is heard no more.' He thought that was it. Macbeth, was it? He wasn't sure, but regardless, it was amazing, he thought, how he could still remember that speech. Life was indeed incredibly short, particularly when he analysed his own experience. Not as short as it had been for the fly or indeed the spider, but it had gone by quickly for him nonetheless. He considered the insignificance of the fly and the millions of other flies that had gone the same way. Of course, his own existence and that of his fellow man was just as inconsequential in many regards. He could not remember the exact details, but he had read an article some time ago which discussed the history of the Earth as though it was a twenty-four-hour clock. Humans had only existed on Earth for the last second or so of the whole twenty-four hours. All humanity had come and gone in the last second of that day. How insignificant we all are, he thought. Even the Earth itself was a mere speck in the solar system and therefore equally unimportant to the universe as a whole.

For a while he pondered his dreams and his memories of the life he had enjoyed. How long ago it seemed that he went to school for the first time, since he first tasted beer, or the first time he had kissed a girl. Relative to his existence, these were a long time ago, although as events they were so important to him the memory seemed not to fade. If anything, as more recent events had become harder for him to recall, these moments strangely became more vivid to him. Occasionally, he might even remember fragments of something he had long since forgotten.

Peter removed his glasses and put them back on the table and as he did so he noticed the sun outside his window still trying its hardest to penetrate the closed curtain. He was considering the merits of trying to get out of bed to open it when he heard the handle of the door turn and looked over as the doctor entered the room.

He was carrying a wooden tray, which he balanced precariously on the tips of his fingers as he shut the door. Holding it now in the more secure grip of two hands, he advanced with renewed confidence into the room and placed it on the dressing table.

"You don't mind if I open this one now, do you, Mr Davis?" he asked as he tugged at the single drawn curtain, allowing the sunlight to flood the room.

"Not at all. I think I must have dozed off for a few minutes, probably only because I didn't have much else to do. Actually, I was just thinking about getting out of bed if you have no objection."

"Excellent. I was hoping you might say that. Although perhaps you could manage something to eat first," he said, motioning towards the tray.

Peter could not see what was on the tray, although he did notice that there was a pot, presumably of tea or coffee. Regardless, he knew that he was both hungry and thirsty and some food was exactly what he wanted.

"Yes, I think I would like something light. Perhaps some tea and toast." He actually really fancied some eggs as well but didn't say anything because he did not want to appear ungrateful in case the doctor had not been able to procure anything hot for him.

"Well, your luck's in. I've brought a pot of tea and a few rounds of toast. I wasn't sure whether you preferred white or brown bread, so I opted for brown."

That sounded good, thought Peter, although he was a little disappointed that the kitchens had not been able to come up with anything more imaginative.

"But perhaps you would like something hot first. I thought you might be able to manage some scrambled egg and perhaps some smoked salmon to go with it," he said, picking up the plate and offering it to Peter.

The steam was still rising from the eggs, so they must have only just been prepared. There was a quarter of a lemon for him to squeeze on the salmon should he wish, black pepper and the dish was even trimmed with some parsley. He made a mental note not to jump to any more conclusions about the standards of the cruise line as he began to salivate.

"That sounds perfect. Thank you," Peter said as calmly and politely as his hunger would allow, keen not to appear too greedy. "Thanks," he added as he watched the doctor pick up the tray and release the legs at either end of its underside before placing it securely in front of him.

While Peter set about the bounty, a piping hot cup of tea was added expertly to the tray.

"Just milk, no sugar?" the doctor asked without waiting for an answer before pouring in the milk.

"Yes, that's lovely. Thanks very much," said Peter gratefully.

For some minutes there was silence apart from the occasional clink of cutlery against china interspersed with satisfying gulps of tea. Peter made short work of the salmon and eggs and as he was rearranging the tray to promote the toast to a position that he could better access, he thanked the doctor again as he moved forward from his seat and topped up Peter's almost empty cup of tea.

When he had finished all the toast and a third cup of tea, Peter leant back on the pillows behind him, feeling both replete and content that his appetite had returned.

"Thanks so much. I think I needed that."

"No problem at all. I'm pleased you enjoyed it."

Peter seemed energised by the meal and was pleased when the doctor suggested he might like to continue the conversation they were previously having while his food digested.

"You were telling me about your dreams," he began, both by way of a recap and also as an invitation to talk.

Peter was happy to chat further, but he did not feel ready to discuss the dream he had just experienced – the one that had inhabited his sleep on and off for the past fifty years. Instead, he settled for some less intrusive disclosure.

"Yes. I was telling you about some of the not particularly pleasant dreams I have. Actually, I had one recently about an incident when an art dealer tricked me and stole one of the pictures I had painted."

"Oh really? Did you paint professionally?"

"Well, I had a full-time job, so it wasn't really my profession. I did make money from it, but it was definitely a hobby first and foremost. Something I had always loved to do, even as a child. I was fortunate to have an extremely good teacher at school and when I was older, I developed a style that people seemed to like. We had my pictures dotted around the house and friends who visited were often complimentary about them. I assumed they were just being polite, but then a few asked if they could buy one. A number did and when their friends saw them on their walls, I was asked to produce pictures for them too. Without really trying, I had a fairly profitable side-line. I never thought of it as a business, although the cash was certainly helpful at times, especially when the children were young. It was the act of painting itself that I loved so much and found tremendously relaxing."

"How nice to have a talent like that in addition to your academic ability. So, what happened with the art dealer?"

"I won't bore you with all the details, but it was quite a blow to me when it happened. I was exhibiting in Paris and one of my pictures won first prize in a competition. The chap who had taken me there disappeared with the painting, which had naturally become quite valuable. I'm pretty sure he was in cahoots with the girl who was curating the exhibition because I was unable to track her down either."

"That must have been upsetting."

"Yes, it was, to put it mildly. They set me up and made a bit of a fool of me actually. In some ways it was the embarrassment that I had been duped that made me feel most angry. I could have done with the money from selling the picture, of course, but what really grated was that I hadn't seen the two of them for the hustlers they were."

"And the picture was never seen again?"

"No. I gave up looking eventually because I couldn't trace either of them and in the end, I had to put the whole sorry affair down to experience."

"Do you still think about it much?"

"It's funny you should ask that because I thought I'd put it behind me a long time ago, but if I still dream about it, perhaps it bothers me more than I thought. I was just so annoyed that they had taken me for a ride. I suppose I do sometimes wonder what they did with the picture and where it is now. It sounds silly, but I had an emotional link with it and not knowing what happened to it nags at me a bit."

"That's interesting. Was there something special to you about the picture apart from the fact that it won the competition and its monetary value?"

"Yes, there was," Peter said thoughtfully. "When I was in my mid-teens at boarding school in Sussex, my parents came down to take me out for the day one Sunday. We went to Cowdray House, which was only a short drive from the school. It was one of the finest Tudor manor houses in the country. Henry VIII had stayed there and so had Elizabeth I. It was like a palace apparently."

Peter picked up the beaker next to him and took a couple of mouthfuls of water before continuing.

"At the end of the eighteenth century, there had been a massive fire and virtually the whole place had burned down. The ruins that remained were still extremely impressive though and much later they were opened to the public along with the rest of the estate. I remember being fascinated by the remains of the building and trying to imagine how it had looked four hundred years earlier. My mother had packed

110

a picnic and we sat and ate it under one of the big oak trees in the grounds. It was a glorious day, and I shall never forget it. I can even remember the potted meat sandwiches and fruit cake that she had made."

"It sounds like a wonderful place. So did you have your paints with you that day?"

Peter shook his head and smiled.

"No, not that day. It was about fifteen years later that I did the painting. I had told Joan about the Cowdray ruins and we decided to go and see them with our own children one weekend. It wasn't always easy to mobilise the family early, so we didn't arrive until mid-afternoon. By the time we had eaten our picnic and taken a stroll in the grounds, it must have been almost five o'clock. Joan and I wandered around the ruins while the children explored and played pretend. I had my watercolours and some pencils with me as I was keen to sketch something to remind us of the day. Most other visitors were beginning to leave, so I was able to position myself right in front of the ruins with an unobstructed view. It had been a very warm day and a magnificent dark orange sun was setting behind the house. It acted like a floodlight and I remember how its rays flickered through gaps in the dilapidated walls as darkness began to fall. It was magical."

Peter noticed the doctor smiling broadly. He was clearly a man who also appreciated the beauty of nature.

"Anyway, I managed to sketch everything pretty well and added some initial colour with my paints. That evening at home, with everything still fresh in my mind, I spent several hours developing the picture. I continued to work on it for a few days until I was happy that I had caught the unique atmosphere of that evening as best I could."

"It obviously must have turned out well."

"Yes, it was certainly one of my best. The subject matter obviously made it, and I was lucky to be there for that incredible sunset, but sometimes there is an extra dimension which is impossible to define that gives a painting an unusual quality. That picture had that indefinable element. I don't know whether it was the story of those ruins or perhaps it was because of my history with them, but there was a refinement beyond the purely visual. I wondered whether it gave me that feeling simply because I loved the place and thought that perhaps others wouldn't see it, but fortunately for me, of course, they did."

"So that was the winning painting that you took to Paris?"

Peter nodded ruefully.

"I have tried to recreate it a couple of times since. On one occasion I visited the ruins on the same day of the year roughly and at the same time in the evening in the hope of experiencing that level of inspiration. It was useless, of course – the sun set behind the ruins, but it wasn't the rich colour it had been on that day with Joan and the kids, and the light didn't move about in the eerie way it had then. That day was freakish. It was a one-off that I was lucky to witness but something that was not destined to be repeated."

Then as if as an afterthought, he added, "The aura around the ruins is extraordinary. If you ever find yourself in that part of the world, I would highly recommend a visit."

"Thanks. I'll make sure I remember that. Now, however, I need to go and see some other patients, but perhaps we could talk further if I come back in an hour or two."

"Yes, of course," said Peter. "I'd like that. By the way, sorry to ask you, but is there any chance you could get someone to bring me something to read? A magazine perhaps."

"Oh, I'm glad you reminded me." Peter watched as the doctor moved purposefully over to the dressing table. "I almost forgot. I thought you might want to read this," he said, passing a large hard-backed book across to Peter.

Peter hadn't noticed him carrying that in and for some reason he had not seen it on the table earlier. He gratefully took the book in two hands and eagerly turned it over so that he could see the front cover. Peter smiled as he read the words 'Artists of the 20th Century'. Below the title were a number of small pictures, liked framed miniatures, intended as an indication to the reader of what they could expect inside. Some of his favourite artists were represented on the cover. Renoir, Monet, Picasso, Klee and probably the two he admired the most, Raoul Dufy and Marc Chagall.

"Thank you. That's perfect," said Peter. "I haven't seen this book before. Where on earth did you manage to find it?"

"It was from our library. It's quite extensive, you know."

Peter had spent some time in the library and had looked at a lot of the books in the art section and he had never seen this one. He thought it was unlikely that he had missed it, but it was possible, of course. Perhaps it was new; after all, these ships stocked up with all sorts of things when they visited a port. That could have happened, thought Peter. Then it dawned on him that the reason he had not seen it there was because someone had borrowed it. Maybe the doctor himself had taken it out and had simply not returned it.

Peter opened the book excitedly and was so engrossed that he did not hear the doctor leave a few moments later.

He decided to start by flicking through it so that he could get a feel for how it was arranged. There was some basic information about the life of each artist, their style and the inspiration for their work. One page of writing, below which were some of their most well-known works, was allocated to each person. Those whom the author considered most worthy of note merited a double page with more detailed background and extra pictures. Interestingly the artists included sculptors and those who worked in other mediums too. He stopped at one of these pages as he recognised the picture of an enormous Henry Moore sculpture. It was in bronze and was entitled *Family Group*. Evidently Moore had sculpted it in the late 1950s, but Peter remembered the impact it had made on him when he and Joan had visited the Henry Moore Foundation in Hertfordshire. The figures of a mother and father with their limbs intertwined around their child perfectly illustrated, Peter thought, the closeness of the relationship between parents and offspring. He spent several minutes just staring at the page then read about the artist. He was already aware of some of the details, but he found it fascinating nonetheless.

Taking a last look at those mammoth figures, he flipped the page back to the letter D to look up Dufy. He was extremely familiar with the history of the artist's life, having read about it on numerous occasions elsewhere, but again it was interesting to scan. He gazed admiringly at the bright colours and the freshness of the open-air scenes Dufy liked to paint. When he did, Peter was always transported to the very places the artist recreated. He thought to himself that if he were able to travel back in time to a location of his choice, he would probably choose France between the two world wars. His parents often talked about how bleak the immediate post World War One years had been in Britain. The wealthy, though, remained in their cocoons, protected against the ravages of unemployment and high inflation. Peter did not know if it was quite the same in France, one of the other supposed victors of the war, but he imagined it probably was. Perhaps it was as an attempt at escapism that inspired Dufy to use the colours he chose and concentrate, as he did, on depicting uplifting scenes of people enjoying themselves. Peter thought how marvellous it would have been to be there watching him as he painted the paddock at Deauville Racecourse or to wander alongside him, barefoot on the sand, as he selected the precise spot where he would paint the pier and the beach at Le Havre.

One of the things Peter particularly liked about this book was that the illustrations were not necessarily of the artists' most famous pictures. There were even a couple that he had not seen before. He couldn't resist turning to Chagall and was disappointed to discover that in his wisdom the author felt that a single page was all his exceptional talent deserved. What a contrast with Dufy who painted what he saw, albeit it in such a dramatically colourful fashion. Marc Chagall was the opposite – he painted things that could not be seen. He created images that told stories of emotions and events that were personal and tended to ignore the logic preferred by most artists. Peter's eyes immediately focused on the deep blue colour of one of the pictures underneath the precis of Chagall's life, but once again, although familiar with that period of his work, he did not recognise this particular painting.

It was entitled *La Barque a Saint-Jean*. He had seen others painted by Chagall at Saint-Jean-Cap-Ferrat in the South of France. He loved them all, but as he looked closer at this one, it drew him in, and he found himself entirely consumed with sympathy for the plight of those involved. Peter knew that Chagall, being a Jew, had fled France for the United States in the early 1940s to escape persecution by the Nazis. Tragically, while he was there his wife Bella, to whom he was utterly devoted, had died. He returned to France in the late 1940s as he was desperate for the spark of creativity that he had lost because of both his exile and the loss of Bella. He threw himself into a series of pictures of her, many of which included reference either obviously or opaquely to himself. This picture, Peter thought, was less of a mystery and more of a statement of the artist's bereavement. A brilliant sun above a village reflected on the water in the harbour where Chagall had positioned boats and an oversized fish. As with many of his scenes, one of the buildings looked like a church – perhaps intended to convey marriage or death. In this case, Peter concluded, it could have been either. Between the sun and an even larger moon was the boat – *La Barque* – in which a man and a woman were lying. She wore a red dress and was obviously intended to be the focal point. Presumably this was Chagall and his wife Bella, thought Peter. It occurred to him that the boat resembled a coffin, perhaps representing that she was dead. A figure stood on the end like a gondolier steering the boat. Whatever it was intended to mean, Peter felt incredibly sad. He admired the artistry, but the pure emotion of the painting overwhelmed him. He felt a bristling in his eye and gathered himself to prevent the tear that was developing there from falling. He reflected on the love and affection shared by these two people, and he could not help but put himself in Chagall's shoes. How would he feel if he lost Joan? What would be left for him if she were no longer there by his side? For a moment he was overcome with anxiety. He would not be able to endure a pain like that of Chagall – it would be too much for him. Then a sudden panic hit him like a bolt of lightning. He could not remember when he had last seen Joan. It felt to him as though he had not seen her for a while, so he must ask the doctor to check how she was. Perhaps he could arrange for him to see her now that he felt so much better. Relieved that it was not going to be long until they were reunited, he turned the pages until he found the letter M. His eyelids were becoming heavy now with all this reading and thanks to the food he had enjoyed, but he needed the comfort of Monet and the beauty of his garden in Giverny. He relaxed and shut his eyes.

We are in our bedroom. Me and Joan. She looks absolutely stunning, her long blonde hair cascading onto her soft, tanned shoulders, gently swishing against the silk of her black evening dress. I am pleased to see she is wearing the diamond earrings I gave her on our anniversary and have a sudden urge to make love to her. I put my arms around her waist so that I can hold her close. She steps backwards, smiling in a way that tells me now is not the right time, but her laughter suggests that it soon might be. I understand why now. She is holding my black bow tie and reaches over to put it around my collar. As always, she ties it perfectly and hands me the jacket of my dress suit. We are obviously going somewhere important tonight.

A new scene now appears with us both in it. We step out of a cab and walk down a short gravel path, then I press the doorbell on the black front door of the house. A small woman in a red dress opens it, smiling politely. She invites us in. Her skin is pale and she has lank brown hair, but her face is pretty and she is obviously happy that we are there. She shows us into her living room, which is full of smoke. Joan is clinging to my arm tightly and, as we enter, for a moment we can't see anything. I hold my breath so that I don't choke on the fumes and the haze clears eventually to reveal a number of other people who are also wearing evening dress. I recognise one of them as my old boss, Beaumont. He approaches us, holding a cigar in one hand which is producing vast plumes of smoke. He is even fatter that I remember, crammed into a tight-fitting dinner suit with a red cummerbund to hold in any excess blubber that threatens to escape. His unshaven face is red because his collar is too tight, and I can see sweat on his face and cheeks. He completely ignores me and with his other enormous hairy hand, he grabs Joan around the waist and pulls her towards him.

One of the other men starts talking to me and I am forced to respond, although I am worried that Joan has disappeared. Beaumont has taken her to a red leather sofa, and I can see her reluctantly sitting there next to him. She looks uncomfortable, so I try to push past the other man, but he stands in my way, continuing to talk cheerily to me, apparently oblivious to my intention. I don't want to be rude, but enough is enough, and I brush past him clumsily and head towards the sofa where Beaumont has now positioned his huge arm around Joan's shoulder. She is trying to move, but his grip is too strong, and she is unable to resist him. Another one of the guests intercepts me and stands directly between me and Joan so that I can't see her and have no idea what Beaumont is doing. This man doesn't want to talk. All he is doing is smirking like some sort of simpleton as though he is ridiculing me. I draw back my fist and smash it straight into that stupid grin. The man falls to the floor, and I can see that hairy bastard Beaumont who is now crawling on top of Joan. His sweaty hands are pawing at her dress, touching her breast, and he is slavering like a wild animal. Joan is crying and thrashing at his hands in an attempt to evade them. Instinctively, I kick him hard and my foot buries itself in his wobbling underbelly. He is hurled backwards by the force of my attack and his body slumps to a halt on the sofa, a satisfied look on his face, still sweating and dribbling with excitement. I hate his smugness and aim another kick at him, harder this time. I don't know where it hit him because I did not feel it land, but when I look up, he has gone. I rush to Joan and wrap her in my arms. She is still shaking with fear, but at least now I know she is safe. The diminutive hostess in her red dress rushes in and apologises profusely and then begins to cry. Although Joan is my main concern, this woman is obviously distraught too, so I tell her that we are alright, and she disappears.

Taking Joan by the hand, I pull her up from the sofa and we run out of the room, down the hallway and out of the front door. There is no cab waiting, so without a clear plan we run away down the street. It's dark and I stumble, barely managing to stay on my feet. Joan is still holding my hand firmly and up ahead it seems brighter. We run as quickly as we can out of the gloom and towards the safety of the street lights we can now see shining in front of us.

Chapter 11

When Peter woke, the art book was still open on the bed next to him, and he realised he had fallen asleep reading it. He looked once more at the waterlilies and the Japanese bridge in Monet's garden, closed the book and carefully placed it on the bedside table. As he did so he saw a small piece of card propped up against the water jug. Being careful not to knock over his beaker, he reached across and picked it up deftly between his thumb and index finger. It was evidently a note from the doctor.

BROUGHT SOME COFFEE BUT DIDN'T WANT TO DISTURB YOU. HAVE LEFT IT ON THE DRESSING TABLE – I THINK YOU SHOULD BE STRONG ENOUGH NOW TO GET OUT OF BED. WILL DROP BY LATER TO SEE HOW YOU ARE. PROVIDED I AM NOT CALLED AWAY, PERHAPS WE CAN CHAT AGAIN ABOUT YOUR DREAMS.

P.S. PLEASED TO SEE YOU ARE ENJOYING THE BOOK
A.S.

That sounded good, thought Peter. He had not had a coffee for what seemed like days. The prospect of not being confined to bed excited him too – he was certainly feeling a lot better. Pushing off the bedclothes, he swivelled and allowed his legs to dangle over the side of the bed. A while ago he had read about the importance of drinking water before coffee, particularly if your stomach was empty. He could not remember the explanation for this assertion, but he tried to follow it whenever he could. Putting the beaker to his lips, he drank what was left. It was a little warm and tasted a bit dusty, but it would do. Dropping his feet to the floor, he pushed himself to a standing position, steadying himself on the table as he did so. He was pleasantly surprised how strong he felt and how well he seemed to have recovered as he strode across the room with conviction. He pulled the curtains open determinedly then had to screw up his eyes for a moment to allow them to become accustomed to the sun's glare.

What a glorious day to be alive, he thought. Hopefully he had not missed any of the shore excursions he and Joan had booked.

He put on his dressing gown, which was conveniently draped over the chair, and poured himself a cup of coffee. He was glad that it was still very hot – he intensely disliked hot drinks that had cooled too much. He could not have missed the doctor by much, he thought as he added some warm milk, which was next to the coffee pot in a small white jug. There were even some biscuits on a separate plate. The doctor had looked after him pretty well, he concluded, eagerly biting into a custard cream.

Peter picked up the cup and saucer along with another biscuit and pulled the chair away from the table slightly so that it was in the sun. Placing the coffee next to him on the table, he retrieved the art book from the bed and sat, one leg crossed over the other, in the full glare of the sun. It felt good and he shut his eyes for a second, letting the rays warm his face. Then he opened the book again randomly, confident that he would find something of interest on whichever page he chose. He was delighted to find himself staring at the unmistakable thin, vertical figures and bleak backdrop of a painting by L S Lowry. No one captured the grim reality of the industrial north of that era like Lowry. It was astonishing that he was able to embody his matchstick people with such sadness and hopelessness. The simplicity of the drawings was magnificent. The thin line of the body at an angle depicting hunched shoulders or at another angle to show the viewer that the person on the canvas was weighed down by their bag of shopping. All the more incredible was that he had only started painting properly in his fifties. Clearly the man had a God-given talent and thank goodness for art lovers that he was eventually able to use it.

Sensing there was someone outside, although he had not heard any footsteps on the carpeted floor of the corridor, Peter tilted his head towards the door just as it opened to reveal the unmistakable form of Archibald Souter as he entered.

"You found the coffee then." And without waiting for a reply, he added, "I'm very pleased to see you up and about. You must be feeling much better."

"Yes, absolutely. Not quite firing on all cylinders, I suspect, but I think I'm getting there."

"That's good. Hopefully we can get you out of here soon. You must be so bored being stuck in this room."

"Definitely. Now I'm on the mend, I can't wait to see Joan. I don't suppose you know how she is?" Peter asked hopefully.

"Oh yes, of course. She is absolutely fine. I spoke to her earlier this morning actually and updated her as to your progress. She was thrilled that she will be able to see you soon."

Peter was impressed that the doctor had been so thorough and taken the trouble to find Joan, particularly since he was clearly a busy man.

"That's great news – thanks so much for doing that. I do miss her. In fact, I've been dreaming much more about her since we've been apart."

"Oh really?" said Souter, inviting Peter to go into greater detail.

"Yes, I dreamt about the night we first met," and then remembering the other dream, he added, "and I had another dream with her in it that wasn't quite so pleasant when I dozed off just now."

"You were going to tell me the story of the first time you met Joan. Where did it happen?" Souter asked, making a mental note to mention the second dream later.

"It was at a dance at the local golf club. I'll never forget the date. It was the 15th of October 1964. I remember the Olympics in Tokyo were on at the time and I think I'm right in saying it was the day of the general election. It was certainly that week if not. Anyway, I was home from university for the summer and about to go back for my third year."

"Wow, that was a nice, long summer holiday. Which university were you at?"

"Oxford," Peter replied without emotion, as though attending one of the world's premier universities was nothing special. "I studied maths, of course – at Exeter College. Anyhow, as I say, the week before I was due to return, my best friend Andy invited me to a dance at the golf club where he was a member."

"You have not mentioned Andy before. I look forward to hearing what you two got up to in your youth."

Peter paused uneasily for a moment before continuing. He was not ready to tell the doctor everything about Andy and decided to concentrate on the dance and the meeting with Joan.

"Andy was a member at the club. Actually, although he hadn't told me, I found out that night that he had he won the club championship earlier that year."

"A modest guy by the sound of it," Souter interjected keenly, wondering whether Peter might tell him a little about his friend.

However, Peter simply nodded in agreement as he took a breath before continuing with his story.

"We were having a drink at the bar, trying to be cool and nonchalant like you do at that age, when we saw two girls across the room. It was Joan, of course, with her friend Teresa. We thought they looked nice, but unfortunately there were a couple of other lads with them. That obviously made it difficult for us to approach them let alone have a conversation."

"Sounds intriguing. You presumably managed it eventually though?"

Peter smiled. "Yes, we did. It's quite amusing actually. The rather snooty club president was attending a committee meeting that night and we moved one of the lad's motorbikes into his reserved parking space. When the president arrived, he was not too happy. The young lad was summoned to move it and while he was gone, we took our opportunity to speak to the girls."

"And I assume the rest, as they say, is history?" Souter asked.

"Yes, that's right. We had a terrific evening and Joan agreed to go out with me to the pictures at the weekend. I remember I took her to see the latest James Bond film – *Goldfinger* with Sean Connery. As I mentioned, a few days later I headed back to Oxford and at the time Joan was working at the Midland Bank and was kept pretty busy there. We wrote to each other while I was away and telephoned a couple of times too, I seem to recall. When I was home for Christmas, we picked up where we had left off. It was as though we had hardly been apart. We've always been like two peas in a pod and I can't recall us having been separated much at all since. A few days perhaps or a week at most, which is why it seems so odd to have been unable to see her while I've been unwell."

"Yes, I can understand that, particularly since you know she is nearby. Never mind, you'll be back together soon enough. It's not at all surprising that she is in your dreams though from what you have told me."

Peter knew what the doctor was getting at, and decided to tell him about the recent dream in which Joan appeared. Much better that than to admit the details of his recurring nightmare involving the wolf that had plagued him for so many years.

"The last dream I had was actually of a very unpleasant experience and I didn't enjoy it very much. Obviously, the dream recreated fragments of what actually happened, but I'll fill in the gaps if you want to hear about it."

"Yes, absolutely," Souter replied politely. "Only if you are happy to share it with me."

"Yes, of course. In actual fact it'll probably do me some good to chat about it."

Peter ordered things in his mind and composed his thoughts before proceeding with his account of the events.

"In the early '80s I was the chief accountant for a building firm in the south of England. They had found a niche in the sector by specialising in the construction of car parks. Multi-storey, underground, even private parking facilities for some of the owners of the swanky houses in places like Mayfair and Knightsbridge. I reported directly to the board and was responsible for overseeing all the figurework on these projects. To cut a long story short, the firm obtained a contract which guaranteed them tens of millions of pounds in revenue. This was quite a coup as you can imagine, and we knew it would put us in the driving seat to secure similar deals provided things went smoothly. My role in making sure we had our numbers right for the tender and my loyalty to the firm did not go unnoticed by the board. I attended most of the high-level meetings in an advisory capacity anyway, but following this big deal, the chairman, Mr Beaumont, approached me privately and said that he was going to recommend that I be made a director.

"The week before my appointment was due to be ratified at the quarterly board meeting, I was invited with Joan to the chairman's house for dinner. A number of the other directors were to attend, and it was obviously intended to reflect that I was now to become one of them.

"We were both nervous but also excited because it meant that we would be set up financially for life. However, when we arrived, it was clear that Beaumont had been drinking. Some of the other couples were there already and they looked as embarrassed as we were at his lewd comments and the rough way in which he spoke to his wife. No one said anything, of course, least of all me as the new boy in the clique. As a majority shareholder, Beaumont wielded complete control over us all and we all knew that if we wanted to keep our jobs, we would have to turn a blind eye to his behaviour.

"Dinner was pleasant enough or at least the food that Mrs Beaumont had prepared was. Her husband continued his verbal assault on her and told a series of extremely inappropriate anecdotes. Quite frankly, we were relieved when the meal was over, and Mrs Beaumont suggested coffee in the sitting room. I whispered to Joan that we would make our excuses and leave as soon as possible, but that we ought to wait for someone else to go first. Fortunately, George Ratnage and his wife declined coffee as they had told their babysitter that they would be home by eleven o'clock. We drank our coffee and another couple, the Bryants, beat us to it by announcing that they needed to be up early the next morning. By now there were only a few other couples and us remaining, so I said that I was going to the toilet and that we would have to make a move too when I came back.

Joan told me what she could recall about what happened next. It seems that the other couples, who presumably had also been discussing their exit strategy, made their apologies in unison and left while I was out of the room. Having seen them out, the Beaumonts returned to the sitting room. Joan told me that Mrs Beaumont stacked up the empty coffee cups on a tray and took them out to the kitchen. Evidently Mr Beaumont saw this as an opportunity to go and sit next to Joan on the two-seater sofa we had been occupying. I had only been gone a matter of minutes, less than five certainly, but by the time I re-entered the room, Beaumont was attempting to force himself on Joan. He was quite a big man and very drunk. Joan explained later that he had almost fallen on her in his attempts to seduce her. She obviously tried to take evasive action, but I could see him pawing her breasts and trying to kiss her on the lips. There wasn't time to think. Even if there had been, I would have done the same thing. I ran over to the sofa and grabbed him by the collar. He was heavy, but I somehow managed to haul him off Joan. She escaped and ran to the door. Hearing the commotion, Mrs Beaumont came in just in time to see her husband climb to his feet and swing a wayward punch in my direction. She was strangely calm, I remember, as though she had seen it all before. I suspect on reflection that she almost certainly had. I dodged him for a few seconds, reluctant to try any offensive manoeuvres of my own, but he was furious. We all knew about his temper. Another of his haymakers narrowly missed me, which caused him to lose his balance again. As he stumbled, I used his own momentum to push him against the wall. He slid slowly down, still conscious and seemingly aware of his surroundings, until he was sitting on the floor with his legs out in front of him. He said nothing, but he glared at me with the look of a man who wanted to do me considerable harm. Joan was already in the hall holding our coats. She opened the front door and I followed. As we looked behind us, we saw Mrs Beaumont waving. We weren't inclined to go back into the house, even though we could hear her calling out her frantic apologies for what had happened."

"Presumably the repercussions from the evening must have been awkward to say the least," Souter said at last, inviting Peter to tell him the rest of the story.

"When I arrived at work on Monday morning, there was a formal-looking envelope with my name typed on the front lying in the middle of my desk. It was from Beaumont in his capacity as chairman of the board. In a few lines it explained that at this time the board had decided to suspend all promotions and wage rises and that this regrettably would include my proposed promotion to director."

Souter shook his head slowly in disbelief and Peter continued.

"I was too useful to the firm to be sacked, so I was to be controlled. Beaumont might have been a vindictive bastard, but he was certainly not completely bereft of business acumen."

"How did things work out in the end?"

"Two of the other directors were in the office that day and I had the opportunity of speaking to them. One said he had not heard anything about the suspension. He clearly thought I was exaggerating about the events at the party and told me that I was being stupid. He suggested I knuckle down and wait until promotions were reinstated. However, the other man, Entwhistle, nodded knowingly when I told him what had happened after everyone had left. Asking me to agree that whatever he said would not be repeated, he told me that he was not entirely surprised, and that Beaumont had a reputation for being a letch within the firm. Apparently, he had tried it on with a number of his secretaries over the years, all of whom had left subsequently. When I pressed Entwhistle for further information, he reluctantly told me that the same thing had happened before, twice to his knowledge, in fact. Both times, the men, and their wives, chose to do nothing. Both became directors, assessing that the mauling of their wives was the price that had to be paid for the fat salary and share options that came with the job. It made no difference to me who they were, only that it had happened, so I didn't press him for their names." Peter sighed.

"That evening Joan and I discussed the situation. We knew that no one would back us up, least of all poor Mrs Beaumont, so there was no point reporting her husband's actions to the police. Even if they did, Beaumont had made it known on several occasions that he played golf with the assistant commissioner, who was apparently a close personal friend. We decided that there was only one thing I could do to control my own destiny and rid myself of that poisonous man. The next morning, I made sure I was first into the office – the cleaners who were finishing their shift were rather surprised to see me, I remember. By the time Beaumont arrived at 8.30, my letter of resignation was on his desk. I carried on with my work as usual for the rest of the day and then about 4.30 my secretary brought in an envelope with a grave look on her face. It was a note from Beaumont accepting my resignation and telling me that I was to leave immediately rather than serve my notice period. I was to be paid what I was owed, but I had to vacate my office by the end of the day. No thanks for what I had done and, as you might expect, no acknowledgement of what he had done. I saw a few of my colleagues who were in the office that afternoon and told them that I was leaving. It was clear that none of them had heard about my departure. Two of them were board members and they were not even aware. There was no future for me after what had happened, that much was clear, so that evening I packed all my personal belongings into my car and drove away from the office for the last time."

"What an awful thing to have happened. Was Joan okay afterwards?"

"Eventually, yes. She was a bit shaky for a few weeks and occasionally I could see in her face that something had reminded her of it. We were fortunate I arrived when I did because I suspect Mrs Beaumont was so scared of her husband that she wouldn't have risked intervening. What he did to Joan was bad enough, but who knows what he was planning. I can still see his face as he sat there, sweaty and drunk, on the floor. He knew he had been thwarted this time, but he didn't need to speak to tell me that there would be other opportunities, other women. He was smirking, I recall, goading me perhaps. I wasn't interested in debating the rights and wrongs with that beast; I just wanted us to be where he wasn't."

Souter could see that Peter looked perplexed. It wasn't simply the telling of the story and the memories that were rekindled. There was something else nagging at him. This was not the time to pry, however, so he waited in the hope that Peter would volunteer whatever was on his mind.

"It was a relief that Joan wasn't badly hurt. As time went by it became less and less important and eventually we hardly mentioned it. What bothers me, though, is the thought of the other women he had assaulted, those who didn't have someone there to help them. How many lives had that pig tainted and how many careers had he ruined? Worst of all is the worry about those who came after Joan. How many of them could we have prevented if we had taken a stand against him? Perhaps none. Perhaps his friends would have protected him, but I feel very guilty that we didn't try. Guilty that we could possibly have protected others from being attacked by such a vile predator."

"Yes, I can understand that, but you did what you thought was best at the time. Your priority had to be Joan's wellbeing. I don't think that you should vilify yourself because you were unable to do more. Think how his wife must have felt. It doesn't sound like she was a bad woman from what you have told me. I suspect she must have thought about telling someone on many occasions but been too scared of the repercussions."

Peter nodded in agreement. "Yes, I'm sure you're right. Poor woman. I had always blamed her because she must have known what her husband was going to do when she and I were out of the room. Of course, the guilt of that knowledge, and of all the other times it had happened, must have been intolerable. Couple that with the terror she must have felt living under the same roof as a man like Beaumont and it's a wonder she didn't go mad."

The two men looked solemnly at each other. "What a horrible experience," Souter eventually volunteered in order to break the silence. "It sounds like the repercussions were probably quite serious for a great many people."

Peter stood up and went to the window. He looked at the perfect blue sky as he reflected on the conversation and thought about those involved. He picked up one of his hairbrushes, enjoying its familiar feel in his fingers. It must have been days since he brushed his hair, although in recent years, as it had thinned, it had needed less attention than in the past. Slowly and methodically, he drew it through the thickest part of his grey hair above his ears, sweeping it flat and tight against his skull. When he had finished, he gently put the brush back with its partner and turned to face the doctor.

"It's astonishing how much impact the actions of one individual can have on other peoples' lives, isn't it?"

126

"Yes, it is," Souter agreed. "Of course, the world also contains a lot of good people and kind actions can be equally powerful in terms of their effect on others."

"Mmm…" Peter hummed thoughtfully as he mulled over the doctor's comment. "Yes, that's very true. I suppose every action has its own consequence. I've always tried to take the view that people are basically good, because most I have encountered have been. Maybe we take the good things for granted, so we don't necessarily appreciate the benefits that come from them. The negative actions of bad people can be so destructive and cause so much pain that perhaps sometimes they have a bigger impact on our lives."

Souter openly withheld agreement with Peter's hypothesis, but he did not intend to contradict him directly after what he had just heard. Instead, he settled for the alternative of a slight change of subject.

"What happened afterwards – once you had left the firm? Did you manage to get another job?"

"Actually, yes, I did. I was approached by another firm, Swithin Holdings, soon afterwards. I had heard of them. They specialised in building leisure complexes, and they clearly thought I had done a good job for Beaumont. The managing director telephoned me at home explaining that my old secretary, Pauline, had given him the number – something for which I was very grateful. He told me that their chief accountant had recently retired early due to poor health and that if I was interested, the job was mine subject to an interview with the board, which he implied was a formality. I never asked him if he knew why I had left, although I understand how word gets around with such things, and he never volunteered the information. It wasn't even a question that came up in my interview. I sensed then and I am certain now that he suspected that Beaumont had been up to his old tricks. As I said, word does tend to get around."

"It sounds as though he admired the way you had handled yourself. That must have been an important factor in wanting you to work for him."

Peter considered this for a second, realising it made sense. "Yes. You are probably right about that."

"How was the new job?"

"It was great once I became used to the new environment. I was welcomed and accepted almost immediately and the atmosphere in the office was completely different. Everyone was friendly towards me, and people genuinely wanted to work as a team. The hotel and leisure business was interesting, and the change reinvigorated me. Also, the money and other benefits were as good as they had been with Beaumont and I was given much greater autonomy. All in all, I was very happy there."

"Did you stay there very long?"

"Yes, I did as a matter of fact. I stayed with the firm until I retired," said Peter, unable to resist a nostalgic smile.

"So, some considerable good came out of what was at the time something so shocking."

"Every cloud has a silver lining, I suppose," Peter replied ruefully.

Souter took a deep breath as though trying to decide whether to say out loud what he was thinking.

"You know, I suspect there is a path that we are all meant to follow in life. On the way down that path, we encounter obstacles as well as happiness. We take the happiness in our stride because it's easy to do so. We enjoy it and usually we are grateful for it, but I think the way we deal with life's difficulties defines our lives and makes them what they are."

"So, do you think our lives are mapped out for us and, regardless of what we do, we are heading down our own specific paths come what may?"

"Partly, I suppose," Souter said, not wishing to appear too dogmatic. "Or perhaps it's what happens and the way we deal with the obstacles that determines how our path continues. Maybe the obstacles are there, but the path continues in different directions depending on how we react to the problems they pose."

Realising that Peter wasn't going to say anything until he had taken this thought process to its logical conclusion, he continued.

"Take this horrific business with Beaumont. You had various options available to you that night. You chose to extricate yourself and did so completely by leaving the company. You could have hit him or called the police and had him arrested. You could have decided not to resign and perhaps you might even have been tempted to tell everyone what had happened. These are just a few examples, but there were numerous things you could have done. What I am suggesting is that the course of action you settled on led to a positive outcome – very positive in many ways from what you have said. Perhaps if you had done something else, the result might not have been so favourable."

"Or perhaps, it might have been even better," Peter said in an attempt to demonstrate that he understood where the doctor was going with this line of conjecture.

"Exactly," Souter said, nodding with appreciation. "Perhaps it's all about what we make of things and sometimes these challenges and our subsequent decisions take us down different branches from our path. It seems to me that your decision was a strong one. You could have perpetuated the problem, argued about it, taken Beaumont to court even. That might have made you feel avenged if you were successful, but it could never have changed what he tried to do to Joan that night. Instead of letting the boil fester, if you'll excuse the medical metaphor, you lanced it. You took positive actions and controlled the situation as best you could. The branch you took from the path gave you a new start. And it sounds as though you seized the new opportunity that presented itself and were all the happier ultimately for doing so."

Peter leant back in his chair and let out a big sigh. "Thanks, Doctor. Did anyone ever tell you that you are extremely skilled at making people feel better?" he asked, grinning widely.

"Once or twice," Souter replied coyly. "Once or twice."

Chapter 12

Souter explained that he had to leave for a while as there was someone else he urgently needed to go and see. He would be a few hours, but when he returned, and as long as Peter felt up to it, he wanted to take him through some final tests. Provided all went well, he told Peter that it should not be too long before he could rejoin Joan.

On his way out, as if as an afterthought, he produced another book from the inside pocket of his coat, mentioning casually that he had found it in the library. Aware that Peter was obviously an enthusiast, he handed him a small paperback entitled *How to Play Cricket* by Don Bradman. It was apparently published by the *Daily Mail* and judging by the price, 2'6, it was quite old and when Peter looked inside, he found that this was indeed the case. The original book, of which this was a 1948 reprint, was according to the flyleaf first published in 1935.

As a youngster Peter had idolised Bradman. Statistically he was easily the greatest batsman ever to play cricket, but the way in which he played and his determination was as much to be admired, Peter thought. He remembered reading as a boy how single-minded he was, practising his batting by continually hitting a golf ball with a cricket stump against a wall. He apparently also put the stump in the ground and practised fielding by throwing balls at it from various distances. This man did not rely on his natural talent alone, immense though it was. He honed it to its maximum potential by applying himself to every aspect of the game and by being a fiercely committed competitor. When England toured Australia in the winter of 1932–33, his resolve was tested to its limit. Bradman was at the peak of his powers and the English, in an attempt to curb his scoring, adopted the so-called 'leg theory' or 'bodyline' style of bowling. In effect they bowled at his body to restrict the space he had to hit the ball either side of the wicket. As he and the other Australian batsmen tried to defend their bodies against the fast bowling of Harold Larwood and Bill Voce, the theory was that they would hit the ball to one of the fielders close on the leg side in an attempt at self-preservation. There were no helmets or chest protectors in those days, which made serious injury an even greater risk. Although England won The Ashes that winter, Peter remembered his father telling him that despite this physical assault on him, Bradman still averaged over fifty for each innings he batted. This was a man who recognised his God-given talent and used every ounce of his fibre to ensure that he wasted none of it.

As he read about Bradman's brilliance in the thin covers of this little book with its small black and white photographs of the author demonstrating his batting technique, he could not help but draw comparisons with his own life. He had been blessed with abilities, top of which, of course, was his aptitude for mathematics. He thought about school again and how easy it was for him to pass exams. University was equally straightforward and then when he left, employers had always been attracted by his intelligence and quick wit. But had he made enough of his talent? Should he have done more with it? Did he coast too much at school and university? Could he have developed his ability and as a result used it to achieve more in life? What would someone with Bradman's attitude have been able to do with his gift? He felt ashamed. Was accountancy a good enough use of his expertise? Who had he helped and who had actually benefitted from his work? He had made a decent living, of course, which had in turn provided a comfortable life for his family, but was that sufficient? Accountancy was intrinsically linked with profit, but the work he had done could really only be measured in terms of the financial effect it had on individuals and corporations. When he thought about it, most of the companies were financially secure and most of the people running them had more money than they needed, with or without his input. Melancholy momentarily replaced his regret. He began to feel anxious that his worth could only be represented by its monetary value. Was that the only way his contribution to the world could be measured?

He leaned back and stretched his legs out, hoping that the change of posture would somehow take away these maudlin thoughts. It did not, so he decided to look out of the window. There was bound to be something out there that would take his mind off things. However, all he could see from where he sat was the edge of the huge yellow sun as it continued on its daily journey from east to west. It was too bright and as he averted his eyes, everything in the room seemed dark for a second or two. He had to blink away the blotchy outlines of objects that this caused before he could see clearly again.

He was finding it difficult to shake this spectre of doubt that had crept up on him. He was an old man now, so there was little he could do to change anything. Perhaps if he had done things differently, he might have been a scientist or an inventor and made a real difference to humanity. Not like Newton or Euclid but something practical and momentous like Alan Turing. He could have been a very good cryptanalyst, he thought. Okay, perhaps not as brilliant as Turing, who succeeded in reversing the outcome of World War Two but something valuable nonetheless. Now he was just being ridiculous. He had talent, but he was certainly not in the same league as these people. What was he thinking even comparing his capabilities with their genius?

He had read an article once and although he was not able to recall all the details, he could remember the gist. The writer described a man who stood before God on Judgement Day. God passed him a piece of paper on which was written all the man's achievements during his lifetime on Earth. He read it and was pleased with himself until God smiled and handed across a second piece of paper with a much longer list on it. The man was puzzled as he read it, then God explained to him that these were the things that he had been capable of accomplishing with the abilities God had given him.

The thought that he had not used the full capacity of his brain during his life weighed heavily enough on Peter, but the possibility of disappointing God in the process was something he found hard to contemplate. His parents were not churchgoers, although he remembered attending Christmas services with them on a few occasions. They did, however, undoubtedly believe in God, although Peter often felt their faith was more a representation of their duty to the society they were raised into and the influence of their families than a determined, unshakeable belief that they had formed themselves. At boarding school religion played a significant part in everyday life for Peter. Every morning before lessons pupils would file into the school chapel for a service which usually lasted about twenty minutes. Following a hymn and prayers, there would then be either a reading or a short sermon from the chaplain, Mr Tennison, with another hymn or occasionally a psalm, which they were expected to sing afterwards. The service always concluded with another prayer and a blessing for the day ahead. No one ever questioned the merits of this enforced religion and even the small number of boys of different faiths dutifully took part. He appreciated now, even if he had not understood it then, that this routine provided not just spiritual guidance for the boys but also enhanced the structure and discipline on which such institutions were founded.

He never felt religion had been forced on him, but it was made available, and he gladly accepted it. It was often embraced more as an obligation than because of faith and he suspected that this was the case with the other boys too, although nobody ever seemed to talk about it much. It was only later in life, when he experienced the pressures of adulthood, that his faith in God began to develop properly. After all, how could such a young boy who had seen so little of life have a profound belief of that kind? It came with maturity and an understanding of life's challenges and could only be fully appreciated when those difficulties arose. It did not seem particularly fair that people only turned to God when they needed help, but Peter comforted himself by remembering that God was always there, and it was an inherent frailty within man that meant that they only sought him when they could not resolve their problems themselves. In his case, he had prayed on and off rather than regularly throughout his adult life. So, although he considered himself a believer, he never classified himself as a practising Christian. He did not particularly like the phrase anyway. Did you have to go to church to believe in God? Who made that rule? Surely because God was all around us and with us all the time, it should not matter one iota in his eyes whether you talked to him in a church or while you were wandering around the garden dead-heading the roses. He appreciated that for many it was important to demonstrate their faith to others, or to have a structured method of worship, but for him that was not necessary. His conversations with God were his and his Creator's business and although occasionally he and Joan had talked about prayer, that was predominantly how it stayed. For Peter it worked. When he needed God he asked for his help, always apologising sincerely that he had not spoken to him for a while, and always first confessing his sins and asking for help for others before himself. Naturally, this strategy was employed largely to ease his own conscience about the process. He knew that God was aware of this but believed that, being merciful, he would not judge him too harshly for it. Peter understood that God could not grant all his requests and if things did not work out as he had hoped, he was quite content to conclude that what he had asked for was not part of God's overall plan for him. Regardless of the outcome, which he found was often positive, the very act of prayer itself was hugely helpful to him. Being able to share his worries and concerns with a higher power made him feel as though he was not alone and that his counterpart in the conversation would ensure that the plan designed for him was implemented.

Naturally, Peter could not know what God thought of him. No better and no worse than the average man probably. Certainly not a bad man – not a murderer, a tyrant or a sadist, for example. He had made mistakes which embarrassed him and caused him a certain unease that he had let God down somehow. But surely that was part of being a human – a mortal man who did not always manage to do the right thing on every occasion. He considered for a moment what was most important. What one quality above all was the one that differentiated between good and evil? A vague recollection of a passage from the Bible came into his head. He could not remember the precise words, but it was something like '…faith, hope, love, these three; but the greatest of these is love…' and another, 'love thy neighbour as thyself…' Wasn't that one of the Ten Commandments? Love was the difference or to be exact the ability to love and the act of loving. Surely the test of goodness was how well a person had loved?

Naturally, Peter knew what love was and that he had not only felt it but at times had been overcome by it. The unconditional love of his parents and his sister Pat and, of course, of Joan and probably most of all his children, Tom and Susan. The only issue with this was that your parents bring you into the world, so there is something of a requirement to love them for this. A sibling is in the same boat and it is expected that there is love between the two even when they disagree or grow apart. A person chooses to love their husband or wife and if they are fortunate enough to have their own children, then that same bond of love that is experienced with a parent is there, only in reverse. He mulled this over for a minute or two and eventually came to the conclusion that the love of a child is probably the strongest if only because you, as a parent, helped make them and they are part you and part another person whom you also love deeply. Children are defenceless and pure when they are born, so they need love and also attract love. As they become older and stronger, the bond of love changes and sometimes it fades, but it never dies. This love, though, was easy to feel because it was largely instinctive and therefore reasonably common in the world. This was not the love that the Bible was talking about. That love was about putting others before yourself even if it was to your own detriment. It was about forgiving your enemies and seeing the best in everyone no matter how devoid of goodness they appeared to be. Surely the acid test of goodness, of true success as a human being, was whether one could love and by doing so improve the lives of others. There was no need to be famous or to do something miraculous to make a success of life. God saw all the deeds of men and these apparently insignificant displays of love in all its different formats were the most powerful acts of all.

Perhaps he had not done so badly. He wondered if his parents would agree. Would they be proud of what he had achieved? They would certainly be pleased that he and Joan still loved each other as much as they did. Tom and Susan had been raised well and he and Joan had ensured their home was a safe, caring environment. The children had developed into decent members of society and had successful careers and children of their own, of course. And so, the cycle continues, he thought, as it has done throughout history.

Peter jumped as his silent contemplation was abruptly disturbed as the door was flung open and Souter bowled in breezily. He had been concentrating so deeply on his thoughts that he had not been aware of his approach outside. Having apologised profusely for startling him, Souter wandered over and joined Peter by the window.

"Everything okay?" he asked.

"Yes, fine, thanks. I'm sorry, I was miles away."

Souter decided not to pry and instead gazed quietly at the world outside. He knew that Peter would tell him what was on his mind if he wanted him to know and sure enough, after a short while, he did.

"I enjoyed the Bradman book," said Peter neutrally to break the silence.

"That's good. I am pleased. I'm not a great cricket aficionado, but I do remember my brother telling me about him. He was quite a man."

"Do you mean your brother or Bradman?" Peter replied jovially with a half-smile.

Enjoying the joke, and with a grin of his own, Souter replied, "Both actually, now you come to mention it."

The two men laughed in unison and the air of sobriety that had filled the room was temporarily dispelled. They continued looking out of the window contentedly, enjoying the aftermath of the joke they had shared. There was, however, something else Peter wanted to say to the doctor, and having constructed a rough sentence in his mind, he spoke again, a little nervously.

"All this time alone has given me the opportunity to think. Our conversations have helped too. I don't think I have ever been so open with anyone other than Joan." Hesitating slightly, and in order to clarify his position, he added, "You know what I mean. About my dreams and some of the things that have happened in my life."

"I understand," Souter said reassuringly. "For what it's worth, I am pleased you felt able to discuss so many of your experiences with me."

"It's been good for me too. Talking to you, I mean. Having the time to think and reflect has enabled me to assess what I have done with my life."

"I am sure there is a lot that we have not discussed, but if what you have told me is a reasonable synopsis, it seems to me you have done plenty with your life. You did well at school, married a wonderful woman whom you clearly love, had a successful career and lovingly brought up a son and daughter who now have children of their own. On top of all that, you have painted, played cricket and, I imagine, been a supportive friend to all sorts of people you haven't mentioned."

Peter nodded reluctantly in agreement.

"What else is on your mind, Peter?" Souter asked, sensing some reservation.

Talk of supporting his friends immediately brought memories of Andy to mind, but he did not want to discuss this at the moment. He did realise that he would at some point be almost obliged to tell the doctor what had happened in the spirit of openness that existed between them. For now, though, he opted for a safer reply.

"I just worry sometimes that perhaps I could have done better. That I wasted my talents and didn't take advantage of all the opportunities that came my way."

"Such as?" Souter enquired thoughtfully.

"You know," continued Peter unconvincingly, "I did well at school and university, but perhaps I could have done better. I often think that I should have pushed myself more and gone into something more meaningful than accountancy."

"Oh, I see. What sort of thing were you thinking of?"

"I don't know really. Just something that would have had a greater impact, I suppose."

Souter understood immediately what Peter was getting at. He clearly assumed that because of his outstanding intellect, he should have done something dramatic, something that brought him fame and public recognition. Experience told him that he needed to be blunt with Peter.

"You mean beyond using your education to provide food and a home for you and your wife and children?"

Peter was taken aback by the sarcasm of this response, and it temporarily angered him. Who did he think he was speaking to him like that? He took a breath and was about to retaliate with a contemptuous remark of his own but stopped himself just as the words were beginning to form in his mouth. The doctor was right. This man, who hardly knew him, was perceptive enough from the little Peter had confided in him to reach the same logical conclusion that he had himself. Instead of arguing, he allowed his frustration to subside then grudgingly smiled and nodded his acceptance instead.

"Do you always tell people what they need to hear?" he asked wryly.

He thought that Souter would laugh at his attempt at amelioration with this quip, but he did not. He remained straight-faced and serious, assuming the question had been asked sincerely.

"I try to, but it's not always possible. Sometimes it is not easy to know what the answer is let alone be able to impart it to someone who might not want to hear the truth." He paused to allow his comment the air space it deserved before continuing. "In your case, though, as I can see you understand, you have done many things of which you can be proud. Those accomplishments are not trivial – you have overcome some difficult challenges and a great many people, in my experience, would have handled them much less well than you."

Sensing that he might have touched a raw nerve, Peter did not want to pursue the matter further. He settled instead for a muffled mutter of approval which he hoped would bring an end to this topic of conversation. However, Souter, who was perhaps more insightful than Peter had realised, was not quite finished yet. Mindful of the trust Peter had placed in him thus far, he trod carefully with his words to ensure that this was preserved.

"I hope you don't mind me asking this, but is there something else that bothers you about your life?"

"Not particularly," Peter said in response to what was a pretty far-reaching question. "I've told you about most of the issues that bother me and I feel happier having chatted about the way I feel. I am very grateful to you. Our conversation has certainly made me feel less of a failure."

Souter inclined his head to one side modestly to acknowledge Peter's thanks. The grin that accompanied this movement soon vanished, though, as he pressed Peter once again.

"Forgive me, Peter, but I couldn't help but notice your use of the words 'not particularly' and 'most'. It sounds to me as though there might be something else you want to share with me. If there is, I am here to listen, you know."

This guy is good, Peter thought to himself. *He doesn't miss a thing*. Hesitantly he answered, realising where this conversation was likely to lead and that the doctor would probably get it out of him eventually.

"No, it's nothing really. Certainly not something that I want to burden you with anyway," he said, putting off the inevitable for a moment or two longer.

Souter looked carefully at Peter, and he could see the anxiety etched in every feature of his face. Whatever this thing was that he did not want to discuss, it clearly distressed him. His use of the word 'burden' was extremely telling and did not go unnoticed. This was clearly not a minor concern, but he knew that if Peter had not mentioned it yet, any amount of badgering was not going to persuade him to do so. Perhaps neutrality and a change of subject was a better course of action at the moment.

"I ought to tell you what happens next. I know you are desperate to get out of this room so that you can see your wife."

He was right. Peter did want that more than anything, but he felt uncomfortable because of the enormous elephant that remained in the room. Both men knew full well there was something he had held back, but only Peter could decide whether they dealt with it.

Souter continued his explanation of the steps that would be necessary in order to allow Peter time to consider his next move. "I need to take you for a few tests before I can formally discharge you. Everything should be prepared for us, so we can leave as soon as you are ready. Provided everything goes well, you can go and see Joan very soon."

He could see Peter was only half listening, so he added cheerfully, "I understand she's very keen to see you."

Peter had heard the words, but instead of elation all he could feel was a ball of anxiety in the pit of his stomach. He considered for a moment that it was probably because he felt bad about not telling the doctor his secret, but in his heart, he knew full well that it was not that. This was something much more profound. This was indeed a burden – one he had carried with him for too many years. Joan was the only one who had any idea what this had done to him, but he had even kept some of his feelings from her. He was not sure why. Probably a combination of embarrassment and pride, he thought to himself. Undoubtedly these two pointless but horribly powerful emotions were in part to blame, but he knew the real reason why he felt as he did. The unbearable weight that had crippled him all this time was a familiar one – guilt.

Souter could see the cogs whirring in Peter's brain. He could sense the conflict of emotions, but it was not his place to pry any further.

"Does that all sound okay to you, Peter?" he said, picking up his notebook and moving towards the door. "Are you ready?"

It was time, Peter thought. Time to see if talking could relieve the weight of the millstone around his neck.

"Yes, I am ready and very much looking forward to seeing Joan, as you know. But before we go, if you can wait a short while, there is something I need to tell you."

Chapter 13

Peter's overriding emotion was one of immediate relief. He was going to do this. He was at last going to tell someone about the guilt he had kept bottled up for such a very long time. A surge of elation entered his body, and rather oddly he found himself remembering the day that his form at school was inoculated against tuberculosis with the new BCG vaccine. It was a relatively new procedure, having only been introduced a couple of years before, but it was common knowledge that it was a highly successful measure to prevent a disease that had killed so many. Naturally, therefore, parents were keen to ensure their children had it as soon as it was their turn. The older boys who had received it before him and his friends told them stories about how painful it was. One insisted that his arm bled so much afterwards that he fainted. Another informed them that boys were crying in agony because it hurt so much. The size of the needle was exaggerated to the point that the picture Peter had formed in his mind resembled a pneumatic drill that would take at least two people to lift in order for the injection to be administered. In the days leading up to the visit of the doctor, the fear levels had been increasing unbearably. As they lined up outside the sanitorium waiting to be called for their turn, Peter remembered being struck by a sudden unexpected wave of relief. He was there now and all the worrying was over. In a couple of minutes, it would all be done and this hideous spectre that had kept him in its grip for weeks would be gone.

The events he was about to reveal to the doctor had affected him much longer, of course. He had tried to rationalise things so often, but nothing ever seemed to dispel the regret he felt. He told himself that he had not committed any sins that might be punishable by God or broken the law in any manner that would interest the police. He also knew that the vast majority of people he knew would probably not feel the way he did, but none of this seemed to help. This burden was his and his alone. It mattered to him even though he accepted that he acted without malice of any kind at the time.

The thought that he might finally be free of his torment energised him and he positioned himself determinedly on the bed, inviting the doctor to sit opposite him by holding out his upturned palm in the direction of the chair. Once both men were comfortable, Peter prepared to begin his account.

"Something happened when I was a young man. Something I haven't mentioned to you because I find it difficult to talk about. I want to tell you now because of all the experiences, good and bad, in my life, this is the one that I dream about the most."

Souter's eyes were fixed attentively on Peter, not wishing to interrupt. Peter was staring blankly at the floor in order to retain his composure, unable to maintain eye contact. He fidgeted on the bed, moving both legs slightly until he was settled. Gathering himself, he raised his eyes so that he could address the doctor directly. Souter's expression was serious but not stern or intimidating. Rather it was encouraging and appeared receptive to whatever Peter was going to tell him, no matter how strange or horrible it might be.

"The dream, or should I say nightmare because it definitely is one, is frightening. The problem is it seems so real when it is happening that often when I wake up, I am hot all over and can feel the sweat on my body. I have experienced a number of different versions of it over the past fifty years or so, but there are certain elements that seem to be constant. It's probably easiest if I start by giving you a rough outline of what happens."

"Okay, that sounds like a good idea. I'm all ears."

Peter took a deep breath.

"Well, it always starts in a pub. Not necessarily one that I recognise, but I am there and so is Andy, my best friend. We are both young – in our early twenties, I should think. Not surprisingly, since we are in a pub, I go to the bar to buy a drink. The problem is that there is a girl on the floor blocking my way and as I try to step over her, she attacks me. Usually, she tries to bite me. On the way to the bar, I manage to avoid her – it's as though she is just making me aware of her presence. More of a threat of violence than determined intent to harm me. However, when I head back with the beers in hand, she is still there. I can usually see Andy, although sometimes I'm just aware of him being there. Whichever it is, I can't get to him with the drinks because of the girl. Then she turns into a wild animal, a wolf to be precise, and attacks me as I try to move towards Andy with the drinks. She bites me and I can normally feel her teeth sink into my calf or thigh and the heat of my blood trickling down my leg."

Feeling that he had provided quite a bit for the doctor to think about, he paused for a few seconds.

141

There was, however, no hint from Souter that he considered any of what he had heard to be particularly unusual, and so, encouraged by this, he decided to tell him the rest of the dream.

"All of a sudden, I am not in the pub and instead I am answering the door to Andy at my parents' house. It's a sunny day and I am always overdressed, usually wearing a tie. Even though I only ever see Andy, I have the impression that there are lots of people around and it's quite noisy. I don't remember if we speak, but Andy leaves, then the wolf from the previous scene returns and tries to pounce on me. My immediate thought is to try and shut the door and most times I manage to do so. Sometimes I feel the door hit the wolf's face and I am sure that a couple of times I've been too slow and he has bitten me again. Occasionally, at this point, I stand behind the door and can still hear the wolf snarling outside. The tie that I am wearing begins to choke me and I pull at it desperately so that I can breathe. Come to think of it, once or twice, I have woken up at this point, presumably because the movements have disturbed my sleep. Usually, though, Joan is involved after I shut the door and return to the living room. When this happens, we are sitting at a large table, which bears no resemblance to the one my parents had. We are having a pleasant enough meal until something goes wrong. It can be any one of a number of things but, as an example, the last time I remember the wine being spilled down me. I was the butt of some sort of private joke they were having, and it made me feel incredibly foolish.

"In the last part of the dream, it's raining, and I am at work. All sorts of things happen, but every time I see a huge lorry outside skidding on the wet road surface. After that it becomes a bit hazy, but I can remember men in top hats and Joan's parents in most of the dreams. Then the weirdest part of the dream happens just before I wake up. I take a phone call at my desk, but the person on the other line is unintelligible. There is just a muffled noise as though someone is talking with their hand over their mouth. I try to speak, but no words come out of my mouth even if I shout. I have had other dreams where I can't make any noise when I open my mouth, but none of them are as frustrating as this. Then finally, to cap it all, the wolf appears again. Over the years I have trained myself to wake up at that point so as to avoid being attacked. Nowadays, I can do it almost immediately, but I always have to see it before I can open my eyes."

Peter took a sip of water and leant back in his chair to make it clear he had finished.

Souter stroked his beard as if deep in thought. "What a terrifying nightmare… dreams often are a jumble of our random thoughts and experiences, aren't they?" Before Peter could respond to what was a statement rather than a question, he asked another to which he hoped to receive a response.

"You know what it means though, don't you? Or at least you think you know why you keep having this dream."

Peter had come this far and he was resolved to tell the doctor everything he could in the hope that there might be some cathartic benefit for him in doing so. He explained that the main events spanned a weekend that was indelibly imprinted in his memory because of its enormity but also because of the continual repetition in his mind of the part he had played in it. Then, a little reluctantly at first but gradually warming to the task, he proceeded to tell the doctor precisely what had happened.

The 23rd of July 1966 had been a good day for English football supporters if not for the game itself. England had won their quarter final in the World Cup against Argentina. The match, though, had been marred by the sending off of the Argentinian captain, Rattin, for dissent against the referee. He had taken nine minutes to leave the pitch and the unsavoury scenes that followed were broadcast around the world for all to see. Andy and his dad had watched the game at Peter's house with him and his father. Peter remembered that the four of them had a great time even though there was a lot of tension because of the importance of it.

Joan was spending the evening with her wealthy friend Melanie, who had just returned from a package holiday in Malta, and although Peter quite liked her, he did not relish the thought of an evening hearing about her romantic dalliances and looking through the inevitable piles of photographs she was bound to have taken. Andy had recently split up from his girlfriend of six months, Tania, a blonde-haired waif who Joan thought always wore far too much make-up, so he and Peter had planned to see each other that night. The quarter-final result made their choice of venue an easy one. The King's Head was going to be rammed to the rafters with proud English men and women celebrating the win. It sounded like an atmosphere that was too good to miss, so around 7.30 the two of them strolled slowly down the road, in the glorious summer sunshine, the quarter of a mile to their favourite pub.

As they approached, they could see that the beer garden was already crowded, mostly with people enjoying a much-needed drink as the heat of the day gradually gave way to a balmy evening. Peter and Andy spotted a group of young men in the far corner well away from the comparative tranquillity of the phalanx of wooden tables, each with their own multi-coloured umbrella. They had a football, which was strictly forbidden as per the 'no ball games' notices dotted around the white picket fence. However, on closer inspection, Peter and Andy could see that they were not kicking the football. Instead, one of them held it in his hand while the others swarmed around him remonstrating with their arms in the air. The performance, although repeated a couple of times for the benefit of new members of their garden audience, was, Peter and Andy realised, a reconstruction of the afternoon's events at Wembley. The lad with the ball at the appropriate time put it down and pointed into the distance, sending off his friend who was playing the part of the Argentinian captain while the rest of the gang expressed, in a much more light-hearted way than was the case in reality, their disagreement with the 'referee's' decision.

Thus it was that Peter and Andy entered the King's Head laughing in appreciation of the impromptu cabaret they had witnessed. The pub was busy, filled with regulars and also some new faces who were out to celebrate. Red and white scarves which had been worn to demonstrate their allegiance to the nation's team had been discarded on tables and chairs, their owners regretting their fashion faux pas in the heat of the throng now filling the bar to the point of overflow.

Peter and Andy scrambled to the bar where the welcome face of landlord Alan greeted them with a smile. They ordered four pints of Harp, two each to save at least one return trip to the bar, and retreated in the direction of one of the small patches of floor that was currently uninhabited. As they placed their drinks on the edge of a table, two girls, one with a red and white scarf firmly secured around her neck, who were bundled into a corner nearby, moved towards them. Peter recognised Sandra, who was a friend of Joan's. They soon established that her fiancé, Dave, who had been to Wembley that afternoon, was due to meet her in the pub but had not shown up yet. Her friend, whose name they gathered was Isobel, started chatting to Andy while Peter and Sandra were talking, and it was clear that she had taken a shine to him. Embracing his newly found single status, and not wishing to appear rude, Andy was only too pleased to play his part in the early exchanges between them.

A short time passed, and Sandra announced that she could see Dave over the other side of the bar, so she headed over to talk to him. Isobel followed dutifully, clearly reluctant to leave Andy. Once they were alone again, it soon became obvious to Peter from their conversation that Andy liked her. Finishing his beer and suggesting that Peter should drink the rest of his, Andy volunteered to go to the bar. On the way, he passed near to the group that now included Sandra, Dave, Isobel and three friends of Dave's who had been to the match with him. Peter watched as Andy smiled and raised his eyes at Isobel in recognition of the boredom on her face. Unsurprisingly, she readily smiled back enthusiastically.

Andy returned with the drinks, pleased to see that Peter had moved slightly to an area that provided a little extra elbow room. They chatted about the usual subjects. Girls, specifically Joan, Sandra and Isobel, Dave's friends, none of whom they had seen before, work, football, cricket and golf. After half an hour of that, it was Peter's turn to get them a refill. As he approached the bar, Isobel, who had sought to decrease the level of the tediousness to which she was being subjected by increasing her consumption of vodka and blackcurrant, stepped unsteadily into his path, stumbling slightly as she did. Fortunately, he was able to prevent her from falling with a carefully placed hand under her outstretched arm, and having expressed her gratitude, she remembered why she had stopped him in the first place. She told him that she fancied Andy and would like to see him again sometime, preferably when she was sober and would not make a fool of herself. Peter, keen to extricate himself, said that he thought Andy would like that, before heading off to the bar. Returning with a pint glass in each hand, he was startled by the sight of Isobel cross-legged on the floor, her England scarf still around her neck. With a biro she was scribbling something on a beer mat, and when she saw Peter approach, she held it above her head for him to take. Smiling, Peter asked her to put the beer mat in his back pocket since his hands were full, which she gladly did, proclaiming that her telephone number was written on it for Andy.

Needless to say, Andy was pleased with both his beer and the accompanying mat. Soon after, Isobel left with her group and the pub began to thin out, much to everyone's relief. Peter and Andy managed to make their way to the bar easily now, deciding to have just one more drink before they called it a night. It had been a terrific day, all in all, particularly so for Andy, whose conversation on the short walk home soon became focused on Isobel's eyes and the length of her legs. They laughed and joked all the way to their front doors, calling goodnight before they disappeared into their houses.

The next morning Peter was woken earlier than he would have liked by the sun streaming in through the curtains in his bedroom. Realising he had forgotten to shut them properly the night before, he went to the window. As he looked onto the street below, he noticed Andy opening his front gate, so, quickly throwing on his jeans and tee shirt from the night before, he ran down the stairs and made it to the door moments after Andy had gently knocked.

Peter had no idea what time it was, but Andy soon informed him it was only 8.30. This amazed him because it was already so warm outside and he asked Andy what on earth he was doing out and about so early. Andy explained that he too had woken early, and heard on the news that the forecast was for a blazing hot day. He had come round to suggest that they took a trip to the seaside. Southend-On-Sea, the Kursaal, paddling in the sea, the pier, ice creams in the sun – it sounded perfect. Peter was sold on it apart from one snag. He had already arranged to have Sunday lunch with Joan and her parents at their house. Naturally, he desperately wanted to go with Andy, but his life would not be worth living if he let them down. Apparently, Joan's mother had been talking about nothing but his visit all week.

He was hugely disappointed, but he had to say no. He watched as the enthusiasm drained from Andy's face and it made him feel horribly responsible for ruining the day for his friend. Perhaps they could try next week and perhaps take Joan and Isobel, he suggested. The weather would probably still be good. Andy smiled cheerfully in agreement as he left, but Peter could tell how deflated he was, having planned the perfect day for them only for Peter to spoil things.

Lunch at Joan's was nice enough. Her parents always dressed smartly for Sunday lunch, so she encouraged him to wear a jacket and tie. It was uncomfortably hot, and he was relieved when Joan's father took his jacket off, thus allowing him to do the same. His tie, however, remained tightly in position around his collar and therefore so did Peter's. After lunch he and Joan went to the park for a walk at her mother's insistence while she and her husband did the washing up. It was good to have some time alone and it gave him a chance to take his tie off for an hour or so. Sitting on the grass, he listened as Joan told him how boring her evening with Melanie had been and about the endless photographs she had been made to admire, each of which came with its own detailed description. In turn, Peter told her about his evening with Andy and bumping into Sandra and Isobel. Joan had taken to Andy as soon as she had met him. He was intelligent, polite and modest. She was glad he was moving on from Tania because in her opinion he could do much better. Peter told her about the idea of going to the coast and she thought they ought to arrange a date as soon as possible and hopefully she could meet Isobel then.

Glancing at her watch, Joan assessed that they had been out long enough and that her parents would be expecting them home soon. The prospect of tea and a piece of the sponge cake Joan's mother had made renewed their keenness to return as they wandered back for another session of refreshments and small talk. Back at the house they found Joan's father busy tending his dahlias in the garden. Her mother was preparing sandwiches for tea and asked Joan to choose a tablecloth to go on the circular metal garden table, around which there had already been arranged four wooden garden chairs. Tea was served at five o'clock and as they ate their cheese and tomato sandwiches and contemplated the cake that was to follow, the four of them wriggled and shifted deftly to try and find a spot that was shaded from the sun's heat by the inadequate umbrella positioned above them.

The ladies cleared away the plates afterwards while Joan's father showed Peter around the garden, explaining in detail why it was important that he cut back his delphiniums and geraniums at this time of year. In his role as prospective son-in-law, Peter stoically feigned interest in all he was told and, by the time Joan and her mother returned, he felt he had accomplished it well. They sat and talked about things of little importance for the next hour as the blazing sun above them reluctantly began to set. As if to draw a line under proceedings, and realising Peter had endured enough, Joan announced that she had a busy day at work tomorrow and ought to think about preparing her things. Peter, recognising their prearranged code instantly, thanked his hosts for a wonderful afternoon and said that it was time for him to leave. He followed Joan, who had already stood up, leaving her parents happily basking in the last of the day's warmth.

The next morning, Peter was woken at 5.30 by the sound of thunder and torrential rain smashing against the windowpanes in his bedroom. Concluding that it was unlikely he would be able to sleep with the noise, he went downstairs and made a drink which he took back to bed. As he sat their sipping his tea in the gloomy daylight, he watched as the rainstorm continued its relentless pounding against the glass.

At a little after eight o'clock, he jumped into his car and drove the short journey to work with extreme care as the storm persisted. He saw pedestrians sprayed with water from cars as they splashed into enormous puddles that had formed and were now making a river in the road that threatened to breach the kerb and spill onto the already saturated pavements. Even though the distance from the office car park to the entrance was less than fifty yards and he was wearing a raincoat, his trousers and shoes were soaked by the time he reached the dry sanctuary of the reception. The only sensible course of action was to go to the toilet and use paper towels to mop as much of the water from his clothes as he could. He was thrilled when he found a towel, which he used to dry his hands, face and hair.

After a few 'good mornings' to his colleagues and some exchanges about the extraordinary weather, he settled down to deal with some reports that were needed for a client meeting at the end of the week. He soon became engrossed in the work, having to force himself to avoid straining his eyes by occasionally looking out of the window. The road was beginning to resemble the local lido when, at 10.15, the phone on his desk rang.

As he reached over to answer what he expected to be an internal call from Mr Rogers asking for an update on his reports, he allowed himself a self-satisfied grin because he had just finished them. He was therefore somewhat taken aback to hear receptionist Carol's voice telling him there was an external call for him. He smiled again when she told him that a Mr Wakely was on the line. It was typical of Andy to announce himself so officially as a joke even though Peter knew he probably wanted to goad him about his afternoon at Joan's. Andy knew them quite well and did a passable impression of Joan's father which he occasionally unveiled after a few pints when they were alone in the pub. In anticipation of the expected barrage, Peter spoke first with a "Hello, mate, I know your day was probably better than mine." To his surprise, however, the line was silent for a second or two and he thought the connection might have been lost. He said 'hello' again, a little louder, hoping to make himself heard the second time and was shocked when a gravelly voice at the other end eventually responded. It was a much deeper voice than Andy's and, before he had absorbed the words properly, he thought Andy was pretending to be someone else. The voice continued slowly, huskily but with unerring purpose.

It was not Andy but his father. As Peter garbled an unheard apology, Mr Wakely's words continued, unabated, to fill the receiver at his ear. They told him that Andy had been involved in an accident on the way to work that morning. A lorry had skidded like an aquaplane on the water in the road, jack-knifing across the highway and hitting Andy's car. His son, Peter's best friend in the world, had been killed instantly.

The words became an undecipherable noise as Mr Wakely, clearly close to tears, asked him quietly if he was still there and whether he was okay. Peter opened his mouth, but he could not speak. Eventually he managed to grunt an acknowledgement, trying to hold back tears of his own, which seemed to satisfy Mr Wakely that he had heard. Peter could not remember either of them saying goodbye to the other as he sat there frozen with the receiver still in his hand. Later on, he would not be able to recall what happened next, but having excused himself from work, he somehow managed to drive home. His mother had been told the news already by Mrs Wakely, so he was saved from the anguish of explaining everything to her. Saying that he needed to change out of his work clothes, he ran to his room and shut the door. He threw himself on the bed, buried his face in his pillow and allowed the tears he had been holding back to flow freely.

Peter spent the rest of the day in a haze of despair, managing somehow to telephone Joan and let her know what had happened. That evening she came over and they sat holding each other's hands, exchanging the information they had gleaned about the accident. The driver of the lorry had survived but was in hospital with severe leg and head injuries. They suspected he was probably driving too quickly given the weather conditions but, whatever the case, the vehicle had spun out of control, ramming into the driver's door of Andy's Austin A30 at great speed and with huge force. His death, they were told, would almost certainly have been instantaneous as Mr Wakely had said, but that was scant consolation and only slightly numbed their pain.

As the week progressed, the world around Peter continued, oblivious to the tragedy that enveloped him. There were celebrations in the street when England beat Portugal to reach the World Cup final at the weekend where they would play Germany. He stared out of his window at the happy faces laughing and congratulating one another as if it had been them rather than Bobby Charlton who had scored their country's goals. All Peter could think about was being with

Andy in the pub just three days before when England had defeated Argentina.

On Wednesday, he forced himself to return to work, hoping that the distraction would help. It did for a while, but the nausea of grief continued to hold him in its unrelenting grip, squeezing the joy of life from him drop by drop.

He managed his first smile shortly after 5.30 on the following Saturday afternoon as he watched Queen Elizabeth present Bobby Moore with the Jules Rimet trophy following England's victory over Germany in the World Cup final. But as people literally began dancing in the streets and the noise of joyful singing filled his ears, all he could think about was Andy. How could he be happy when the person he most wanted to celebrate with was not there?

The funeral took place on Wednesday of that week, only nine days after the accident. As they drove to the church, the world outside the car, full of happiness, flags draped from windows and scarves hanging from fences, did not represent reality for Peter. It was not a world in which he could exist, at least not yet. Looking back, he could remember remarkably little about the day itself beyond the look of excruciating pain on Andy's parents' faces as they sat in front of their son's coffin. The wake took place at the golf club, the scene of some of Andy's happiest moments. Peter looked fondly at the honours board where Andy's name was now written more than once in gold lettering, but he could not help reflecting on the contrast of this sorrowful occasion and the joy of the last time he had been there with Andy. He remembered meeting Joan and the prank they had played and his mouth widened into a thin smile for just a moment as a picture of the irate club president standing by his parking space entered his thoughts.

Only when he was sure that Peter had finished did Souter speak.

"Thanks for telling me about that, Peter. It must have been difficult for you."

In fact, in a perverse way, Peter had actually enjoyed speaking about that awful time. The act of doing so, after all these years, removed a weight from deep within him, the existence of which he had learnt to ignore. He felt reinvigorated somehow by the process.

"I just wish I had gone with him that day and made some excuse or another to Joan's parents. I can't remember him ever letting me down, which is why the guilt I have felt is so strong."

"You couldn't possibly have known what was going to happen to Andy though."

"I know, but that doesn't stop me regretting that decision even though there is nothing I can do about it now."

Then as if to draw a line under the business of the dream, the sadness and the horror of that time, even if only for a while, he stood up with clear intent and fixed the doctor with a determined stare.

"Shall we get going then? The sooner these tests are done, the sooner I can see Joan and tell her how much I love her."

Souter was pleased at this reaction and vigorously nodded in agreement. Placing his palms on his knees, he pushed himself up from his seat.

"Good idea," he said as he opened the door for Peter, adding breezily, "I think it's about time we did precisely that."

Chapter 14

The door clicked satisfyingly as it shut behind them and with a slight stoop which suggested forward motion and an inviting thrust of his upturned hand, the doctor urged Peter to come with him. The corridor they found themselves in was longer than Peter remembered as he recalled the difficulty with which he had last walked down it. The carpet felt soft under his shoes as they passed closed doors and turnings to both left and right, but the pattern and colours seemed unfamiliar to him. The fabric was gold with double chevrons alternately of blue and green which were pointing in the direction they were walking, and even when they turned a corner, the arrows continued to indicate the direction they should follow.

This was the first time he had moved any appreciable distance for quite a while, but his legs seemed to be handling the outing well. The rest had probably done them a power of good, he thought as he progressed easily and without the usual soreness in his knees. The doctor was not exactly sprinting, but his pace was steady enough for Peter to be aware that he saw no need to take it easy on him. Regardless of this, Peter not only managed to keep up but he also was not unduly out of breath and the contrast of this with the coughing and spluttering he had experienced during his recent illness was remarkable. He looked over at the doctor, who was cheerfully humming a tune quietly to himself, his pursed lips protruding slightly from their bearded surround. Peter could not identify it and assumed it was probably one of those melodies we all made up from time to time to bridge a gap when conversation was difficult or, as it was in this case, superfluous. He was immensely grateful to the doctor for his care during his recovery, but his role as confidant had been unexpectedly helpful. Perhaps it was all part of his job, but Peter was particularly thankful to him for his patience and marvelled at his incisiveness and ability to listen. His combination of skills had made Peter feel optimistic about his physical and psychological wellbeing in a way he had not been able to for some considerable time.

Souter spied Peter in his peripheral vision as he looked over at him.

"Everything okay? You must be pleased to be up and about again."

"I feel marvellous actually, thanks to you," Peter replied animatedly.

"Kind of you to say so," said Souter, leading Peter through some swing doors with circular panels of glass positioned at eye level.

Peter gradually became conscious of some noise up ahead and, as he listened, he could hear the murmur of conversations from a room that was just coming into view on their right. The doctor slowed as they approached the room which Peter could now see had a double-door-sized opening, but no doors. Peter chopped his stride and came to an abrupt halt slightly closer to the doctor than he had intended. Stepping back to a more comfortable distance, he caught a glimpse of the people he had heard and was further heartened by the prospect of at last being in the company of some fellow passengers. As he stood expectantly on the threshold, Souter turned to face him.

"Shall we stop here for a moment?" he said, his question sounding more like a statement of his preference than a request for agreement. Even so, Peter was very happy to comply, as he was eager for some more human interaction.

"I'm sure you'll forgive me, but I wanted us to take this little detour." Then, stepping aside so that Peter's view of the room was unobstructed, he added, "I hope you don't mind, but there are one of two people I'd like you to meet."

"Not at all," said Peter, flattered that the doctor had arranged this. If they were friends of his, they were bound to be interesting. Perhaps they were his colleagues or possibly his family, Peter thought as he tugged at his trousers and smoothed down the front of his shirt in an effort to ensure he was reasonably presentable.

With a clear view Peter could now see the whole room. He certainly had not been in this part of the ship before because the décor was completely different to the areas where he and Joan had spent most of their time. However, it was the lighting that struck him as most unusual. Just inside the door, a few yards from where he was, it was well lit, slightly brighter in fact than in the corridor. It was not oppressive but was certainly in stark contrast to the far side of the room. In the corner Peter could only just make out the silhouettes of those sitting in chairs and on settees, who it seemed were responsible for the conversations. Unfortunately, he was not quite close enough to hear what they were discussing, which he found a little frustrating. There were three settees and an array of chairs, illuminated by two dim lamps which produced barely enough light for those talking to see each other. Peter could hear the rattle of teacups, then some laughter as two companions shared a joke. They were obviously enjoying each other's company and Peter smiled as he wondered if he might be offered the opportunity to join them for a cup of tea.

"We won't disturb the whole group if you don't mind, Mr Davis. There are just a couple of people who I want to introduce to you."

"Yes, of course," replied Peter, disappointed that he probably would not be invited to join everyone but nonetheless intrigued and excited to meet the individuals in question.

"If you don't mind waiting here, I'll just pop over there and ask them to come across for a quick chat."

And with that he entered the room and strode resolutely towards the seating area, leaving Peter in the doorway to await his return. As he approached the settee where his friends were sitting, he slowly became a silhouette himself in the half-light. Peter could still see him, though, as he stopped to speak to someone who then rose to his feet, exchanged a few brief words with the doctor and began to follow him back towards the doorway. The poor light did not make it easy for Peter to clearly see the person, but he managed to discern that it was a man who looked, Peter estimated, roughly the same age as himself. He followed close behind the doctor as the two men began to walk in Peter's direction.

At first, the doctor partially obscured Peter's view of the newcomer, but as they reached the brighter part of the room, the angle enabled him to see the man more clearly. They were still in the partially dark part of the room, but Peter saw a large man who, as he had guessed, was probably about eighty years old. His frame looked as though it had supported more weight in the past than it did now, and his broad shoulders were slightly rounded and hunched, giving the impression that the man had raised his collar to shelter from a sudden rainstorm or a chilly breeze. His grey hair was curly and surprisingly thick for a man of his advanced years and his mouth was pursed, Peter noticed, which made him looked very serious and determined. He did not seem to be having any trouble moving, thought Peter, because his gait was that of someone, not necessarily in their prime, but certainly much younger.

Peter examined him intently as he and the doctor approached. Eventually the two men breached the invisible barrier caused by the stronger lighting in Peter's half of the room and as they did so Peter narrowed his eyes, focusing his gaze on the figure of the newcomer.

Something, a trick of the light or perhaps Peter's failing eyesight, made the man look completely different. He was in the light now about thirty feet from where Peter was standing, and his hair was much less grey than it had seemed a few seconds before. Oddly he looked less hunched too. Peter guessed he was nearer fifty than eighty. A few steps further and Peter realised that he did not now have grey hair after all, but instead a thick mop of very dark hair curly covered his head. He was much younger too and carried more weight than Peter had originally thought. He was less than ten feet away and Peter's gaze became transfixed on the person who was now shuffling along slightly pigeon-toed next to the doctor. It was clear that he was much shorter up close and intriguingly was wearing a blazer and tie that Peter immediately recognised. Peter realised that he had become completely mesmerised and was also conscious now that his mouth had been open in amazement at what he was witnessing. Five feet away and Peter was able to distinguish the emblem on the tie, and as he looked up, the face he saw was of a young boy dressed in the familiar uniform of Tinniswood Manor. He looked again, distrusting his eyes, and could see that the young man was holding the school cap tightly in both hands. Utterly bemused, Peter examined his face once again. It had been many years, but the jowly flesh and the unkempt mass of black curly hair were unmistakable – it was Blackshaw.

Peter stared at the schoolboy, unable to understand what had just happened. Questions filled his head, but they were too numerous for him to successfully isolate any one in order to vocalise it. Eventually, he turned to the doctor in the hope that an explanation might be forthcoming. To his surprise, though, Souter turned instead to the boy.

"It's Alistair, isn't it?"

"Yes, Sir," the boy replied hesitantly. "Alistair Blackshaw, Sir."

"This gentleman, as you know, Alistair," he said, aiming his outstretched palm in Peter's direction, "is Peter Davis."

"Yes, Sir," responded Blackshaw, trying not to look directly at Peter. "I understood that you were keen for me to meet Peter again, Sir. I expect it is because of what happened between us when we were at Tinniswood Manor," the boy said contritely. Then, in a manner that seemed completely inappropriate to Peter, the young boy looked over and addressed him as an equal. "Hello, Peter, it's good to see you again."

Souter confirmed with a slight tilt of the head that Blackshaw was indeed correct in his assumption. "Yes, thank you for coming."

Peter, however, did not share Blackshaw's enthusiasm for the reunion. "What on earth is going on?" he said in a voice that was sufficiently raised for a lady occupying one of the settees to turn her head. "I must be dreaming. I can't think why else you would want me to meet him," he said contemptuously, flicking his head in Blackshaw's direction.

Then for the first time since Blackshaw's arrival, Souter spoke directly to Peter.

"Firstly, let me assure you, Peter, that you are not dreaming. I know this must be difficult for you to comprehend at the moment, but I promise all will become apparent in due course."

"Are you going to enlighten me as to how he became seventy years younger in less than ten seconds?" Peter asked in disbelief.

The doctor smiled. "Yes, of course, Peter, all will be revealed if you could be patient with me for a little while longer."

Unexpectedly, it was Blackshaw who spoke next: "Perhaps I can help with some of Peter's questions, Sir," and deferring to the doctor's authority, he added, "if that would not be overstepping the mark, Sir."

This cannot possibly be Blackshaw, Peter thought to himself. He had never been this polite at school. On the contrary, his arrogance was trumped only by his insolence with teachers and his indifference to his classmates. It was entirely out of character, to say the least, for this disgusting child to help anyone.

"I think that is an excellent suggestion, thank you, Alistair. Please do explain to Peter what you can."

"Thank you, Sir," said Blackshaw and he turned again to address Peter face to face.

"You are quite right. I am considerably older than the boy you see before you now, but I think that is one thing that is probably best explained by someone else."

He glanced at Souter, who gave a nod in agreement.

"I was invited to come and meet you today, Peter, because of what I did to you at school. For that reason, I am physically as I was then even though you are not. I am here to try and explain why I acted so appallingly towards you and to ask if you might be able to forgive me."

Peter was so completely bewildered as questions flooded his mind again, but he was not going to let Blackshaw lie his way out of things a second time. He might be able to fool the doctor, but Peter was all too aware how deceitful he could be.

"Forgive you?" Peter asked incredulously. "Forgive you?" he repeated slightly louder, causing some more of the people on the other side of the room to turn their heads to see what was happening. Self-consciously, Peter moderated his tone but not his anger.

"Do you realise what you did to me? What my parents had to sacrifice for me and how much they were hurt when I was expelled? We were completely cut off with no recourse to anyone after your appalling dishonesty. I had made friends there, David Samuels, Edward Aplin, Charles Taylor. One day I was there, part of a group that looked out for each other, the next I was gone. I never saw any of them again, all because of your lies. So, you'll understand if I don't shake your hand and tell you everything is fine and dandy because quite frankly, Alistair, it is not."

Blackshaw was undeterred by Peter's outburst, clearly expecting this sort of reaction. He had been told he was here for a purpose, and he needed to do his utmost to fulfil it. He waited a few seconds before he replied, allowing Peter's words to settle.

"I understand completely. What happened to you was unfair. You did nothing wrong and yet you became the victim of my misdemeanours. I lied and you suffered because of it. My actions were totally reprehensible, and I can only hope that when I tell you honestly why I acted the way I did, that you have it in your heart to forgive me."

Nice words, thought Peter, but his scepticism level remained high. "Okay, I'll listen. If nothing else, I'm intrigued to hear the excuses you are going to come up with."

"Thank you, Peter," said Blackshaw. "I appreciate that very much. My family was extremely wealthy. My father was a very successful businessman and had a lot of people working for him. He often told me as I was growing up that one day, when he retired, the firm would be mine and his plan was that I should work with him in order to learn the ropes as soon as my education had finished. I was an only child, so there was no one else to share in his dream – in that regard my life was mapped out for me. It did not take me long to establish that whatever I did at school was largely irrelevant. I didn't need to do well academically because I would never need any formal qualifications to inherit the family business. The education that mattered, according to my father, was the one I would receive from working with him. I did reasonably well at school for a while and I hoped my father would be pleased, but he never was. He would say that it was all well and good, but none of it mattered as much as learning about business. I remember once being so proud to score nineteen out of twenty on a history test, but when I told him, he said that history was a waste of time and what I really needed were lessons in dealing with lazy employees or negotiating deals with suppliers."

Peter looked impatiently across at the doctor. Blackshaw's sob story and insincere platitudes were not convincing him one bit.

Sensing what Peter was thinking, Blackshaw continued before he was interrupted.

"I am not asking for sympathy. I know in many ways I had a very privileged upbringing, but my father's attitude eventually made me stop wanting to try. So that is precisely what happened. I turned my attention towards ridiculing others for their achievements and being as disruptive as possible. I became envious of the boys whose parents loved them enough to praise them when they did well and commiserate when they did not. Then you came to the school with your scholarship, and you were from a different social background too, which seemed to make matters worse. You never had to try like everyone else and that made you stand out from the crowd even more. It all came to you so easily and when your parents came to pick you up, I could see delight on their faces. How much you meant to them. I admit that I was overwhelmingly jealous of you and what you had. Then at the Christmas party, when you won the signed cricket bat that I wanted, I decided that I was going to do something to get back at you."

Peter felt uncomfortable. He had not realised that anyone at school had thought of him like this. There was also a part of him, albeit very small, that, for the first time, felt the minutest fragment of sympathy for the child standing in front of him.

"My opportunity came when you saw us stealing from the sweet shop that afternoon. I knew you had witnessed everything, so I convinced my friends to lie with me if we were asked about what happened. Of course, they did what I wanted and when the headmaster asked if anyone knew who the thief was, we all said that we had seen you taking the money and the sweets. Unfortunately, the headmaster did not believe us at first – perhaps our stories sounded too similar. He suspected we had concocted our accounts, mainly, I think, because he did not believe that you were capable of doing something like that. I didn't really care what happened to me, but I wanted you to suffer, so I confessed to my father, hoping he would be pleased that I was able to be as underhand as he was. Instead, and much to my surprise, he took a different course of action. He threw me over the large oak desk in his study and beat me with his belt so hard on the back of my legs that they bled. He was furious because he knew that if the headmaster put two and two together, he would expel me. My father at the time was standing for election as a town councillor and had aspirations to become an MP at some point. A scandal of that kind could have ruined his chances – people would certainly question the morality of a man whose son was accused of being a thief by one of his classmates. I cannot recall ever being as scared before or afterwards when he told me that I was to stick to my story and make sure that my friends did too. The next day he went to see the headmaster, who told him that he suspected the thief was in fact me and not you. My father feigned incredulity at first but had to accept the truth when the headmaster explained that one of the other boys had given them an honest version of events in exchange for lenient treatment. Faced with the prospect of my expulsion, my father did what he did in any difficult business negotiation. He resorted to unscrupulous tactics – in this case blackmail. The school had been raising funds to renovate the gymnasium. You probably remember the poster on the wall outside the building showing how much was needed and how much had been received. My father said he would donate the remaining £5,000 that was required if the headmaster accepted that it had been you that stole the money. Mr James was a good man, but my father knew his weakness and that he would probably be willing to expel one innocent boy in exchange for a facility that would benefit thousands of boys in the future."

Blackshaw paused for a moment, but it was clear to Peter that he had not quite finished.

"So that's what happened, Peter. That was why you were expelled. I do not want you to think I am trying to make excuses for what I did – it was entirely because of my jealousy of you and because I did not appreciate the impact my actions would have. I am truly sorry though, Peter, and it would mean a lot if you were able to forgive me. It is impossible for me to change what happened now, but I would like you to know that my duplicity has been a source of great regret for me ever since."

Peter looked at the boy, but all he could see was the same poisonous youth that he had encountered at Tinniswood Manor. His reference to the passage of time since the incident alongside his unchanged appearance made this meeting feel even odder.

"How old are you now, Blackshaw?" he enquired with interest.

The response when it came from the mouth of the boy further confirmed how surreal this conversation had become.

"I'm eighty. I'll be eighty-one in a couple of months."

Peter glanced at the doctor for some sort of input that might help explain what this was all about. Was it a joke? Or was this really Blackshaw? Souter, however, again remained silent.

"Oh, okay, so you are eighty then, are you?" he said, ridiculing the boy. "Well, if that's the case, perhaps you could tell me what you have been doing since we were children."

"Yes, by all means," replied the boy, ignoring Peter's sarcasm. "After school, I went into my father's business just as he had intended. I worked with him for ten years before he retired, and I took over the firm. During that time, I watched him bribing people, breaking his word and worst of all treating those who worked for him with utter contempt. He became ill and was forced to retire early, so I was only in my late twenties when I became managing director. I was fortunate to find an ally in Mr Spears the office manager, and he helped me enormously. We immediately set about reversing as much of my father's bad practice as possible. Over time the clients and suppliers we dealt with began to see a difference and knew that they could trust me to honour our agreements. Unlike my father, I intended to be honest and most importantly I kept a promise to myself to never lie or cheat again. I wanted my staff to know they were valued, so once I had implemented a new health and safety policy, I improved their financial packages so that there were annual pay reviews, a pension scheme and sick pay should it be needed. None of this would have happened under my father's regime. The investment we made in this way was the best thing we ever did and the company continued to thrive until eventually I retired and passed it on to my own son. I made sure he could choose what he wanted to do with his life and he went to university to study, would you believe, maths. I expected him to forge a different career for himself, but to my surprise he asked if he could join the family business. I was delighted, of course, and I made absolutely sure he understood what made the firm successful. On his first day he was shown around by one of our managers and introduced to as many of the staff as possible. It was them who made the firm what it was, and I wanted him to appreciate their importance.

Afterwards, I asked him to come to my office. I sat opposite him and as we drank a cup of tea together, I told him for the first time what I had done to you. I admitted to my son that I had thought about my wrongdoing almost every day of my life, which incidentally I had, and that I regretted my actions deeply. I wanted him to know. I needed him to know in case it changed his mind about working with me."

Peter had not expected this revelation, but while he was trying to process the information, Souter spoke unexpectedly.

"How did your son react, Alistair?" he asked.

A tear appeared in Blackshaw's eye as he struggled to utter the words that were forever imprinted in his memory. Eventually he managed a staccato version of his son's response. "He... said he forgave me. Said I... was a... good... man... a good... father and that although I had wronged Peter... I had made a lot of people's lives... better since."

Blackshaw puffed his cheeks out, releasing the emotion he felt at sharing this with them, and then averted his eyes to the ground in order to try and hide the fact that he was crying uncontrollably.

Peter looked at the boy and, although he did not understand much of what was going on, could sense the anguish that he had been carrying all these years. This was no act and Peter realised that what Blackshaw had done had resulted in trauma for him too. At least for Peter it had been relatively short-lived. The immediate aftermath of his expulsion was a hurtful time for his family, but he had gone on to Rosehill Grammar, where he had thrived. He made new friends and met Mr Carling, who had given him so much encouragement to paint. Every cloud, as they say. Perhaps, if he had not been expelled from Tinniswood, his life might not have been so fulfilling. In some senses, maybe he should be thanking Blackshaw for what he did.

He could also see now that, for Blackshaw, the reverse had happened. Apart from the unplanned beating he received from his father, he had achieved exactly what he had intended by ensuring Peter was expelled. For him, though, as time went on and he became an adult with a family of his own, he could never escape the horrible guilt he felt for what he had done. It was there with him constantly and haunted him, often in quiet moments when he least expected, exposing vulnerability that could not be repaired. Peter knew only two well the torturous nature of that burden and he found he was able to empathise with him.

It was clear that Blackshaw's contrition was genuine and Peter decided that he had carried the memory of the wrong he had inflicted on him for long enough.

He leant forward and placed a hand on the boy's shoulder. Blackshaw's head was still bowed, but when he felt Peter's touch, he slowly raised it so that they were looking at one another.

"I know you are sorry, Alistair, and you have paid a heavy price for what you did to me. I think enough is enough. Please try not to think about that time again. Although it made things difficult for a while, I did perfectly well at another school. Then I went to university, and had a pretty decent career one way and another. Like you, I am lucky enough to have a wonderfully supportive family – my life has been good, and I am grateful for it."

Blackshaw had been unable to look at Peter while he was speaking and his chubby chin had fallen to his chest once again, hiding his tears.

"Look at me, Alistair," Peter said kindly.

The boy slowly raised his head once more and Peter saw that the tears had not yet cleared from his eyes.

"Your son sounds like an extraordinary man – you must be very proud of him. For my part, I know how much courage it must have taken to have that conversation and I believe that you are truly sorry. As far as I am concerned, your son is absolutely right, and it is clear to me what I need to do." He paused for a fraction of a second before very deliberately adding, "I forgive you, Alistair."

Blackshaw could not speak at first and as the doctor was clearly not going to say anything either, Peter decided to continue.

"It sounds like you have a lovely family – perhaps you could introduce them to me some time."

Blackshaw managed a smile as he wiped his eyes and took a deep breath. "They are not with me at the moment, but I would like to do that in the future perhaps."

Peter smiled in approval of Blackshaw's suggestion then looked in the doctor's direction once again in the hope that he would intervene. This time he did speak, although his words when they came were formal as though he was oblivious to the emotional effects of the reunion on the other two men.

"A quick reminder, Alistair, in case you have forgotten. One of your companions would also like to speak to Peter?"

"Oh yes. You are quite right. I had forgotten," said Blackshaw, pleased now to have something else on which to focus.

"Thank you, Peter, your forgiveness means everything to me." The octogenarian held out the podgy hand of the boy he had been when they last met and Peter grasped it warmly in his own, now bony fingers. Each gripped the other tightly, reinforcing the bond of their new relationship.

"I'll go and get him, Sir," said Blackshaw, glancing at the doctor, and then with a final nod to Peter, he turned and walked back in the direction of the seating area.

Peter could not see Blackshaw's face, but he noticed that as he moved away from them, his physical shape changed, and he was walking much more slowly with the same slight hunch he had seen earlier. Peter watched as he spoke to another man who then stood up. Blackshaw eased himself carefully into a chair and the other man began walking towards them. The notion suddenly struck him that he might know who this man was and if his assumption was correct, he needed to prepare himself.

"It's his father, isn't it? I don't know if I can forgive him," he said to the doctor without waiting for a reply, as the man was halfway across the room now.

"No," replied Souter. "It's not him, Peter." Then in a noticeably quieter voice, he added, "Mr Blackshaw Senior is not here."

Relieved to hear this, Peter studied the elderly man who, unlike Blackshaw, had changed surprisingly little as he made his way over to them. Perhaps he looked a little younger than when he first stood up, but there were still flecks of grey in his hair. He was tall with unmistakably long, thin legs which Peter recognised as soon as he could see him properly. The memory of what the boys called him when there were no teachers around immediately came to mind. Their last conversation had cast a terrible shadow over Peter's life, but now that he had spoken to Blackshaw and understood what had happened, he smiled warmly as the headmaster of Tinniswood Manor, Mr James, the 'stick insect', now joined him and the doctor.

Even though Peter was almost eighty, he greeted him in the only manner that was acceptable.

"Good morning, Sir," he said with deference.

Mr Milson opted for the same protocol in response.

"Good morning, Davis."

Souter smiled at this most English of encounters before effecting his contribution to the introduction.

"I believe, Mr Milson, that there is something you would like to say to Mr Davis."

The headmaster coughed to clear his throat, simultaneously raising his eyebrows in the doctor's direction in thanks and to express his acknowledgement of his words. Then, looking directly at Peter, he spoke.

"I know that Blackshaw has explained the circumstances to you of the awful events in which we three were involved. He has just told me that you were able to forgive him, which makes me very happy for you both. I too regret that time immensely and knew full well that you were not capable of stealing. I am very grateful to have the opportunity of speaking to you because I wanted to ask if you also felt able to forgive me."

Peter tried to interrupt, but the headmaster had something else to say. He needed to explain his actions to Peter.

"You have been told, I understand, that Mr Blackshaw, as chair of governors, exerted some considerable pressure on me to deflect the blame for the theft from his son onto you. I want you to know that I initially told him that I was not prepared to do that and that I found the suggestion reprehensible. But, as you can probably imagine, he was persistent, and he knew how important it was to me that the new gymnasium was built – you probably recall the tatty building that we had in those days."

Peter nodded encouragingly in an attempt to help Mr Milson say what was on his mind, remembering the damp walls and splintered wooden floor.

"There is no hiding from it. I allowed him to bribe me. It would have taken ages to raise the rest of the money we required, almost certainly beyond my retirement. He dangled the carrot in front of me and with this one misdeed, the building work could be completed for the start of the next academic year with an injection of money from him. The benefit of doing this for the boys was an enormous incentive for me and I deluded myself at the time that their gain was worth the blemish on my integrity. But it is important to me that I confess to you the other reason why I went along with his deception. You see, I wanted to be known as a headmaster who had achieved something tangible during his tenure at Tinniswood. Beyond that, I sought the approval of parents and the wider community for being the man who had helped make the new building possible. I hoped that people would remember me for years to come as one of the most successful headmasters the school had ever known rather than the effective but somewhat nondescript leader that I actually was."

He paused momentarily before pressing on with his admission.

"The gymnasium was built, and it served the school marvellously for many years, but for me the satisfaction of providing it was always tainted and I was never able to explain to anyone, not even my wife, why that was. In my heart I knew that I endorsed your expulsion for personal gain and in the quest of praise which I certainly did not deserve. My mistake and the feeling of guilt has remained with me to this day."

He paused for breath before his final appeal to Peter.

"I know I have no right to do so, Davis, but I ask you please to forgive my weakness. Please be assured that I will always regret the impact my lack of fortitude had on you then and subsequently."

It seemed very odd to hear the man of whom all the boys at Tinniswood were so in awe speak to him in this manner. He was a little uneasy with the reversal of roles that had taken place – somehow it just seemed wrong for Mr Milson to ask him for anything rather than to give him instructions. Regardless of this, the decision was very simple for him to reach, and he replied with gusto.

"Headmaster, I always assumed that the decision to expel me was Mr Blackshaw's rather than your own. I can recall the look of disappointment on your face when you told me I had to leave, and I have never harboured any malice towards you for the way things worked out. You were an excellent headmaster, a little scary at times for a nine-year-old boy, but compassionate and understanding when you needed to be. I have no hesitation whatsoever when I say that yes, Sir, I do forgive you, without reservation. As far as I am concerned, you have nothing to admonish yourself for, so please do not do so any longer."

"Thank you, Davis," the headmaster said gratefully with a slight quiver in his voice. "You were a great loss to our school as a pupil and you have become a fine man, just as I hoped you would."

With that, the headmaster nodded to both Peter and the doctor, realising that the matter was concluded, and walked back gratefully to rejoin his friends. In the gloomy distance Peter could just make out the shape of Mr James embracing the woman who had risen to hug her husband. Even from that distance and being unable to see either of their expressions, Peter could sense their combined relief.

"Thanks for that, Mr Davis. Everything went rather well, I thought," said Souter very matter-of-factly but with a smile now on his face.

Peter felt invigorated somehow by the experience. He was inwardly lighter at having confronted and dealt with the anger he had felt over that chapter in his life.

"Yes, it did," he replied, "and thank you for going to the trouble of arranging this for us. I think it has done us all a lot of good."

Peter paused before he spoke again a little hesitantly.

"I do have one or two questions though."

Souter stifled a chuckle. "Yes, I thought you might, Peter."

Chapter 15

As the two men stood in the doorway, Souter knew that this was the time to answer Peter's inevitable questions. He edged into the corridor, gently placing an arm on Peter's shoulder, encouraging him to follow. Once they had exited the room, they were out of earshot, which allowed Peter the freedom to ask whatever was on his mind about the strange events that had occurred during his meetings with Blackshaw and Mr Milson.

"I assume you saw what happened when they came over to us just now," Peter blurted out for want of anything more cohesive to say. Although the statement was phrased as a question, the requirement for an immediate reply was delayed by a further query hot on the heels of the first.

"You told me that I was not dreaming, but when Blackshaw stood up, even though the light wasn't great, I could see he was an old man like me. By the time he was standing next to us, he was the young boy I had detested seventy years ago. What I want to know is, did you see that too? Did you know it was going to happen? And, incidentally, how did it happen? How can people transform like that? Has someone invented a drug that does it or perhaps it was time travel?" he said sceptically, emphasising how ridiculous he considered the situation to be. Peter had jettisoned any attempt at structure, preferring this combined outpouring from which the doctor could take his pick of questions. He took a deep breath, as much for his own sanity as to allow Souter the chance to reply.

"They are all good questions and rather than answer them individually, I believe I might be able to deal with them more effectively together if that is okay with you."

Peter nodded eagerly, although he remained doubtful that any explanation would satisfy him adequately.

"What I am about to tell you is going to be difficult for you to understand, let alone believe immediately. I do promise, though, that in due course, all will become clear," he said by way of preamble and to ensure he had Peter's full attention before continuing.

"Naturally, I saw what you saw, and I confess that I did know it was going to happen. As a matter of fact, I have seen it happen many times before. The how is a little harder to explain, I'm afraid, but perhaps I could ask you for now to accept that what you watched was real. No drugs were involved and there was no trickery. It's just that there is a lot the human race has not yet accepted as normal or indeed possible."

"Hang on a minute. The human race? You are speaking as though you are some sort of alien. Are you an alien?"

"In a manner of speaking, I suppose you could call me that, but not in the way that I think you are imagining," said Souter, well aware that it was unlikely that Peter would be satisfied with such a cryptic response.

"Can I be direct, Doctor?"

"Yes, of course, Mr Davis, by all means be as direct as you like."

"We have only known each other a short while, but I think it's fair to say we get on pretty well. You have looked after me and I am extremely grateful, but there is something very odd going on here. If it's all the same to you, rather than us pretending there was nothing unusual about my meeting with Blackshaw, perhaps you could tell me straight who you are and what is going on. I don't mean to be rude, but I think that would be easier all round, don't you?"

Souter inclined his head and smiled to demonstrate his agreement to Peter's request.

"Well, the first thing to say is that you are not where you think you are."

"Yes, I understand that. I knew I hadn't seen this part of the ship before. Where are we then?"

Souter spoke in a very relaxed manner when he responded. After all, he had heard this question many times before.

"The simplest way for me to explain where you are is to tell you the three other pieces of information that you need to know. Firstly, I am not a doctor. Not at least in the conventional sense of someone who cures physical ailments. Secondly, you are not now, nor have you recently been on a cruise ship."

That didn't make any sense, thought Peter. He was feeling so much better. His cough and shortness of breath had gone, his joints did not ache as they normally did, and his brain felt agile just as it had when he was younger. Perhaps that was all due to Dr Edgeman rather than him, but who was he if he was not a ship's doctor?

"And thirdly," Souter continued before Peter could interrupt, "the cough and the difficulty you had breathing were in fact the early signs of pneumonia."

"Well, it seems to have gone now, doesn't it?" Peter exclaimed abruptly, becoming rather exasperated with this mysterious explanation.

"Yes, it has gone now," Souter admitted. "You might have noticed that your joints don't ache as much as they did and perhaps your short-term memory is better than it has been for a while."

Peter knew this was true. He felt better in himself than he had for ages and his mind was much less fuzzy than usual.

"The reason for this is, Mr Davis, that despite the best efforts of Dr Edgeman, the pneumonia killed you." He paused for a second to let Peter absorb the shock these words always created and then, as he usually did at this point, he provided the additional clarification that he knew would be required.

"Mr Davis, since you are obviously keen to know everything, I will not sugar-coat this. You are dead."

Peter said nothing and Souter knew that this was the moment when people needed to be allowed some time to process the enormity of what they had been told. Peter's response, though, came quicker than he had anticipated.

"But I feel fine. Better than that, I feel fitter than I have for ages."

The men looked at one another and simultaneously became aware of the loud thud of the penny that had dropped in Peter's brain.

"So that is the reason why I feel so good. No aches and pains and no illness."

"Yes, that's quite right. You will not be affected by any of those things anymore."

He paused again, giving Peter time to consider this before he came out with the second most commonly asked question in this situation.

"So, this is Heaven?" Peter asked hesitantly.

Souter knew that these were difficult words for someone to say, mainly because it was one of those questions they had never asked before. People often thought themselves silly at first, at least until they had grasped the fact that the life they had always known was now over. For this reason, he did not intend to rush his reply. He preferred instead to treat the enquiry sympathetically, knowing also that it was important that Peter listened properly to his explanation.

"The simple answer to your question is, no, this is not Heaven. The place we are in at the moment is one of a number that people go to before they move on to what you refer to as Heaven. You have already seen some of the others here, and I have more people for you to meet shortly."

"So, this is purgatory then?"

"In a way I suppose you could say it is, in that while people pass through here, they are encouraged to cleanse themselves of certain issues that have arisen while they were alive. It is not, however, like the purgatory that you are probably imagining where sinners are forced to suffer and prove they are worthy enough to enter Heaven. Everyone sins – it's almost impossible not to as a human. But not all sin is of the extreme kind that comes from being more evil than good. A lot of sin is mundane, the odd lie here and there, being uncharitable and unloving or simply not doing enough good when you have the opportunity. While you are here you will have the chance to confront some difficult things and at the same time you will be allowing others to do the same."

"I'm not sure I follow you, Doctor," Peter said, pushing his fingernail into the palm of his hand to see if he could still make it hurt as much as it did when he was alive. He was oddly satisfied that it did and even more pleased when it remained sore even when he stopped. Then before continuing he remembered that this man had just told him he was not in fact a doctor.

"You're not a doctor though," Peter said, correcting himself. "So, what do I call you? Mr Souter?"

"If you wish, but quite honestly, I would much rather keep things informal if you are happy to. After all, I have just told you that you are dead, so we do have a rather special relationship. Most people tend to call me Archie from this point and, to be honest, that is what I prefer."

Peter had no idea what the protocol was in purgatory, or whatever this place was called, and since he already liked this man and assumed their relationship was going to become closer, he decided to follow suit.

"Fair enough, Archie it is, and I think you ought to drop the Mr Davis and call me Peter, since it sounds like we are going to be together for a while."

"Excellent. Thank you, Peter. That will make things much easier."

"Actually, Archie, I was just about to ask you what you meant when you mentioned that I would have the chance to confront some difficult things. Perhaps you could explain."

"Yes, of course, Peter," Archie said. "Take the conversations that took place a few minutes ago with Alistair Blackshaw and your old headmaster, Mr Milson. I know there were some awkward moments in there, but don't you feel better having heard what they both said and being able to forgive their actions?"

"Yes, I can't deny that, I suppose. I told you that those events have played on my mind for a long time, quite apart from the effect they had on my family when they happened," Peter conceded, rubbing his hand on his thigh in an attempt to mitigate his self-inflicted pain of a few moments earlier. "To understand what motivated them and to be able to forgive them does feel pretty good. The extreme anger for Blackshaw that I felt has definitely lessened and I am pleased that he told his son what he did to me. It's as though telling someone he loved how much he regretted it was in some way an admission to the world that he knew he was wrong."

"I am glad you have used the word forgive, Peter, because forgiving sins and wrongdoings is of great importance in this place. I am sure you will have noticed that your forgiveness had an enormous impact, not just on you, but also on both Blackshaw and Mr Milson. I saw the relief on the faces, Peter, and I saw the anger you refer to being dispelled. In its place you showed great compassion in allowing them to unburden themselves of a guilt that had weighed them down. What happened was not just part of a process for you; it was also a significant step on their journey through here."

"So, are you telling me that the headmaster, Blackshaw and all the others they were talking to are all dead too? Not only that, but they have also ended up here like me?"

"Yes, that's exactly right. They are all dead, although some have been here longer than others, of course. Alistair Blackshaw did not die that long ago, but he has had to wait for certain people to arrive so that he can speak to them. It's very comfortable here, as you can see, and although everyone is keen to leave for the obvious reason, their stay is always made as pleasant as possible."

"So how long does this process normally take?" Peter asked, feeling heartened by Archie's words but also keen to obtain as much detail as he could.

"There's no fixed time, I'm afraid. It depends on a number of factors, the main one of which is how many people are on your 'list'."

"List?" queried Peter. "I have a list?"

"Yes, everyone has a list made up of the people they need to settle things with before they can move on. In addition, occasionally you might be asked to come back to help someone who has recently died with their list. The headmaster, for example, died over thirty years ago and was able to work through his list reasonably quickly. I don't think it was particularly long and once he had forgiven those who had wronged him and unburdened himself of his own guilt with those who were available, he was able to progress. Interestingly, I think you were possibly the last person he had to come back here for."

"I liked him at school," Peter said, remembering the strict but fair man he was at Tinniswood. "He was a kind man and I can see he did what he thought was right at the time for the benefit of the school. Mr Blackshaw took advantage and manipulated him for his own means, I suspect. Talking of him, I assume that he is on my list of people to forgive, so why was he not with his son today."

"Actually, Peter, I don't think he is on your list, at least not yet. If he had been, you would have met him just now with the others. It is possible you might be asked to talk to him in the future, but for the time being he has gone to a different place. Whether you need to see him largely depends on what he does there."

"Do you mean that he is in Hell?" asked Peter, now no longer concerned as to whether his queries sounded ridiculous.

"I don't know for sure where he is at the moment, but certainly it is somewhere considerably more austere than here and his tasks there will be much more arduous. He could be there for some time and there is no guarantee that he will ever move on. You might be asked to forgive him one day, but in the meantime, the knowledge of his current situation has probably made you feel somewhat differently towards him already."

Peter thought for a moment, reflecting on the mental picture he had formed of the hideous suffering to which the man was being subjected.

"Yes, I think I do. The place I am imagining and the thought of what he has to do there if anything makes me pity him. From what you suggest, if I ever am asked to forgive him, I should find it comparatively easy knowing that he has perhaps literally been through Hell to get here."

"Yes, exactly, Peter, and because his current location is no fault of yours, the fact that you have encountered him in your life will not prevent your progression when the time is right."

Peter was in the practical mindset he had adopted at school and during his working life. He was concentrating much better than he had for years and was entirely focused on gathering all the information he might need.

"Do you know how many people I have to meet here?"

"Unfortunately, no, I don't have that precise information, I'm afraid. It will become apparent to me, however, when you are nearing the end and I promise that I will let you know when that happens."

"So, you are going to be with me throughout and help me to navigate this place," said Peter, the relief evident in his voice.

"Yes, Peter, I will be your guide here and I will do what I can, within the rules, of course, to help you."

"Okay, thank you," Peter said, slightly embarrassed. "So, when do I see the next person? That meeting was not easy, but I am keen to get on with things and do what I need to."

"That's quite understandable, but why don't we go and have a cup of tea first? There's a good place up ahead," he said, pointing to a door that Peter had not noticed earlier.

"If you want to, but honestly I am fine to carry on if you are, Archie."

"If it's all the same to you, Peter, I think a hot drink would be a good idea because there is something else I need to talk to you about before we continue."

"Right…" said Peter suspiciously.

"To be precise it's someone rather than something that I need to tell you about."

Peter wondered what he could possibly mean and eyed him now with concern. Archie had also been through this part of the process many times before and knew that it was best not to prevaricate.

"Peter, I need to speak to you about Joan."

Peter was both stunned and ashamed. He had been so preoccupied about his own situation, not unsurprisingly, that he had completely forgotten about what would happen to Joan now he was dead. He had left her well provided for financially, of course, so at least she would not have to worry about that. She had her state pension and his work pension continued to pay her a significant income, which they had both agreed would be plenty to ensure she could continue to live at home if she wanted to. They had no debts and a decent level of savings which she would almost certainly never need to touch. She knew where all the paperwork was, and their son Tom had a copy of everything in case she needed any help. Running quickly through the financial plan they had put in place together calmed him slightly, but he felt guilty that he had not thought about her earlier.

He was still a little dazed as Archie led him into the room he had indicated. Peter did not know what to expect since this would be his first experience of a post death cup of tea. He had assumed there would be other people in the room, perhaps chatting as Blackshaw was with his acquaintances. He was a little surprised, therefore, that the room was much smaller than the last one they had been in and that there was no one else inside. As far as he could tell, there were no windows, but the lighting was soft and more reminiscent of an early summer morning than the harsh glare of artificial light. There was a series of nondescript pictures in frames dotted around in order to break up the colour of the pale blue walls. The cream carpet on the floor looked inviting, a fact that was confirmed as Peter passed through the doorway and stepped on it for the first time. It felt as though it was brand new, although the familiar 'new carpet' smell was missing. All the same, he wondered whether he should take off his shoes and leave them in the hall. The only items of furniture in the room were two comfortable-looking armchairs and a round Victorian wooden table on which stood two cups and saucers, a bowl of sugar and a jug of milk. On a mat next to them was a teapot from the spout of which Peter could see a gentle puff of steam rising into the air.

Archie beckoned Peter to take the chair of his choice and remained standing himself so that he could pour the tea more easily.

"I thought it was best that we had some privacy so that I can explain things and answer any questions that you have. Before we get started, it's just milk, no sugar for you, isn't it?"

"Yes, thank you, that's right," replied Peter, still a little bewildered and realising that he was actually rather thirsty.

Archie passed Peter his cup and saucer then poured one for himself, to which he added a decent splash of milk and three lumps of sugar that he dropped in expertly using the silver tongs that were in the bowl for that purpose. He then took his seat opposite Peter, stirring his tea methodically as he did so.

"How could I have not mentioned Joan? I was so caught up with everything else that it never occurred to me to consider how she must be feeling," said Peter.

"Don't be so hard on yourself, Peter. After all, I have just sprung something of a shock on you. In any case, I think once I explain things you will feel differently."

"Perhaps," said Peter. "I know she won't have any practical worries, but I hate to imagine what she is going through at the moment. We've been together over fifty years, you know, so it's going to be so difficult for her not having me there. Sorry, that sounded conceited, but you know what I mean."

He paused for a moment then added, "And it works both ways. How am I going to get on without her by my side?"

"I am glad you ask because that's what I wanted to talk to you about. You see, the thing is that Joan has already been through this place. She passed on from the life you and she had together two years ago and has since moved on from here."

A cold shudder went through Peter's body as the words were, one by one, processed by his brain so that eventually they became a cohesive sentence. He tried to speak but was unable to do so. Instead, he sat staring open-mouthed at Archie. "I am sorry if that was a bit abrupt, Peter, but in my work, I find it is usually best to be honest and up front with people."

He sipped his tea and suggested Peter might feel better if he did the same. Still feeling numb, Peter managed to stretch a hand rigidly towards the cup and take a gulp. Archie was right; the tea was good, and its warmth shook him from his temporary stupor. After a second sip he found he could talk again.

"I don't understand though. She's not dead. I only had dinner with her a few nights ago. She'll still be on the cruise, unless, that is, time passes differently here."

"Time does pass at a different speed here, oddly enough, but that has not affected things regarding Joan. I understand this is incredibly confusing, but please take my word for it that Joan, like you, was not on a cruise."

"But that makes no sense. Surely, I would know if Joan had died. And it was two years ago, you say?"

Archie nodded, smiling sympathetically as he did so.

"Well, if Joan died two years ago, where have I been since and with whom? Was someone impersonating her or are you suggesting something else?"

Archie gestured defensively with his palms raised in front of him in an attempt to prevent Peter from 'shooting the messenger'.

"I understand that this is the second bombshell that has been dropped on you in a short space of time and I will do my best to make things as easy as possible for you. Firstly, I need to warn you that there will be other surprises on this journey, but I believe absolutely that you are very capable of dealing with all of them. You are bound to be apprehensive, but I am confident that you will soon move on. With regard to Joan, what I have told you is true and once you have done what you need to here, all will become clear to you, and hopefully you and Joan will be reunited."

Peter still felt uncertain about this explanation. This was not a comprehensive answer to his question, but it seemed as though it was all that Archie was prepared to offer. He was confused about Joan, but perhaps it was best to simply go along with things. He could not think of any good reason why this man should deceive him, and he obviously knew how things worked here. Having considered the problem that confronted him, he arrived, as he always had, at the only sensible solution.

"Okay, I'm going to go along with whatever you say."

Peter hesitated and, sensing a follow-up question, Archie waited patiently for him to continue. Peter drained his teacup and placed it back on the saucer.

"Can I just clarify something? You said that I will be reunited with Joan soon, but you have already told me that she is not here now, so presumably…"

Peter stopped in the hope that Archie would finish the sentence for him, but when he did not, he forced the words out himself.

"Presumably she is in Heaven?" he asked.

For once, Archie's reply was refreshingly unequivocal.

"Yes, Peter, she is in the place you know as Heaven. She is waiting there for you and I sincerely hope that you are able to get there too, preferably as soon as possible."

Rising to his feet, Peter smiled with determination at Archie, who was still seated opposite him.

"If it's okay with you then, Doctor, I mean Archie, I'd like to get cracking."

Archie returned the smile with satisfaction.

"Excellent. I think it's time I introduced you to someone else who I believe is extremely keen to speak with you."

With that he stood up straight and walked briskly towards the door with Peter following keenly behind him, intrigued as to who he was going to meet next in this odd halfway house of a place.

Chapter 16

To Peter's surprise, instead of continuing down the corridor, Archie turned right and led him back towards the room where he had spoken to Blackshaw. A few yards down the hall, he leant on a set of swing doors, holding one open as he did so, inviting Peter to come through with him. The passage they walked down was now brightly lit with candle-shaped lights that were fixed to the wall at regular intervals. They passed a mahogany table on which Peter noticed was a huge ceramic bowl full of fruit. He was tempted to reach out and try an apple, but then, checking to see if the doctor had seen him looking, he remembered where he was and resisted the temptation. After a while, he became vaguely aware of the sound of voices in the distance. It was a low-level hum of polite chatter, he realised, but he could not hear what was being said. The passageway opened out a few yards ahead of him, giving way to a large space of some kind and he sensed that the sound, which was now becoming louder, was coming from whoever was there.

A few moments later, they were standing in what looked like an auditorium of the sort that might be used for a conference or perhaps a musical concert. Peter could see people milling about, some of them talking to each other animatedly in small groups. The majority were walking around the perimeter of the room looking at the vast array of pictures adorning the walls. Peter scanned the enormous space, trying to take in his surroundings. The floor, walls and ceiling were all white, which accentuated the colour that came from the paintings and other artwork. Performing a quick calculation in his head, he estimated conservatively that there must be almost a hundred exhibits and his eyes were drawn to the centre of the room where a series of sculptures, one or two of which were at least fifteen feet tall, were being admired by those who circled them.

Archie watched contentedly as Peter absorbed everything. He never tired of the look of awe on peoples' faces when they first entered this room. For a true art lover like Peter, he imagined the impact was even greater than usual.

"Welcome to our gallery, Peter. I think you are going to enjoy spending some time here," he said, waving his arms in different directions to ensure that Peter was aware of every part of the room. "You might be impressed to know that all the artwork has been produced by those who have passed through this place. Many have moved on elsewhere by now, of course, but some are still here, and new items are added all the time," he added cheerily.

Peter looked left and right again, noticing that the room seemed to extend much further than he had thought at first. Another quick addition in his head told him that his initial guess at the number of pieces on display was a significant underestimation.

"I know you have a real appreciation for art of all kinds, but there is one picture here that I think will be of particular interest to you. It's over there," he said, thrusting his hand to the right and simultaneously beginning to move in that direction.

Peter gazed in wonder at the exhibits as he followed, trying to take in the array of watercolours, oil paintings and sculptures as he passed them. Unannounced, Archie suddenly stopped and turned to face the wall to his right. He approached the picture hung there and beckoned Peter to join him for a closer look. Peter recognised the subject of the painting long before he was in front of it. His eyes had become so much sharper than before and he thought how marvellous it was that he did not seem to need glasses. Archie observed him with interest as he stooped to read the small white card to its left that bore its details, patiently waiting as Peter's assumption about the subject was proved correct. The words read:

'COWDRAY PARK BY DIMITAR ZHECHEV'

Peter could not think straight for a few moments and had to compose himself in order to make sense of what he was reading. It was most certainly as he had suspected, a picture of Cowdray Park – but why was Zhechev's name on it? It was not the picture that he had stolen from him in Paris, so at least Zhechev was not trying to claim the credit for his work, but the man was not an artist himself as far as Peter could recall, so why did the card say that he had produced it? Looking again at the picture, he could see the familiar white stone of the ruins in the top left corner, but the picture was dominated by a group of people in the foreground among the swathe of white ox-eye daisies and pale blue forget-me-nots. Two adults and a baby were sitting on a blanket having a picnic while another small child who had gone to retrieve a ball stood holding it proudly in front of him.

Peter jumped, feeling a hand rest on his shoulder, and turned suddenly, expecting to see Archie. Instead, though, he found himself face to face with someone much less agreeable, the man who had run off with his picture all those years ago in Paris and whose recreation of its subject he had been admiring. Dimitar Zhechev, the Bulgarian art dealer who had disappeared without a trace, was right there in front of him. The shock of seeing him was quickly replaced by anger as Peter appraised him in an instant despite being caught by surprise. It was strange, Peter thought, that he looked no older than the last time he had seen him, and the charming smile confirmed that this was indeed the same person he had known then. Keen to give him a piece of his mind, Peter opened his mouth to speak, but he was beaten to it by his adversary.

"Hello, Peter. It's good to see you again."

Peter did not know what to say, but he was sure that he certainly did not share that particular sentiment. Realising that Peter was not ready to reply immediately, and keen to avoid the barrage of abuse that he suspected was about to pour from Peter's mouth, Dimitar continued.

"I hope you don't mind that I painted the place you loved so much. It's not particularly good, I know, but much of it is from memory and, of course, I am not really an artist. I think so often about your extraordinary picture and how much Cowdray Park meant to you and your family."

"So do I," Peter replied curtly, having gathered himself sufficiently to speak. The nerve of the man knew no bounds, he thought to himself. "In fact, as Mr Souter knows, I have never really been able to forget about that painting and what happened to it after the exhibition in France," he added, deciding to get straight to the point.

"Yes, I am certain that you do, Peter, and I can assure you that I do too. Such a fantastic victory at the exhibition tainted by what occurred afterwards."

"Precisely," said Peter sarcastically, anticipating a string of excuses as to why he took the picture and disappeared.

"You must wonder what on earth happened after we parted in Paris all those years ago and I have been waiting for so long to explain everything to you. I was so excited when word was sent for me to return to meet with you here."

Return? thought Peter quizzically to himself. How could a crook like Zhechev have been let in here in the first place let alone be asked to return? Where had he returned from? Surely not Heaven. He recalled that he was taught at school that it was written in the Bible that a sinner who repented was a source of joy for God, but surely there had to be some sort of sanction against the underhand activities of someone like Zhechev. Perhaps the reason that he was so pleased was because it had given him a break from Hell or some other horrible existence that he had been made to endure as punishment. But he was being so pleasant, so reasonable, so apparently devoid of remorse that Peter was intrigued to hear what he had to say for himself.

"I am sure you would like an explanation of the events that followed our trip to Suresnes, and if you will indulge me, after all this time, I would like to tell you all I can."

When Peter demonstrated his agreement, albeit with a rather impatient nod and an uninspiring downturned mouth, Dimitar eagerly began, keen to tell the story even if his audience did not seem overly enthusiastic at the prospect.

He recalled that Peter had left early on Monday morning, the day after the exhibition, because he needed to be at work on Tuesday. At 11.00 am, Dimitar explained that he had checked out of the hotel and taken a cab to the station in order to catch the Paris train. The previous evening, he had spoken to a wealthy collector he knew, Monsieur Joubert, who had told him he wanted to buy the picture without even needing to see it. Provided the painting could be delivered to his hotel in Paris the next day, before he headed south for a few weeks, he had agreed to pay fifty thousand francs.

It had been an extremely hot day in Paris and Dimitar had needed to pause by a newspaper vendor to mop his brow with his handkerchief before carrying his suitcase in one hand and the carefully wrapped picture under his other arm when he exited the station. Monsieur Joubert was a man of significant means and spent most of his time in Monte Carlo or Nice, but when he came to Paris, he always took a suite at his favourite hotel, Le Royal Monceau. The hotel was on Avenue Hoche, just a stone's throw from the Arc de Triomphe, which looked stunning in the intense spring afternoon sun. Monsieur Joubert, despite his immense wealth, was from a relatively humble family, but a good education and an incredibly shrewd eye had enabled him to assemble one of the best private art collections in the world. Dimitar had known him for more than ten years, during which time he had helped him acquire a number of items for his collection and trust had never been an issue between them. If Joubert said he would buy something, he bought it. If a price was agreed, there was never any attempt to renegotiate afterwards. Apart from being an excellent client, Joubert always ensured their meetings were enjoyable and was an extremely good host. Dimitar was, therefore, in high spirits, if uncomfortably hot again, when he arrived at the grand entrance of the hotel and stepped into the imposing lobby. Having left his suitcase with the concierge, he took the lift to Joubert's suite with Peter's painting of Cowdray Park ruins still clasped firmly in both hands.

The sale of the picture took less than five minutes to complete. Joubert held the painting close and examined it for no more than twenty or thirty seconds, which was all he needed to see why the Louvre's expert had awarded it the gold medal at the exhibition. Before Dimitar knew it, Joubert had thrust a banker's draft for fifty thousand francs into his hand and was pouring them both a glass of champagne to celebrate the deal. For a while, they chatted, mainly about Joubert's collection, finishing the bottle of Dom Perignon 1966 in the process. It was only then that Dimitar looked at the carriage clock on the sideboard in the sitting room of the suite and realised that he only had twenty minutes until his train left for Boulogne. Joubert was his normal jovial self, telling him that he did not need to be embarrassed as they hurriedly said their goodbyes and Dimitar left. He only just made it in time. In fact, he recalled he had needed to run as quickly as was possible, with his suitcase in hand, almost the whole length of the platform to find his carriage. He was relieved, if sweaty and out of breath, to find his seat just in time to feel the juddering movement of the train pulling gently out of the station.

The journey to Boulogne was more stressful than he would have liked. There were two families with young children sitting nearby. If the baby was not crying, one of the toddlers was screaming, which made it impossible for him to relax. Even without their noise the almost constant foot tapping of the two older children who had been positioned directly behind him would have prevented him from sleeping. He did turn and glare at them on a number of occasions, but rather than deter them his attempted intimidation had the reverse effect. He had clearly become a source of amusement, which made them do it all the more, the ultimate goal being to make Dimitar lose his temper. He considered talking to the parents, but he always preferred to avoid confrontation when possible, so instead chose to ignore them in the hope that they would eventually become bored.

This tactic worked periodically but overall was not a resounding success.

He had allowed plenty of time to catch the overnight ferry, but a delay near Amiens had meant that when he arrived, he had to hurry again to get to the ferry port on time. Matters were made worse by the fact that he felt slightly nauseous, which he put down to a combination of champagne, a lack of food and the attentions of the children on the train. He had to run again to make it, but eventually, though sticky with sweat, he found his cabin. He was a little dizzy and remembered he had not eaten since breakfast, so he decided that it would be a good idea to try and find some food.

"That was the last thing I remember," Dimitar explained when he had finished.

"The rest of the story was told to me by my brother Stoyan, with whom I have since been reunited."

Seeing now that he had Peter's attention, he pressed on with his account.

"I was evidently found the next morning on the floor of my cabin by one of the stewards who had come into clean. Apparently, I had suffered a huge heart attack which had killed me almost immediately. The ferry manager found my wallet in my jacket, which contained my brother's details as he was my next of kin. By the time Stoyan arrived, my possessions had been transferred to a room in the ferry terminal for him to collect and my body taken to the mortuary at a nearby hospital."

Peter had not expected this and felt the colour draining slightly from his face. He had always assumed that he had been swindled by Dimitar and that the art dealer had been in cahoots with the beautiful curator of the exhibition, Sophie. What he had just heard was a very different version of events. It sounded uncomfortably plausible to him, and he felt so ashamed of having harboured nothing but malign thoughts about this man who, far from being the rogue he had imagined, had in reality died trying to do exactly what he and Peter had agreed.

Dimitar could see that Peter was somewhat perturbed and decided that it might be best to tell him the rest of the story as quickly as possible.

"When Stoyan unpacked my things, he found a large zip-around document holder containing various notes I had made and two signed bills of sale. Fortunately, I was always quite good with paperwork and each document had a banker's draft attached to it with a paperclip. One was for a small picture I had sold the evening before we left for France. The other, of course, was for the sale of *The Ruins at Cowdray Park*. As soon as Stoyan, who was also the executor of my will, was able to do so, he ensured that both were declared to my bank and added to the value of my assets they held. Of course, he didn't have any idea the money from Joubert was mainly yours. I am so sorry about that, Peter, but it really was not his fault."

Peter felt more wretched by the minute. If this story was true, it did not sound like Dimitar, let alone his brother, had anything in the least to be sorry about. On the contrary it was he who should ask to be forgiven for the conclusions he had reached about him. He had only ever disclosed those thoughts to two people, Joan and Archie, but that did not help to ease his conscience now that he had heard the truth.

"No, please, Dimitar, you do not need to apologise," said Peter, desperately trying to begin to make amends.

"I went to the shop to try and find you but, of course, you were not there," he said, frantically attempting to add something useful to the conversation.

"Yes, I believe Stoyan had a lot of problems while he was trying to sell the shop, but he got there eventually. It must have been awful for him, and I am very relieved that I have been able to tell him how grateful I am for what he did."

"I tried to contact Sophie to see if she knew anything, but she had changed employment by that time and I could not trace her," Peter said, wanting to explain his side of the story as though this was somehow relevant to Dimitar.

"Had she?" replied Dimitar. "I didn't know that, and I haven't spoken to her since we left her that evening at the chateau. It doesn't surprise me though. She made such a good job of curating the exhibition that someone there was bound to snap her up. I guess she would probably be in her sixties or seventies by now judging by your appearance, if you don't mind me saying so, Peter, so I suspect she is probably still alive."

Archie had remained a short distance away while the two men spoke, but at this point, he made sure they both saw him slowly nod his head to confirm that this was indeed the case.

"Incidentally," said Dimitar, "I still see Joubert from time to time. He left his chateau and collection to his wife and then his children, with strict instructions that it should be maintained and displayed. We discussed your picture and he was sad to hear what had happened to me. He told me how much he admired *Cowdray Park Ruins*, so much so that it was in his favourite place in the chateau, the morning room. I had visited him there some years before and he showed me a Matisse and a Monet that were in there, so it sounds like you were in pretty good company. Perhaps I might be able to introduce the two of you some time. I think you would enjoy talking to him."

This was too much. This poor man even wanted to introduce him to his friends. Peter could wait no longer; he had to come clean with Dimitar about the animosity that had consumed him, even though he was probably not going to thank him for it. He realised then that not only did he need to be honest but that it was him, not Dimitar, who needed to ask for forgiveness.

"Look, Dimitar, I need to be straight with you."

He waited to make sure he had Dimitar's full attention before continuing.

"The thing is that I had always presumed that you had stolen the picture and either kept it yourself or sold it and made off with the proceeds. I assumed that was why the shop was closed. That was why I tried to come and find you there. All these years I have believed that you conned me. I even thought that Sophie was in on it and that you had asked her to show me the town that morning to distract me so that I would not suspect what you were going to do. The story you have just told me, the true story of what happened, never even occurred to me as a possibility."

Dimitar could clearly see Peter's evident discomfort and he interrupted, smiling broadly before allowing himself to laugh for a moment.

"How could you have imagined that I would die like that? You must not be so hard on yourself. I probably would have thought the same myself if the boot had been on the other foot, as you English say."

"That might be the case. Nevertheless, I want you to know how very sorry I am. Can you possibly forgive me for thinking so badly of you?"

Dimitar smiled again and, as he did so, exhaled loudly as if he had been holding his breath and could do so no longer.

"Peter, I reckon that you are well aware by now of the importance of forgiveness. You must realise that I am delighted to forgive you because I know how much it is going to help you. You must not think about this thing again until perhaps one day you are summoned back here to meet Sophie, that is," he said, looking at Archie with a mischievous grin. "Forgiving makes me feel great and to be honest with you, the thoughts you had were quite understandable. You could not have expected me to literally disappear off the face of the earth."

Peter offered his hand in gratitude and Dimitar immediately grabbed it warmly, pulling Peter into a hug. The two men embraced then released. Peter sighed deeply with relief.

"Thank you, Dimitar. I am beginning to understand what a waste of time some of the anger I have harboured throughout my life has been and, most importantly, how misguided it was."

"That is good, my friend, and if Mr Souter doesn't mind me saying so, I suspect you are well on your way to working through the tasks before you in this place."

Peter glanced at Archie, hoping for an indication as to what he thought about Dimitar's theory. Unfortunately, there was not even a flicker from him as he caught Peter's eye, but he did get the distinct feeling that Archie was reasonably satisfied with how things had gone with Dimitar.

Chapter 17

With Archie's blessing, Dimitar and Peter completed two circuits of the enormous room, examining the art that had been created by those who had been there. Peter was pleasantly surprised by the quality of the work, and he recognised a few of the artists' names, including that of Madame Vermeiren, the Belgian lady who had won the silver medal at the Suresnes exhibition. Her picture was of a series of three-dimensional shapes which, with an ingenious use of light and shade and set on a flat background, appeared to advance towards the eye, leaving what was behind them to recede into the distance.

At the end they returned to look again at Dimitar's representation of Cowdray Park, and he explained to Peter that he had deliberately not painted the ruins for two reasons. Firstly, that they were special to Peter and no one else could possibly convey that connection as well as he, and secondly because even if he had tried, his skill was so inferior to Peter's that it would never be anything but a poor imitation.

Dimitar told Peter that he still thought about his painting and would occasionally recall small parts of it in his mind's eye. Naturally enough, Peter could remember every inch as clearly as the unforgettable day he had painted it. One thing they had in common, though, was a profound happiness that the painting was still being enjoyed by Joubert's family. For Peter, knowledge of the picture's continuing existence brought him an immense sense of relief. No longer did he have to imagine the awful fate that might have befallen it. It was safe and appreciated and that was all that he had ever really wanted.

Archie had not joined them on their tour of the gallery's exhibits but reappeared now from the corridor and approached the two men. As if previously primed to do so, Dimitar immediately took this as his cue to leave but not before he shook Peter by the hand and told him that he hoped to see him again soon. Peter assured him that he was equally keen that this should happen, and they parted, he thought, much firmer friends than they ever had been when they were alive.

"That seemed to go well," said Archie, once Dimitar was out of earshot.

"Yes, I reckon it did. To think I had held that grudge against him for so long and all the time he had died. I can't believe how stupid I was. You know I thought that he had almost certainly disappeared because of some shady underworld deal and even considered the possibility that he had been killed because he had crossed the wrong people. Whatever scenario I visualised, I assumed he was a crook, and that I was the victim of one of his scams. It never occurred to me to consider that he was just a hard-working man doing a decent job, and that there was another explanation. It's not an excuse, but because he always looked so flashy, it was too easy to assume he was a con man. I feel so ashamed that I didn't see the honest man he was and that he was genuinely doing his best for me. I am glad I was able to be straight with him and that he forgave me for thinking the worst of him."

"Yes, that's a wonderful thing, isn't it? I know Joan will be particularly pleased because she understands better than anyone how much that picture meant to you," said Archie, ignoring Peter's attempts at mitigation and instead pinpointing the most important thing he had said.

To this point, it had not occurred to Peter that Archie might have met Joan, but it made sense now he thought about it. His casual reference to her inferred that not only had a meeting taken place but that she had perhaps confided in him, possibly as much as he had himself.

"Have you spoken to her about it?" he asked.

"No, I haven't, Peter, but one of my colleagues who helped her while she was here was able to tell me about some of their discussions."

Peter wanted to know what else Archie's colleague had said, but it did not seem quite right for some reason. This was Joan, the woman he loved and knew so intimately, and he was sure that if there was something she wanted to tell him, she would have done it while they were alive. Furthermore, if she had moved on from this place, she had clearly resolved any problems for herself, so it was not relevant anyway. Besides, there was probably some confidentiality code that Archie was obliged to follow, so he decided not to pursue the matter.

"Incidentally, while you and Mr Zhechev were looking around the gallery, you might have noticed that I disappeared for a while," Archie said, implying that an explanation was probably in order.

In fact, Peter had been so engrossed in the art and his conversation with Dimitar that he had not been aware of Archie's absence.

However, he did not want to appear rude and in reply offered a non-committal nod accompanied by a close-mouthed 'mmm' which he felt conveyed the right level of acknowledgement. Archie was not easily fooled but appreciated Peter's efforts to spare his feelings.

"Yes, well, I received word that the people I would like you to talk to next have arrived, so I wanted to make sure all was well with them," he explained while rooting deeply in his left ear with his index finger for something that made him shudder a little as he spoke.

People plural? thought Peter, but before he could ask anything about the specifics of the meeting, Archie had more to tell him.

"There aren't too many more things that you need to do here, and I suspect you might have worked out who you are likely to see, but just to caution you if you don't mind, you are going to need an open mind for this next encounter." He inspected his finger before rubbing presumably a stubborn piece of wax that he had retrieved between it and his thumb. Satisfied that it had either magically disappeared, or more likely fallen on the floor, he continued with a summary of Peter's progress so far.

"I feel sure you are going to be fine, though, so please do not be concerned. Based on the way you have dealt with some of the surprises sprung on you, it seems you have grasped the importance of forgiveness both for the person receiving it and the person granting it."

Peter reflected for a moment, composing his reply in his mind before speaking.

"I know, because you have told me, that forgiveness is extremely important. More than that, you have explained that it is vital in terms of getting into Heaven, or at the very least, moving on from this place."

He looked hopefully at Archie for either confirmation or contradiction of the validity of his assessment. When neither was offered, and Archie inserted his finger in the other ear, presumably for the same purpose as before, he thought it best to carry on with his own synopsis.

"You have certainly helped me to realise how good it feels to forgive someone, and I want to thank you for that. Getting rid of the burden that has been weighing you down is such an incredible relief, but when someone forgives you, the picture becomes complete. You realise the benefit of both because when you have offended or harmed someone else and they decide to overlook it, the feeling of wellbeing doubles. You feel content yourself, but you also appreciate their fulfilment."

"That's great to hear, Peter," said Archie, suddenly abandoning his aural excavation. This was very good – this man was beginning to understand.

"I don't know if you realise, but the importance of forgiveness is inherent in almost every religion on Earth. You asked God as a Christian at an Anglican school when you said the Lord's prayer to 'Forgive us our trespasses as we forgive those that trespass against us.' You learnt, I am sure, from your studies that as he was dying, Jesus asked God to forgive those who crucified him. Forgiveness is embedded in the religion that you have been taught, just as Buddhists believe that the anger experienced when you are unable to forgive harms your wellbeing or Karma. Mahatma Gandhi, a Hindu, was persecuted horribly, but instead of returning the hostility, he chose a path of peace and reconciliation in order to achieve his aims. Many religions believe in a formal atonement for their sins on Earth and this kind of acknowledgement for one's wrongdoings is appreciated by God. However, remember that God is merciful and what you do in this place is hugely significant. Forgive others, and God will choose to forgive you for your wrongdoings even though he knows that they have happened."

Archie watched Peter carefully and had the distinct impression from his expression that he had heard a version or perhaps a number of versions of this idea before. He definitely did not want to preach to him; that was not his job. It was, however, important that while he was here, Peter had a good understanding of the place's relevance. For now, though, he had made his point and that was, he considered, probably sufficient.

"I must apologise, Peter – I get a little overenthusiastic sometimes," he explained.

Then, thinking it best to avoid further theological discussion, he suggested that perhaps it might be sensible for them to move on to the next meeting. Peter had in fact been listening intently and had some follow-up questions about the forgiveness of major sins. On reflection, though, since he was fairly sure nothing he had done would be considered as being in this category, and because he desperately wanted to see Joan, he decided that he would save these for another time.

"It's about a ten-minute walk, but to save us time I have arranged some transport for us," Archie explained, motioning towards a large wooden door partially hidden behind a life-size bronze statue of a young man and woman dancing.

Peter had been fascinated by the statue and studied it for some time with Dimitar. It reminded him of the evening he and Andy had spent at the golf club and his first dance with Joan, even though the sculpted figures bore no physical resemblance to either of them. He had noticed the door at the time but thought little of it as he was well aware by now that corridors, rooms and doors had a habit of appearing and disappearing here.

As he ambled past the bronze, he took a last appreciative look at the intricate detail of the smiling faces of the couple. Then, realising that he was in danger of being left behind, he hurriedly had to quicken his pace to catch up with Archie, who was already at the exit. Unlike most of the doors, which were on hinges, allowing them to swing backwards and forwards, this one was fixed and needed to be opened with a key, which Archie had imperceptibly produced from his pocket. Peter was just in time to hear the lock click and see him pulling the heavy door open. Curious as to what was beyond, he strained his eyes, gazing into the gloom ahead. All he could establish with any certainty, though, was that it was pitch black on the other side, the light from the gallery managing to illuminate only the area immediately around the threshold.

Fortunately, and to Peter's amazement, as they entered the room, a series of lamps suddenly burst into life, presumably operated by some kind of sensor, providing enough light for them to see each other. Once Peter was safely inside, Archie leant in front of him, pulled the door shut and then, somewhat unexpectedly, locked it behind them. As Peter became accustomed to the comparative darkness, he could see that the room was vast with passages, some lit, others unlit, diverging from it at irregular intervals. It was as though they had reached the middle of a maze and now needed to find their way out. Making sure that Peter was following, Archie headed to the right, ignoring the first two passageways they passed. When he reached the third, with Peter a couple of paces behind him, he stopped and turned to face the entrance. As he did so, the uncarpeted walkway ahead brightened and a long line of torches, their flames flickering against the walls on which they were positioned, stretched ahead in front of them. The floor, Peter could see, like the walls, was made of stone. It was cold and the air was filled with an oppressive haze of smoke that was emanating from the torches. It felt to Peter as though they were in a medieval castle and a slight tremor of fear entered his body as he thought that these could even be the dungeons. Perhaps Archie was intending to give him a taste of another world, more like Hell, as part of his 'journey'.

For the first time since they had entered this new location, Archie spoke.

"We could walk from here, Peter, as I said, but it's quite a way and you have probably noticed that the air is not the cleanest."

Without waiting for a response, he entered the passage and turned immediately to his left where there was a recess in the stone wall. As Peter peered more closely into the dimly lit space, he saw what looked like the wheels of a vehicle of some sort. Confused for a second or two, he watched as Archie approached what he could now see was a small two-seater car not unlike a golf buggy.

"It'll be much quicker and easier if we use this. Unless, that is, you would rather walk," he added with a playful smirk.

"No, no, I'm sure you are right," Peter replied, climbing expectantly into the passenger seat next to him.

On first inspection, it was not clear what was powering the vehicle as there seemed to be very few controls and no ignition for a key that Peter could see.

"All set?" asked Archie, simultaneously pressing a small green button that protruded from the central console between the two seats.

Inaudibly the car lurched slowly forward from its position in the alcove and then, like a boat from a slipway, shot forward and started to move steadily along the smoky passage. The floor was extremely uneven, but Peter's assumption that the ride would be a bumpy one was soon proved to be unfounded as the vehicle weaved its way effortlessly through the winding tunnel. He stuck his head out, over the door, and looked at the wheels, which were moving exceptionally fast but apparently not making contact with the holes and imperfections of the stone floor. He could not work it out. It was as though there was a layer of something invisible just above the floor that was providing them with a completely smooth ride. He presumed the vehicle must be some kind of hovercraft, but the engineering and the mechanics of their movement were beyond him. Before he could ask any of the questions that came to mind, Archie suggested he might be safer if he did not try to lean out again as there was a stretch coming up where they would be going very close to the wall. No one was steering, so whatever force was propelling them along the passage was either being controlled remotely or their journey had been pre-programmed. In places the ceiling became lower and Peter instinctively ducked to avoid decapitation. This amused Archie, who remained motionless throughout, no doubt very familiar with the route they were taking, and Peter felt some sense of security much like the comfort one obtained from watching the unworried conversations of cabin crew during aeroplane turbulence.

The trip had lasted no longer than a minute, two at most, when they rounded a bend and the vehicle slowed, gradually coming to a halt. Archie opened his door and climbed out.

"Just a quick warning, Peter, you might find your legs are a little wobbly for the first few steps. Best to hold on to the side of the car for a moment."

Peter stepped out and, sure enough, felt his legs give way slightly just as Archie had predicted. They were like a disobedient jelly sliding around on a plate, and he had to grab the door to keep himself upright. It reminded him of the sensation he had experienced following a particularly hair-raising roller coaster ride with his son Tom during a holiday they had taken one year in Blackpool.

"That's the way. That usually happens when you aren't used to this type of travel. It'll be okay in a few seconds." Sure enough Peter was soon conscious of the strength returning to his limbs and was sufficiently confident to gingerly release his grip on the car door and stand unaided.

"It's just through here when you are ready, please, Peter," Archie said as he wandered over to a small opening in the wall opposite them.

Pleased that his legs now seemed to work properly, Peter followed, cautiously placing one foot in front of the other as he became used to walking again.

Archie passed through the arched opening in the stone wall and Peter could see that there was light coming from inside. As Peter stepped through, he became aware of the distant sound of music playing. Assessing his surroundings, he could see that it was much the same as the passage they had just left. The only difference was that the air seemed a little warmer in here and it was much less smoky. Archie approached a big oak door that instantly reminded Peter of the enormous entrance to the chapel at Tinniswood Manor. Anticipating that he might require some help to open it wide enough for them both to enter, Peter moved closer to offer his assistance. Archie knew what he was thinking and gave him a broad smile before flamboyantly flinging the door wide open with apparent ease.

"I think you understand by now, Peter, that not everything is quite as it appears." He chuckled. Then he continued in a business-like fashion, "If you could just follow me, please, they are just in here."

As he passed it, Peter pushed at the door a little, curious to see what it was made of. To his astonishment it was solid oak, just as he had assumed initially, and although he pushed hard and even leant on it with his full weight, he found that he was unable to move it an inch. He shook his head with incredulity.

The floor of the chamber they had entered was covered patchily with clusters of patterned rugs of different shapes and sizes. Weirdly, the apparently haphazard manner in which they were scattered worked well. Peter wondered if they had interior designers here or were bothered by things like feng shui, but he decided that now was probably not the time to express his curiosity in words. The room was large, easily the size of a tennis court, he calculated, and at the far side he could see a long wooden table with benches either side. He thought, from this distance, that it looked as though it was laid with plates of sandwiches. As the two men moved nearer, this suspicion was confirmed, and Peter was particularly pleased to see that in addition there were some small cakes covered in delicious-looking butter icing.

On one of the benches sat an elderly man dressed very ordinarily in a pair of dark grey slacks and a nondescript light grey pullover. Seeing Peter and Archie enter, he rose from his seat to greet them, and Peter noticed there was another, much smaller stone arch behind him which presumably led to a further room. The music Peter had heard outside was undoubtedly coming from there. He strained, but through the thick walls, he could only make out the sound of a piano being supported by a variety of other instruments which he could not quite distinguish.

Peter turned his attention back to the man in front of him and immediately froze in horror as he looked closely for the first time at his face. He was much thinner now, but the plump rolls of flesh around his jowls told of the barrel of a man he had once been. Quite unnecessarily for either party, Archie effected the formal introductions.

"I am sure you remember Mr Beaumont," he said, turning breezily towards Peter.

Peter stared at Beaumont, undecided as to whether the best course of action would be to reach over and punch him as hard as he could immediately or to tell him what he thought of him first and then hit him. He could feel the anger boiling up inside as he took half a step closer to the man who had forced himself on Joan all those years ago.

Aware of the potential confrontation, Archie moved nimbly alongside him and touched his arm lightly in an attempt to defuse the situation and remind him where he was. Then he tactfully suggested that Peter might be more comfortable taking a seat on the bench opposite Beaumont. Remembering his warning that this meeting would be difficult and pleased that he was concerned sufficiently about his welfare to have provided it, Peter's anger gradually dissipated and was replaced by curiosity. At the same time, he was struck by the realisation that this meant that Beaumont was also dead. He was at least twenty years older than Peter, so it was to be expected, he thought to himself, regaining his composure and starting to focus on the inevitable conversation between them that was to follow.

Peter duly took a seat, aware that he was nevertheless still glaring in disgust at the man who sat across the table. Two plates, one of which looked like it held cheese and pickle sandwiches, formed an incongruously inviting barrier between him and his foe. A jug of water from which a glass had been poured for each of them completed the barricade, ensuring that peace would at least be given a chance.

Mindful of the tension, Archie spoke first.

"Peter, you were good enough to confide in me the details of the evening that you and Mr Beaumont last met, and you also explained how angry you were then, and afterwards, about what happened."

Looking towards Beaumont now in order to include him in the conversation, he continued.

"I don't need to remind either of you about the importance of forgiveness. I believe you have both had adequate opportunity to form an appreciation of that. It is for this reason that Mr Beaumont has been asked to return here to see you today, Peter."

He certainly had Peter's attention and his reference to that night gave him some justification inwardly for feeling as incensed as he did by the sight of his old boss.

"Quite simply, Peter, I would like you to listen to Mr Beaumont's account of the night and the circumstances leading up to it in the hope that you can reconcile any differences that exist between you. As you can see, refreshments have been provided in case you are hungry and I am going to be close by should either of you need to speak to me."

With that he walked slowly towards the doorway which was about ten feet behind Beaumont and peered in as though checking on something. Returning his attention to the two men, he remained leaning there against the wall. Perhaps, Peter thought to himself, he was simply enjoying the music.

Beaumont took a sip of water before he spoke.

"As Mr Souter has explained, Peter, the main reason I am here is to apologise to you for what happened that night and its effect on you and your wife subsequently. I hope when you hear what I have to say, you might be able to forgive me for my actions."

Peter thought this was a reasonable start. He had already acknowledged that what he did was wrong, which was something. However, he was not going to let him off the hook easily. This would have to be good if he was going to be able to begin to forgive his actions. Peter remained impassive, trying to subdue the animosity that was once again beginning to build inside him at the thought of what this man had done to Joan.

"I am asking for your forgiveness for the completely unacceptable manner in which I conducted myself that evening when you, Joan and the others came for dinner. It was boorish and my behaviour was thoroughly disgraceful and I can only apologise and hope that you are able to show me the same generosity of spirit that you were renowned for in the office. I know that I scared Joan and you must have wanted to kill me right there and then for what I did."

There was a pause, during which Peter weighed up his anger against the purpose of being there and his ultimate goal of being with Joan again.

"Okay, Beaumont, I intend to try because of what Mr Souter has said, but you are going to have to do better than that, I'm afraid."

He was annoyed by Beaumont's use of Joan's Christian name, the informality suggesting a casualness that seemed entirely appropriate. This irritation spilled over, and he could not resist a barb of his own, which he knew was more bravado than truth.

"Incidentally, how do you know she was scared? She was a much stronger woman than you think. It would have taken more than the attentions of a beast like you to frighten her."

Beaumont was relieved that the aggression he had seen rising in Peter had at last been released a little and responded calmly to the question in the hope that what he said next would reduce his former employee's agitation.

"The reason I know that she was scared was not as you might assume that I had seen it in her eyes at the time. I admit, much to my regret, that I was so out of control I did not notice it then. No, it was not that. The reason I understand how frightened I made her feel is because she has told me."

Peter screwed up his face to show both confusion and contradiction, looking over to Archie as if appealing to a tennis umpire for an incorrect line call. Joan had been so stoic about Beaumont's attack on her and had never wanted to admit how awful it must have been for her.

"How on earth do you know that? Did she tell you while you were pawing at her?"

Beaumont winced at the recollection of the assault before composing himself and responding in the same controlled tone of voice.

"No, Peter, she did not. The reason I know is that she told me during the conversation she and I had some time ago when she sat precisely where you are now."

It took a few seconds for the full weight of this admission to sink in. Hesitantly Peter began to put the pieces together in his mind as he realised that Joan and Beaumont must have spoken after her death. Beaumont could see that Peter was struggling and decided to confirm the conclusion Peter was gradually reaching.

"Yes, Peter, I spoke to Joan when she passed through this place. We discussed the evening and how she felt, and I asked her to forgive me just as I am asking you. I have also asked the same of some of the other unfortunate women who I hurt in that way. Joan told me how my actions had also made you leave the firm and about the impact that the whole affair had on your lives and those of your family. She was exceptionally understanding and kind, much more so than my conduct deserved."

"Joan is one of the kindest people I ever met," Peter responded indignantly, "but surely you are not trying to tell me she forgave you just like that."

"Actually, Peter, she did forgive me, which I suspect is why she has been able to move on from here. She understood once I had explained everything to her."

Peter shook his head slowly in disbelief. It could not possibly have been as straightforward as he was making it sound.

"Come on then, let's hear it, Beaumont. Tell me how you can in any way justify such vile behaviour. I'm all ears."

Beaumont remained stony-faced despite being disturbed by Peter's use of the word vile, determined that he should hear the truth.

"Thank you, Peter," he said, suitably chastened. He took another sip of water followed by a deep intake of breath before he began to speak again.

"Something I suspect you don't know, because I never really spoke about it much, is that I was born in Germany not long after the end of World War One. My father was a civil servant who had been transferred to work at the British embassy in Berlin in the early '20s. It was obviously a pretty turbulent time, as you can imagine, but he had only been there a short while before he met my mother, who was working as a nurse in one of the city's hospitals. They fell in love, married, and the following year I was born. In many ways my childhood was extremely privileged because of my father's work, but we were also treated with suspicion as a family. The British were not thrilled that my father had married a German, and the Germans were, naturally enough, hostile towards the British, who they blamed, along with the other Allied powers, for the unreasonable way in which their country was treated when it lost the war. My parents adored me but were keen that not only should I speak both English and German but that I also had an understanding of the culture and history of both countries of my heritage. By the end of the decade, Germany had gone through a huge amount of change, and it was clear by the beginning of the '30s that Hitler and the National German Workers' Party were looking to change society fundamentally. My parents did not like Hitler, believing, unlike most of the population, that he was dangerous and certainly not the positive influence he purported to be for Germans. Consequently, when, in 1931, my father was offered the opportunity of a promotion in London, he took it, and we came to live in England."

Peter did not know about Beaumont's family and childhood, and, interesting though it was, he wondered when he was going to get to the point. He was also hungry and was finding it increasingly difficult to sit in front of the cheese and pickle sandwiches any longer without trying one. He reached forward, took two and put them on his plate.

"You don't mind, do you?" he asked belatedly. "I am listening, but I think if I don't eat something, I might pass out."

"Not at all,'" Beaumont replied, putting a couple on his own plate. He was pleased that Peter was prepared to listen, but his own hunger would have to wait a while.

"Things went well for us. School was enjoyable, I met my English grandparents, and we lived in a lovely neighbourhood. Then, of course, in 1939 everything changed. I joined up like most men of my age and, at the end of my initial training, was told to report to London. It was all a bit 'hush hush', but I learnt quite soon that I was known because of my father. After a few weeks I was told to present myself at an address in Baker Street where I was informed that my ability to speak German fluently could be useful to a new organisation that had been formed, known as the Special Operations Executive. I won't bore you with all the details, but suffice it to say, I was sent on a number of unusual missions, mostly in Germany, with the aim of acquiring intelligence about the German war effort."

He took a large bite of one of his sandwiches then finished it with a second, washed it down with a gulp of water before, suitably sustained, he continued. He did not notice that Peter was now listening much more attentively.

"On one such mission, I was parachuted behind enemy lines in order to obtain intelligence about the position and strategies being adopted by the German army. I was accompanied by an Austrian prisoner of war who wasn't a fan of the Nazi regime which had annexed his fatherland. Our mission was to pose as members of a German battalion. The German army was not in a good way by that time. The soldiers were hungry, tired and overworked. The flagging troops were a huge problem for them, and they had for some time employed amphetamines as a means of reducing pain and increasing the length of time their men could go without sleep. The drugs also made the men more aggressive. Hitler soon realised he could turn men into killing machines who lacked any morality or conscience, which might help them to understand or have remorse for the atrocities they were ordered to perform. When we received our meagre food rations, we were also given the amphetamines. When able, I concealed them, but usually I had to take them to avoid suspicion. We were forced to march for days sometimes without sleep, so through necessity I needed them sometimes so that I didn't collapse when all the Germans around me were full of energy.

"The mission went well – so well, in fact that it was extended, and I spent almost a year traipsing backwards and forwards across Germany with the battalion. During this time, I continued taking the amphetamines, along with my 'comrades'. Towards the end of the war, I was pulled out, for my own security. I was shipped back to England but, although considerably safer, I began to find life without the amphetamines extremely difficult. I had become reliant on them and, still having quite a quantity secreted, I continued to take them. Unfortunately, my supply only lasted about a month, at which point things became even harder for me. I told my commanding officer, who was as sympathetic as he could be, bearing in mind all the other things he had to deal with, including soldiers who were much worse off than me. The army could only provide limited help, which was not of much use in my predicament. Despite the horrible effects of doing so, I decided to try and wean myself off them. It worked for a while, but unfortunately the amphetamines I had been given were incredibly addictive, and I continued to crave the feeling of power and euphoria they gave me. I managed to find a man who could supply me with what I needed and through him I was able to keep taking them. They made me aggressive and violent and occasionally completely out of control, but I was hooked and kept taking them for years.

"Then came the '60s when all sorts of new substances were readily available. I abused many of them just to survive each day. On one occasion I took so many pills that my heart nearly stopped, and I was rushed into hospital. The consultant managed to revive me and recommended a programme to get me off them. It was the ultimate cold turkey scenario. Complete deprivation and close monitoring. It was hard and the effects on my body were horrendous. After three months I was discharged, apparently cured. They had done their best given the resources available, but I knew that the craving inside me was still there, and I had to constantly fight to suppress it."

The second sandwich disappeared as quickly as the first and Beaumont pressed on with his story.

"I had found it difficult to build close relationships for the obvious reason, but when I met my wife, it seemed like I had turned a corner. It transpired, I am afraid to say, that I was mistaken. I started taking amphetamines again and although I tried hard to give them up, I could not do it. Sometimes I managed a few weeks, occasionally a month.

Often, in order to compensate for the lack of a high from the drugs, I would drink heavily. It wasn't the same though. Instead of making me more alert, it had the opposite effect. If I had a skinful on a Saturday, I would usually sleep most of Sunday, just so that I was in a fit state to return to work on Monday.

"Like most addicts, I was very ingenious when it came to hiding my problem. I suppose my army wartime training also helped with that. Eventually, though, I became aware of the talk in the office, which I am sure you heard too. I was unpleasant, abrupt, aggressive, not at all the sort of person you or anyone else wanted for a boss. The amphetamines occasionally also made me somewhat over-amorous towards women."

He stopped for a moment as if considering what he had said.

"That's rubbish, sorry, Peter. I became a beast. I couldn't stop myself. You must have seen the number of women who left the firm in a hurry."

He looked across at Peter, who was nodding thoughtfully to indicate that he did.

"Almost all of them left because of me. I have apologised to one or two who have been here, but there is still quite a number that I will need to see in the future."

Hoping that Peter could show him some sympathy, even though he was not particularly convinced himself that he deserved it, he decided to talk about the night he and Joan had come for dinner.

"The afternoon of the party you attended at our house, I tried not to take anything but, and this is not an excuse, the conversation at dinner was so boring it almost sent me to sleep."

"Ah yes, I remember that myself," Peter interjected helpfully. "Who would have thought that David Greig and his wife could talk for so long about their holiday in Skegness, let alone bring all those photographs with them?"

"Quite," smiled Beaumont, grateful for the brief humorous interlude. "Before the dessert was served, I slipped out to the toilet and took a pill. I don't remember making a conscious decision to do it, but sometimes the cravings just overcame me. By the time I was left alone with Joan, I had become a different person. The life of the party, the man no woman could resist and who was free to do anything and everything, regardless of the consequences. At least that is what the drugs made me believe. I cannot tell you how bitterly I regret what I did and the damage I caused to all those concerned."

Peter needed to think. This was certainly a compelling story, but Beaumont had acted so disgracefully time and time again, forcing himself on women and treating his male employees like they were dirt. Could he forgive him for all of that? After all, he had made the decision to keep taking the amphetamines. But had he? Peter had never been addicted to anything, so how could he truly appreciate the compulsion that overtook an addict? What made a gambler keep placing bets even when they had no money, what made an alcoholic keep drinking despite the damage it was wreaking on their body? The man sitting opposite him, nervously taking a bite of another sandwich and sipping water, was presumably the real Beaumont. A reasonable man by the sound of it, who certainly bore no resemblance to the bully Peter remembered. Was this the man he would have been had he not become hooked on drugs? Probably – based on what Peter knew of this place. He had not been born an addict, and even if he were, was that really his fault? In Beaumont's case addiction had overpowered him while he was fighting to defeat one of the most evil regimes in history. Whatever happened as a result, despite his best efforts to 'get clean', there was no getting away from the fact that the change which created the monster he became occurred because he was a good man doing a very brave thing for the ultimate benefit of so many. Peter wondered if Beaumont had been so candid when he apologised to Joan and concluded that he must have been. This was not a place for deceit or half-truths, so of course she knew everything. Not only that but she, the person who had been most hurt, had chosen to forgive him.

Peter drained the water that remained in his glass to signify that he had reached a decision.

Beaumont stared at him through piggy eyes, his jowls appearing to wobble slightly of their own accord as he apprehensively awaited the verdict. Even Archie straightened discernibly from his slouching position against the wall in anticipation.

"I was warned that I would encounter difficulties with some of the meetings Mr Souter had organised for me and now I can see what he meant. What you did was so grotesque on the face of it and it affected my family so much that I could never have conceived of forgiving you while I was alive. Now, of course, things are different, and we are encouraged to forgive while we are here. It's easy to go into these meetings with the intention of forgiving just so that we can progress to wherever we go next, but that is dishonest, and I suspect Mr Souter and his colleagues would be able to detect this tactic in some way."

Archie avoided eye contact, looking at the floor as if forensically examining a minute crack which had formed miraculously in the stone that had been laid there many centuries ago.

"However, your story is, I can see now, an extremely tragic one and the man that attacked my wife is neither the man you were before the war or indeed during it. I can see too that he is also not the man sitting opposite me now. Mr Beaumont, I do forgive you for what you did, not because I think I should or because of your past heroics but because I want to and also because I honestly believe that you deserve to be forgiven."

He spoke the last sentence looking directly at Beaumont, emphasising how earnestly he meant what he said. He could see now the tears in Beaumont's eyes and he understood then if he had not been certain before that this was indeed a good man who was worthy of his forgiveness. Peter reached across the table, awkwardly avoiding the plate of sandwiches, and grasped Beaumont by the hand. He had not been sure what it would feel like, but in fact it was just a normal hand – warm flesh with the moist residue of nervousness still lingering on the palm.

"Thank you. Thank you," said Beaumont, letting the tears fall onto his chubby cheeks from where they bounced a little before trickling towards his ample chin.

Peter was pleased and felt a contentment inside which invigorated him. So much so that he had almost forgotten about Archie, who had been observing events from a distance. Only now did he move from the archway and approach the table.

"Well done, gentlemen. It looks as though you have reached a very satisfactory resolution to an awkward situation. I think you should both congratulate yourselves."

They turned to him simultaneously with relieved expressions that confirmed beyond doubt that they were indeed in agreement both with him and each other.

"Do please continue to eat all you want. In fact, perhaps I will join you for a while," he said jovially.

Then tapping Peter on the shoulder as he swung his leg over the bench next to him, he added, "There is, however, one other thing that we do need to explain to you, Peter."

Then, allowing Peter a second or two to understand, he finished what he needed to say.

"It's about the person in the room next door."

Chapter 18

It took Peter a few moments to fully register what he had just heard, by which time Archie had helped himself to, and bitten into, one of the sandwiches. A small smudge of pickle stuck to the corner of his mouth and threatened to become embedded in his beard until a skilful flick of his tongue drew it back into his mouth. Beaumont decided that, as Mr Souter was temporarily incommunicado, he should pick up the reins of the conversation.

"The point is, Peter," he began tentatively, "you have heard about the events as they relate to my behaviour, but that is only part of the story. There are a few other things you need to know about that time and also the unfortunate events that followed."

Peter was vaguely aware that he was staring at Beaumont and that his mouth was betraying both his concentration and shock by remaining partially open. He made a conscious effort to shut it, checking for any escape of dribble with his index finger as he did so. He rationalised. There was something else, but he did not see how it could possibly affect him, or Joan for that matter. They had left the dinner party and soon after he had left Beaumont's firm. This thought comforted him a little and he relaxed. In the meantime, Archie was on his second cheese and pickle sandwich.

"The person Mr Souter is referring to, Peter, is in the room behind me," he motioned with a slight turn of his shoulder and head, "and also needs to talk to you."

So, there was more, thought Peter, and it sounded as though it did involve him after all.

"Shall we?" said Archie, suggesting, rather unfairly Peter thought, that it was him who had been waiting for them, and not the other way around.

"Yes, of course," Peter replied, still a little bemused.

The three men reverse-straddled the benches and extricated themselves from the table. Archie led Beaumont and Peter to the doorway. The music was clearly audible now, but Peter could still not quite place the tune.

"Would you like me to make the introductions, Mr Beaumont?" Archie asked without turning around.

"No, thank you, Mr Souter," Beaumont responded hastily. "I think on this occasion it's right that I do that," he added, pushing carefully past Archie and taking Peter with him through the entrance.

As they walked in, Peter noticed that the temperature was much cooler and the two torches on the walls provided far from adequate lighting for a room of its size. There was no furniture to speak of except a small side table on which stood a CD player, the source of the music, and four wooden chairs. One of the chairs was occupied by a frail-looking woman with slightly unkempt grey hair. As they approached, Peter noticed her keen, intelligent eyes and realised that she was in fact considerably younger than he had first estimated.

"Peter, I hope you remember my wife, Phyllis."

This suddenly makes sense, thought Peter. Naturally, she would be with her husband. She was obviously waiting for them to finish their chat.

"Yes, indeed," said Peter as cheerfully as he could manage. "How nice to see you," he added politely, glossing over the fact that they had actually only met once before, some forty or fifty years ago.

"Hello, Mr Davis," she said in a hoarse voice.

"Oh, please do call me Peter," he replied.

"Thank you, Peter, I will," she said, reaching across and turning off the music. "I do so love Beethoven and I don't get the chance to listen to him as much as I would like nowadays."

"Ah, I wondered what it was. I knew the tune, but I couldn't remember the piece or the composer."

"It's one of my favourites," she replied. "His Piano Concerto Number 5. You might know it better as the Emperor Concerto, although I believe it was actually dedicated to his patron and pupil Archduke Rudolf rather than the Emperor," she added unsentimentally.

"I am impressed. You obviously know your classical music."

Phyllis Beaumont smiled at him, taking a moment or two to enjoy the compliment. Her father had been a music teacher and both he and her mother were very accomplished violinists. Phyllis could play the instrument too, but her great love was the piano. As a youngster she had hoped to play professionally, but for one reason or another, that did not happen. Today, however, was not a day for romantic thoughts of that kind.

"Perhaps we should get on with things, gentlemen," she said. Then looking towards Archie for his permission to proceed, she continued to speak as the three men each took a seat.

"I am sure by now that you have heard my husband's story and I presume, since you have now come to see me, that you have been gracious enough to forgive him for what he did to Joan."

"Yes, that's right," Peter responded, wondering if the woman's use of his wife's first name meant that they too had met.

"I am pleased, thank you. He is a good man," she said as if this was a fact rather than something that was open to speculation. She took a deep breath, preparing herself for the account she had been brought here to deliver.

"Firstly, Peter, I need to tell you that, as you probably know, I was fully aware of my husband's addiction to amphetamines. He will have told you that despite his efforts and my attempts at support, he simply could not stop taking them. I have always loved him, but as you can imagine, life with him was extremely difficult. He was often aggressive towards me and regularly did to me what he tried with your wife and the many other women that he assaulted. As his wife, and because I loved him, I let him. On a number of occasions, he defiled me horribly. He hit me if I did not appear willing, and sometimes he hit me even when I submitted without a fight. I considered going to the police and, once or twice, told him I might. This normally led to a further beating and he convinced me that no one would believe me. Even if they did, he was close friends with quite a number of senior police officers who he was confident would ensure this was the case."

The words were delivered with little emotion – these were further facts that were part of the fabric of her life. Mr Beaumont stared at the floor in shame, unable to look anyone in the eye, least of all his wife.

"I am telling you this not because I want your pity or to excuse myself for my actions but simply so that you are aware of what drove me to them. I reached a point where my life was spent either anticipating or recovering from my husband's attacks on me. I just needed some respite from time to time so that I could recover a little. That is why I started to turn a blind eye to the attention he showed other women. I became aware that although it was hideously cruel, when he had his way with them, he left me alone. My life was better for a while. As time passed, I took the decision that in addition to condoning his activities, I would actively encourage them in order to protect myself. I started to plan and engineer scenarios in which he would be alone with a woman in order that she should be the object of his disgusting urges rather than me. That is what I did with your wife Joan and it is for that reason that I beg you to forgive me."

Peter looked blankly at her. He had to think about what she had said before he could voice any sort of opinion about what he had heard. Mrs Beaumont, sensing his hesitancy, took the opportunity to elaborate.

"I knew that my husband had taken a pill during the meal, of course. I was all too familiar with the signs of boredom that tended to come before and the brashness that followed. Some of the guests had left, as you might recall, and when you went to the bathroom, I distracted the others by insisting they go and see the magnolia and wisteria in the garden. That left only me, my husband and your wife in the living room. It was easy enough for me to make an excuse to go to the kitchen, leaving the two of them alone. I understand that you know what happened next, so I assume I do not need to repeat the details."

She paused and leant forward in her chair as if to reinforce the importance of what she was about to say next.

"I had completely lost my way, Peter, and in desperation I wilfully deflected my own pain and suffering onto others. I have tried to explain why I did this and, although I do not in any way seek to defend or play down my disgraceful subterfuge, I want you to know that I am now and always will be ashamed and profoundly sorry for those actions."

Beaumont raised his head, transferring his gaze from the floor, for the first time, to his wife as he did so. His face was once again streaked with tears, this time of tenderness and love for his wife. He pursed his lips, trying to force a smile at her supportively while resolutely attempting to maintain his composure. She saw him in her lateral vision but dared not catch his eye for fear of breaking down herself. She would not cry. She would not diminish the wickedness of her crimes by appearing weak.

Peter could see the pain in their expressions, and he began to comprehend how awful the whole business had been for them. It was patently obvious that they were ashamed, embarrassed and, most importantly, full of remorse.

"Thank you for explaining everything to me so honestly, Phyllis, it has helped me to understand things much more clearly. I can see that, like your husband, you are undoubtedly sorry for what you have done. I just have one question. Mr Beaumont mentioned his recent conversation with my wife and I wondered whether you too had met her again?"

"Yes, indeed. I had the opportunity to speak to her in much the same way as we are talking now."

"And can I ask, did she forgive you?"

Mrs Beaumont glanced at Archie, seeking his permission before answering. Seeing him nod his consent, she continued.

"Yes, she was extremely understanding, and she forgave me more readily than I suspect I deserved," Phyllis replied thoughtfully.

"I am pleased about that," said Peter, "because I can see, as she clearly did, that you are both profoundly sorry for your actions. Phyllis, please do not think about what happened again. I forgive you for your part in it. You must have been at your wit's end and, from what you say, it is clear to me that you were simply trying to survive."

She leaned back in her chair, exhausted by the ordeal of confession but at the same time enormously relieved to receive Peter's forgiveness.

"Thank you so much, Peter. That means more to me than I can adequately put into words. You and Joan are wonderfully kind people. I only wish we had met under more pleasant circumstances."

Peter beamed contentedly, pleased to have been the cause of some happiness for this woman who had evidently experienced so much difficulty in life.

He was a little startled when Archie rose abruptly to his feet, signalling, it appeared, that the meeting was over. He was even more taken aback when both he and Mr Beaumont were asked to return with him to the other room, as he had assumed Beaumont would be staying with his wife. No words were spoken to Mrs Beaumont as they left, although her husband, he noticed, managed to smile reassuringly at her before he was hastily ushered out. Bewildered by the whole incident, Peter was about to ask what was going on when Archie spoke.

"Mr Beaumont, thank you for your attendance. We have to leave now, but one of my colleagues will be along in a minute to take you back."

Peter expected Beaumont to object to this perfunctory attitude, and his impolite attitude when they had left his wife, but instead he replied rather meekly.

"Thank you, Mr Souter. I'll wait here." He offered Peter his hand and the two men shook with affection.

"Perhaps we will meet again," said Peter.

At this unexpected offer of friendship, Beaumont was momentarily overcome before he pulled himself together sufficiently to respond.

"I hope so, Peter." Then he turned and shuffled over to the table to reassume his seat on the bench, rubbing the moisture from his face as he did so.

Archie was already halfway out of the room and Peter had to walk quickly to catch him up. By the time he reached the doorway, Archie was in the car waiting for him. As Peter approached, he sought to pre-empt the inevitable questions by speaking first.

"I apologise if I seemed a little brusque in there, Peter. I would like to explain why before we move on if that is okay with you."

"Yes, please do," Peter said as he climbed into the passenger seat, still reeling from his uncharacteristic display of rudeness.

"Firstly, it is important for you to know that confidentiality is something we take very seriously here. As you are well aware, the matters we deal with are extremely personal, so in virtually all cases they are not discussed with anyone other than those involved."

"That's very comforting to hear," replied Peter with a hint of sarcasm.

"There are, however, certain exceptions to that rule and one of those is Mrs Beaumont."

"Mrs Beaumont?" Peter asked quizzically, emphasising the MRS. The thought of her being a special case intrigued him as much as it shocked him.

"Yes, Mrs Beaumont. You see, you have only heard part of the story. I cannot tell you everything, but I am permitted to disclose to you the reasons why she is being treated rather differently to her husband. No doubt you noticed this."

Peter was glad he had not imagined Archie's unusually discourteous manner towards her and the contrast of her being in a separate room without refreshments now began to make some sense.

"I had wondered," admitted Peter. "Please go on."

Archie readily continued, glad that Peter understood the situation, and returning to the story of the couple, he explained that Mr Beaumont had continued to take amphetamines and, as a result, his abuse of his wife had worsened considerably. He had struck her several times when he was unable to control the outbursts of anger that they prompted within him. On one of these occasions, he had bruised her face so badly that she felt unable to leave the house for over a week. Beaumont had always shown contrition subsequently, but as time went on, he became less regretful after such episodes. A relatively minor incident, if it could be described as such, during which he pinned her against a wall while squeezing her throat, was the last straw. As she collapsed to the floor, breathless and battered, waiting for the front door to slam, signalling that her husband had stormed out of the house, she decided that she needed to do something to put a stop to his actions.

The next day, she visited the library and researched the particular amphetamines her husband acquired most regularly from his dealer. Over the course of the next few months, the beatings continued, but determinedly she began to build up a cache of pills by moving a few at a time from the different locations where he kept them around the house. In order that he did not notice, she was careful to never take too many from one place in case this aroused his suspicions. The process took longer than she wanted, but eventually she calculated that she had all the pills she needed.

While her husband was at work one day, she went to her hiding place and retrieved the pills. To be absolutely certain, she added some which she had found by chance that morning and went into the kitchen to count them. She had a little over a hundred 25 mg tablets, which she had calculated should easily be enough. Having crushed them painstakingly into a powder using a pestle and mortar, she then set about preparing dinner, which she knew only too well her husband would expect her to have ready for him as soon as he arrived home from work.

Early that evening they sat down to dinner in silence and Mr Beaumont ate the vegetable soup to which his wife had liberally added the powder she had prepared just before serving. There had been some excess, which she tipped into the bottle of claret that had been breathing for the past few hours on the sideboard. He had already drunk two glasses of the wine and was nearing the bottom of his bowl of soup when the inevitable cardiac arrest that she had read about in the library books suddenly struck her husband. It was, as she had hoped, relatively quick, although from the grimace on her husband's face, not without pain. Within three minutes she had cleared away the bowls and glasses and disposed of the remains of the wine. She then half-filled two clean bowls with the soup that remained in the saucepan on the stove, ensuring that both spoons were immersed in it and one placed on the floor by her husband's body. She dropped her husband's bowl, making it seem as best she could that he had pulled it over as he had fallen from his chair. She was careful to cover the spoon in soup, knowing that her husband's fingerprints would not be on it. Only when she was satisfied with the crime scene did she telephone for an ambulance. By the time she replaced the receiver, less than seven minutes had elapsed from the time of her husband's collapse.

She knew it was not the perfect crime, but she hoped that the packets of pills concealed around the house with presumably only his and his dealer's fingerprints on them would deflect suspicion from her and towards the possibility of an overdose by an addict. His previous hospitalisation and time spent in rehabilitation would back this up, as would the injuries she had been careful not to conceal from her more talkative friends over the years.

It was only following a police investigation and coroner's inquest that the funeral was allowed to take place and Mrs Beaumont began to believe that she might actually avoid prosecution for her husband's murder. As the weeks passed, she found herself able to relax in a way she had been unable to for years. One evening, following a resting day at a health spa, she settled down contentedly to watch television. Just as she did, there was a knock at the front door. She remembered that her neighbour Doreen had promised to return a casserole dish she had lent her, so although a little exasperated, she felt confident that she would be able to deal with her and be back in her seat in time for the start of *Coronation Street*. So as not to waste time, she raced to the door and opened it eagerly. As she did this, she was violently pushed backwards with such force that she stumbled. Two burly men followed by a younger, skinnier man with spectacles burst into the hallway and shut the door behind them so that they could not be seen from the street. As she struggled to regain her balance, one of the men hit her hard with a baseball bat. She slumped to the ground in agony, her kneecap shattered. Pieces of bone protruded through the bloody mess that had previously been her leg. The thin man calmly asked her where her husband was but was not convinced that she was being honest with him when she hysterically responded that he was dead. A further thump with the baseball bat, this time to her torso, initiated the internal bleeding which would ultimately kill her. She heard them ask once more where her husband was before she lost consciousness.

Absurdly, her death provided indisputable corroboration of the story she had told the police. It seemed that the bespectacled assailant was in fact Mr Beaumont's dealer. Unbeknown to Mrs Beaumont, her husband was heavily in debt to the man both for the provision of his usual large supply of amphetamines and also for a significant quantity of cocaine which he had also apparently started to use. The dealer was a pragmatic businessman who knew Beaumont had a good job and always paid him even if a gentle reminder was occasionally required. His client, however, had taken liberties for too long this time and his debt needed to be settled. While Mrs Beaumont lay dying, they ransacked the house, taking jewellery, cash and anything else of value they could carry. The dealer appreciated the irony when he found a cache of pills he had sold Beaumont hidden in the cistern of the downstairs lavatory.

"The next morning, the Beaumont's cleaner, Mrs Bartlett, had quite a shock when she opened the front door and found her employer's battered body in the hall," Archie added by way of conclusion.

"So, she killed Beaumont and then, because of his drug addiction, was also murdered herself," said Peter, slowly assimilating all the facts.

"Yes, that's the long and short of it, Peter. I thought it was important that you knew how the story ended since you and Joan were caught up in it."

"Yes. Thank you," was all Peter could manage to say. It was an incredibly grotesque tale. He felt the most intense, almost painful, pity for the Beaumonts but simultaneously was enormously grateful that his problems in life by comparison had been so minor. He was tempted to ask why she had been detained in a separate room, but he decided that it would probably be best not to pry too much. In any case, he had formulated his own theory about her fate and did not really want to know any more.

As he considered the situation further, Peter remembered Beaumont's emotional reaction to what his wife had said during the meeting. Surely he should hate his wife for killing him, but that reaction and the look on his face did not seem to Peter to be the response of a man whose heart contained such animosity.

"Beaumont has forgiven her, hasn't he? For murdering him, I mean," Peter added by way of clarification.

Archie smiled. "I think you are beginning to understand how things work here rather well, Peter," he said, confirming that this was true without actually saying so. "Of course, you also know full well that I am not at liberty to share those details with you though, I'm afraid." He added another conspiratorial glance as he said this, which removed any doubt Peter had as to the accuracy of his assessment.

Something else, though, was still nagging away at Peter. At first, he was not sure what it was and then quite suddenly it came to him.

"But she hasn't been able to forgive him yet, has she? That's it, isn't it?" he persisted.

"As I say, Peter, it's not my place to divulge that information, I'm afraid."

Peter knew he was probably right, but before he could continue his questions, Archie silently started the car and they pulled away smoothly, leaving Mr and Mrs Beaumont behind them.

Peter was content with the knowledge that he had probably been a little closer to the truth than was comfortable for Archie and he certainly did not want to upset him by becoming impertinent. After all, he thought to himself, there was nothing he could do about the Beaumonts now and he probably ought to concentrate on what was expected of him rather than their business.

The return journey was taking much longer than their earlier ride, but Peter had long since resigned himself to the conclusion that all was not as it seemed in this place. The road ahead was well lit now, and the floor was no longer stone but a silver synthetic-looking substance that resembled lino but appeared soft like a thick carpet. Fascinated by its structure, he looked behind him curiously as they passed over it. He could see that there were ripples, which were presumably caused by the air, that gave it a liquid quality unlike anything he had ever seen. He estimated that they had been driving for at least ten minutes when, having just taken a tight turn to the right, they approached a dead end. To Peter's horror, instead of slowing to a halt, the car, which was not being controlled in any discernible manner by Archie, accelerated alarmingly.

Archie's expression did not alter at all as their speed continued to increase. They were now about fifty yards from the jagged rock that formed a huge barrier blocking the entire tunnel ahead of them. As they closed further, a thought randomly came to Peter's mind that the rock ahead resembled the cliff that he clambered down to get to the beach at Polzeath when he and Joan used to holiday in Cornwall.

When they were only ten or fifteen yards away, he shut his eyes to await the certain collision that was to follow, holding on, for some comfort, to the memory of the white Cornish sand where he taught his children to play cricket and the rock pools where they had searched for crabs.

A few seconds passed, but the horrific crash he had expected strangely did not transpire. He opened his eyes and could see that they were now in a high-ceilinged area that felt like a warehouse. As the vehicle slowed, Peter looked over his shoulder to see the rock through which they had driven seal itself up like the two doors of a London tube train closing for departure. Turning to ask Archie for an explanation as to what had just happened, he was greeted by a mischievous grin which his companion was unable to hide.

"I am sorry, Peter. I can never resist doing that." He sniggered. "The rock parts like a door as we approach. Seeing people's reactions is such fun."

Peter was less amused, but now that they were safe, his main feeling was one of relief rather than annoyance at Archie's practical joke.

"So, it's operated by a sensor then?" he added as calmly as he could, oblivious to the fact that injury from a potential crash would have been irrelevant to him since he was dead already.

"Yes, something like that," Archie said vaguely. "Come on, I've brought you here for a reason," he added in an attempt to erase the frivolity of his prank.

In front of them was a pathway leading to a single-storey building with a slate roof from which a small chimney protruded. It was constructed of the type of creamy white stone Peter had often seen in the Cotswolds during his time at university. It was neat and tidy with a central wooden door which had been painted blue, either side of which were rectangular windows. He wanted to know who or what was inside, but annoyingly the thick net curtains hung behind them prevented him from being able to see through.

After a quick glance across to check that Peter was following, Archie strolled confidently up the path, removed a very old-looking house key from his pocket and inserted it in the lock. The door creaked as he pushed it open and cheerfully invited Peter to enter first. Once inside, Peter found that the ceiling was much lower than he had anticipated as he took in his surroundings. To the right, two powder-blue upholstered armchairs were positioned to the sides of an unlit fireplace. Facing it was a settee covered in ivory linen with a brightly coloured floral throw draped over the back. A thin green carpet which showed considerable signs of wear covered the floor throughout. To the left was a pine table and chairs which no doubt served as a dining area. A stone wall divided it from another room that Peter could not see properly but which he assumed was probably a kitchen. His supposition was confirmed by the sudden appearance from the doorway that connected the rooms of a wizened old lady carrying a huge tray which held various items of crockery and a steaming pot of tea covered by a bright yellow woollen tea cosy. There was a jug of milk and a small pot of sugar lumps, spoons and a plate piled high with some extremely good-looking buns.

"Tea's good'n 'ot," she said without looking at either of them as she arranged the items carefully on the table, adding butter, knives and a pot of jam that had been concealed behind the crockery. "There's a plate of prupper Cornish saffron buns. 'Ems made with extra clotted cream, me own recipe," she added proudly, rubbing her palms dry on her apron. "Let me know if yer wan' anythin' else, my luvvers."

Archie smiled his thanks and the woman returned to the kitchen, leaving the two men to help themselves. He poured the tea as they each took a chair at the table. The saffron buns were delicious, and Peter was about to reach for a second when the progress of his outstretched arm was temporarily interrupted.

"I expect you are wondering why we have come here," Archie announced, breaking the silence.

In all honesty, Peter was not really thinking beyond his second saffron bun but decided it might appear rude if he did not agree.

"Yes, I must admit I didn't expect you to bring me somewhere like this," he replied, "but I'm getting used to that feeling," he added with a wry smile.

Archie did not return the humour, choosing instead to remain serious. "You will be meeting some more people here, Peter."

Peter was a little disappointed that there were going to be other guests and could not imagine who else Archie was going to wheel before him.

"Don't worry though. These meetings should be much simpler. Just a few 'I's to dot and 'T's to cross," Archie added quickly, attempting to dispel the concern on Peter's face.

"We are expecting a small number of visitors to discuss what are fairly minor matters with you. Nevertheless, it's important that you all have the opportunity to speak before we move on," he explained as cryptically as ever.

As if rehearsed, the end of his sentence was punctuated with perfect timing by a firm knock on the front door.

"That will be the first person," he said. "Why don't you take a seat over there?" he suggested, gesticulating vaguely in the direction of the armchairs.

Peter had taken a liking to the saffron buns and was rather disappointed to be parted from them, but Archie was on his feet now and moving towards the door. Not wishing to seem unprepared, Peter hurried across the room so that he was safely in one of the armchairs by the time the person outside was admitted.

The man who entered was tall and angular with a black moustache which was perfectly groomed. He was in his forties, Peter guessed, dressed immaculately in a blue pin-striped suit. His double-breasted jacket was done up neatly and drew the eye to the red tie and white shirt it framed. Peter instantly had a sense of recognition but could not put a name or a place to the individual that Archie was now beckoning towards the other armchair.

The spark needed to ignite his memory came with his introduction.

"I'm sure you remember Mr Galsworthy – he was an auctioneer."

That's it, thought Peter. This is the auctioneer who had sold his mother's diamond ring for him after her death. The details of their previous encounter came back to him as though it had occurred only yesterday. He recalled that Mr Galsworthy had provided an estimate of £5,000, which, in 1981, was quite a sum. There had been a lot of interest in the room, Peter remembered, but for some reason when the bidding was significantly below the estimate at a relatively meagre £3,000, he had banged down his gavel despite there being at least two other bidders with their hands in the air at the time. Peter had confronted him about this afterwards and had not believed him when he apologised, explaining that he simply had not seen the other bidders. He had no choice but to accept this as the sale had been legitimately concluded despite one of the ignored bidders confirming to him that she would have paid much more than the final sale price. Peter had long since wondered whether he was simply incompetent or if he had deliberately sold the ring cheaply to someone he knew, presumably for a cut of the profits. He was pondering whether his suspicions had any foundation when his thoughts were interrupted by Mr Galsworthy.

"Mr Davis," he began, "it's about the sale of the diamond ring you brought to my saleroom."

Pleased to see some recognition in Peter's eyes, he continued, clearly keen to tell him what was on his mind.

"No doubt you remember that you suspected I had acted dishonestly and that at the time I denied any wrongdoing." Peter nodded neutrally, which was enough encouragement for Galsworthy to proceed.

"I have been given the opportunity to come here today to explain to you why I ignored the other people who wanted to bid and sold your ring at a lower price than I might have."

"I see," said Peter, limiting his contribution to the conversation so as not to distract Galsworthy from his purpose. Even so, he felt vindicated that his suspicions had at last been confirmed.

"I am afraid that I was a bit of gambler back then, something my wife helped me to straighten out some years later. I had lost more than I could afford a few nights before the auction playing poker with a man who had the sort of friends one did not want to irritate, if you get my meaning. I have felt awful about what I did ever since, but a message was sent to me by one of his henchmen that, if I sold your ring, and I confess a number of other items that day, for a knock down price to a particular person, my debt would be waived. The offer was too good to refuse, not that I was given much choice in the matter. I was told that the auction house and all its contents would be burned to the ground if I did not cooperate. Of course, I did exactly as I was told, and my debt was expunged. Doing this got me out of a hole at the time, but I know it was wrong. I should have been strong enough to go to the police and face up to my stupidity, but I was not. I was scared and convinced myself that my indiscretion was a fair price to pay to be free of the threats of these people."

Mr Galsworthy looked across at Archie as if checking that he had been sufficiently detailed before concluding.

"That is the whole story, Mr Davis, and I can only hope that having heard it that you might consider forgiving my deceit and my weakness."

Peter considered things silently for a few moments. The ring had, in fact, not been his mother's favourite and he would have been very pleased with £3,000 for it had Mr Galsworthy not told him it was worth more. In addition, he had not been hard up for money, unlike the auctioneer, and had simply invested the proceeds, which were excess to his needs. As time passed, he had become quite philosophical about the incident. Neither he nor Joan much liked the ring either and were only too pleased to exchange it for what was a decent sum of money. Mr Galsworthy, on the other hand, had carried the guilt of his actions with him all this time and Peter knew only too well how that must have felt. His decision was therefore not a particularly difficult one to reach.

"Thank you for telling me that, Mr Galsworthy. I had suspected something odd was going on but resigned myself to it just being one of those things. Knowing and understanding the predicament you were in has clarified things considerably for me."

He paused, not for dramatic effect but so that Mr Galsworthy would believe that he was sincere in what he said next.

"I am only too happy to forgive you, Mr Galsworthy. Try not to think about it again."

Mr Galsworthy smiled with relief rather than joy and his shoulders, which had been tense and rigid, now relaxed as he sat back in his chair. "Thank you so much, Mr Davis, I appreciate your generosity very much."

Another one off each of our lists, Peter thought to himself with satisfaction. He returned the smile and was about to speak when Archie unexpectedly cut across him.

"Okay, Mr Galsworthy. We need not detain you any longer. Perhaps you could ask the next person to come and see Mr Davis."

Clearly appreciating that this was likely to be a fleeting visit, Mr Galsworthy rose to his feet, nodded to Peter and left, shutting the door gently behind him.

"Crikey," said Peter, "I see what you mean by 'simpler'. He didn't hang around, did he?"

"No, he did not," Archie smirked, "but we are on quite a tight schedule, so I don't want to encourage any unnecessary delays."

Over the course of the next half an hour, the small cottage was reintroduced to a variety of men, women and children from Peter's past, many of whom he had forgotten. Firstly, a young boy named Apton, wearing the familiar school uniform of Tinniswood Manor, admitted pouring half a bottle of ink into his satchel because he was jealous of Peter's academic ability. Apparently, he had been the top of the class prior to Peter's arrival and thought he would pay him back by ruining a number of his books and his PE vest, which were inside it at the time. Mr Bayford, a middle-aged school teacher wearing a white cricket umpire's coat, apologised for giving him Run Out when he was in fact safely back in his crease during a cricket match that he needed his school to win in order to qualify for a national cup competition. He explained that he had seen Peter as the main obstacle to his team's success and had let his partisan emotions get the better of him. Then Peter's neighbour of some fifteen years, Mr Sharma, told him that due to some imaginative rewiring by the previous occupants of the house, the Davises had been paying for his electricity all the time he and his family lived there. He should have said something, but by the time he realised, he could not afford to pay Peter the lump sum owed. Peter liked Raj Sharma very much; he was a cricket fanatic and he always enjoyed having that interest in common with his neighbour. Peter forgave all of them once he had heard their explanations and in Raj's case had to issue a counter apology for regularly adding garden cuttings to the Sharma's green waste bin for which the council charged Raj £100 a year. They laughed and had a quick chat about the most recent test series which had finished one-all between England and India before Raj left, telling Peter that he hoped to see him again soon.

"That's all from that list, Peter," Archie declared with satisfaction once Raj had left. "There's another short, slightly different group now."

Peter had given up trying to work out what was happening here and had resigned himself to going with the flow on the basis that he had little alternative.

"Okay – whatever you say."

Almost immediately there was a very loud and deliberate knock at the door.

"Perhaps you wouldn't mind answering that, Peter, while I go and see if Agnes could bring us some more tea."

With that Archie disappeared into the kitchen, leaving Peter no option but to answer the door. When he opened it, he saw a very slight-looking elderly man who could not have been more than five and a half feet tall. His grey hair was wiry, and he was wearing a pair of very thick-rimmed glasses.

"Hello, Davis," the man said as he confidently walked in. "You don't recognise me, do you?" he asked. The blank look on Peter's face confirmed the accuracy of his supposition. "No reason why you should, of course. We've both changed quite a bit over the past fifty-odd years."

The man headed towards the sitting area without hesitation while Peter shut the door, still none the wiser as to the identity of the gentleman. When he turned around, however, he stopped in his tracks as he looked over to where the man was now sitting. The strong spectacles he wore looked a little different and his grey hair, although retaining its coarse appearance, was now a mousey shade of brown. Peter was frozen for a moment, examining him as the realisation of his identity slowly dawned on him.

"Clive Mansell," he exclaimed. "I recognise you now," he added, bristling at the memory of the time they had met.

"I thought you might," Mansell replied just as Archie re-entered with Agnes following close behind, holding another tray of refreshments.

"Good, you've introduced yourselves," he said, keeping one eye on Agnes, who was carefully depositing the tray on the table. "Many thanks, Agnes," he called, although she seemed not to hear him.

"Peter, I think it's fair to say," he continued, "that when the two of you last met at university, you were not particularly kind to Clive."

That is an understatement, Peter thought to himself. At Oxford, Clive had been an apparently hapless weed of a young man who had tried to latch on to Peter's group of friends. He was studying law from what Peter could recall, so he was obviously clever. The problem was that Clive was, no doubt due to a regime of constant study that had gained him his university place, completely unaware of the ways of the world. Everyone poked fun at him and although Peter was not the worst by any means, he certainly had his moments. Clive had never drunk alcohol, so it was fun to spike his orange juice with vodka sometimes and then, when he passed out as a result, deposit him in someone else's bedroom or in the middle of the lawn of the college quad. On one such occasion they even put him in a boat and pushed it out onto the River Cherwell – in hindsight an incredibly stupid and dangerous thing to do, thought Peter.

Clive, though, was desperate to belong and would keep appearing when they went out, trying to be one of the gang for the night. At first, he annoyed Peter and his friends, but they soon realised they could have a lot of fun at his expense. One evening they were in the pub and a middle-aged woman started trying to chat up one of Peter's friends. She was not particularly attractive and the fact that she was at least thirty years older than any of them did not add to her appeal. What made it worse was that she was extremely drunk and was followed everywhere she went by the overpowering stench of fresh vomit, which they all assumed was her own. Unfortunately, as with many drunks, she was very persistent. Peter overheard the young man in question, a Scottish student of economics called Doug, asking one of the others how on earth they could get rid of her. They were pretty sure Clive was still a virgin, so Peter suggested that perhaps the perfect solution was to fix him up with the woman, thus getting rid of two birds with one stone. It was cruel and Peter regretted it later, but at the time, and after plying him with a few drinks, they had ensured Clive was suitably inebriated before taking him to the gents and leaving him in one of the stalls. They then sought out the ghastly woman and informed her that one of their friends was keen to spend some time with her and explained where he was. They said they would stand guard outside but that she would need to be relatively quick.

She was in with Clive for a little over fifteen minutes and no details were exchanged about what went on, although suffice it to say, she seemed very content with the outcome when she left. Clive was somewhat dishevelled, and one particular item of his anatomy needed to be carefully examined and returned to its usual home before they helped him back to his room. None of them, least of all Clive, precisely knew the extent of the violation he had been subjected to, but after that night he stopped appearing quite so frequently and instead relied on his usual regime of study for the provision of his evening entertainment.

"Yes, I certainly do owe you an apology, Clive, for the horrible way we all treated you," Peter said sheepishly. "I can't speak for the others, of course, but I have thought about you occasionally over the years and have always been embarrassed by my behaviour. I try to blame it on the exuberance of youth but never really succeed in convincing myself of the validity of that excuse. You were less worldly than the rest of us and an easy target, but we were, quite simply, bullies. I regret immensely my part in that bullying and have often worried about the damage we did to you."

It sounded sincere as Clive listened to each word intently, establishing in his own mind whether he felt Peter's level of remorse was sufficient. He still shuddered when he thought about his time at Oxford and in particular that cubicle in the toilets of the Rose and Crown.

"Actually, Peter, you and your friends probably did me a favour. I was weak physically, although I compensated for that with my intellect, of course. I didn't have any other friends either, so I decided to put all my efforts into ensuring that I left university with the best possible degree. In the legal world my outstanding qualifications bought me respect and in time my confidence grew. I landed a fantastic job and no one cared about my stature or the way I looked. All they cared about were my results. Of course, as a barrister I was highly paid. I had time to join a gym and although I was still small, I became physically much stronger. I successfully represented a large modelling agency in a huge case, which gave me great standing in the legal community. I also started dating one of the models I met on my many visits to their offices and the next year we were married. In fact, we were happily married for fifty-two years, had three wonderful children and five grandchildren. Another is on the way now, I understand."

"Wow, that is so good to hear, Clive. I am so pleased for you," said Peter, beaming widely. "It sounds like you had a pretty decent career too."

"Yes, I did. I won't bore you with the details, but as my reputation grew, it wasn't long before I became a recorder and, five years later, I was made a circuit judge. I was in that position for about ten years before being made a High Court judge and receiving the customary knighthood from Her Majesty the Queen. I was assigned to the Family Division where I worked very happily until I retired."

Peter was amazed by the calm and modest delivery of this information. What a fantastic life this man had forged for himself. Anxiety about his own underachievement threatened to grip him momentarily and he had to focus on the positive things he had done to push it to the back of his mind.

"So, I should call you Sir Clive then," he said.

"No, there's no need for all that, Peter, none of that stuff matters here. You didn't do too badly yourself, did you? A loving family and a good career. I have had the good fortune to meet your delightful wife Joan and I know she is looking forward to seeing you."

The thought crossed Peter's mind for a second or two that everyone seemed to have met Joan except him. Then he remembered there were rules he had to observe first. He chuckled inwardly. Of course they had all met Joan. She wasn't the type of person to be shy and unassuming. He had a surge of love for her so strong that for a few moments it overwhelmed his body with emotion. He had to gather himself so that he could speak again.

"I am so glad to have heard your story, Clive, and that our stupid antics and our callousness had no lasting effects on you. I hope you can forgive me, and the others, for our foolishness."

"Funny you should say that because I met Doug six months ago and did precisely that. I haven't seen any of the others yet, but I'll tell you what I told him. I thought about that time continuously throughout my life, but instead of letting it depress me, I used it to spur me on to greater things. I developed a steely determination because of those events and that is what helped me to be the person I became. In many ways I have you and the other reprobates who bullied me at Oxford to thank for toughening me up – I'm not sure I would have done it otherwise. How could I not forgive you?"

Peter felt the worry and the discomfort of those memories melt away at these words, releasing them from his body with the tears that now gently fell from his eyes. He was overwhelmed by the generosity of this man and overcome with a sense of relief that was completely unexpected. Any embarrassment that he might have felt at this uncontrollable emotional outpouring was banished completely by Archie's voice.

"Well done, gentlemen," he said. "It sounds to me as though we have reached a very satisfactory conclusion to this matter."

Both nodded their agreement very enthusiastically.

"Good," he said, looking at them in turn. "Now, who's for another of these delicious saffron buns?"

Chapter 19

A quarter of an hour later, the number of saffron buns left on the plate had diminished to one. The three men exchanged surreptitious glances, hoping that someone would say he was too full for another or perhaps suggest that they cut it into three. No such compromise, however, was forthcoming and Clive thought it was probably time for him to be on his way. He and Peter exchanged pleasantries and having also said goodbye to Archie and called out to Agnes, who did not answer, he left.

Archie spent the next ten minutes summarising Peter's progress, which gave their stomachs time to digest the avalanche of buns. He knew that there was one more important hurdle that Peter needed to cross, and he wanted to make him feel at ease before he mentioned it. He complimented him for the manner in which he had conducted himself, and they talked briefly about some of the people he had met. Despite his best efforts, it was all a little too contrived and he sensed that Peter could tell he was building up to an important announcement.

"There is, of course, the matter of your feelings of guilt about the days leading up to your friend Andy's death," he said as casually as he could, aware that this conversation would not be easy for Peter. "From what you told me, you were plagued for many years by your recurring dream about it and you know as well as I do that this was fuelled by the self-reproach you could not shed."

To his great relief, Peter seemed more cooperative than he had feared and his answer when it came was an honest one.

"Yes," he replied, sighing loudly. "Meeting all these people again who I encountered during my life has shown me that things are not always what they seem, but I just cannot shift the horrible burden I feel internally whenever I think about Andy."

"It's odd," Archie observed, "that a man who has such a skill for the logic of mathematics and learning can be so illogical over something like this. I'm sorry," he added, worried that he might have overstepped the mark. "I don't mean to sound rude, but when you decided to stay with Joan and her parents that day, it was impossible for you to anticipate what was going to happen to Andy. You must realise that surely?"

"I know you are right," Peter replied gravely, "but in my mind and my heart, logic does not seem to play a part for me where Andy is concerned. I have tried to rationalise it and tell myself repeatedly that I am not to blame, but for some reason it doesn't work. It's as though the guilt has become part of me, and I don't know that I will ever be able to let go of it."

Archie thought this was a rather good assessment of the situation, but it was important that Peter did not simply accept it as final. Perceptiveness of this kind was unusual in his experience, and he allowed Peter's words the space they deserved before he responded.

"What if I told you that it is imperative that you resolve this issue and that it is impossible for you to move on until you have at least dealt with the lack of logic behind your preoccupation?" he asked, dangling a carrot.

"I'd say I was afraid you might say something like that," replied Peter with a resigned grimace.

"Cheer up, Peter. You can do this; I am certain of that. You have achieved so much already since you died, and I might just have a way of helping you overcome this difficulty."

A glimmer of hope flickered across Peter's face.

"It's not, shall we say..." Archie hesitated, trying to find the correct words, "totally orthodox, but this process has worked well in the past for some of those with similar difficulties."

Peter sat forward in his chair expectantly. "I could do with all the help I can get, please, Archie, even if it is unusual. What do you have in mind?"

Keen not to suggest that this was a panacea for all woes, Archie wanted to ensure that he managed Peter's expectations carefully.

"You must understand this can only assist you. It's not some sort of magical cure for your anguish."

"Absolutely. I completely understand," Peter said, a little too eagerly for Archie's liking.

"Okay," said Archie decisively. "There is a way in which you can relive a day from your life. Just one. It does not change what actually happened, but it can show you what events would have been like if you had acted differently or if circumstances had been altered. In that regard it's a bit like a dream, I suppose. The hope is that the fulfilment of the experience that someone desperately wants might help them to deal with the associated worry and anxiety," he explained, deliberately leaving feelings of guilt from his list of ailments.

"So, what you are saying is that I could choose any day I wanted and see what might have happened if I had done things differently?"

"In essence that is precisely what I mean. Do you have any thoughts as to what you want to see changed?" he asked coyly.

"You know very well that I do. If I could have done one thing differently, even though it won't actually change anything, I would have taken the trip to Southend with Andy the day before his crash. It's the biggest regret of my life that I didn't go with him."

"Right then," Archie said resolutely. "Let's do this, shall we? Bring your chair a bit closer to the fire and get comfortable."

Peter did as he was told, somewhat surprised that this could be arranged so quickly, and awaited further instruction.

"Lean your head back and shut your eyes." Peter obeyed. "Now you need to concentrate hard on the precise moment in time that you want the day to start."

Peter opened one eye. "Just one quick thing. How will I know when this is going to stop?" he asked.

"Ah yes, that is a good question. Unfortunately, I am unable to be exact, although I can assure you that it will not be over until some good has been done and hopefully you feel happier about the day."

Peter nodded his understanding and shut his eyes again, deep in concentration. He decided to focus on the sound of Andy's knock on the front door of his parents' house. For what seemed like almost a minute but what was probably only about twenty seconds, nothing happened. The room was silent, and he was tempted to ask Archie if he was doing it properly when, quite abruptly, he heard it. Instinctively, he opened his eyes and sat upright, strangely startled by the noise he was hoping to hear. He looked around. He was there in in his old bedroom – it had worked. He looked closely at the books on the shelf, his discarded clothes from the previous night scattered on the floor, even the World Cup wall chart, which now showed that England were in the semi-finals. He felt drowsy but was acutely aware of the bright summer sun outside trying to penetrate the drawn curtains.

He jumped excitedly out of bed and headed for the door, glancing at himself in the mirror as he did so. He had to think for a moment to remember how old he was. He double-checked the mirror, pausing to stare at the twenty-three-year-old version of himself. So, this was really happening – exactly as the doctor had explained. He ran down the stairs, jumping the last couple to test his young body to its full potential. *That felt good*, he thought to himself as his knees absorbed the shock of the landing with ease. Hardly out of breath, he yanked the door open and there in front of him, as he knew he would be, was Andy. For a while Peter was unable to speak. All he could do was stare as the memory of this meeting the first time around flooded into his mind.

"You okay there, Peter?" Andy asked cheerily. "Looks like I woke you up. Or perhaps you're a bit hungover."

"No, it's fine, I was just dozing," Peter replied, all too conscious of the trance he had been in.

"Good night, wasn't it?"

Peter had to think for a moment before he could respond. What happened last night? Of course. The pub and England beating Argentina.

"Yeah, great," he said hesitantly.

"Blimey, Peter, you are still half asleep. Anyway, you'd better wake up because it's a fantastic day, as you can see, and I thought it would be a shame to waste it."

Peter knew what was coming next and he could barely contain himself long enough for Andy's suggestion.

"How do you fancy a trip to the coast? I thought we could go to Southend. There should be a good atmosphere down there. What do you reckon?"

This was feeling very strange to Peter, although from here onwards he would not know what was going to happen or what Andy was going to say. This was where the day would change.

"Sounds great to me. I can't think of anything else I would rather do."

"Great. I knew you would be up for it. I thought we could leave as soon as possible. That way we'll be able to park easily before the crowds arrive. My dad has agreed to lend us his car."

"Good thinking," said Peter. "Give me forty-five minutes to get ready and have something to eat and I'll knock for you."

"Lovely. See you then and don't forget to bring a hat – we'll need them in this sun," Andy replied with a wide grin on his face as he headed back down the pathway.

Peter showered and dressed in less than fifteen minutes, spent another five minutes locating his sunglasses and a hat, and made himself some toast and marmalade, which he washed down with a mug of tea inside a further ten minutes. That left him ten minutes to telephone Joan and apologise that a crisis had occurred with Andy and he needed to spend the day with him. He did not enjoy lying to her, but he assuaged his conscience with the knowledge that he and Joan might be able to laugh about it all quite soon. Then he remembered that Archie had said that history would not actually change and inwardly ridiculed himself for being bothered in the first place.

When he knocked for him around quarter to nine, Andy was waiting, car keys in hand. He called cheerio to his parents, who were having their breakfast, and shut the door behind him.

"I see you've got the essentials," Andy observed as they walked over to the car.

"Don't think we'll need much more than a few quid, will we?" Peter replied, tapping the bulge of his wallet in his pocket.

"Yeah, that's exactly what I thought," said Andy, smiling.

They drove with the windows down and the radio on, chatting excitedly about how they would spend the day. It was surprising how many cars were on the road given the time, but the weather had brought people out in their droves. They passed children playing football by the roadside and groups of men carrying their Sunday papers under their arms, laughing and joking, animatedly reliving the previous afternoon's victory at Wembley. There was an air of optimism all around, which they both sensed as they approached the seafront and vast numbers of day trippers with the same idea as them, wandering towards the beach. Fortunately, Andy's dad had told him the best place to park, and he found a spot without too much trouble.

"Glad we left when we did," he said. "I reckon anyone arriving in an hour or so will have to park at least half a mile away."

As they got out of the car, the warm breeze from the sea gently buffeted their faces with its saltiness. There was little doubt as to where they were heading first, but it was still a source of some amusement to them both when they turned to each other and asked the same rhetorical question. "Kursaal?"

The Kursaal Amusement Park was the most popular destination in Southend for young people. Peter had only been there once before and it was soon clear to him that Andy knew the place much better than he. Andy suggested they headed straight for the Water Chute on the basis that it was not only a great ride but also offered the distinct possibility that they would get wet and thus cool off a little after their journey. Peter could see the sense in this and it transpired that his friend was right on both counts. So much so that having been on the Cyclone rollercoaster and the aptly named ghost train 'Laff in the Dark', where they did to extreme what the name suggested, they returned to cool off once again under its inevitable splash at the bottom. The Kursaal was filling up by now and they decided to have an ice cream while there was not too much of a queue at the kiosk.

Behind the ice cream stall there was a crazy golf course which caught Andy's eye. Ice creams in hand, they wandered over to take a look. There were only a few people waiting, so once they had finished their cornets, they decided to have a game. The one proviso Peter had, though, was that they operated some sort of handicap system because of Andy's superior ability. Andy offered him a shot a hole, which he readily accepted. Wandering to the window to pay, they passed a sign which read 'Today's Best Scores'. Underneath the sign was a list of names and the current leader was someone called Billy Richards with a total of '33' for the eighteen-hole course.

"Not a bad score," said Peter, "but I reckon you could beat it, don't you?"

"You never know," said Andy cagily. "Let's give it a go then, shall we?"

They paid their money and received a putter and golf ball each from a young girl who seemed to take a shine to Andy. Peter reflected that this was often the way of things when they went out together, but needless to say, he did not begrudge him one bit even if he did feel a little like a spectator. He stood a pace or two behind but could see that the girl was extremely pretty. Not only that but she was also smiling encouragingly as the two of them chatted. Eventually, as Peter hoped he would, Andy remembered they were supposed to be playing golf and pulled himself away from the conversation.

"Nancy was just telling me that the person with the lowest score today qualifies for a regional competition next month," he said, handing Peter a scorecard and pencil.

"That's interesting," Peter replied, his lack of enthusiasm matching his personal expectation that he might be that person. He had been so caught up in the day that it did not occur to him immediately that Andy would not be around then even if he won. A sudden wave of sadness smothered him and he had to remind himself that all that mattered was today. He was confident that he and Andy would meet again soon enough, so there was no time for melancholy thoughts.

"But not as interesting as the fact that you already know that her name is Nancy." He smirked.

Andy looked at him, trying not to laugh. "You know me, Pete. I don't like to waste time. Talking of which, shall we play? I reckon '33' could be tough to beat."

The irony of what Andy had said was not lost on Peter. He could not help but think about how little time Andy had left in this life. He was pleased when his friend's voice distracted him again from his dark introspection.

"There are eighteen holes and each one is a par two, so that means that this Billy has had at least three holes-in-one, which is pretty good. Still, if he can do it, I'm sure we can," Andy said confidently, putting his ball on the ground for his first shot.

The first hole looked quite simple but for the fact that the path ahead of them narrowed and would prevent any ball aimed imperfectly through the gap from threatening the hole. Andy's ball crept safely through and straight into the middle of the hole, exactly as he had intended. Peter, however, failed to negotiate the gap with his first shot and had to settle for a rather ignominious three. They laughed and joked as they navigated the course in the sunshine. Peter improved, managing a hole-in-one of his own on the seventh, hitting his ball perfectly through the mouth of a wooden crocodile so that it crossed a narrow bridge over a small pool of water and had just enough momentum left to drop into the hole on the other side. Unfortunately, his round was dogged by a number of catastrophes, including a five on the apparently simple ninth where Andy had once again holed his first shot.

By the time they stepped onto the eighteenth tee, Andy had taken only thirty shots, so a par two would be enough to beat the high score. Peter was quite content with his respectable forty-two to that point and was much more interested in his friend's score. The hole was situated on the other side of a ship, on board which a grizzly-looking pirate stared menacingly at them. To overcome this obstacle, they needed to hit their ball against a raised bank with sufficient speed for their ball to climb the slope but not so hard that it flew past the hole the other side. Peter's immediate reaction when Andy hit his shot was that it was not going to reach the top of the slope in order to flop over the other side, but it seemed to gather pace from somewhere as it approached the summit, and its weight was perfect. It trickled over the top and was heading straight for the hole. For a moment it looked like it was going to miss, but then it curved fractionally to the left and caught the lip of the hole, horseshoed around it and eventually fell in for Andy's fifth hole-in-one.

"You've done it!" Peter shouted, slapping Andy on the back in celebration. Casually he played his own shot without looking and it too climbed the slope and tiptoed over, nestling alongside the hole so that he could easily tap it in for a very creditable two.

Excitedly, they totted up the score and double-checked it before Andy returned triumphantly to the delectable Nancy and announced that he had scored thirty-one. She took his card and pinned it on the wall with a number of others, then came outside to join them. They both stared at her as she moved gracefully but with purpose, writing his score at the top of the leader board slowly so as to ensure that Andy had plenty of time to look at her. She brushed lightly past him on her way back to her post, lingering just long enough to ensure that the alluring fragrance of her Estee Lauder Youth-Dew filled his nostrils. Then, as she sat down again, she stared directly at him and smiled seductively.

"Make sure you come back by five o'clock when we shut to see if you have won, won't you, Andy?" she said, carefully imparting to him not only this essential information but also the time that her shift ended.

"I most certainly will, Nancy," Andy said playfully, leaving her in little doubt that he was glad he knew when she finished work and that he would indeed return at the requisite time.

"You are incredible," Peter said, shaking his head with admiration.

"Well, I do play a lot of golf, so it's not that surprising."

"Not that, you idiot," Peter said, gently punching Andy's shoulder. "I meant with the girl."

"Oh, did you?" Andy replied innocently, knowing full well what Peter had meant. "She's nice, isn't she?"

"Nice? She's absolutely stunning, as you well know." He laughed.

"What's so funny?" Andy asked.

"Sorry, Andy, it's just that sometimes I can't keep up with your love life. I thought you had made pretty good progress with that Isobel last night and now you are off chasing Nancy."

Andy smirked. "I think 'chasing' is a rather unpleasant way of putting it. I am merely making friends with a beautiful young lady, and we will just have to see where it goes from there."

Before Peter could consider the ethical considerations involved, Andy was two or three steps ahead of him, fuelled by the relentless energy of youth. Peter watched with affection before using his new-found athleticism to sprint so that he could catch up.

"Fancy a trip down the pier on the train?" Andy asked once Peter arrived alongside him.

"Why not? We can't very well come to Southend and not go on the pier."

They wandered over to the kiosk and bought their tickets from an elderly man with huge clumps of dark grey hair protruding from each ear and both nostrils. In between customers, he displayed extraordinary dexterity as he alternately took large gulps from a cup of steaming hot tea and deep drags on a cigarette which he kept in an ashtray next to the long string of tickets that he was employed to sell. Peter had to pull himself away, so impressed was he by this astonishing feat of co-ordination to which the man duly returned, having pushed their tickets under the window of the booth.

Peter joined Andy, who had already taken a seat and saved one for his friend, in one of the green-and-cream-coloured carriages waiting on the track. Five minutes later they arrived at their destination just over a mile into the Thames Estuary at the end of the pier. After a short discussion, they decided to head for the ever-popular Hall of Mirrors where they spent twenty hilarious minutes looking at the distorted reflections of themselves and others. Still laughing, they stumbled out into the sunlight again and Peter, seeing the Dolphin Café directly opposite them, suggested they had a cup of tea.

It was a lot cooler inside the café, which made a welcome change from the heat outside. After a quick glance at the menu, they each ordered tea and a bun then sat down at one of the round wooden tables. As they took in their new surroundings, Peter noticed three mods who were clustered around the fruit machine, their drinks arranged precariously on top. He was just about to point them out to Andy, when he was beaten to it by the loud rat-a-tat-tat of coins pouring into the tray at the bottom of the fruit machine. He and Andy looked over and saw the young lads congratulate one another as they stuffed the coins into the pockets of their immaculate silver-grey mohair suits.

"Alright for some by the sound of it," said Peter, raising his eyebrows and glancing over his shoulder at them.

Andy, who was sitting opposite, could just see them by looking past Peter. With an expression of curiosity on his face, he responded, still looking at the mods, who were continuing to put coins into the machine. "Yes, sounds like they've won the jackpot judging by the amount of noise, so why would they still be playing?"

"What do you mean?" Peter replied, unclear as to the relevance of his friend's observation.

"It's just that everybody knows, once you win the jackpot, you might as well walk away and let some other unsuspecting punter put their money in because it's not going to pay out again for a while."

Peter had limited experience of fruit machines but had played a few before and had found them to be a quick way to lose money rather than win it. He assumed this was often because the activity had tended, for him, to be accompanied by alcohol as most machines were in pubs or clubs.

Twenty minutes later they had eaten their buns, both of which were accompanied by strawberry jam, and drained their mugs of tea. They were contemplating whether to leave or have another drink when the fruit machine erupted again with the distinctive clatter of falling coins.

"That can't be right," said Andy. "They can't possibly have put enough money back in for it to pay out that much again."

Peter was a little bemused by his friend's interest but could not really add anything to the conversation other than suggesting that the mods must have been particularly lucky.

Andy was not convinced. "I'm just going to nip to the loo before we go. Won't be a minute," he said, pushing back his chair and standing up.

The toilets were situated to the rear of the café and to get to them it was necessary to walk past the fruit-machine-playing mods. Peter craned his neck and watched as Andy paused momentarily, quite unnoticed by the group, as he passed them. He did the same on the return journey before retaking his seat opposite Peter.

"I knew it," he whispered triumphantly to Peter, leaning across the table. "Those lads," Andy continued, "they're working a scam on the fruit machine."

"How do you know?" asked Peter, intrigued that such a thing was actually possible.

"I've seen it done before, that's how. At the golf club. A chap was caught by the steward doing exactly what those three are up to." Encouraged by the interest Peter seemed to at last be showing, he explained what he meant. "One of the members, or should I say ex-members because he was thrown out of the club, kept winning on the machine in the Spike Bar. He always seemed to be on it and never walked away when his money ran out. The reason for this baffled us all, but the answer was in fact extremely simple – his money never did run out."

Andy could see Peter was becoming confused so provided the additional details to make things clear.

"He used to have a coin on a piece of cotton which he wrapped around his finger. He would carefully lower the coin into the slot until he heard it click then pull it out again on the cotton. The machine thought it had taken the money and the reels turned, but the coin had never dropped. He could play all night without spending any money and that is exactly what he did until he didn't hear the steward behind him one time and was spotted. He let the coin drop into the machine, as part of the trick was to tie it loosely in case this happened. Unfortunately for him, the steward, who was an ex-military man with excellent eyesight, knew he had seen something attached to the man's finger. Suspicious of his continued success on the machine, he challenged the man and opened up the machine. When he did, he found the coin with the string and that was that. One of the other members was a pub landlord and had seen this done on his premises, so the chap had to admit his crime when he was summoned to appear before the committee. They threw him out and, in exchange for not informing the police, took a donation from him towards club funds. He was very lucky and probably made money on the deal, but he was never allowed to set foot in the golf club again."

"People actually do that sort of thing?" Peter exclaimed in amazement.

"Oh yes. And that's precisely what those lads are up to. Why don't I take the cups back to the counter? I'll see you outside."

Peter didn't argue because he suspected that Andy was going to tell the café owner what was happening. Five minutes later his friend came out grinning from ear to ear. The owner of the café, who tended to stay in his small office by the kitchen, was a retired professional wrestler known now as Billy Bradley but in his previous incarnation had gone by the name of the Canvey Crusher in recognition of his former home town. As they strolled down the pier, having decided not to take the train back, Andy explained, between fits of laughter, how he had watched the man-mountain deal with the mods. They were scared out of their wits and confessed immediately, apparently offering to give him their winnings. The Crusher, being a pragmatic individual, had a better idea and had grabbed two of them by the collar and deposited them by the kitchen sink, informing them as he did that they would be doing the washing up until closing time. The third lad, sensing the inevitability of his predicament, followed them sheepishly rather than risk being manhandled. Mr Bradley had apparently been so grateful to Andy that he tore up his bill and told him the tea and buns were on the house.

By the time Andy had finished telling Peter the story, they were virtually back on the seafront. They stopped to look over the rail at the beach, which was now packed with day trippers. Most of them were lying on towels, bathing in the sun, although a few brave individuals were splashing around in the sea, which did not look particularly warm in spite of the heat of the day. There were a couple of games of football and one of cricket being played in addition to numerous children with spades digging holes, building castles and burying assorted family members in the sand.

"Let's go for a paddle. We have to while we're here, don't we?" Andy said, nudging Peter playfully in the ribs.

"I suppose so," Peter replied. "It'll cool us down a bit, I should think."

Sitting on the wall by the beach, they took off their shoes and then held them aloft while they descended the two or three steps onto the warm sand. Weaving their way in and out of groups of people, trying not to stare too obviously at the numerous scantily clad young women, they eventually made it to the sea. The feel of the sand underfoot reminded Peter of his childhood and family holidays in Cornwall, but the sudden rush of cold water on his feet and calves took his breath away. Fortunately, after a few seconds, his body had acclimatised to the temporary sensory overload and he felt more comfortable.

"Quite bracing, isn't it?" Andy chuckled, making sure he kept moving so that he didn't feel the cold so much.

It was, but they were able to warm up their feet by stepping back onto the sand now and again so that future incursions into the water were welcome rather than traumatic. Feeling quite invigorated, they wandered back after a while, stopping for a couple of minutes to help two young boys dig an enormous moat around a huge fortification of sandcastles they had built. The tide was coming in and it would not be long before it began to fill.

They wiped the sand off their feet and sat down on a wall again to put their shoes back on. Peter looked across at Andy who was tying his laces and at the same time bobbing his head left and right, in front and behind, excitedly trying to decide where they should go next and what they should do. He stared for a moment, unable to believe that this lively young man, so full of energy, would be dead by tomorrow. Andy caught his gaze.

"You alright there, Pete? You having another one of those turns like this morning?" he said, unable to resist pulling his friend's leg a little.

"Don't be stupid," Peter replied with more bravado than he actually felt. "I was just thinking about what we ought to do next," he added, making light of his momentary lapse. As he did so, he reminded himself that they were both dead anyway, so it was pointless wasting time on such matters.

"What do you reckon then?" Andy asked.

"I think food might be a good option. How about you?"

"You read my mind, matey. Let's go and see what we can find."

They crossed the road in search of some shade and to survey the array of eating options opposite the seafront. A seafood stall caught their eyes for a moment until they saw a lump of ash fall from the cigarette in the proprietor's mouth and nestle in a pint of cockles he was passing to an unsuspecting customer. The air was full of the smell of salt and vinegar, and minus the ash, those cockles did look good. Fifty yards further on they came to a shop with a similar menu on the board that stood outside on the pavement. Satisfying themselves that none of the staff seemed to be smoking, they bought a pint of cockles and whelks to share, and some chips. There was a vacant bench in the shade, so they sat looking contentedly across at the sun glinting on the sea, allowing the salt and vinegar in which everything was liberally doused to caress their tastebuds.

Another group of mods walked past, the smartly dressed young men, holding the hands of their equally well-attired girlfriends. One of them stared aggressively, presumably to deter them from looking at his girlfriend. Peter quickly broke eye contact with him but continued to observe the group as they walked away from them. He felt wonderfully vindicated when they stopped to sample the menu at the cigarette ash seafood stall. He kept looking until he saw them pay for and began to eat whatever they had bought before recommencing their parade along the front. Their misfortune made him feel very satisfied. He knew he should not feel like this – they hadn't really done any harm – but he could not resist it. His contemplation of the unpleasantness of their food was broken by Andy, who very resolutely announced that he was going to pop into the pub and buy them a beer each to wash down the salty food.

When he returned a few minutes later with two lagers, he explained that he had only bought halves because he needed to keep a clear head for the drive home later. As they quenched their thirsts, it occurred to Peter that life did not get much better than this. A family wandered by, the mother pushing their baby in a pram while the father held his son's hand, proudly clutching under his other arm a large toy monkey which he had no doubt won playing one of the amusements. Domestic bliss, Peter thought to himself. How he missed that.

"We should have a go at some of the games and see if we can win one of those. If he can do it, I'm sure we can," Peter said confidently.

"Well, I have already excelled this morning, haven't I?" Andy replied, referring, Peter assumed, to the crazy golf rather than his romantic dalliance with Nancy. "So perhaps it might be your turn to have some success."

Peter had forgotten how much he enjoyed this kind of banter with Andy – it had been a long time. Resolving to pick up the gauntlet that had been thrown down, he finished the last few glorious drops of his drink and scrunched up his chip wrapper.

"Fair enough. You take the glasses back and I'll find a bin for our rubbish, and we'll see what I can do then, shall we?"

They each gave the other the momentary glance that was customary at such times before erupting into fits of laughter. Then, clasping one another around the shoulders, they set off back down the road in search of the arcades.

Every other building they passed contained amusements. Some were clearly aimed at younger children and were filled with sit-on rides for toddlers. Others had a more serious layout with banks of fruit machines for the discerning adult gambler, but the majority had a mixture in order to appeal to a broader clientele. They walked past a few of the less interesting arcades until they saw one with a long line of crane machines.

"Those machines look like they have been filled up recently," observed Andy. "It shouldn't be too difficult to win something there."

On closer inspection, his assessment proved accurate, but the main problem, apart from the fact that the prizes were relatively small, was that it was frustratingly difficult to get the claw to pick anything up, let alone successfully deposit it in the chute where it would be relayed to them. They spent twenty minutes, and more money than was sensible, trying to get a miniature replica of the Jules Rimet trophy out of one machine, only to walk away in disappointment when it somehow managed to wedge itself under the arm of a large rag doll. Refusing to be disheartened, they then decided to try their luck at a shooting gallery. Suspended from the roof above the rifles were stuffed animals of almost every species known to man. There were lions, tigers, bears, frogs, dolphins and even caterpillars. To win the biggest version they needed to hit and knock down all six of the targets rowed up opposite them. It did not seem to be beyond them, even though, as they were both well aware, the sights on their rifles were not exactly in perfect alignment. Peter managed two while Andy knocked down a respectable four, which secured him a small brown bear. He held it jubilantly for a moment before realising that its size told more of failure than skill. Fortunately for him, the family they had seen earlier were outside and he was able to pop it into the pram with a smile to the mother as they made their exit.

Peter remembered taking Tom and Susan to Southend once when they were young, and a thought occurred to him.

"Let's try Peter Pan's Playground. I know it's for smaller kids, but I'm pretty sure they have some sideshows in there too."

"That sounds like a decent idea," Andy said. "I doubt we can do any worse than we have already."

The game that Peter and the children played involved throwing hard baseball-like balls into milk churns. It sounded and looked simple and you only needed to get one ball in to win a big prize. Unfortunately, it was nothing like as straightforward as people thought. Susan was determined that she should win the pony that hung tantalisingly above them, so they kept playing, he recalled, for some considerable time. On a number of occasions, he walked away but returned, certain that he could win the toy for his daughter. Eventually he had spent so much money, probably enough to buy three of the ponies, that the stall holder took pity on him. The man explained that it was necessary to impart back spin on the ball as it was thrown so that when it hit the rim of the metal churn, it went upwards rather than bouncing back or to the side. From a position above the churn, it had a much better chance of falling in, particularly since its momentum had been stalled by the spin. Peter remembered feeling annoyed with himself at the time, thinking that he really should have worked that out for himself. He bought another three balls and tried the technique.

None of them went in, but the third was closer than any other he had thrown before. He bought another three as Susan looked on in hope. He had felt quite a bit of pressure, not just to pacify his daughter but also because he had been given inside information which he wanted to put into practice properly. The first two balls stalled again but fell away. He was getting closer, and his confidence began to grow. His third shot felt good as soon as it had left his hand with the extra back spin he decided to impart. They all watched, mesmerised by the ball's trajectory, as it hit the back rim of the churn, popped up a few inches and dropped into the centre. Susan was beside herself when the man reached up and unfastened the pony before passing it across to her. Peter had a few more turns before another ball was successful and he was able to let Tom choose a similar-sized tiger. He remembered exchanging a nod of recognition with the man as he suggested they moved on to another stall. Although silent, it said 'thank you' and confirmed that their secret would not be shared with anyone.

Peter wondered excitedly if the game would be there in 1966 as they entered the playground. He strode over to where he remembered it would be ten years later, but in its position was a stall selling rock. He turned around and scoured the park with his eyes, more in hope than expectation. Then he saw it. In a completely different, quieter section of the park was a stall with milk churns. Surely it had to be the same one.

Not wishing to give the game away because he wanted this to look good, he calmly pointed past the merry-go-round in front of them. "That one over there might not be too difficult – it looks like you have to throw balls into those churns," he said nonchalantly.

Andy was prepared to have a go on anything to win a proper prize and liked the look of the size of the toys that were amassed around the stall.

"Great, let's give it a try then, shall we?"

As they approached, Peter saw the young man who was running the game and wondered if he was the same person he would meet on his visit with Tom and Susan. He could not remember much about the chap's features, just his generous manner and his big smile as he told him the secret of getting the balls in the churns. He was therefore none the wiser as the man noticed them approaching.

"You go first, Andy. I reckon you'll get a prize in no time," said Peter, unable to resist having some fun at Andy's expense.

Andy had five turns, incredulous that he was incapable of doing something that appeared so simple.

"I don't understand," he said. "I'm probably trying too hard. Here, you have a go, Peter."

Peter moved forward, feigning indifference regarding his chances, paid the man his money and took hold of the three balls he was offered in return. He deliberately threw the first one underarm just as Andy and everyone else they had watched had chosen to do. It hit the rim and was not too far away from the middle of the churn but, because of the speed at which it was released, it bounced off and fell to the floor. With his second throw he flicked his thumb under the ball, deliberately imparting insufficient backspin for the ball to go in but to give those watching an idea of what he had in mind. A couple who had finished their turn walked away shaking their heads, oblivious to what they were about to miss. Before he threw his third ball, Peter checked that the only people paying attention were Andy and the stall holder. After all, he did not want to ruin the man's business. He flipped his hand round so that instead of holding the ball in his palm, he formed a claw around it with his fingers over the top. This he found, ten years later, to be the best method of generating the maximum backspin. Having lined up the shot, he let the ball go from underneath his fingers with a skilful flick of his wrist. The ball ballooned from the front of his hand, his fingers having moved suddenly through ninety degrees, and took a looping path towards the milk churn. Peter could tell immediately it was straight and knew as soon as it hit the far rim of the churn that the spin and reduced speed would stall it in its tracks. As it struck the tin of the churn, there was one exquisite fraction of a second when Peter knew it was going in immediately before it popped up in the air over the hole and fell inevitably into the body of the churn with a satisfying thud.

Andy was the first to congratulate him, of course, slapping him heartily on the back. The stall holder, who had never come across the technique before, checked that no one else had seen what Peter had done before speaking quietly so as not to attract attention.

"Nice throw, young man. Which prize would you like?" he asked, casting his eyes towards the menagerie of stuffed toys attached to the roof.

"I'll take the lion, please," Peter replied quickly, almost toppling over as Andy released his congratulatory arm from around his neck.

"It looks a bit like World Cup Willie – you never know, it might be a good omen for the England team," he added.

The man unhooked the huge lion and with two hands passed it over to Peter, who positioned it victoriously in the loop of his left arm.

"I have to try that," said Andy. "You made it look so simple. Show me exactly how to hold it."

The stall holder winced and scanned the area nearby to see who was watching or listening to the instructions that might threaten his game's profitability. He did not have to worry, because Peter was aware of his unfair advantage and was only interested in telling his mate.

Andy paid his money for another turn but failed with all three balls, although the second one hung in the air nicely but was not quite straight enough to go in.

"I'll have another go, please," he said to the man, holding out the coins in his hand.

His first two shots showed some improvement, but his third was perfectly straight, bounced softly above the churn's opening and dropped in with a resounding clunk.

"Yes!" he cried out as he punched the air with joy. Peter slapped him, thrilled to see the delight on his face.

"Nice one, Andy. What prize are you going for?"

"I think I'll have the elephant, please," he said with a slightly self-satisfied tone.

The man untied a few pieces of string and eased the toy down before speaking.

"Do me a favour, please, lads. Show other people that you have won, by all means – it'll encourage them to play themselves. But please, whatever you do, don't tell them how you did it."

Enjoying this new-found sense of power, Andy replied first. "No problem. I am sure we can do that." Then turning to Peter with a grin, "Particularly if you let us have one free turn each before we go." The man was reluctant at first as he calculated the potential downside of six large toys. He was, however, something of a gambler and liked Andy's cheek.

"Go on then." He laughed. "Three balls each and you don't tell a soul."

As it turned out, both of them had a further success and two near misses, so it didn't cost the man too much to secure their silence.

Nevertheless, Peter walked away with a whale under his other arm and Andy had a giraffe to go with his elephant.

"I meant what I said about the lion being an omen for England," Peter called to the man, feeling a little guilty as they left with their spoils. "I wouldn't be at all surprised if they win the Cup."

The man raised his eyebrows, pleased to see the back of them, and Peter wondered if he would take any notice of the tip he had given him.

"That was great fun, Peter. We might as well go on a few rides now we are here. That one over there looks good," he suggested, pointing at a sign for The Whip, which appeared quite gentle until, on the bends, the cars flew sharply round the corner, almost causing their passengers to fall out of the side. They each took a car and arranged the soft animals amusingly next to them as though they too were passengers.

By the time they had been on the roller coaster and a water ride not greatly different to the one in the Kursaal, it was quarter past four.

"We ought to be thinking about getting over to the crazy golf soon, Andy, to see if you've won," Peter said, as Andy was circling the park with his eyes to select their next destination.

"Blimey, Peter, you're right. Time flies when you're having fun, doesn't it? I think we could probably have a couple of those doughnuts first, don't you?" he said, pointing towards the large kiosk by the exit.

"Definitely. I'm feeling a bit peckish myself after our exertions and judging by the queue they must be pretty good."

They were good, but because of the queue they had to eat them quickly as they dashed back to the crazy golf. Wiping the sugar from around his mouth and then transferring it to the back of his shorts with his palm, Andy could see Nancy was just closing up as they arrived on the dot of five. There was a middle-aged man with her who Andy presumed was the owner collecting the day's takings. She smiled as he and Peter approached, laden with the stuffed toys they had won.

"Looks like someone has had a good day," she said, looking directly at Andy as if reassessing him. Then turning to the man who had not yet finished loading his car, she explained, "This is the lad I told you about, Mr Harwell. The one who shot the lowest score of the day."

The man eyed Andy and Peter suspiciously.

"Did you really go round in thirty-one? Honestly?" he asked sternly.

"Yes, I did," said Andy. "Ask my friend if you like. He's training to be an accountant, so he should be able to add up properly."

The man looked over, trying to decide whether this was true, when Peter piped up.

"Andy's been the champion three years running at Clayton Manor Golf Club," he announced in an attempt to both satisfy the man's questioning looks and to give Nancy something else to find interesting about Andy. "I'm sure the club secretary will confirm that if you contact him. What's his name, Andy?"

"David Chatworth," Andy replied disinterestedly, preferring to concentrate on Nancy's admiring eyes rather than such trivial matters.

The man calmed down and explained that he did not intend to check but felt he had to ask because it was only the second time anyone had scored thirty-one since the course had been open. He jotted down Andy's contact details, which he told him would be passed on to the sponsors of the regional finals.

"They'll be in touch with you within the next week or two, I suspect. Good luck – see if you can't win for us," he said as he wandered over to his car lugging a large canvas bag full of coins.

There was silence for a moment or two as the three of them were left together. Peter broke it tactfully with an excuse he had planned.

"Sorry, Andy, I forgot, my mum and dad wanted me to pick up a few things for them while I was here – I've got a list somewhere – you know, some cockles for tea and sticks of rock for some of their friends. I might be a while. Is that okay with you?"

"Yes, of course, Pete," Andy replied, trying to hide the smirk on his face needlessly because Nancy knew as well as he did that no such list existed. "Shall we meet back at the car in, say, an hour?"

Peter agreed readily, said goodbye to Nancy and began to walk back in the direction of the shops. He was pleased to be alone for a while and he reflected on how much fun the day had been. The guilt that had beleaguered him for so long had been replaced with a sense of happiness. He was grateful to Archie for arranging this and pleasingly satisfied that he had been able to make things up to Andy. Smiling to himself, he imagined what he and Nancy were up to and considered that he had indeed well and truly redeemed himself as a friend today.

The sun was still hot, if a little lower in the sky, and he thought he ought to at least buy a few things to take home just in case he saw Nancy again later. He went into one of the shops on the seafront and bought half a dozen sticks of Southend rock and a bar of chocolate which he planned to eat himself. There were fewer people around now as most of the day's visitors began their journeys home so that parents could prepare for work the next day and children could be put to bed. He noticed two benches side by side facing the beach and the sea. They were both free, so he sat down to kill some time. What a sight it was, he thought as he stared across the estuary. It was incredibly bright though and he popped his sunglasses back on before breaking off some of the chocolate and putting it in his mouth. Contentedly, he leaned back on the seat and shut his eyes with the heat of the afternoon sun on his face and the salty smell of the sea filling his nostrils.

He woke himself up and realised that he must have dozed off for a few seconds because as he sat there with his eyes shut, he became aware that it was much quieter now and the sun had gone in. He exhaled and was about to take off his sunglasses when he heard a familiar voice.

"Hello, Peter. How are you?"

He was startled for a moment and abruptly opened his eyes to find that he was no longer sitting on the bench and the beach and sea had disappeared. Instead, he could see that he was back in Agnes' cottage. Reluctantly but still hugely thankful, he realised that his day with Andy was over and that the voice he had heard was Archie's.

Chapter 20

"Here you are, Peter, Agnes has made you a cup of tea. You must be thirsty after a day like that," said Archie, holding out a steaming cup and saucer.

Still slightly groggy, Peter pushed himself up in the chair, aware that he had been slouching. His mouth was dry and as soon as his eyes focused properly, he reached for the mug and took a sip.

"Thanks. I needed that," he said, nodding gratefully, taking another sip of the tea.

"Was everything as you had hoped?" asked Archie.

Peter thought for a moment, remembering the laughs he and Andy had shared. "Yes, thank you, Archie, we had a wonderful time." Then with a slight grimace, he added, "But I didn't say goodbye to Andy – I didn't realise it was going to end when it did."

"No, of course not, but I can assure you that Andy was in no way offended. You might recall he was otherwise engaged with the beautiful Nancy at the time, so I certainly do not think you need to concern yourself with anything like that."

Peter relaxed and leant back in his chair. "Yes, of course. I shouldn't think he gave it a second thought."

He was just reflecting quietly that Archie clearly knew about the events in Southend, when the tranquillity of the cottage was shattered by a loud noise coming from the kitchen. It sounded like a plate or a tray hitting the floor and Peter assumed poor Agnes had probably dropped something. Archie, however, did not look at all surprised by the sound – it was almost as though he had expected some sort of commotion.

"If my ears don't deceive me," he began, "Agnes might be in need of some assistance," he said, raising his eyes to the ceiling in mock exasperation.

Then, before Peter could react to this cryptic statement, Archie leapt to his feet.

"Why don't we go and see what's happening?" he said, walking towards the kitchen without waiting for a response.

Peter was curious to find out what he had meant, so he hurriedly stood up just in time to see Archie disappear through the kitchen door.

As Peter reached the threshold, he could see a saucepan on the slate floor and next to it the hot strawberry jam that up until a few seconds ago had been contained within it. Agnes wielded a wooden spoon in her hand, which she brandished like a club as she menacingly approached a young man who was standing with his back to Peter and Archie. Sensing trouble, Archie reacted in the nick of time, narrowly managing to prevent Agnes unleashing her first blow on the unfortunate individual.

"Agnes!" he bellowed authoritatively.

The old woman froze and lowered the spoon, realising the futility of her planned assault now that there were two witnesses.

"But, Sir, he crept up on me like he always does," she pleaded, "and he gave me such a fright that I dropped the pan of boiling hot jam I was about to put into jars."

Archie nodded and frowned in an attempt to ameliorate her.

"Yes, that is most unfortunate and not the sort of behaviour we encourage at all. Totally unacceptable," he said, managing to subdue the smirk which threatened to appear on his face. Pulling himself together, and now addressing the offender sternly, he added, "I think an apology might be in order, don't you?"

The young man turned to face them for the first time and began to speak. "Yes, of course, Archie… I mean Mr Souter. Agnes, I am extremely…"

But the remainder of his apology was drowned out by Peter's cry of "Andy!" as he ran over and hugged his friend. Andy was momentarily taken aback as he tried to work out who this strange old man was who clearly seemed to know him.

"I'm sorry. I don't recognise you," he said.

"It's me, you fool," Peter replied.

There was something in the expression, the man's movement and the way he spoke that, in an instant, erased the chasm of time that had passed since they had last seen each other, and in that moment Andy understood.

"Peter? Is it you?" he said tentatively.

"Yes, of course it is. Don't you recognise me?" he replied with a smile as it dawned on him why Andy had been confused.

"No, I'm sorry, I didn't at first. You certainly have changed a bit since the last time I saw you. What a fantastic day that was we had in Southend. Do you remember it? We never got the chance to talk about it afterwards. By the way, remind me to tell you what happened with Nancy after you left."

Peter looked at Archie for some sort of guidance. Did this mean the day in Southend was real?

Unhelpfully, Archie raised a non-committal eyebrow and Peter turned back to Andy. It didn't matter one way or the other. As confusing as things were and regardless of what was real and what was not, all that was important to him was that Andy could remember the day they had spent together in Southend.

They hugged again and as they parted Andy said: "It's so good to see you, mate. Not that I mean it's good that you are dead, of course, but you know… good to see you at last."

"Ahem." Agnes coughed to remind them that she was still waiting for her apology.

"Ah yes, Agnes. I am terribly sorry. I promise I won't jump out on you like that again." Then as only he could, he turned on the Andy charm that Peter had missed so much. "It's just that those saffron buns of yours are legendary and I was desperate to try one."

Agnes smiled and blushed a little at the compliment, just as he had intended.

"Of course, I'll help to clear up too and I can also make some more jam with you if you would like."

"That won't be necessary," she replied hurriedly. There was absolutely no chance that she was going to let him anywhere near one of her batches of jam. "Just leave me to it and as long as it never happens again, we'll say no more about it," she said, opening a large cupboard and pulling out a blue mop and bucket.

Andy winked at Peter.

"Thank you, Agnes. That is most generous of you," said Archie.

"Yes, thank you," said Andy. Then turning to Peter, he continued, "Let's go out into the garden, shall we? It's a beautiful day and we've got a lot of catching up to do."

Peter had not noticed a garden, but through the open kitchen door he could see a beautifully manicured lawn bordered by the most striking assortment of flowers. In the distance he could see some mature fruit trees either side of a pathway that led invitingly into a concealed area beyond. It was sunny and a gentle breeze was flickering through the leaves and making the flowers sway rhythmically. The effect was hypnotic.

He was just about to follow Andy when he remembered that Archie was in charge of his itinerary, and it occurred that he ought to check with him first. "Is it okay with you, Archie, if I take a stroll with Andy in the garden?" he asked.

"Yes, of course, Peter. Please carry on. I'm going to stay in here for a while. There are just one or two more things I want to do. I expect I'll see you later."

Peter stood for a moment considering this reply which seemed unusually vague. No mention of the next task that he was to confront, no indication as to when they would be moving on, and what were the other matters he had to sort out? Were they anything to do with him? It sounded to him like Archie did not necessarily have anything else planned for him, so perhaps he had done everything that was required of him. He decided to test the water.

"Thank you, Archie." Then he carefully added, "For this, of course, but also for all the other help you have given me."

"You are most welcome, Peter," said Archie with a smile that certainly suggested some finality. He then turned and was about to leave the kitchen when Peter called out to him.

"Wait, Archie, please." He walked over to him hesitantly, uncertain as to what the appropriate convention was with angels or heavenly beings or whatever this man was.

"I don't know if this is the done thing, but thank you so much for everything again," he said, embracing Archie warmly in a heartfelt hug. "I really am so grateful."

Archie nodded in appreciative acknowledgement. "I'm sure I'll see you again some time, but for now, I suspect you two must have plenty to talk about, so why don't you catch your friend up before he gets himself into another scrape?" He grinned.

"Okay, I will." Peter laughed as he headed towards the garden. At the doorway he turned again, unable to leave without knowing for sure if he had done everything that was required in order to progress from this place.

"Archie, does this mean that I…" he managed before focusing and looking up to see that the kitchen was empty. Archie had gone. His momentary confusion was removed by the bustling figure of Agnes entering the kitchen with a tray of cups.

"You still here?" she asked unnecessarily. "Be off with you now. I need to do some washing up and clean up the rest of this jam."

He felt oddly happier now that she had told him to go too and, thanking her again, he hurried out to find Andy.

It was warmer outside, and Peter could hear birdsong coming from the trees. The garden was vast, both in length and width, much larger than it had appeared from inside. He was trying to work out how far it extended when he heard Andy's voice.

"Come on, Peter. I've got a surprise for you."

This whole experience has been full of surprises, so what's one more? he thought to himself as Andy led him across the lawn. He turned round to make sure he hadn't left Peter behind before continuing through a gap in the middle of a clump of apple trees. Peter was aware of the comforting hum of the bees on the white blossom as he walked under the branches. A couple of yards further on, there were two well-trodden paths in the grass, one heading to the right and the other to the left.

"You can thank me later," Andy said, mischievously grinning at Peter.

"What do you mean?"

"Well, it's like this. I'm going this way," he pointed to his left, "and down that path," he said pointing to the right, "is your surprise."

Peter knew there was no point in arguing or asking questions, so he resisted the temptation. "I'm going to see you later though?" he said.

"Yes, absolutely. We are going to have plenty of time for a decent chat. We've got so much to tell each other. Go on – trust me, you are going to like this. It's good."

Then spotting that Peter was a little wary of his new surroundings, he added, "Pete, when have I ever let you down?"

Peter racked his brains for a witty response, but there wasn't one – Andy had never let him down. "Okay, okay, I'll see you later then. Incidentally, how will I find you?"

"Just come down this path when you are ready and I'll be waiting for you," he said, beginning to walk away.

Before Peter had the chance to say anything else, Andy disappeared. He was on his own now and he knew that he had to see what it was that Andy had arranged for him. Cautiously he began to follow the path to the right. The scent of flowers was all around, and the warm breeze was at his back, encouraging him forward. He had gone no more than twenty yards when he could see open land ahead and he realised he was entering what looked like a meadow. As he drew nearer, he caught sight of a building up ahead. A sudden rush of emotion filled his whole body as he recognised the ruins of the old building that he loved so much. This was Cowdray Park on the most perfect summer's day. *How on earth did Andy manage this?* he wondered, conscious of the irony of the phrase.

This is astonishing, he thought to himself – *good old Andy*. And then he noticed that someone was waving and calling to him. It was a woman, standing next to a picnic blanket. He increased his pace, first jogging and then running on legs that were strong now. He could see her face and, with recognition, tears of joy began to pour from his eyes as he reached her. Her arms were outstretched waiting for his to envelop her. As they touched and he held her, his heart was filled with happiness so intense, so powerful, that at first he could not say anything. Eventually he was able to breathe again, although as he opened his mouth, he did not know whether he would actually be capable of speaking.

"Joan. My darling. I have missed you so much."

Epilogue

Tom pulled into one of the bays of the small car park and switched off the engine. He recognised a couple of the other vehicles, including that of his son Chris, who unusually for him appeared to have arrived early. No doubt, he thought to himself, that was due in no small part to the positive influence of his new girlfriend Julia. Her father had been a captain in the RAF, and the importance of punctuality had been instilled in her from a young age.

"Shall we?" he said, turning to his wife Caroline, who was sitting in the passenger seat next to him.

They got out and walked across the tarmac, which was covered with piles of brown leaves that had fallen from the ancient trees around its perimeter. The tall oaks in particular had witnessed this scene many times before and the idea that this was just another normal day for them comforted Tom. When they arrived at the three stone steps, Tom waited so that his wife could go first before slowly following himself. As they walked hand in hand across the churchyard, with its variety of gravestones, some upright, others at odd angles created by the passage of time and the movement of the soil, Tom stopped and pointed to the cross that was prominently positioned in front of the church.

"That's a Cornish cross," he proclaimed very seriously. Caroline dutifully looked across at the monolith, feigning interest, well aware of the humour intended by her husband's announcement.

"Do you remember, every time we came here Dad would remind us that it is one of the oldest of its kind in the county?" Tom added.

"I certainly do," said Caroline. "Apparently, it dates back to the eighth century..." She grinned as they shared the joke and the wonderful memory of those conversations.

The vicar, whose name was Alan, was waiting for them in the porch.

"Welcome, Tom. Welcome, Caroline. I see that you were admiring our wonderful Cornish cross. It dates back to the eighth century, you know."

They looked at each other, trying desperately not to laugh.

"Hello, Alan," Tom said, suppressing a giggle marginally more effectively than Caroline.

"Come in, please," Alan said, assuming that these were the kind of nervous laughs often associated with days like this. "There are a few early arrivals, including your son and his delightful girlfriend. And of course, your sister and her family."

Tom and Caroline said their hellos, administering hugs, kisses and handshakes as appropriate when people arrived, then took their seats on the front pew with the rest of the family. As he waited, Tom looked around. The church was not big and the relatively small number of people who had been invited would probably make it look quite full. There was a singing gallery but, as requested, there was no choir present because it had been agreed that there would be no hymns. In places the walls were in such poor condition that Tom wondered how much repair work, if any, had been done since the church was built almost five hundred years before.

Caroline noticed that he was distant and gave his hand a slight squeeze to remind him she was there. Then the music started, a classical piece he did not recognise that his sister had chosen, and the undertakers slowly brought in his father's coffin.

The service was as pleasant as it could be and did not drag on like so many have a tendency to do. The vicar energetically said his father's favourite Psalm 23 and also read a relevant passage from one of the Gospels before asking Tom to join him at the lectern to give the eulogy.

Smiling at Caroline more confidently than he felt, he leapt to his feet. Realising that this probably looked over-eager and out of keeping with the tone that had been set, he paused before very deliberately shuffling at a sedate pace to the front. He looked directly at the congregation, forced a smile in an attempt to put everyone, including himself, at ease, and then began.

"Dad was born during World War Two, which was, of course, a time of great uncertainty for everyone. Our grandparents, fortunately, were both stoic and incredibly loving, qualities he championed whenever giving advice to me and Susan when we were growing up. When the war finished and he started school, much to everyone's surprise, I understand, it became apparent that he was extremely gifted academically. In fact, he was something of a genius. He won scholarships to two very prestigious private schools and, of course, finished by winning a place at Oxford where he studied mathematics.

"As well as being an excellent cricketer at school, he discovered another of his life's passions at this time, painting. He obviously had considerable natural artistic flair, but he was lucky enough to be shown how to refine his skill by his school's art teacher, who was himself a successful artist. Many of you will have one of my father's pictures hanging on your wall and there is no doubt he produced some outstanding work. My own memory of him as an artist, though, will be of the man who, almost wherever we went, would produce a sketch book and pen, and begin doodling as though it were the most natural thing in the world. It was amazing how, with a few swishes, he could create what to someone with my lack of artistic ability looked like a masterpiece.

"Cornwall was somewhere he had always loved and a frequent destination for family holidays when we were young, so I was not at all surprised that when he stopped work, he and Mum retired here. They made some wonderful friends and adored being able to visit the beautiful coast or a National Trust property whenever they fancied.

"When his short-term memory began to desert him, he was still able to remember a specific game of beach cricket we'd had as children or the names of people we met on our holidays, just as he could tell you about the time he and his friends scrumped apples at school. As dementia took hold of him, he remained incredibly brave – it must be hideously scary to lose touch with things in that way, especially, I imagine, for someone who had always had such an agile mind.

"Fortunately for him, he had my mother to help him through most of it and we would all try and do our bit when we visited. We started to holiday again together, three generations of the same family, and we all discovered the pleasures of cruising. We went to some fantastic places and enjoyed some terrific food and wine, which many of you will know he also loved. I think going on those cruises gave my mother a much-needed break from looking after him when things became worse because they were structured and so it was relatively easy to keep an eye on him.

"By the time Mum died, his dementia was pretty bad and, in a way, perhaps that was a Godsend, since I am absolutely certain he didn't realise she had gone.

"We are grateful to all of you who visited him at Rose Lodge, the wonderful care home where he spent the final phase of his life. I would also like to thank Grace, and her team, for the compassion they showed my father and continue to show their other residents. You are all extraordinary people and each of you made such an enormous different to Dad at the end. Norbert, for example, who is sitting over there next to Grace, would spend hours painting and drawing with him even after his stroke made it difficult for him to hold a pencil. We were allowed to take him in two of his great loves, chocolate and wine. I can vividly recall sitting in the garden one beautiful day and watching him eat a bar of chocolate, savouring every mouthful with his eyes shut and the sun on his face, telling me it doesn't get much better than this.

"Often when we visited, he would point to one of the female residents and ask me to go and check that Joan was alright. Most of the time he believed he was on a cruise ship, holidaying somewhere exotic, no doubt. It was such a blessing that even after Mum's death, he thought she was there with him. We would often be sitting together chatting about something and he would ask how she was. Was she at one of the craft classes on board or getting him a coffee? I shared the meals at Rose Lodge with him occasionally and he would usually tell me Mum was having lunch in another restaurant with one of the friends she had met on the ship.

"I honestly don't think he could have spent his final days anywhere better in reality and also in his mind, on a holiday he loved and with the woman he adored."